GU00775859

DESPERATION IN DEATH

Mina Rose Cabot, age thirteen, is a good girl from a good family. Walking home from soccer practice in Devon, Pennsylvania, she disappears.

Eight months later her body is found in Battery Park, New York, speared through the chest by a three-inch piece of wood.

Lt. Eve Dallas knows that whoever abducted Mina is responsible for her death. But who took her — and just where has Mina been for eight long months . . . ?

DESPERATION IN DEATH

Mina Rose Cabot, age thirteen, is a good girl from a good family. Walking home from soccer practice in Devon, Pennsylvania, she disappears.

Eight months later her body is found in Battery Park, New York, speared through the chest by a three-inch piece of wood.

Lt. Eve Dallas knows that whoever abducted Mina is responsible for her death. But who took her — and that where has Mina been for eight long months . . . ?

J.D. ROBB

━━━━━━━━━━◆━━━━━━━━━━

DESPERATION IN DEATH

Complete and Unabridged

LARGE
PRINT

ISIS
Leicester

First published in Great Britain in 2022 by
Piatkus
an imprint of Little, Brown Book Group
London

First Isis Edition
published 2022
by arrangement with
Little, Brown Book Group
London

A catalogue record for this book is available
from the British Library.

ISBN 978–1–3991–2542–0

Published by
Ulverscroft Limited
Anstey, Leicestershire

Printed and bound in Great Britain by
TJ Books Ltd., Padstow, Cornwall

This book is printed on acid-free paper

A simple child,
That lightly draws its breath,
And feels its life in every limb,
What should it know of death?
— William Wordsworth

Abandon hope, all ye who enter here.
— Dante Alighieri

1

When they made the bargain, they knew they risked death. But living — if you could call existing in the Pleasure Academy living — wasn't much of a bargain.

Sure, she had three squares a day — like fricking clockwork. A bed at night — Lights Out, ten o'clock! She had clean clothes, and even the ugly uniform ranked higher than whatever she'd scrounged or stolen when freedom hadn't been just a concept.

School — mostly bullshit — but she secretly liked the French lessons. Auntie (top bitch) claimed speaking a second language helped create a sophisticated, elegant female.

None of that made up for the fact that she hadn't breathed outdoor air for . . . She couldn't say exactly, but they'd scooped her up just before Christmas when the easy pickings on the street were abso gargan.

Which is how she'd gotten scooped up because, yeah, maybe a little careless.

The girl they'd brought in the week before claimed it was May — maybe — but her brain was still addled from Orientation. Plus, the new one was really young — seven or eight maybe — and cried a lot.

It didn't seem possible she'd spent a whole winter, a whole spring inside. Then sometimes, at night, in the dark, it all got blurry, and felt as if she'd lived her whole life inside the Academy.

Up at seven sharp! Make your bed and make it right, or earn a demerit. Ten demerits earned an hour in the Meditation Box.

Shower, dress, which included hairstyling and makeup appropriate to the tasks of the day. Breakfast at eight sharp. Arrive late, demerit. Poor table manners warranted a quick jab with the shock stick or worse.

She'd had it all, and worse, before she'd learned to pretend.

On uniform days you took classes, like French or Polite Conversation, Deportment, Style, Personal Hygiene, Skin and Hair Care, and Weight Management.

Every week they measured, weighed, evaluated. And after that came Salon Day, whether you wanted one or not.

They'd had to strap her down and tranq her the first couple of times when they blasted some flaws — blemishes, a birthmark on her thigh. When they'd cleaned her teeth and did something to straighten them that ached for days after.

But the day she dreaded most? Intimacy Practice.

Sometimes it was another woman, an Academy graduate, who 'taught' the proper way to undress yourself, or undress somebody else.

She'd earned the prod and an entire day in the Meditation Box for punching her instructor when the woman put hands on her.

Sometimes it was a man, and that was somehow worse because you had to touch him, too.

They made you do things — all kinds of things — except actual sex. If they had to tie you down for it, they said that served as another lesson. Some owners enjoyed tying down their consorts.

Sometimes they paired you with another student

2

because some owners were women, or just got off watching two girls together.

And that's how she connected with Mina.

Naked in the bed, the cameras recording it all for Evaluation, Dorian resisted, turned her face away from Mina's lips.

Mina just rolled on top of her, pressed those lips to Dorian's ear. 'I hate it, too. I hate it,' she said, then moaned, rubbed her body against Dorian's. 'Pretend you don't, it'll be over faster. You have to go somewhere else in your head, you have to pretend it isn't you. Because it isn't.'

'Get off me.'

'Then we both end up in the damn box. You're going to roll over, get on top. Put your hand down there between us — just do it. I'm going to make myself come. That's what they want.'

She rolled over, and pulled Dorian's hand down — stronger than she looked. Then she bucked, made crazy sounds, flung her head side to side.

To Dorian's shock, Mina wrapped her legs around her, ground their centers together. 'Fake it,' Mina hissed. 'Now, fake it now. And we're done.'

Humiliating, yes, but better than being tied down, better than the shock stick or the box.

So she cried out as Mina had done, and if a couple of humiliation tears escaped, it didn't matter.

'Well done.' Auntie rose from her observation chair. 'Very well done, both of you.

'Trainee 232, as expected. Trainee 238, much improved. Enough to erase one demerit, and hopefully move you beyond the restrictions of Bondage Only status.'

She waited, eyes keen.

3

'Thank you, Auntie,' Mina said dutifully, and with a hand between their bodies, pinched Dorian.

'Thank you, Auntie.'

'You're quite welcome. Now, shower thoroughly. You can have ten minutes in the Relaxation Area before you dress for dinner.'

The showers in the Intimacy Area ran plush — a small benefit. Cameras recorded, of course, as the small benefit never included privacy.

But water ran hot, and steam rose.

Mina spoke in whispers under it as she shampooed.

'I'm Mina. I've been here six months and ten days, I think.'

'Dorian. I'm not sure, maybe five months.'

'I've seen you in some of the classes. You have to pretend better. If you keep getting tossed in the box, drugged up, or smacked around, you'll never escape.'

'There's no way out. I've tried. I've looked.'

'If there's a way in, there's a way out.' She sent Dorian a sidelong look as she carefully worked conditioner through her long red hair. 'Maybe I've got a plan I'm working on, but I think it needs two.'

Then she smiled, poured liquid wash onto a pink pouf. 'You're doing really well in French class,' she said in normal tones.

Since Dorian didn't need to get hit with a brick to catch on, she shrugged. 'I really like the French class. Polite Conversation is boooring.'

'Oh, it's not so bad, and it's nice to have conversation. You know, you could maybe help me in French, and I could help you with the other. Improvement means more time in the Relaxation Area, which is totally iced.'

Which was beyond boring, but Dorian shrugged

4

again. 'I guess. Is it allowed?'

'Auntie let me help a trainee with reading, so I guess. I'll ask.'

'Yeah, you ask. She likes you.'

'I'm likable.' Her pretty, heart-shaped face lit up with a smile that fell short of her eyes. 'I like being likable. One day I'll have a master who'll like me, and give me beautiful clothes and lots of orgasms. I can't wait!'

Dorian saw the lie. Mina wanted out, and so did she.

So they formed an alliance.

As Dorian saw it, they had nothing much in common.

She was Black — or mostly — and Mina was as white as white got. Through snippets of conversation, she learned Mina had lived in a nice house in the 'burbs of Philadelphia.

She'd been scooped up walking home after soccer practice from her school. Private school. She had a younger brother, and two parents, four grandparents, and three best friends. She had a sort of boyfriend, too.

Dorian had lived on the streets for months before she got scooped. She'd run away from her hard-handed mother and her mother's series of idiot boyfriends and a craphole tenement in Freehold.

She'd made it to New York only a few weeks before the scoop and had just started finding her feet. She'd found her freedom, then bam, she'd come to strapped to a bed inside the Academy.

She'd thought hospital at first, because it looked like one.

Auntie told her differently.

5

As she saw it, she and Mina practically came from different planets. But they had a few things in common. Hatred for the Academy and a desperation to escape it. And smarts.

Over the next weeks, the alliance grew into a friendship.

Dorian learned to pretend, and learned the benefits of pretending.

She got praise, she got little rewards. And better, even better, the sharp eyes of the instructors, the guards, the matrons, of Auntie didn't look so often in her direction.

She built up a little trust. Not the big pile of it Mina had, but enough. If someone said something careless around her, she filed it away and told Mina.

Mina did the same. And piece by piece they put together a blueprint of the Academy. In their heads only, but they had smarts.

Then Mina found out about the tunnels.

'Number 264 killed herself. Or she's dead anyway. She used bedsheets and hanged herself.'

Dorian felt her chest burn. 'Which one is that?'

'One of the newer ones. We're luckier because we're in the Pretty Ones and they don't hurt us as much as they do the Servants and Pets. Yesterday I was with Auntie, in her office, for a special evaluation, and one of them came to the door. She went out, but I listened.'

'If she'd caught you —'

'She didn't, and there aren't any cameras in her office. Nobody watches Auntie. She said use elevator three to take the body down to the tunnels tonight, after Lights Out, and to the crematorium. She said how the dead girl was a street rat anyway, and a waste of time and resources.'

The burn in Dorian's chest erupted into fire. 'I'm going to kill her one day.'

'Dorian, grip it. Tunnels. That's a way out for sure.'

'You need a swipe for the elevators.'

'That's where you come in. That's what you do, right?'

Maybe she'd worked the streets, the tourists — and maybe exaggerated her skill just a little — but this was different.

'You want me to lift a swipe card?'

'The plan doesn't work without it.' Mina's absolute confidence radiated, and infected. 'You get the swipe as close to Lights Out as you can.'

'Even if I get the swipe, it doesn't work inside our rooms. We're locked in at night.'

'Tonight we won't be. I've got that part. You get the card, and at ten-thirty, take the elevator down to the infirmary. Pick me up there, then we go all the way down, and we get out.'

They'd talked too long, both knew it, but Mina risked another minute. 'We've got to get out, Dorian. I was telling Auntie how much I wanted a handsome master to buy me beautiful things, and she said the auction was coming up soon. I wouldn't have much longer to wait.

'They'll sell us. We have to get out now.'

Sold, Dorian thought. No more pretending then, and no more Mina to help her stand the pretending.

'I'll get the swipe.'

'Ten-thirty, infirmary. Something I ate didn't agree with me.'

It didn't seem real. For months she'd dreamed and schemed of a way out. But now all she could think of

7

were the punishments if they got caught.

More likely when.

But they had to try. They had to or Auntie would sell them like — like a candy bar in a twenty-four/seven.

She knew, of course she knew, her ancestors had been sold into slavery, and when she'd still gone to regular school, she'd studied about the whole damn war fought over it.

But this was 2061, for fuck's sake! People couldn't just sell people.

But they would. They would.

She felt sick to her stomach, and really hot — like maybe she had a fever and she needed the infirmary for real.

But she reminded herself that she had a talent for one thing. She knew how to pick pockets. She knew how to take something from a mark and move on.

With fifteen minutes to Lights Out, Dorian scurried down the corridor to her room carrying a small bag. Since scurrying broke the rules, she knew the hall matron would stop her, issue a demerit and a warning.

'238!'

Heart pounding, Dorian skidded to a stop.

'Running in the hallways, one demerit. How many does that make this time?'

'Three, Matron. I'm very sorry.'

'You should be. What do you have there?'

'Hygienic supplies, Matron.' All innocence, Dorian held out the bag containing a small roll of toilet paper, a tiny tube of soap, and a tube of facial cleanser.

As the matron — a big, beefy woman with a shock stick strapped to her belt — grabbed the bag, Dorian shuffled an inch closer and, ears ringing, palmed the

8

swipe card hooked to the woman's left jacket pocket.

'I was getting ready for bed, and saw I was out of some supplies for hygiene and skin care. I needed to —'

'That's two demerits, 238, the second for carelessness. It'll be three if you're not in your room and properly prepared for the night by Lights Out.'

'Yes, Matron. Thank you.'

She walked blindly to her room — cell, she corrected. And didn't allow herself to shake until she'd closed the door.

She prepared for bed as usual because the hall bitch might check on her. But she kept her clothes on under the ugly nightgown.

When the lights blinked their one-minute warning, she got into bed, pulled the sheet and thin blanket up to her chin.

And as she'd feared, her door opened.

Fear exploded inside her as the matron marched to the bed.

She knew! She knew!

The woman stared down at her with mean eyes — monster eyes to Dorian's mind. She braced for the fire of the shock stick.

But the matron just peered at Dorian's face, swiped a finger over her cheek.

Her mouth thinned as she nodded, and without a word walked out.

Dorian heard the locks snap. And the lights went off.

She lay trembling in the dark, staring up at the faint numbers illuminated on the ceiling.

10:00 P.M.

9

She didn't know. She didn't know. Yet.

Dorian watched those numbers change, minute by minute, and visualized the Matron Monster checking each door — twenty-eight on this floor. Then she'd use the stairs — please God don't let her decide to use the elevator this time. And check the other floors. Probably.

There had to be other floors with other rooms because she'd counted at least sixty trainees. And she didn't think she'd seen all of them. This floor held the Pretty Ones. But there were Servants, Breeders, and Pets.

Since none of the cells had soundproofing — they wanted to hear you — she listened for voices, footsteps, alarms, any sounds.

She heard the heavy door of the stairway thump shut, and closed her eyes as tears leaked.

She still didn't know.

★ ★ ★

In the infirmary, on the narrow exam table, Mina rolled on her side, stuck her fingers down her throat, and puked on Nurse's shoes.

'Goddamn it, 232!'

'I'm sorry.' She added a few pathetic moans. 'I'm sorry.'

Nurse shoved a slop dish into her hands. 'Use this if you have to vomit again. Stay there!'

Since the door to the infirmary was locked — the drugs, the supplies, the everything locked — where would she go?

She moaned, held her breath, moaned, then leaped up, dashed to the computer on the desk. Nurse had

had to check her in, so no passcode needed.

She'd paid attention in computer class, had a geek friend. She knew what to do.

She pulled up the locks, hit the release for Dorian's door, crossed her fingers for luck, then yanked open drawers.

Nurse chewed gum. All the damn time.

And there was a pack of it. Mina grabbed two sticks and, chewing madly, dashed back to the exam table.

She had time to tuck the wad into her cheek when Nurse came back — wearing fresh shoes.

'I'm so sorry, Nurse. I'm sorry, but I feel a lot better. Just really tired and sort of weak, but my stomach doesn't hurt anymore.'

Nurse grunted, took her temperature, checked her pulse.

Mina knew her skin felt clammy — but that was fear, and excitement.

'I'm not hauling you upstairs, then having somebody haul you back down again if it starts up again. You'll stay in the sickroom tonight.'

'I just want to sleep.'

Nurse helped her up, and Mina leaned against her as they went across the hall to the sickroom. Half the size of her bedroom upstairs, it held a cot, a rolling chair for a medical.

At the door, Mina swayed, leaned a little more weight on Nurse as she covered her mouth with her hand, spit out the gum.

'I thought . . .' She breathed out as she shoved the wad of gum against the latch. 'False alarm. A little queasy, but not like before.'

Nurse dumped her on the cot, used the mini tablet in her pocket to record the sickroom stay. She set a bucket beside the bed.

'You have to go, you have to vomit again, use that. If you need medical assistance, press the button on the bed guard. Don't bother me unless you need medical assistance. Understood?'

'Yes, yes. I'm so tired. I just want to sleep.'

'Easy for you. I have to clean up your mess. Lights, ten percent,' she ordered. 'So you don't miss the bucket.'

She stalked out.

Since Mina didn't have a clock, she counted off the minutes.

Nurse had to get cleaning supplies, mop up the puke, then she'd probably go back and clean up her shoes. She had a little room with a sleep chair and a screen.

Maybe she'd sit at her desk first, write up the report on the puking incident, but if she did, she'd face the comp screen, not the glass door.

Quietly, Mina slipped off the cot, moved to the door. She pressed her ear to it, heard nothing.

Now or never, she told herself, and eased the door open a crack.

No alarm sounded, so she picked the nasty gum off the latch, then crept out. Nurse sat at the desk, and everything inside Mina trembled.

She pulled the door closed behind her, heard the lock click. Though it sounded like an explosion in her head, Nurse didn't even glance away from the screen as she worked.

Mina made the dash to the elevator.

'Come on, Dorian. Please, please, please.'

If Dorian didn't come —

No, no, she would. She *had* to. They had to get out,

go to the police. She had to call her mom and dad. They'd come get her. And Dorian, too.

They'd be safe, and all these terrible people would go to jail.

But the minutes ticked by.

What if Nurse decided to check on her? What if someone else got sick, and a matron brought them down? What if Auntie —

She heard the elevator hum, and instinctively stepped back, looked wildly for a place to hide.

Then braced her shoulders. If the doors opened and she didn't see Dorian, it was over anyway. Everything. She'd be punished, beaten, tossed into the box. She'd be sold at auction like a — like a painting or some fancy necklace.

A thing. She wouldn't live as a thing.

When the doors opened, she nearly cried out. Slapping a hand over her own mouth, she leaped in with Dorian.

Forgetting the gum, she gripped Dorian's hand.

'What the —'

'Sorry. Gum. I used it on the latch. SB? Sub-basement, right? That's got to be it.' Mina pressed the button.

Authorization required for that level.

They both jumped a foot.

'Swipe card, try the swipe card on the pad. It has to work. It *has* to.'

Dorian gripped her own wrist to steady her hand, swiped the card. Mina pushed the button again.

Authorization verified.

13

The elevator started down.

'Someone could be down there,' Dorian said. 'What do we do if somebody's right there?'

'I don't know. We — we run, or try to fight. I don't know. We got this far. Oh God, oh God, I guess I never really believed we'd get this far, so I don't know.'

It took forever, or seemed like it as they wrapped arms around each other.

Then the doors opened, and still wrapped around each other, they stepped out into dim light.

'It really is a tunnel.'

'It goes both ways.' Dorian pointed right, then left. 'Which way is out?'

'We have to pick one. You pick. I feel like I might puke again.'

Dorian chose right. 'We should run. We might not have much time. The Matron Monster might need her swipe.' She shoved it in her back pocket in case they needed it again. 'Maybe she'll think she dropped it, but maybe she'll put it together.'

Hands clasped, they ran. The tunnel echoed, so they spoke in whispers, filling each other in.

Then the tunnel forked.

'You pick this time,' Dorian said when they stopped.

'We went right,' Mina replied, 'so this time left. It has to lead somewhere because that's how they removed that poor girl. We just keep going until we escape. Then we have to determine where we are. You were in New York, I was in Devon. We could be any-where now. We break free, find out where we are, get somewhere I can call my parents. And the police.'

'The police? But —'

'All the others, Dorian.' In the dim, yellowish light, Mina's soft green eyes went fierce. 'We have to think

14

of all the other girls, like us.'

Maybe she felt bad for them, but Dorian's instinct said just get out and run.

'My parents will know what to do,' Mina told her. 'They'll come get us, no matter where we are. I miss them so much, and my stupid little brother, too. I know he's a pest and annoying, but not always. And I know I get pissed at my parents sometimes. I mean, so clueless, right? But I never ever felt afraid until the Academy. They never ever hurt me. And your mom —'

'She's not like them.'

'You've been gone all this time. She's got to be worried. She —'

'She's not like your parents, okay?' Everything inside Dorian hardened, coated over even the fear. 'I felt afraid plenty, and she hurt me when she felt like it. If we go to the cops, they'll send me back to her or toss me in juvie or a foster. I might as well stay here.'

'Don't say that, don't. My parents will take care of you, too. I promise. I swear it. Nobody's going to screw with you. They won't let that happen. And they won't let these — these *fucks* get away with everything they did.'

Rather than argue, Dorian shrugged. Mina had plenty of smarts, but she didn't know how the real world worked.

'Did you hear that?' Dorian's hand vised on Mina's.

Voices echoing, footsteps running.

'They're coming. We need to run.'

'No, no, they'll hear running,' Mina hissed. 'Like we hear them. Keep walking, close to the tunnel wall, keep moving, but quiet, quiet. Look, look up there! A ladder in the wall. We climb up, right? It has to be a way out.'

15

When Mina reached it, she gripped the sides. 'There's a cover on it. We'll need to push it off. Careful, it's a little slippery.'

They wedged together on the narrow ladder.

'It's not heavy. I'm taller, let me.' Dorian gritted her teeth, shoved. 'I've got it. I've got it.'

As she used both hands to push the metal cover, Dorian's foot slipped. Even as Mina grabbed for her, she went down, banging her knee on a rung, then feeling her ankle twist and go out from under her on the fall to the concrete.

She bit back a scream of pain as Mina pulled her up. 'You're okay, you're all right. I see light. We have to go up now. They're getting closer.'

She shoved Dorian up, climbed behind. 'Hurry. You have to hurry.'

The pain made her sick, made her dizzy, but she climbed. Climbed into pouring rain and roaring thunder.

Mina popped out like a cork behind her, then dragged the cover back in place.

Through the storm, they saw what looked like a huddle of derelict and abandoned buildings, a couple of rusted-out cars slumped on weedy gravel, a heap of busted-up planks, a lot of trash.

It smelled like a broken recycler filled with rotten fruit.

But in the distance, lights gleamed through the wall of rain.

'That way!'

'I can't run, Mina. I can barely walk. I maybe broke something.'

'Lean on me. If we can get to those lights —'

She broke off as the cover shifted. With an arm

16

around Dorian, she dragged her friend to the old lumber pile.

'We hide,' she whispered. 'Stay down until they go away.'

A man pulled himself out of the hole. Spoke to someone below him. 'There's blood on the ground, the ladder. One of them's hurt.'

The Matron Monster climbed out. 'I hope to fuck it's the little shit who stole my swipe. She's going to pay for it.' Already soaked to the skin, she spoke into a 'link. 'We found their exit, and one's banged up.'

The man gave a location and orders to send more for the search. Ordered vans for a street sweep even as a third climbed out.

'They didn't get far,' he said. 'We were a minute behind them. Spread out and find those bitches.'

'They'll find us,' Mina whispered in Dorian's ear. 'I'm going to lead them away.'

'No!'

'I can run faster than they can, and it's raining so hard, I can get a head start maybe. Stay here, stay quiet. I'll make them think you're with me so they'll stop looking. I'll send help.'

'You can't —'

Mina picked up a broken piece of wood with a jagged edge, and shoved at the bright hair the rain plastered to her face. 'Stay down, stay quiet. We got out, Dorian. We're not going back.'

She gripped Dorian's hand one last time. 'Partners,' she whispered, then ran.

'There! I see one!'

'Go, Dorian,' Mina screamed. 'Keep going! Don't stop!'

As Mina ran, Dorian squeezed her eyes shut. She'd

tried praying a few times in her life, and it never worked. But she tried again, as hard as she could.

She heard a shout, and then a scream. Mina? Following her gut, she lurched to her feet, managed one running step before her leg crumpled under her. Her head cracked hard against a plank on the way down. She saw stars. Then nothing at all.

Under a black umbrella, Auntie stood over the body. The trainee she'd put so much time and effort into, had such high hopes for, lay like a soaked rag, impaled with a jagged spear of wood.

Useless now, she thought. Useless.

'No sign of the other one.' Her head of security stood next to her. 'What a fuckup. I'll have a full report for you after I debrief. Do you want her taken to the crematorium?'

'No. 238 may go to the police. It's not her nature, but in case she does, we'll turn this on her. Have that idiot Nurse get the last blood draw from 238. When the cops find the body where you'll deposit it, it'll have 238's blood on it. And have whatever 232 was wearing when we recruited her brought up. Get this disappointment in a van. You'll take care of this tonight.'

'Yes, ma'am.'

'I'll relay precise instructions. I want no more carelessness. Understood?'

'Loud and clear.'

'Stupid, ungrateful bitch.'

Auntie kicked the body once, viciously, then walked away.

18

2

Dorian woke with her head pounding like an airjack. Her knee felt sick and squishy, like her stomach. She didn't know where she was or what had happened. For a terrifying few minutes she didn't know who she was.

Everything went blurry when she tried to sit up, so she lay still. The air smelled bad, and the ground felt rough and bumpy under her. Her ankle throbbed.

She tried hard to think of the last thing she remembered, but just couldn't, so she concentrated on what she did know.

Somebody had hurt her, and she didn't want to be wherever she was. That somebody might come back, hurt her again.

This time when she sat up, she braced against the dizziness, hissed her way through it. She saw some buildings — crapholes — some junk.

She wore gray pants — they looked like good pants except for the bloody tear in the left knee. Wet and clingy pants, like her shirt — her white shirt.

She pressed her fingers to her knee, squawked in pain before she could stop herself. She wore plain white sneakers, and the ankle above the left foot swelled like a balloon.

She'd had bumps and bruises and swollen parts before. Her mother got pissed and dealt them out like a hand of cards.

Had her mother done this to her?

No, no, she didn't think so. She'd gotten away, again.

Spend Christmas in New York. Wasn't she going to do that? But it didn't feel like Christmas. It felt hot. Even though she couldn't stop shivering, it felt hot.

Maybe she had a fever.

Wherever, whenever, she had to move. Maybe find a place she could steal some medicine, an ice pack.

She picked around the woodpile — got a splinter for her trouble — until she found something she could use as a kind of crutch.

Tears streamed, watering the pain as she used the wood to pull herself up. She hobbled her way toward the lights in the distance.

Lights meant people, people meant pockets to pick or stores with ice packs and blockers. Once she had those, she'd find a hole somewhere and sleep. Just sleep until the pain went away.

Dazed, her mind heading toward numb in defense, she walked.

And walked. And walked.

* * *

About the same time Dorian crawled through a broken window in a condemned building and fell into a blocker-and-tranq-induced sleep with ice packs strapped to her knee and ankle, Lieutenant Eve Dallas stood over a body on the north edge of Battery Park.

Last night's storm had cleared the worst of a late June three-day heat wave and left the air in Lower Manhattan oddly refreshed.

Wouldn't last, but it made a nice morning.

20

Except for the kid — just a kid, Eve thought. Hair in a frizzy red cloud around a sweet, heart-shaped face. Green eyes stared out behind the film death smeared on them.

Blood stained the white shirt, spreading out from the spear of wood in the girl's chest.

No blood on the grass or ground, she noted. Could've washed away in the rain, but the body lay fairly sheltered under the leafy branches of a tree near the bike path.

She glanced toward the path — light traffic at this hour — then at the uniform who stood by.

'What do you know?'

'Sir. Not a hell of a lot. Guy decides to do some yoga in the park at sunrise.' The uniform chin-pointed at a man of around seventy in compression shorts and tank holding a rolled mat. He stood by a second uniform. 'Wilfred Meadows. He lives a couple blocks away and says he likes this spot for his, ah, sunrise salutations. He saw the body, contacted nine-one-one.'

The officer cleared his throat. 'When we arrived on scene, the witness was sitting cross-legged a few feet away from the victim, with his hands pressed together.'

The officer demonstrated. 'He said he was trying to send positive energy to her spirit on her journey. And he cried a little because she's just a kid. Says he's got a redheaded granddaughter about her age.

'He comes here most mornings, he said, and rides his bike on the path three afternoons a week, leads a tai chi class in the park two afternoons a week. He hasn't seen the victim around before. He thinks he'd have noticed because of the hair and his granddaughter.'

'Okay, get his information and let him go home. We'll follow up. Wait.'

21

She spotted her partner, Detective Peabody, walking fast toward the crime scene tape. 'We'll follow up now. Peabody.' Eve crossed to the tape.

'Sorry! Subway glitch, so I ditched it. I put half a mile on my feet and shift just started.'

'Yoga guy there found the body. The uniforms got his statement. Follow up before you let him go.'

'Got it.' Peabody took off her rainbow sunshades, slid them into a pocket of her jacket. Maybe the sun beamed, but she knew how Eve felt about rainbow sunshades on the job. 'She looks like a kid.'

'She was. Twelve, thirteen, fourteen. I'll take the body, you take the wit.'

Eve turned, walked back, crouched down.

Opening her field kit, she took out her Identi-pad first and pressed it to the victim's right thumb.

'Victim is identified as Mina Rose Cabot, age thirteen, of Devon, Pennsylvania. Caucasian, red and green. Five feet, four inches, a hundred and six pounds. Parents, Rae and Oliver Cabot, same address, one sib, Ethan, age eleven.'

She got out her gauges. 'TOD, twenty-three-oh-six. COD appears to be the approximately eighteen-inch-by-three-inch piece of wood or wood product impaled mid-chest. ME to confirm, lab to verify weapon.'

With her sealed hands, Eve picked up and examined the victim's. 'Some bruising on the knuckles, some dried blood.' She took a sample of the blood, sealed it, then put on microgoggles, studied both palms. 'Looks like a couple splinters in the palms, both hands. Blood on the shirt around the wound consistent with the injury. Some drops on the cuff of the shirt, some on the pants. Not consistent with the wound.'

22

She shook her head. 'Where the hell did that spear thing come from?'

She sat back on her heels. 'Put up a fight, didn't you, Mina? Grabbed for the spear of wood — or maybe you held it to begin with and the killer used it against you.'

'Victim has pierced ears — two on the left, one in the right. No earrings. No shoes, no 'link, no wallet or purse. She's got a little — looks like silver — heart on a chain. Chain's broken.

'So the killer takes her earrings, her shoes, whatever else she had on her, but doesn't take the necklace. Maybe heard somebody coming and ran before he could grab it. Maybe.'

She replaced her tools. 'No visible facial wounds or other visible injuries. Clothes are intact. ME to check for sexual assault or rape, but it looks like a mugging gone way wrong. What the hell were you doing in New York, Mina from Pennsylvania?'

Family trip, Eve thought, a runaway? She sure as hell didn't look like a kid who'd spent any time on the streets.

She pushed up as Peabody walked to her.

'Mr. Meadows's statement jibes. I've got all his information. He's lived here for eighteen years, works as a life coach for Healthy You and Me — thirty-three years there. Married for forty-one years. His wife's a fitness coach, same company. His wife's a redhead, so are their daughter and their oldest granddaughter. He said he had one horrible instant when he thought the victim was his granddaughter, Abigail. He knew it wasn't — but he had that instant.'

'She's Mina Cabot, from Devon, Pennsylvania. Looks like a mugging, but . . .' Eve looked back. 'See how she's laid out? Not posed or anything, but it's still neat. Not like she took the spear in the chest and fell. And no grass stains on her clothes. No blood on the ground — we'll have the sweepers check that, but . . . Let's roll her.'

Together they went back to the body. Peabody sealed her hands with the can Eve passed her, then they carefully turned Mina on her side. 'Let's amend the size of the spear to closer to twenty-four inches,' noted Eve. 'Look at the blood on the back of the shirt. It pierced her back. But there's no blood under her.'

'Dump site?' Peabody asked.

'Her shirt's damp — hasn't dried through — and TOD confirms she died during that storm last night. But the pants? They're dry, and the blood on them? Rain didn't hit that.'

'They fit her though. Well, maybe just a tad short, like she had a little growth spurt.'

'Her ID lists her at five-four. Morris to verify.'

'They're good pants. School-uniform navy.'

Eve's eyes narrowed. '"School uniform"?'

'That's how they strike me. Private school uniform. They're usually navy or gray, maybe khaki for the summer. These aren't summer weight though.'

'Not summer weight,' Eve repeated thoughtfully. 'Morris will check for rape. Why change her pants? Take her shoes — you can see by the condition of the bottom of her feet she wasn't walking around the city barefoot. Why take her shoes, remove her earrings, take her ID, her 'link, if she had all that, but take the time to change her pants? Because I'm damned if she died in these. Or died here.'

'Pretty kid,' Peabody said. 'Seriously pretty.'

'Yeah, she was. Look at her nails — fingers and

toes. Perfectly kept, clean, neat. Soft hands. She hasn't spent any time on the streets. Check with missing persons in Devon, see if they have anything on her. I'll call for the dead wagon and the sweepers.'

Moved her here, Eve thought as she made the contacts. Set it up to look like a mugging. But it wasn't about a pair of shoes or a pocket 'link.

'Dallas. There's been an Amber Alert out on her since last November. November nine. She didn't come home from school. Bester Middle — private school. I've got the names of the detectives assigned. And there's a notation the parents have offered two hundred thousand to anyone with information that leads to their daughter's return.'

'This kid hasn't been on the streets for over seven months. A runaway, possibly. We'll see what the investigators say. But she's had a decent place to stay. You know this shit — is that actual wood or composite?'

Peabody crouched down.

'It's pine,' she said. 'The real deal. Looks like it has some age on it. The lab'll have to pin that down. I think it's an old stud.'

'Like your grandfather?'

'Ha! Funny! Like a wall stud maybe, and somebody who didn't give a shit about decent wood ripped it out. Somebody rehabbing a building — like we're doing with the house, but we'd never treat material like this. It's warped some, so it's been out in the weather. Probably for a while.'

'Another point she was dumped. The killer didn't just happen to pick that up lying on the ground here. We'll have uniforms canvass, but somebody brought her here, after that storm blew out, dumped her under that tree.

'Could've weighed her down, dumped her in the river — it's close enough.'

'They wanted her found.'

Eve nodded at her partner. 'And why's that? She was out in that storm, and she fought. Nothing under her nails, so she didn't get any scratches in — or the killer cleaned them before the dump. No facial bruising, just a little on her knuckles.'

'Fight didn't last long,' Peabody concluded.

'No.' Eve looked down at the body again. 'Not long.'

* * *

Eve waited until she got to Central, into her office, grabbed some life-giving coffee from her AutoChef, before making the first contact.

Rather than start with the notification, she contacted the lead detective on Mina's missing persons case.

'Ah, hell. Ah, fuck it all to hell.' Detective Sharlene Driver scrubbed her hands over her deep brown face, then pressed her fingers to eyes several shades darker.

Then she dropped them, and the eyes went cop flat. 'I'd appreciate the details, Lieutenant.'

'And you'll have them. My partner's writing the report now and will copy you. I'll answer any questions you may have. I have some of my own.'

'How about I anticipate some of them, answer — and reciprocate by sending you our files?'

'Appreciated.'

'It's a good family, Lieutenant. Mother's a civil rights attorney — does a lot of pro bono work. Father's a doctor, a GP, has his own practice. They're financially solid, but not crazy rich — not kidnap a kid for

26

a big, fat payday rich. Mina did exceptionally well in school, had a solid circle of friends — no serious boyfriend, but she was sweet on a guy in her class. We talked to him, his family, the friends. Nothing pointed to her running off. Nothing.'

Driver paused. 'You have to look at that. Kid gets pissed off, takes off, but not here. She'd negotiated a vid date — her first group date with the boy and two other couples, and was looking forward to it. She was walking home from soccer practice.'

'Usual time and route?'

'Yeah, and that's a thing. It's only about a half mile, nice neighborhood — with this little grove of trees along her way. The other thing is while the parents had the talk about strangers and all that, and Mina was a sharp kid, she was also the type — look at her parents — to try to help somebody she thought needed it.'

'Somebody knew her route, used her nature, grabbed her up.'

'That's how we saw it. No ransom demand. We got some hotline calls, but mostly bogus, and nothing panned out. The closest we came is somebody thought they might have seen a van in the area. Either a black or brown or frigging blue van. With windows, no windows.'

'I hear you.'

'The dad picked up the son at his friends' — where the kid habitually went after school — just before five. Mina was due home by five, but he didn't worry until about five-thirty when his wife got home. They called Mina's 'link — but couldn't connect. Started calling her friends, her soccer coach, then while Oliver — the dad — went out to drive around the area, Rae called the police.

27

'They haven't given up, Lieutenant. This is going to crush them. If you could do me a solid, let my partner and me notify them. We have a relationship.'

'I'll make sure you get the report quickly. I'll want to talk to them, but it can wait until later in the day.'

'I'll tell you they're going to be on their way to New York today. They won't wait.'

'Give them my contact. I'll make time.'

'They're going to ask me if she was raped.'

'I can't give you that information. She's with our ME now, and he'll determine that. What was she wearing the night she went missing?'

'School uniform — she'd have had her soccer clothes in her bag. White, long-sleeved shirt, navy pants. She had a habit of shoving her school blazer in her backpack — because it was lame — and wearing a white zip-up hoodie. Same with her uniform shoes — dark brown loafer style. She'd more likely have worn her white kicks.'

'Jewelry?'

'Three earrings — studs. Two silver hearts, one blue star, a silver heart on a chain. She'd have had her 'link, her ID, under twenty in cash, her tablet, schoolwork — assignments, a binder to hold assignments — earbuds, the makeup she was allowed — and what she snuck in, which her mother knew about. Hairbrush, hair ties, and a small first aid kit. Her father insisted both kids carry the basics. We didn't find a trace of any of it.'

Whoever grabbed her wanted it to look like a runaway at first glance, Eve thought when she ended the call. Like the killer wanted it to look like a mugging.

To buy time, she assumed, in both cases.

And that led her to believe the snatch and the

murder rested on the same person or persons.

She got up to start her murder board.

She kept at it when she heard Peabody clomp down the hall to her office.

'Send the report to Detective Driver.'

Peabody pulled out her PPC and did so.

'Devon's going to do the next of kin notification, and reciprocate by sending us their files. They concluded a snatch, not a runaway. I'm going to agree with that. The victim didn't strike out for the bright lights of New York after soccer practice with under twenty in her pocket.'

Eve didn't turn. 'I can feel you giving the AC begging glances. Get your damn coffee. Get me more.'

'It was more like longing glances than begging.'

'We're going to run the parents to cover it. Look for any debts, any payouts that don't square. Devon's done that, but we cover it. She had a boyfriend — sort of. We're going to look at him and see if he has a perv older brother, uncle, father. Run her coaches and teachers, same deal.'

'Okay.'

'And we look for any connections to New York, because they brought her here, and they kept her here. No signs of restraints or force — so far.'

'Maybe kept her drugged.'

'The tox will show it, just like Morris will determine if somebody used her for sex. Why do you grab up a pretty young teen if not for ransom — and no ransom demands made — or sex?'

'Like a house droid? Slave labor?'

'Not with those hands and nails. If anything, she'd had some pampering there, with that — what do you call it — kind of manicure deal.'

29

'French. You're right. She had a classic French manicure — fingers and toes. Nothing flashy, all classy.'

'Classy,' Eve repeated, and grabbed her coffee. 'If it was for sex, he wanted that classy. Or . . . let's check child pornography. Thirteen's on the cusp of that. It's more pubescent porn. Photos, vids.'

Eve looked at the ID shot on her board, that young, fresh, open face. 'Pretty redhead, clear white skin, some curves. Youthful but what — budding?'

'It's so sick.'

'Yeah, and so's jamming a sharp piece of wood in a kid's chest. McNab did some time in Vice — check with him.'

Since the EDD ace was Peabody's cohab and main squeeze, checking with him added a plus.

Eve stepped back from the board, studied it.

'A pretty young girl walks the half mile home from school — same route every day. That makes a snatch easy. But the nice neighborhood makes it stickier. Somebody took some time, to watch, to plan. Had transportation. I'm betting somebody's done this before. Maybe selling the kids he snatches. For sex, for underground porn sites.

'It has to be worth it, to keep her for months, to keep her clean and healthy, closed in or drugged, or convinced she's living the high life. Has to pay off. Has to pay enough to transport her out of state.'

'Maybe that just happened,' Peabody suggested. 'And something went wrong there, and she got away.'

'Could be. Could very well be. You've had her all this time, you maybe get a little careless, and she tries to bolt.'

She looked at the picture from the crime scene.

30

'Where the hell did that weapon come from? Close to where she bolted, if so?'

She went back to her desk to open the murder book on Mina. 'Check with McNab, and let's put together a list of known pedophiles — in and around Devon, in New York.'

'Holy shit, that's going to be a long list.'

'Girls — eleven to fourteen. Younger won't work, older's beyond that scope of sick. No brutality — unless Morris turns some up. He kept her school uniform,' Eve murmured. 'The pants. But the shirt? Roe said long sleeves when she was snatched — we need to verify that absolutely, because she had on short, cuffed sleeves when she was killed. Maybe we can track the shirt.'

'They could change the pants, but not the shirt,' Peabody concluded. 'But why keep the pants?'

'Maybe he has a collection. That's the file from Devon coming through. Go.'

Eve read the files from the initial incident report through the steps and stages of the investigation, the interviews, statements, the timeline the investigators put together. She studied the map of the neighborhood, the location of the house to the school, both to the grove of trees.

Thorough, she decided. The Devon detectives weren't morons or slackers. They'd worked it, and hard, covered the ground, then covered it again.

And attached to the file, she found a list of known pedophiles that included nearby Philadelphia.

She'd go through those interviews, too, but first she entered the list, then ordered a new search narrowing it to her parameters.

Females between eleven and fourteen.

She did the same for New York, restricting it — for now — to Manhattan.

Then, testing her tech skills, ordered one more for any connections between the narrowed Pennsylvania list and New York's.

While the computer worked, she put her boots on her desk, picked up what was left of her coffee, and studied the board.

Pampered hands and feet, no signs of restraints, no outward signs of malnutrition, violence.

Morris would confirm or refute that, but for now . . .

What kept a thirteen-year-old girl with an abductor for months?

Someone she knew, trusted. But nothing in Driver's report indicated anything like that, and she and her partner hadn't missed a trick that Eve could see.

No physical restraints didn't mean she hadn't been locked up, or fed drugs to make her compliant. Brainwashed, threatened.

School uniform pants and a plain white shirt. The necklace. Odd, really, they'd allowed her to keep the necklace but not the earrings.

Because it sure as hell hadn't been a standard botched mugging.

'You got outside, didn't you, Mina? And you fought back when they caught you. Died for it. Maybe you still had those pants, or maybe they put them on you to make you look like a runaway. Left your necklace with a broken chain to make it look like a mugging or fight.'

Just another kid, Eve thought, who takes off and comes to a bad end.

'But that's not you. Look at that face. Pretty girl with skin like white rose petals. And a body just barely

32

past the first bud. Whoever took you kept you pretty and prime for a reason.'

When her computer announced the completion of her first search, she dropped her feet to the floor, swiveled back.

She'd find the reason.

3

Peabody came back in while Eve worked another series of cross-checks.

'McNab gave me a contact, Detective Willowby. She just transferred to Central from the four-oh-six. She's in SVU, mostly on crimes against minors. I reached out.'

Because Peabody knew the perils of Eve's ass-biting visitor's chair, she perched warily on the very edge. 'She'll run Mina's picture against any of the vids or photos they've got. And there are dark web chat rooms — sharing sites. They —'

'Share or trade slaves — sex or domestic.'

'You knew about that. Jesus, Willowby says some of the minors they pull out claim it's consensual, or ordained — or whatever they've been indoctrinated to believe. Sometimes they start them off really young, even babies they . . .'

As it struck her, Peabody forgot about the chair, had her ass bitten, pushed up. 'Sorry. Sorry, Dallas.'

'Nothing to be sorry about. It gives me insight. I probably had a couple more years before he put me on the market. He fucked that up by raping me, so he couldn't market me as a virgin. They're usually worth more. Then again, some like them broken in.'

Or just broken, she thought. She'd sure as hell qualified.

'But this wasn't that,' Eve continued. 'Probability's high she was snatched because of her looks and her

34

age — twelve at the time of the snatch. But why keep her so long if you're going to put her on the market? Personal use and/or porn profit hits the highest on the scale. And when she ages out of kiddie porn and your preferences, you pass her on to the next.'

'That's more or less what Willowby told me. She also said, when I told her about the mani-pedi and her general condition, the victim fits what they call the Princess category.'

Intrigued, Eve stopped, swiveled around. 'Princess — as in treated as such?'

'Yeah. Compliance drugs probably, at least at first. But pretty clothes, makeup, some sparkles, a fun room — no windows likely, locked door for sure. Toys and stuff for younger ones.'

'The carrot instead of the stick. I never get why it isn't candy or ice cream instead of the stick. Who really can't wait to eat a damn carrot?'

She considered it, tossed carrots aside. 'The stick comes in for lack of cooperation. A street kid — they're likely to wallow pretty deep in all the goodies. But somebody like Mina wouldn't be as easily turned.'

She glanced at her wrist unit. 'Let's see if Morris can tell us any more.'

Even as she started to stand, her 'link signaled. She looked at the display. 'The victim's parents. Hold on. Lieutenant Dallas.'

The man on-screen looked ghost pale, the blue of his red-rimmed eyes glassy. 'Lieutenant Dallas.' His voice cracked. 'I'm —'

'Mr. Cabot. I'm very sorry for your loss.'

'Sharlene — Detective Driver said you were absolutely sure.'

'Yes, sir. I understand how difficult this is for you

and your family. I can promise you that finding out who took Mina from you is priority for me and my partner.'

'She — our Mina — was she —'

Raped, Eve finished in her head, because she understood the father couldn't quite say the word. 'Mina is with the chief medical examiner of New York. Let me assure you she couldn't be in more skilled or compassionate hands than Dr. Morris's. My partner and I are about to go there now.'

'We need to see her. We need to bring her home.'

'You won't be able to take her home at this time, but I can arrange for you to see her. I can arrange transportation for you, Mr. Cabot, and accommodations if you plan to stay overnight.'

'We won't come home until Mina comes with us. We need to bring our girl home. We need —'

He broke off, broke down. While he struggled, Eve continued to speak.

'We need to keep Mina here for a while. When we speak with Dr. Morris, we'll let him know you're coming in to see her. It would be helpful if I could speak to you and your wife, your son if he's coming with you. I understand you've gone over everything about her disappearance with Detective Driver and her partner, but it would be helpful.'

'We need to know what happened!'

Grief, immense and unimaginable, ripped through every word.

'We're going to do everything we can to find out. Do you want me to arrange transportation and accommodations for you, Mr. Cabot?'

'No, I— We'll drive in. We'll drive in. If — if — if you could give me the name of a hotel near Mina. I

36

think we should stay near Mina. I don't know where she is.'

He covered his face with his hands.

'I still don't know where my baby is.'

'Mr. Cabot, we're going to book rooms for you at the Hanover Hotel. It's very near Mina. Is your son coming with you?'

'Yes, yes.'

'We're going to arrange two bedrooms, with a family area. Will that work?'

'Yes, thank you, yes.'

She shot a finger at Peabody as she gave Oliver Cabot the address. 'They have a parking garage. I can arrange for someone to meet you there and take you to Mina. It's only a few blocks.'

'You're very kind.'

'Just contact me when you arrive. Again, we're very sorry for your loss.'

'I think you mean that. Lieutenant, can you tell me fairly, are you good at what you do?'

'I'm good at what I do.'

'I hope you mean that, too. Thank you. We'll leave here within the hour.'

When Eve ended the call, Peabody sighed. 'That was almost as rough as a notification. He tried so hard not to lose it.'

'Did you get the rooms?'

'Two-bedroom suite. I went with the concierge level. They're going to want quiet.'

'Okay. Let's go be good at what we do.'

★ ★ ★

Eve knew Morris was good at what he did, and hoped, as she and Peabody walked down the white tunnel of the morgue, he could tell them more about Mina Cabot.

The air smelled of chemical lemons and death sneaking under it, with an overlay of bad coffee. Their footsteps echoed off the glossy white tiles.

Behind the doors of Morris's autopsy suite, music played. Something Eve found almost obsessively cheerful with a lot of guitars and young female voices harmonizing.

With a clear protective cape over his sky-blue suit, Morris closed his Y-cut on Mina with meticulous stitches. He'd done a trio of braids today in his long black hair and joined them together with a thick band that matched his precisely knotted — she supposed it was mauve — tie.

He looked up, paused. 'It's hateful, always, when it's a child, so I'm giving her music girls her age generally enjoy. Cut volume by half,' he ordered, and the voices went to murmurs.

'Her parents, maybe her younger brother, are coming in. About three hours, I'd say.'

'She'll be ready for them. Such a sweet face.' He touched the back of his sealed hand to Mina's cheek. 'Peabody, get us all something cold, would you? The killing blow had some force behind it, enough the tip of the sharp end went through her and pierced through her back between her shoulder blades. A slightly upward trajectory.'

'From below.'

'Face on, slightly below the entry point.'

'She had splinters in both palms.'

Morris took the ginger ale Peabody knew he

38

usually preferred, cracked the tube. 'The lab will analyze the weapon, but the edges were rough. She grabbed it, picked up the splinters as her hands slid over it.'

Eve nodded, paced, visualized. 'Most likely? She was the product. She had value. She had the weapon first to fight someone off or defend herself. The killer gets it away from her, she fights — bruised knuckles — tries to get it back — splinters. And in the struggle, it ends up in her.'

'With some force,' Morris added.

'Somebody's pissed enough, or distracted enough trying to control her, it rams into her.'

'It hit her heart — a blessing, I suppose, as she wouldn't have suffered.'

'But she didn't fall — after the blow,' Eve said. 'I didn't find any injury to indicate she fell. And I'm looking at her bare knees now — so she didn't go down on them, either, so the killer didn't just let her drop. But there's a bruise on her hip. From a blow, maybe a kick?'

'A kick, likely from the slightly rounded toe of a shoe. Postmortem, but very close to TOD. No other injuries,' Morris confirmed, 'other than the killing wound and her knuckles. A product, you said. Of value.'

'Abduction, not runaway. Everything points to abduction. No ransom demand, and the family would have scraped together a decent amount. She was worth more than that to somebody else, somebody who kept her in French manicures.'

'Yes, I noted that. They also kept her healthy. Body, hair, skin. No signs of illegals abuse. And she's a virgin. No sexual penetration, no rape, no signs of sexual assault.'

Didn't take her for personal use then, Eve concluded.

'Virgins are usually worth more. What did she eat last?'

'Now, there's something interesting. She had a green salad with carrots, tomatoes, cucumbers, chickpeas, a portion of grilled white fish and brown rice, sautéed spinach — very healthy — and a mixed berry tart.'

'Dessert?'

'A healthy, rounded meal — no alcohol in her system. Herbal tea, unsweetened. However, there are traces of vomit in her esophagus and in the back of her throat. Some scrapes on the back of her throat.'

Morris lifted two fingers, mimed sticking them into his mouth.

'She stuck her fingers down her throat.' Eve moved closer to the body. 'Puked up some dinner, faked being sick. She had a plan.'

'Since I see no signs she binged and purged on a regular or habitual basis, I agree.'

'Distract whoever's holding her long enough to make a break for it. She got outside, but he caught up with her.'

'I'll mention her underwear.'

'Her underwear?'

'Her clothes are, certainly, conservative, but age appropriate. Under them, the bra and panties? More mature, sexier. I sent them to Harvo.'

And the Queen of Hair and Fiber would tell Eve everything there was to know about them.

'She also has the clothes, and a sample of Mina's hair. You'll have the tox report shortly, but as I said, there's no signs of illegals use or alcohol use — not habitual.

'She was healthy, had good muscle tone, excellent dental hygiene — some minor straightening there about two years ago. No broken bones in her short life. What, I wonder, might she have done if allowed to live the rest of it?'

'Can't know, but we're damn well going to find out who took the rest of it from her. Did you measure her — height? Peabody said the pants she was wearing — and they're going to turn out to be the ones she wore at the snatch — were a little short. Her ID said five-four.'

'She added a half inch since then. How long ago was she taken?'

'Last November.'

'Not surprising she'd gain that half inch.'

'Okay. Good eye, Peabody. Would she have added elsewhere?'

'Developed more? Very likely at her age, yes. She was just beginning to bloom.'

'Appreciate it. The father's going to let me know when they get in. They're going to stay at the Hanover. I'll give you a heads-up.'

'We'll take care of them. And her. I'm going to wish you good hunting, both of you.' He looked down at Mina again. 'Such a sweet face.'

As they left, Eve heard him order the music up again.

'Let's hit the lab. We may be able to give Dickhead a shove on the tox and the blood.'

'Got a bribe ready?'

Since she knew how it worked, Eve rolled her shoulders instead of her eyes. 'It's baseball season. I

41

can toss out a couple of box seats. We hit him first,' she continued as they headed down the tunnel. 'He got so damn pissy when we went straight to Harvo before, and I want the blood and tox reports.'

'And the underwear,' Peabody added. 'What Morris said fits in with the porn theory, especially since she hadn't been raped or had sex.'

'There are lots of ways to rape without penetrating.'

Understanding her lieutenant had firsthand knowledge, Peabody fell silent.

Through the buzz of activity and sea of white coats in the lab, Eve spotted the dome of Dick Berenski's — chief lab tech's — head.

It moved right, paused, moved left as he used his rolling chair to cover his work counter. Maybe she'd have preferred to go straight to Harvo, but antagonizing Berenski — he'd earned the name Dick-head — wouldn't get her the reports.

He might have sensed her, as his gaze flicked up, then narrowed on her as she and Peabody moved through the maze toward his workstation.

He'd shaved the molting caterpillar off his top lip so at least she didn't have to test her willpower by not looking at it. His spidery fingers continued to work as he curled that naked top lip.

'You know how long ago we got those samples? How many cases are ahead of yours?'

'The victim's parents are on their way into New York. I'm checking in with you before we see if Harvo's got anything on hair and fiber. The victim's clothes are an angle we need to pursue.'

'Harvo's got a load of her own. You're not the only cops who want results yester-fucking-day.'

'Right now, to my knowledge, we're the only cops

who have a thirteen-year-old victim who was abducted walking home from school, brought to New York, and held for over seven months before she got a jagged plank of wood through her chest.'

She started to bring up the box seats, but wanted to vent a little first.

'Right now our theory is a kiddie porn operation, and I'm going to ask Harvo to prioritize the sex underwear she had on, as we might be able to track that back to the sonofabitch who snatched her so some other sonofabitch can pay to jerk off looking at her in the goddamn sex gear.

'And,' she added, fired up now, 'since you made it clear you're king of the lab, we're notifying you of same.'

'Jesus please us, take it down a notch.' He hunched his thin shoulders and scowled. 'I got your tox results right here.' He jabbed a finger at one of his screens. 'Clean. No alcohol, no drugs, legal or otherwise. I bumped you up. Vic's a kid, vic goes to the front of the line.'

Not a complete Dickhead, she thought. This time.
'Nothing?'

'Nada. No way to tell if somebody dosed her previous — say, forty-eight hours before TOD — with something that dissipates. But her tox is clean. So's the blood samples you sent in that aren't the vic's.'

Eve's antenna quivered. 'Which weren't hers?'

'I did the blood myself. My people are jammed.' He rolled down the other end of the counter, nodded at another screen.

'The sample from the shirtsleeve, the pants — both right side — don't match the vic's. Wrong blood type.'

'I need DNA.'

43

He sent her a sour look. 'Are you *looking* at the screen, Dallas?'

'If I knew what the hell's jumbling around on there, I'd be sitting in your chair.'

'I'm running the DNA. You shoulda paid more attention in science class.'

'I have people like you for that. How long before you ID the blood?'

'I just started the run, for fuck's sake. Takes time, doesn't it? Even if the DNA's flagged for prior bad acts and whatever. I'm damn good, but I'm not a magician.'

Then his machine dinged.

DNA sample identified.

'Well, kick my ass and call me Sally! There you go.'

'Dorian Gregg,' Eve read. 'Age thirteen — a few weeks younger than the vic. Freehold, New Jersey, mother Jewell Gregg, professional mother status. Father unknown.'

'She's got a sheet, Dallas.'

Eve nodded, studying the thumbnail photo on-screen. 'That's why she popped so quick.'

'Shoplifting.' Peabody scanned her PPC. 'Age ten. Truancy — got nailed twice there. Runaway — twice there, too, ages nine and eleven. She's got an assigned caseworker.'

'Kids killing kids,' Berenski muttered.

'I don't think so. She was there,' Eve said. 'Same age as the victim, and look at her. That's a really pretty girl. This one likes really pretty girls. Morris said that wood spear went into her with some force. Maybe another kid could manage it, maybe. But she's five-six and a buck ten. That's slender.'

'They got away together,' Peabody concluded.

'That reads more probable to me. Maybe, in the heat of battle, one kid could ram that weapon into another, but no way this kid then manages to get the body to another location. Not alone anyway.

'Thanks for the quick work,' Eve told Berenski. 'Send me the reports, and copy Mira. Peabody, send Mira what we've got and let her know I need a consult. If not late this afternoon, tomorrow morning.'

'You figure some doucheball's snatching little girls and using them for porn shit?' Berenski curled his lip again, but in disgust. 'You get anything else on it, front of the line.'

'Appreciated. Let's see if Harvo has anything.'

'Tell her I said it's priority,' Berenski called out.

Peabody trotted behind Eve's long strides. 'You didn't have to use the box seats.'

'So they'll be handy next time. It's going to be more than one.'

'More than one kid.'

'It already is more than one kid as I see it.' Eve worked her way through the counters and cubbies. 'More than one running this, or grabbing girls. Pennsylvania, New Jersey. Close enough to New York, but different locations. You have to see to want, you have to study to get. And Mina wasn't restrained.'

'Not like Mary Kate Covino and the others. Not like with Dawber.'

'Exactly. They've got a way to keep them contained. Maybe Mina managed to avoid the drugs if they use drugs. Cheeked them or dumped food. Two different types of girls — body type, coloring. Need to think.'

She checked the time. 'We need to talk to Dorian

45

Gregg's mother and her caseworker, then speak with Mina's family.'

Harvo sat in her fishbowl, keyboarding something while one of her strange tools hummed merrily along.

She'd kept the purple hair, at least on the top and a thick, eyelash-skimming fringe, but had gone pale pink on the rest.

Rather than a lab coat she wore a pink T-shirt and purple baggies, purple sneaks with pink laces.

She spotted Eve and Peabody.

'Yo, detecting duo. Figured you'd do the drop by. I'd've leapfrogged you on this one, but the chief beat me to it.'

'So he said. It's appreciated.'

Harvo shrugged. 'I have to try not to think too much when it's a kid. It gets inside you. Hair, no issue. Natural color, healthy. It got soaked with rainwater, but I found some traces of argan oil and linseed extract.'

'In her hair?'

'Frizz fighter, right?' Peabody said.

Harvo did an air check mark with a purple-tipped finger. 'You got it in one. A hydrating leave-in spray to kick the frizzies. I'm running the compound for brand ID.' She jerked a thumb at the humming machine.

'Nailed the pants, but can't take credit. They had a label. Wool blend, navy, size five, regular. Morsett Uniform Suppliers. They have their main branch in Philadelphia.'

'That fits.'

'They'd been professionally hemmed — a good inch, so I'd say the regular length was too long — but short, too, you know, short. The shirt? A hundred percent cotton, broadcloth, and that'll cost ya.'

'How much?'

46

'Well, considering the stitching, the buttons, the cut? I'm going to say a solid two-fifty. No label, which is a little odd, right? No evidence a label was removed. It's a size medium, I can give you that, and I can tell you it had some tailoring for fit — taken in some at the torso, shortened about a half inch. Damn good job, too.'

'Like it was made for her?' Eve asked.

'Tailored to fit, abso-poso. And no manufacturer or brand label's either a glitch or deliberate. I can run a search, but you're gonna end up with multitudes for a white, short-sleeved, cuffed cotton broadcloth shirt. It's a staple, right? You'd have zillions more in a blend, but higher-end, still multitudes.'

'Run it,' Eve decided. 'Stick with outlets in the city to start. We could get lucky.'

'Here to serve. Now, the undies? Who puts sexy virgin undies on a kid that age? Pervs, sick fucks.' Harvo put up both hands, closed her eyes, took a breath. 'Have to stop thinking. No labels.'

'No labels in the underwear?'

'Nada. You've got a silk georgette, white push-up bra with white lace trim, size thirty-two-A, and matching thong, size five. I'm giving you US sizes.'

'Okay.'

'These are high-end, the material, the design, the craftsmanship. I'm going to be able to narrow them easier than the shirt on a search. Best guess, the bra's going to go for seven, eight hundred, even up to a grand.'

'Dollars? *Dollars?*' Eve repeated. 'For a tit lifter?'

'A silk tit lifter with exceptional architecture and construction. The thong's an easy three hundred.'

Eve jammed her hands in her pockets. 'Three hundred for something designed *not* to cover your ass.

People are just screwed up.'

'I've got a black thong and a baby-pink one so I have a choice on my tonight's-the-night undies,' Harvo commented. 'But thirty bucks for a thong's top of my limit.'

Eve just nodded. 'I'm going to file that data away, somewhere I never think of it again.'

'Hold on.' Harvo pushed her stool over to the machine. 'Hair product's Gretta Giselle's Hydrating Frizz Barrier Spray. Retails for two-fifty — and yeah, dollars — for a sixteen-ounce bottle. Higher-end retail stores, salons, and like that.'

She pushed back. 'I'll need some time to get you manufacturers and outlets on the shirt and the undies. Undies, like I said, should be quicker.'

'As soon as you can. This is good information, Harvo. Thanks for the quick work.'

'It's what I do. Hey, Peabody, next time I want some pictures of the Great Mavis and Peabody House Project progress.'

'Oh, I got them. I'll text you some.'

'Solid.'

As they headed out, Eve ran it all through her head. 'Tailored a pricey but basic white shirt. How much, you figure, for that end?'

'Taking it in, shortening it? At least fifty. If you had basic skills, it's an easy do-it-yourself.'

'Maybe, maybe whoever had her knew how to tailor, or had somebody on tap who did. That's about three-fifty for the shirt. No label, so yeah, maybe somebody knows how to sew, how to tailor. But it has to be different for the bra, right? Even the thong deal, but the bra, that's got the tit-lifter stuff, the hooks.'

'More specialized,' Peabody agreed. 'I've never

48

made one — I mean, why would you? Well, no,' she considered. 'Maybe you just can't find one that fits right, so you learn to make them, or pay someone to custom. Getting the right fit in a bra is like everything.'

'They just keep tits from jumping around.'

Deliberately, Peabody aimed a solemn look at Eve's chest. 'Easy for you when your girls are high, firm, and small. Those of us with big, bouncy girls need a good fit so we don't spend our days hauling it up, tugging it down, or just suffering.'

Peabody changed the solemn look to a sorrowful glance. 'And the suffering's real.'

'The vic was just thirteen — she had girls, but I'm going with high, firm, and relatively small. No way she needed a custom bra.'

'My big, bouncy girls and I can't argue that point.'

'Maybe whoever took her and/or held her works in a place that makes underwear. Maybe runs a company that does. You could get products made or make them, without the labels if you wanted to keep that part of your life hidden.'

When they got back to the car, Peabody strapped in. 'I don't know. Why not just go to one of the places that sell sexy bras and thongs and buy them? You buy a standard-type brand, we'd have a hell of a time tracking it. And the shirt, that bugs me. So it's a little wide, a little long. Why go to the trouble to tailor it?'

'Good questions. First, we make sure they weren't hers to begin with. Odds are low, but we cross that off when we talk to her parents.'

Eve considered the time. 'Plug in Dorian Gregg's address in New Jersey. Get the estimated drive time.'

'Looks like it'll take close to an hour, traffic depending.'

49

Not if they ran hot, Eve thought, at least until they got out of the city. 'I can cut that down,' she said, and hit lights and sirens.

'Oh Jesus.' Peabody grabbed the chicken stick.

'Mina's family's on their way, but they have to get here . . .' She paused, shot around a maxibus, hit vertical to stream over a line of traffic. 'And they have to check into the hotel, get to the morgue. They'll want to spend some time there, and Morris will make time for them. We're grabbing this lead while we've got it.'

Peabody tightened her safety belt a little more. She didn't let out an easy breath until they hit the interstate. Eve still streaked down the road, but without the obstacle course of cars, trucks, cabs, buses, pedestrians, and bike messengers.

'Okay! Road trip. Can I have a snack?'

'You want a snack?'

'How about some chips?' To help ignore the speed hovering at about ninety — and she herself didn't have the wheel — Peabody hit up the dash AC. 'No-fail road trip food. We'll go for the classic. You never cracked your tube of Pepsi. I'll get that for you.'

'What's the ETA now?'

'We should make the trip in about thirty-seven minutes at this speed.'

'That'll do.'

'Do you think Dorian Gregg would go back home?'

'We find out why she took off — if she took off. No missing persons filed on her, but it could've been another abduction. If she and Mina broke out together, if that's how it plays, home might be her first thought. That's if they didn't grab her up again, and that's just as likely.'

Focused on the road, Eve ran through her thoughts.

'Same age group, both really attractive young girls. And look at them together. The contrast in coloring, in body types. If you're making porn, they'd make a good girl-on-girl duo.'

'No drugs in the vic's system, but —'

'That doesn't mean they weren't forced. It doesn't mean they weren't willing, either. 'You do a few of these, we pay you, you get to wear sexy stuff, then we'll let you go.''

'But.'

'Mina was taken months ago, so willing doesn't cut it for me, unless they managed to indoctrinate her. Add they got out, and she's dead. Willing goes bottom of the list. No rape, no penetration strikes me as a marketing tool. Maybe any photos or vids they made, if they made them, serve as the same. Because there's a serious investment here. Investments need a payday.'

'There could be others. Other girls. Boys, too.'

'Hard enough to hold two for all that time — no drugs, no restraints. But yeah, it's possible. Maybe they have more locations to keep them, a network. Richard Troy didn't get the idea of making me, selling me out of thin air. It's a business. An old, tried-and-true business.'

'It has to cost, a lot, to buy a human being. Especially a young girl or boy, then it has to cost to keep them somewhere. Feed them, clothe them. You could get a licensed companion who'd do role-playing. You could buy a damn sex droid.'

'Those don't hit the mark,' Eve said simply.

'What I mean is, it costs. So you have to have that kind of money. Maybe Roarke —'

Eve shot Peabody a look that had Peabody mentally rolling up in a ball.

'I don't mean Roarke — not like that. God. I just mean maybe he heard some stuff about somebody with that sort of money. Or he could, in his Roarke way, dig around in that pool. And you probably don't want that. That's a terrible idea. Delete.'

It took Eve a minute, a struggle against her personal feelings, those flickers of her past. 'No, I can't say I want it, but it's a good idea. He's got connections, not just with stupidly rich people, but with the shelter, the school. And he does have a Roarke way. Let's see where we are after we cross some of these angles.'

'All right.' Peabody waited until Eve blew past a pair of eighteen-wheelers like they were parked.

'And maybe we could have like a safe word if I say something or suggest something that hits you wrong on this. Like 'aardvark.''

''Aardvark'?'

'It's the first thing that popped into my head.'

'What's wrong with 'shut the fuck up, Peabody'?'

''Aardvark' could be code for that. So coworkers, suspects, and witnesses wouldn't know. And if I shut the fuck up when you said 'aardvark,' you wouldn't feel obliged to put your boot up my ass, which is painful.'

'I might feel obliged to put my boot up your ass before I said 'aardvark.''

'Yeah. There's that.'

Eve let silence hang for nearly a mile.

'We don't need a safe word, Peabody. And we're not doing the job, not putting the victim first if you're afraid to say or suggest something, or I'm touchy about what you say or suggest.

'What happened to me happened. I got through it. Whatever happened to Mina, she didn't. We do the

52

job and find out who and why.'

She waited another beat.

'That doesn't mean my boot won't meet your ass for other reasons.'

'I'm aware.' Then Peabody brightened. 'But it's a little bit of a smaller target now.'

Eve just smiled. 'I have excellent aim.'

4

They found Dorian's building on the sketchy edge of the city. The eight-story concrete block tower butted up against a strip mall and faced a road thick with grumbling traffic. It looked as if it had seen better, brighter days — and all of them had passed half a century earlier.

Considering the gray dinge over the peeling puke-green paint and the visible weeds growing out of sagging gutters, whoever owned the building didn't trouble with pesky details like upkeep.

They parked at the strip mall, walked and stepped over a low, pitted concrete curb.

Eve mastered into a skinny lobby and eyed the pair of elevators. The skull and crossbones painted on one of the doors had her aiming for the stairs.

More dinge, she noted, some grime with it, and a lacing of trash. The tenants, at least some of them, didn't appear to worry about upkeep, either.

They hiked to the fourth floor.

By her eye, she judged the industrial beige walls hadn't seen a fresh coat of paint in over a decade. Most of the doors — army green — had numerous locks.

Not a camera or palm plate to be seen.

She knocked on 412.

It took several more knocks before the door across the hall creaked open a few inches and thumped against the security chain. Eve saw a single eye, the side of a nose, and the corner of a tight-lipped mouth.

'She's in there all right.'

The door creaked shut again.

Taking the neighbor's word for it, Eve gave the door a solid pounding. 'Ms. Gregg, this is the police. We're here about your daughter, Dorian. Open up, or we'll come back with an entry warrant.'

An empty threat, but it got the desired result, as locks snicked and clacked, a chain rattled, a bar thumped.

The door opened, and Jewell Gregg barred the way. A tall, mixed-race woman with a headful of gold-tipped black twists, she folded her arms over her chest. She wore snug red shorts that showed off the snake tattoo slithering up the outside of her left leg, and a tight white tank.

Despite the pouches under her eyes smeared with yesterday's mascara, she owned a dissipated sort of beauty. Behind her the apartment smelled of stale smoke and last night's Chinese.

'That girl's in trouble again, and it's nothing to me. I'm done. So you can tell her, since she thinks she's so smart, to figure it out herself.'

'Ms. Gregg.' Eve held up her badge. 'I'm Lieutenant Dallas. This is Detective Peabody. We're NYPSD.'

'This ain't New York City.'

'We believe your daughter's in New York. Can we come in?'

'I don't have to let you in, do I?'

Not going to budge, Eve thought.

'No. We can talk right here in the hallway.'

'Fine by me. Can you hear all right, you nosy bitch!' Gregg shouted it as she sneered at the door across the hall.

55

To Eve's amusement, the woman behind the door called back. 'Yeah, I can hear just fine, thanks.'

'When's the last time you saw or spoke with Dorian?'

'I don't know. Last summer, maybe. Don't know, don't care. That girl's been nothing but trouble to me since the day she was born. A thief's what she is, a sneaky little thief.'

'Your — at the time — twelve-year-old daughter goes missing last summer — you think. You didn't file a missing persons report, go to the authorities?'

'I said I'm done, didn't I? They find her whiny ass, haul her back, she brings trouble before she takes off again. I got a life of my own, and I'm living it. She can live hers.'

Peabody tried to insert a little soothing balm with the placating tone of her question. 'Does she have friends or other relatives she might go to?'

'Got some bitchy little sneaks for friends.'

'Names?'

Jewell sneered at Eve's single, snapped word. 'How the hell do I know? They don't come around here. That girl says we live in a dump and how she doesn't like who I date. Well, la di da, maybe she can go live in a palace like a princess.'

'Relatives?'

Gregg shrugged. 'My grandmother's somewhere. Queens, maybe Yonkers. She doesn't approve of how I live my life, so fuck her. We don't speak, maybe ten years now. Who needs that?'

'Would Dorian know how to contact her?'

'Don't know how, don't know why she would. That old lady's got nothing except bad knees from scrubbing other people's floors. Ran my own mother off, too, with all her 'Do this, do that,' and God knows where

56

she ended up. I got away from the old bitch. Probably should have left the brat with her. I'd be better off.'

'If we could come in, see Dorian's room, her things, it might help us locate her.'

'She ain't got no room here, not anymore.' Jewell fisted her hands on her hips. 'I said I'm done! Got rid of her things. And you don't come in here without a search warrant.'

Before Jewell could slam the door, Eve slapped a hand on it.

'You continue to hold professional mother status and collect your payment for same every month.'

'Why the hell wouldn't I?'

'Because, by your own statement, you're done being Dorian's mother. She's been missing for nearly a year, but you filed no police report. You said she no longer lives here, and you've tossed out her belongings.'

'So the fuck what? I'm still a mother. Gave birth to her, didn't I?'

'You've willfully defrauded the federal government and the state of New Jersey. Believe me when I tell you I'm going to report same, and you'll be getting another visit from the authorities. You'll also face questions on the fact you haven't reported a missing minor child in your custody — all while reaping the monetary benefits.'

The look in her eye, ice-cold rage, had Jewell backing up a step.

'You're going to do some time, Jewell.'

'I am not! You shut the fuck up over there,' she shrieked as a burst of laughter erupted behind the neighbor's door.

Instead of shutting up, the woman shoved the door open.

She had an easy decade on Jewell Gregg and lacked her tired beauty. In its place was cool dignity.

'She smacked that child around. I saw it myself.'

On a howl, Gregg shoved Eve with murder in her eye for the neighbor.

'That's called assaulting an officer.' Eve spun her around, slapped restraints on her. 'Peabody, notify the locals so we can get the ball rolling here on Ms. Gregg.'

'Happily.'

'Stay there, would you?' Eve asked the neighbor, who beamed smiles.

'Happily.'

'Jewell Gregg,' Eve began, 'you're under arrest for assaulting a police officer. Additional charges to follow will include filing false reports on your minor child's status in order to receive the monthly stipend for professional parent, failure to report a missing minor in your custody, destroying or removing evidence.'

'You're not in New York! Get your hands off me.' She tried to jab Eve with an elbow.

'And now top it off with resisting arrest.'

'Bullshit. This is bullshit. I know my rights. I know my rights.'

'Yeah, well, I'm going to read them out to you anyway. You have the right to remain silent.'

Two other doors opened. A young woman juggled a baby on her hip in one. A man who'd surely hit the century mark watched from another.

'This is harassment. You all see this harassment? I'm getting a lawyer. Lawyer, lawyer, lawyer!'

'Heard you the first time. One'll be provided for you, as since you owe the government every dollar you raked in since Dorian went missing, you may not be able to afford one.'

58

'I don't owe nothing to nobody!'

'Add the fines — pretty steep — plus the interest on the money you took by fraud?' Eve sucked in a hissing breath. 'Ouch.'

Down the hall, the old man applauded.

'Any charge for being mean as a snake?' he called out.

'You shut up, you old fuck, or I'll shut you up.'

'You really don't want to threaten physical violence on your neighbors in front of the police.' Peabody spoke cheerfully. 'Freehold officers on the way, Lieutenant. And I've notified the Professional Parent Service for this county of the fraud.'

'Good. Contact Dorian's caseworker. I want a conversation. In New York,' she added as she calculated the time. 'He or she can get his or her ass to us.'

It took time, more than she'd bargained for, to brief the local cops, file the assault and resisting charges, and turn Jewell over.

But she took more to speak to the neighbors, starting with the one across the hall.

'Ms. Rhimes —'

'Just call me Tiffy. I feel like we've been through a battle together. I told the social worker that woman mistreated that girl. Smacked her in the face — I saw it myself more than once. Last time I saw her shove that girl out the door, smack her twice, and tell her to get the fuck out. How that man — can't remember that one's name — could stay as long as he wanted. I know it was after ten at night when she booted her out the door.'

Tiffy sighed.

'I waited till she'd shut the door again — you could hear her laugh through it while that little girl's on the floor there where she went down. I asked Dorian if she wanted to come in. I told her she could sleep in Edwin's room. Our son,' she explained. 'He's in college, gonna be a teacher. But she said she'd be okay.'

'Did you see or speak to her after that incident?'

'Once or twice. I work at home four days a week, so I'm mostly here. You ask anyone on this floor, or my friend Karlie two floors down, or Mr. Brewster on the first, that girl never caused any trouble around here. And you'd see her with bruises, or a split lip — one time a damn black eye. I told that social worker, but that woman, she said Dorian was clumsy, and she got into fights, too. I guess Dorian didn't say different.

'I last saw her — I think it was last August. I know it was hot because Hank and I — my husband — went out to sit on the fire escape to get some air. Building's going to hell as you can see. It didn't used to be this way, but it's going to hell now. We saw her walking toward the town center. She had her backpack. I never saw her come home. Never saw her again. I hope she's all right.'

'So do we.'

'I know I'm no relation, but I'd sure appreciate it if you'd let me know when you find her. Let her know Tiffy and Hank and Ed, too, are thinking of her.'

She had Peabody talk to the woman with the baby while she took the old man.

Statements and memories ran close enough to Tiffy's to solidify the pattern.

The Freehold police secured a search warrant, and opened the door for New York.

It didn't surprise her to find no trace a kid ever lived there. Or to find Jewell had a closet full of clothes and shoes. A decent supply of wine and beer. And a tidy

60

supply of illegals.

'No wonder the kid took off,' Peabody said as they got back in the car. 'I mean, if she took off.'

'She took off. She may have gotten snatched up before she got far, might've spent some time on the streets first. But she took off. And no, it's no wonder.'

'That woman? It's like she hated the kid. Not just she didn't love her or take care of her, but there was real animosity there.'

'The kid was a meal ticket.' Eve didn't hit the sirens because she needed time to settle. 'Nothing more than a way to pull in a monthly check without doing anything for it. She abused a program set up for parents so they can opt to stay home full-time, so they have that choice. Or because the job they can get won't cover child care. It was a damn good day for her when Dorian took off. Now she could get the check and not have the annoyance of the kid.'

'I thought you were going to punch her.'

Surprised, Eve glanced over. 'Did I look like I was going to punch her?'

'No, that's why I thought you might. You were so pissed, and not letting it show.'

Eve looked at the signal on her in-dash. 'The Cabot family's on their way to Morris. I imagined punching her,' she added. 'Arresting her, knowing she'll probably do two to five for the fraud — and that's before they found her illegals, and doesn't include charges, if they go for it, of child abuse, neglect and so on. I'm going to imagine she does a solid five inside.'

'Better than a punch,' Eve decided, then hit the sirens.

Peabody grabbed the chicken stick. 'Here we go again.'

61

* * *

When Eve walked into Homicide, Jenkinson's tie assaulted her eyes. He'd outdone himself — if such things were possible — with a single, huge, atomic-pink, googly-eyed cat staring out from a neon-purple background.

She pointed at him. 'My office. Peabody, set up a conference room.'

She went straight to her AutoChef, waited as Jenkinson shuffled in.

'You like cats,' he began.

'I like my cat. I mostly like cats. That cat looks like somebody shoved a shock stick up its ass.'

Desperate to ignore it, she jerked a thumb at the AC. 'Want coffee?'

Suspicion flickered into his cop's eyes, but he stepped over to program some. When you got a shot at Dallas's coffee, you took it.

'Give me a roundup.'

Suspicion flickered away again. 'Carmichael and Santiago just caught one. Headed out about ten minutes ago. Stabbing death, a customer in one of the fancy boutiques in the Meatpacking District. Baxter and Trueheart are in Interview A, pushing the prime suspect on the one they caught a couple of days ago.'

'Strangling, loft apartment, East Village.'

'That's the one. They liked the ex for it all along, but he's been slippery. But the slippery slipped up, and they think they've got him. Me and Reineke, we pulled out a cold one until something comes in hot.'

He eased a hip on the corner of her desk. 'Remember that double, seven years back? Married couple, well-off, both about fifty, bound and gagged in their

62

living room, throats slit.'

Eve flipped back in her mental files. 'Upper East Side, private residence. Looked like a break-in, but that didn't jibe. Was that yours?'

'Yeah.' He shook his head in disgust. 'Knew it had to be the son but couldn't shake his alibi. Insurance money, that's why he did it. Five-million-dollar policy on each of them, with double indemnity. He walks away with twenty. He just had to slit Mom and Dad's throats to get it.'

'Got a new angle on it?'

'He thinks he's in the clear, right? Smug bastard. He's got himself a fancy penthouse — same building as Nadine.'

'Nadine?'

'That's right. Fancy digs, keeps a boat, too. Living the high life, but not with the skirt he used for his alibi back then. He dumped her a while back. He's got a new one now.'

'And maybe the old one will find her memory adjusting.'

'That's the hope.'

Eve nodded as she programmed coffee for herself. 'It's worth the push. Meanwhile.'

In defense, Jenkinson pressed a hand over his atomic cat. 'Now, boss.'

'It's not about the damn ties. Don't make me think about the damn ties.'

'They brighten up the bullpen.'

'They burn the air in the bullpen. However, I've put you up for the sergeant's exam, and I'm asking you to seriously consider taking it.'

He looked pained — like the cat had given him a quick, sharp swipe. 'Aw now, Loo, why'd you do that?'

63

'I'm going to tell you why. Your end first. You're the highest-ranking detective in my bullpen, and with the longest tour of duty.'

'Just because you figure I'm old —'

'Shut up. It's about experience, instincts, skill, and knowledge. You have all of what's needed to make DS. If you're thinking you'd outrank your partner, I outrank mine by a lot more. It doesn't matter.'

Studying him, she drank some coffee. 'It's the rhythm,' she continued, 'the relationship, and the trust. You know that. And you're not going to stand there and bullshit me saying you don't need the boost in pay.'

He shuffled his feet. 'More money's always a plus. You'd have gotten a nice boost if you'd taken the captaincy when they offered it. I hear things,' he added. 'I know Whitney offered it — and it was overdue — and you turned it down. I figure it's because they'd boot you upstairs and take you off the streets.'

'You figure correctly, which is another reason I want you to take the exam. I'm a street cop. So are you. I don't intend to change that. I run this division, and I'd be stupid to take my most experienced detective away from what he does best just because he makes detective sergeant. You'd do what you do now, but with a boost in pay and rank. Don't you be stupid.'

He rubbed the back of his neck. 'The administrative shit.'

'Yeah, and that's my end of why we're having this conversation. Unless you're out in the field, you already handle things when I'm jammed. I've got a family coming in shortly — I've spent most of today away from my desk on their daughter's murder.'

'The kid in Battery Park. Fucking fuck does that

64

to a kid needs to fucking rot in a cage for a couple lifetimes.'

Since she agreed, wholeheartedly, she nodded again.

'I hope to make that happen. I have more room to because I know damn well I can come in here and ask you to catch me up. You can and will. I can ask you to take charge if I need to, and the rest of the bullpen respects that, because — despite the damn ties — they respect you. And goddamn it, I'd fucking love to dump some of the paperwork on you now and then.'

He smiled at that. 'You're the boss. You could do that anyway.'

'You make sergeant, and I can dump some of it now and then without feeling guilty about it. So that's my end, but it circles around to this. You've earned it.'

He stared down into his coffee. 'I'll think about it. I'll talk to my other boss — the one at home — and we'll think about it.'

'Good enough. Now take your electrified cat and get out of my office. I don't have much time.'

He drained his coffee first. 'I appreciate you putting me up for it. I appreciate that.'

The minute he walked out, she switched gears, updated board and book, wrote everything up with a copy to Mira. She considered more coffee — boots up, time to think — and heard Peabody coming.

'Heard back from the caseworker,' Peabody told her. 'Pru Truman. She's coming in. It'll take some time, but she's coming. I got the feeling her supervisor ordered her to come.'

'If the supervisor's not an idiot, that's a good call. Her charge is missing, and has been, yet no report on that? Custodial parent's arrested — which would've happened before if the caseworker paid attention. Yeah, she's under the hammer on this, and so's her department.'

A few hours, she thought. She'd have the victim's family, then Dorian Gregg's caseworker, and the day was bleeding away. She needed a consult with Mira, and had to find a way to squeeze it in.

'We'll keep the conference room,' Eve decided. 'I ought to put her in the box, but we'll keep it cool and professional. In the meantime —'

She broke off when Roarke appeared in the doorway.

You never heard him — those (former) cat burglar moves. So seeing him could come as a jolt to the heart.

Those wild blue eyes, that mane of black hair, that incredible face, and a mouth sculpted by artisan angels that curved for her in a smile that could turn the brain to mush.

He said, 'Lieutenant,' and the whisper of Ireland made her want to nibble on that excellent mouth. 'I'm interrupting.' Then he smiled at Peabody, gave the flip of her hair — the hair she insisted on streaking with red — a flick of his finger. 'I'm hoping to get to the house and see the current progress.'

'The kitchen cabinets.' Peabody spoke as if she spoke of gods. 'They're just so mag. Ours and Mavis and Leonardo's. I can't believe it's really happening. Sorry,' she said to Eve. 'But wait till you see. I'll go extend the conference room.'

'You're pressed for time,' Roarke observed as Peabody hurried out. 'I expect this is new.' He stepped to the board. 'Children? Ah, God, she can't be much more than twelve.'

66

'Thirteen. Both of them. I don't know the status of the other as yet. I wasn't expecting to see you until I got home.'

'I was in the area.'

'That's happening a lot.'

'A project,' he said vaguely. 'Am I seeing this correctly? The second girl's blood found on the first's body? You don't think one child killed the other.'

'I don't. Not that it can't and doesn't happen, but not here.' And since he was here, why not use him? 'Tell me what you see when you look at them — the ID shots.'

'Lovely young girls. Exceptionally lovely. Different types, certainly. The second looks defiant, a little angry, while the first seems happy to pose for the ID.'

'I think the exceptionally lovely plays in. Mina Cabot was abducted last November — early November — on her way home from soccer practice. Devon, Pennsylvania. Nice, affluent neighborhood. I think Dorian Gregg — Freehold, New Jersey, the hard side of town, abusive, neglectful asshole of a mother — ran off. She had a history of it — then got grabbed. I don't know where or when, but I think the two of them got out from wherever they were being held together.'

Considering her time, she filled him in quickly.

Even before she'd finished, he took her by the shoulders. And the worry in his eyes had those shoulders going tight.

'Eve, working a case like this? Young girls, abductions when you've barely come off another abduction investigation. Add the high probability of rape, abuse, trafficking. I can already see it's wearing on you.'

'I can handle it. I am handling it.'

'Don't ask me not to see it wearing on you. Don't

dismiss that.'

She heard the edge, and stepped back from him. 'I'm not.' Bullshit, she admitted. 'Fine, I am, because I have to work the case. I don't have time to delve into my psyche. I don't know Dorian Gregg's status. Did she get away, get caught? Is she alive, is she dead? I don't know, and until I do, I've got two victims.'

His voice stayed absolutely, perfectly, infuriatingly calm.

'It never occurred to you to assign another team to this, or give Peabody the lead?'

She didn't know exactly what hackles were, but she knew when hers rose, hard and sharp.

'No. You need to back off because I don't have time to get into this with you right now. I have the family coming, then the second girl's useless excuse of a caseworker. I've got some threads to pull, and I need a consult with Mira, and she's probably going to be gone for the day before I get through the rest.'

'Invite her and Dennis to dinner.'

Annoyed and cruising toward pissed, Eve shoved at her hair. 'I don't want to socialize with her. I need a consult.'

'A working dinner,' he countered in that same even tone. 'I'll grill some steaks. I've got the hang of it now. Summerset can take care of the rest. You'll have time to do what you need to do.'

'And you —' She knew him. 'You'd see what the shrink thinks about how I'm handling it.'

'Yes. If you don't think I'm entitled to that, you're wrong. It's probably even somewhere in your bloody Marriage Rules. I'll stop by her office and take care of it.'

'Good luck getting past her dragon. Her admin,'

Eve said when he looked blank.

Then he smiled, and she hissed out a breath. 'Never mind. You won't have any trouble there. But I haven't said this works for me.'

'You want me to back off? Make it work. I'll see you at home.'

Pissed at her, she thought when he walked out. A little bit — maybe more than a little — pissed at her. And damn it, if anyone should be pissed, it was her. Nowhere in her Marriage Rules did it say he could walk into her office and question her competency on a case.

Nowhere.

And they'd get down and dirty on *that* one the minute she had time.

She started to sit, to take two minutes to clear her head, when Peabody signaled from the bullpen.

'The Cabots are here, Lieutenant.'

'Take them to the conference room. I'll be right there.'

5

The Cabots sat at the conference table with their son between them. A unit, Eve thought when she walked in, bound together by grief. Each carried the pallor of the exhausted, and the stricken eyes of the shattered.

She saw Oliver Cabot reach for his wife's hand when Eve approached the table.

'Dr. and Ms. Cabot, Ethan, I'm Lieutenant Dallas. Again, I'm very sorry for your loss, and appreciate you coming in to speak with us.'

Eve took a seat next to Peabody. Instinct had her speaking to the mother first. 'This is hard, and the questions we'll ask may make it even harder. I promise you, they're necessary for us to find who hurt Mina.'

'Nothing you can say or do could make this harder than it is.' Rae Cabot, her bright hair drawn severely back in a tail, held Eve's gaze with her devastated eyes. 'All these months we believed — had to believe — we'd find her and bring her home. Now that's gone, and Mina's gone. Nothing can make it harder.'

'Do you know if Mina had any contacts or connections in New York, or any reason to come here?'

'She was taken from us. She was brought here. If you think she ran away —'

'I don't.' The simple response tempered some of the fire that leapt into Rae's eyes. 'I've read Detective Driver's reports and agree with her conclusions. But it's a question I have to ask.'

'She didn't know anyone here.' Oliver spoke now.

70

'We brought the kids to New York a couple of times a year, to see a show, to visit museums.'

'She always wants to go shopping.' Head down, Ethan mumbled it, then knuckled his eyes.

'She does.' With a ghost of a smile on her face, Rae stroked his thatch of red hair. 'And you always want the pizza. We'd come in as a family,' Rae continued. 'Sometime during the holidays to see all the decorations and a Christmas show, and early summer, after school let out. She's smart, and could have figured out how to get from home to New York on her own. But she didn't.'

'We know, from Detective Driver's files, the police conducted a thorough search on all of Mina's devices and found no questionable correspondence or activities. But there are other ways for someone to connect with a young girl.'

'The investigators looked at that, and they — and we — talked to all Mina's friends, her classmates, her soccer team, teachers, coaches, neighbors.'

'And she would tell us.' Rae interrupted her husband. 'I'm not saying Mina didn't have some secrets, some things she didn't tell us. But she wasn't sneaky.'

'It could have been very innocent on her part,' Peabody put in. 'Something she didn't mention because it didn't seem important or unusual. Someone she passed on the walk home from school.'

'She'd never have gone with someone willingly, or gotten into a stranger's car. Never. The short distance she walked is in a neighborhood,' Rae insisted. 'It's residential and quiet. It's safe. It's always been safe.'

As silent tears slid down Rae's cheeks, Eve laid the printout of Dorian Gregg's ID photo on the table. 'Do you recognize this girl? Any of you?'

'I don't. Oliver?'

'No, she doesn't look familiar.'

'Mina has lots of girlfriends, but not this one,' Ethan said.

'Who is she?' Rae demanded. 'Does she have something to do with Mina?'

'We have reason to believe this girl was abducted also. Evidence indicates she was with Mina last night.'

'What does that mean?' Oliver demanded. 'Do you think — is this girl a suspect?'

'At this point we consider her a witness.'

'Do you think Mina knew her? There haven't been any other child abductions from our area,' Rae added. 'We'd have heard. She looks about the same age as Mina. If they went to school together . . .'

'She wasn't from your area.'

Rae's eyes narrowed. 'Where?'

'New Jersey.'

'Oliver, why don't you and Ethan go grab a snack?'

'You don't want me to hear, but I'm *not* going. I'm not.' Ethan's face reddened with temper under a scatter of freckles. 'She's *my* sister. And I was mean to her that morning. That morning before school I said how Nick was gonna try to touch her boobies.'

'Oh, Ethan.' With a sobbing laugh, Rae laid her cheek on the top of his head.

'I've got a sister,' Peabody told him. 'And two brothers. Sometimes we said silly and mean things to each other because it's what you do. That's all. But I love them, and they love me, just like you love Mina and she loves you.'

'I'm not going. Somebody killed my sister, and I'm not going out for a stupid snack.'

'Okay.' Oliver leaned over, got his arm around both

of them. 'It's okay. We'll stay together.'

'All right. All right.' Rae straightened in her chair. 'You're considering the possibility of child trafficking.'

'We are. So were the investigators on Mina's abduction. The investigation's in its very early stages, but we consider this a high probability.'

'She hadn't been raped.' On the table, Oliver clutched his hands together. 'Dr. Morris confirmed that. You may not think that should be important to us after —'

'No, sir. I understand it's important to you as her family. It's also important to Detective Peabody and me as investigators.'

Eve took out another photo — this of the underwear. 'Mina was wearing her school uniform pants and a white short-sleeved shirt, not the shirt she wore when abducted. She also wore these. Do you recognize them as hers?'

The instant Rae took the photo, she shook her head. 'God, no. Mina would never — she's much too young. She most usually wears a sports bra, cotton blend panties — hip skimmers they call them. And from the look of these, she couldn't afford them on her allowance. She liked young, sporty, nothing like this.'

Rae looked back at Eve. 'She had a French manicure. I didn't think — I couldn't think when we saw her. But she had a French manicure. Fresh, wasn't it?' She rubbed a hand on her temple. 'Mina thought they were boring and old. Whenever we went to the nail salon, or she went with her friends, she got color. I usually got a French, and she'd roll her eyes. 'Boring, Mom.''

Now she looked down at her son again, then took a

long breath. 'They were grooming her. Whoever took her, they were grooming her, for trafficking, for sexual slavery.'

'Why would they want her in traffic?'

Oliver rubbed Ethan's arm. 'It's not that kind of traffic, baby. Don't interrupt now.'

'We're working on that possibility,' Eve told them.

'Could I see the photo of the other girl again?' Rae asked. Then nodded when Eve showed her. 'Yes, she's striking, isn't she? A strikingly pretty girl, like Mina. You haven't found this girl?'

'Not yet.'

'Why do you think she and Mina were together when Mina was killed?'

'We're not going to share certain details with you at this time, but we believe she was.'

'Maybe they were friends, Mom. Mina liked her girlfriends. She talked to them *all* the time.'

'Yes, maybe they were friends. Maybe she wasn't alone.'

Eve stayed where she was after Peabody escorted them out. They'd held up better than she'd expected. She could be grateful for that, just as she was for the opportunity to see and judge the family dynamic.

Close, tight, but not smothering.

Peabody came back with tubes of Pepsi and Diet Pepsi. 'I didn't program your coffee into the AC in here.'

'This is fine, thanks.'

'They're going to stay, at least a day or two. They're going to visit the spot where we found her body.'

'Did they tell you that?'

'They didn't have to.'

Nodding, Eve cracked the tube. 'The possibility Mina ran or got into a vehicle with someone was always low. It's now below zero for me. She didn't run from that, from them, and everything says she had too many smarts to climb into a ride. The mother? She's smart, sharp, and observant.'

'She knows her kids.'

'That's right. The underwear, the manicure — not a choice. Adds weight.'

She pushed up, drank from the tube as she paced. 'Roarke's asking the Miras over for dinner tonight.'

'Oh. Nice.'

Eve shook her head. 'Working dinner — consult dinner. I don't much like the combination, but it got away from me. He got away from me. He keeps popping up here at Central unexpectedly lately. Have you noticed that?'

'Well, not really, but I guess.'

'Projects, meetings.' Eve waved a hand in the air. 'Whatever. Bad timing on this. He's decided he has to worry about me given the circumstances.'

Peabody followed the dots. 'Hard to blame him.'

'Not for me it's not. He —' She broke off when her comm signaled. 'Looks like the caseworker got here a little early.'

'I'll go bring her back.' Peabody stood. 'You know, my mom's pretty smart.'

'Scary about it,' Eve agreed.

'She's proud of me. She and my dad didn't really want me to be a cop, much less in New York, but they let me choose, and they're proud of me. But she worries, and I know it. She says worrying is part of loving.

'So. I'll bring Truman back.'

'He's not my mother,' Eve pointed out as Peabody

walked from the room.

'But he loves you.'

Yeah, yeah, she thought, then put it away.

She sat, started reviewing the file she had on Dorian as Peabody brought the caseworker in.

Pru Truman looked like a human rag that had been wrung dry too many times and tossed aside. Pale and bony in what even Eve's unfashionable eye noted as an ugly suit, she clutched an ancient briefcase and kept her thin mouth pursed tight.

If Eve hadn't skimmed her data, she'd have gauged the woman as early sixties. But her bio claimed a decade younger.

'I'm Lieutenant Dallas. Thanks for coming in, Ms. Truman. Have a seat.'

'Can I get you coffee?' Peabody asked her. 'A soft drink?'

'I don't consume caffeine, faux or otherwise. Still water, please.'

Because she found herself taking an instant dislike, Eve took a slow sip of her Pepsi.

'This is all very inconvenient,' Truman began.

'What's that?'

'Being obligated to come all the way into New York. I had to reschedule several appointments.'

'I have a thirteen-year-old girl who'll never have to worry about appointments again, seeing as she's dead.'

'This unfortunate girl wasn't one of my charges.'

'Dorian Gregg is.'

'Yes.' Truman reached into the briefcase, took out a disc file. 'I have all my files on minor female Gregg, going back nearly five years. As you'll see, I conducted numerous home visits over that length of time, arranged meetings and interviews with the teachers in her schools. I recommended, I believe you'll find three years ago, for the custodial parent to attend and complete an addiction program, which she did.'

'You did all that?' Eve said, very pleasantly. 'Oddly, we found a number of illegal substances in Jewell Gregg's apartment, along with cheap wine and brew.'

'Perhaps she had a recent relapse, as often happens.'

'No mandatory testing?'

'She had completed the program.'

'Perhaps she had a recent relapse,' Eve repeated.

'And we will look into the matter.'

'A little late for that, isn't it, since Dorian hasn't been in that apartment since sometime around August of last year.'

Truman's pointy little chin jutted up. 'I was not aware of that circumstance.'

'It's your job to be aware.'

Annoyance flashed, and Truman's thin lips vanished as she pressed them together. 'I won't tell you how to do your job, you won't tell me how to do mine. Minor female Gregg —'

'She has a name. She has a goddamn name.'

'Be sure I'll report your language,' Truman responded with a sharp nod. 'I do not refer to charges by name in order to keep a professional distance. She is a difficult, recalcitrant child,' Truman continued. 'And as you can see from my files, and her juvenile record, has a history of truancy, of running away, of petty theft.'

Eve found the words, the tone, the voice pounding in her head. Except for the petty theft, Truman might have spoken of minor female Dallas.

'There's also documentation of sporadic physical

77

and verbal abuse of the custodial parent by the minor female.'

'Are you fucking kidding me?'

'I won't tolerate that language. You have copies of my files, so we're done here.'

'Sit your tight ass down, Truman, or I'll not only see you're cited for dereliction of duty, I'll bring charges of my own and toss you in a cage.'

'You threaten me!'

'I promise you. Whatever your files say, you haven't conducted a home visit for months.'

'I certainly have.'

'Not with Dorian present. And if in those files you claim otherwise, or claim to have spoken to her since last August, I'll charge you with conspiracy to defraud the government.'

'I'm not a criminal!' She squawked it, and made Eve think of the chickens on the Brody family farm.

'I'm a public servant. I had no idea the female — the child,' she amended, 'wasn't in parental custody. Ms. Gregg said they were trying tutors and homeschooling, and it was working better.'

'And isn't it your duty to speak to the child?'

'The child was, as I said, difficult. And very, very rude to me. I had no reason not to trust the custodial parent.'

'A woman with a history of illegal and alcohol abuse. One reported to you by witnesses of striking Dorian.'

Truman lifted her chin. 'Neighbors have agendas, and will gossip.'

'Did you ever see bruises on Dorian?'

'She's a clumsy child, and in addition, often got into physical altercations with other children.'

'Who says?'

78

Truman looked away. 'Her custodial parent.'

'The one smacking her around, booting her out of the apartment when she wanted alone time with her newest 'date,' the one pulling in a monthly check even when the kid doesn't come home for months? The one who never bothered to file a missing persons report on her own daughter, send up an Amber Alert? That custodial parent?'

'Obviously Ms. Gregg wasn't forthcoming and failed to inform me, and the authorities. Naturally, she'll be disqualified as a professional parent, and I will certainly recommend foster care for the child.'

'The missing child. The child who may be dead because you couldn't be bothered to do your job.'

'I did my job!' Truman's face bloomed red at the accusation. 'You have no idea what goes into my job! The stress, the hours, the unruly, difficult children, the careless parents and guardians. I'm not responsible if that girl ran off again, or if she met a bad end because of it. She had choices, and made poor ones.'

With everything inside her burning dark, Eve got slowly to her feet. 'Now would be a really good time for you to leave.'

'I will not have some — some New York City bully accuse me of —'

'You need to get out, and now.'

'I'll be reporting this treatment, your language, and your behavior.'

'Yeah? Same goes. Now get the fuck out of my house.'

Moving fast, she got out.

'Peabody, get me that fucking negligent asshole excuse for a human being's supervisor. Get me her boss. Now.'

'I'll do that, but do me a favor, and take five minutes first. Just five minutes,' Peabody repeated, standing up and standing firm when Eve rounded on her.

'I feel what you feel. You feel more of it, I get that, but I feel it. I wanted to pound her with my fists, choke her till she popped, then kick what was left of her into squirmy pulp. She needs to be reported, she needs to be fired, and I think, I really think, brought up on charges. But that part, that last part's not our call.'

She could barely find her breath. All she could find was rage.

'Fuck that.'

'I want to fuck that, I do. And if you'd told me to toss her in a cage, I'd've done it. Hopefully you'd have covered me when she sued our asses off for it, but I'd've done it either way. It's not that she didn't help Dorian, and who knows how many others, but that they weren't kids to her. They were just charges. Nameless charges.'

Because Eve paced, said nothing, Peabody kept going. She'd get that five-minute cooldown.

'We've worked with Child Services before, and we know most of them are dedicated, caring, compassionate, overworked. Some of them burn out, sure. And maybe, maybe there are more like that piece of shit out there. But she's the first for me.'

'Not for me,' Eve muttered. 'Not for me. But she ranks high on the worst list. You're right, most of them go into it because they care and want to help. It's not like it pays the big bucks. And that's just one more reason she's revolting.'

Eve stopped pacing, turned. 'I don't need the five.'

'Dallas —'

'No, you did the job, and it's appreciated. I can

be outraged, but not throw a tirade, and that'll have more impact. I'd have you do it, but I'm rank, and that'll have more impact.'

'Okay, I'll get you her boss.' Now, for the first time, Peabody let out a breath. 'You scared the crap out of her.'

'Did I?' Eve pressed the knuckles of her fist to the headache drilling between her eyes. 'She's lucky I told her to get out. I was close to pounding her, then I'm the one you'd be tossing in a cage.'

'She's not worth it.'

'No. It would have felt good, but she's not worth it. I'm going to need to pound something.'

'Please, not me.'

'I'll bust up another sparring droid when I get home. Thanks, and I mean it.'

'I'll get the boss. You want to take it in your office?'

'Yeah, better.'

'And I'm going to write all this up. I'm going to do Truman first because we want copies of that going to her boss, to the cops in Freehold, and to the Professional Parent Service.'

'Good thinking.' And now with the red haze of fury subsiding, Eve could think, too. 'Copy Mira and Whitney on it. I'll write up the interview with the Cabots. You can take off and go visit your kitchen cabinets and whatever.'

'That can wait.'

'No, we're already near end of shift, and I'm going to work from home. But first I have a date with a sparring droid.'

Since the meeting with Truman had lit a fire in her, Eve willed a coating of cold professionalism over her tone when she spoke to Truman's supervisor.

She knew the heat burned through in spite of — maybe because of — the supervisor's shock and lame — to her ear — excuses.

Maybe she found some satisfaction in Truman's immediate suspension and the internal investigation to follow, but not enough.

She drove home pissed, which suited the traffic that snarled and bitched all the way uptown.

Most days, driving through the gates, winding up the drive toward the castle-like house that was home brought relief, even gratitude. She had a home, and she had all its beauty, its grace, its peace.

But tonight, it made her feel itchy. She firmly believed Roarke had pushed buttons he had no business pushing, and now she'd have to slog through the whole thing with Mira instead of just getting down to work.

And fine, fine, she thought as the lush green lawns spread and the glorious flowers bloomed, slogging through the whole thing with Mira equaled work.

But.

She didn't know exactly what followed *but* because she was too itchy and pissed to think about it.

Her go-to solution when something stuck so hard in her craw to make her itchy and pissed? Punch something. An inanimate something.

She parked, and with visions of beating the crap out of a sparring droid in her head, walked into the cool, lightly fragrant air of the foyer.

Summerset stood, of course, the black-clad, silver-maned scarecrow with the pudgy gray cat at his feet.

It occurred to her Summerset could almost qualify as inanimate.

The cat pranced over to wind between her legs

before she headed for the stairs.

'The Miras will arrive at seven-thirty. That should give you enough time to make yourself presentable.'

She kept walking. Punching him could be fun, but — and she knew what followed this one.

She'd feel guilty, then be duty bound to arrest herself on assault charges. And Roarke would be — justifiably pissed.

Instead of a punch, she threw out a rhetorical question as the cat bounded up the stairs ahead of her.

'Do all those suits come with the stick up your ass, or do you just interchange it?'

'Seven-thirty,' he said as he watched her head up. 'Cocktails on the patio.'

'Yeah, yeah, fucking yeah.'

Galahad perched on the bed when she walked in, and gave her a long stare with his bicolored eyes. She walked over to give him a scratch and a stroke.

'Crap mood. Need to work it off.'

She turned to grab shorts and a tank, caught a glimpse of herself in the mirror, and frowned. Summerset didn't know she had a date with the sparring droid. Why the hell wasn't she already presentable?

No visible blood, no rips or tears.

She shrugged out of her jacket, tossed it on the bed, removed her weapon harness, and stood in a sleeveless white shirt and khaki trousers.

Presentable, she thought.

'Stick up the ass,' she muttered as she changed, and took the elevator down to the gym.

Moments later, Roarke walked in the front door.

'The lieutenant seems a bit off-kilter,' Summerset told him.

'I'm not surprised.'

'You'll straighten that out before your guests arrive.'

As Eve had, Roarke strode straight to the stairs. 'And why, I wonder, am I the one always obliged to straighten the lieutenant's bloody kilter?'

Summerset lifted his eyebrows. Apparently, the lieutenant wasn't the only one off-kilter.

'Children.' With a shake of his head, he headed back to the kitchen to ensure at least his part of the meal passed muster.

Upstairs, Roarke noted Eve's work clothes on the bed with Galahad keeping guard.

'Gone down to the gym, has she?' Just like Eve, he gave the cat a scratch and a stroke.

As he loosened his tie, he considered joining her. He could take twenty or thirty minutes to sweat out some of the day's annoyance.

Stripping off his suit coat, he called for the gym on-screen.

He watched Eve execute a side kick to the sparring droid's breastbone, pivot, then follow up with a left jab to the jaw.

She'd chosen a beefy female he'd yet to try out himself.

And obviously programmed for full contact, as the droid's countered right cross slipped by Eve's guard and connected high on her cheekbone.

'Bloody hell.'

Eve went for a leg sweep that knocked the droid off-balance enough for her to land a body blow and a solid uppercut before the droid's elbow jab snapped his wife's head back.

He took two steps to the elevator before he stopped himself.

He could go, shut down the droid, turn Eve's

obvious fury on himself. They could go a round, and Christ knew he wouldn't plant a fist in his wife's face.

'Hell with it. Let her do it her way.'

He turned off the screen and took himself off to the shower.

When she came up, he finished buttoning his jeans.

'Your mouth's bleeding,' he said as he reached for a T-shirt.

She swiped the back of her hand over it. 'The droid said it needed some minor repairs and needed about twelve hours to deal with it.'

'Might take you a bit longer,' he said in a voice like a shrug. 'You've got a black eye coming on, and your jaw's swelling.'

'It's got a sneaky left.'

'You might opt for light contact rather than full next time.'

'What's the point in that? Look —'

'I am, and I take it you feel getting punched in the face multiple times was somehow worth it.'

'I figured it for a better choice than punching you or some innocent bystander.' Planting her feet, she prepared to stand her ground. 'How would you react if I came into your office and told you what to do, what not to do?'

He held up a finger, turned, and walked into the bathroom. He came out with several cold packs, tossed them at her.

'First, I didn't tell you what to do, or what not to do. I asked if you'd consider doing something.'

'That's a real slippery line.'

'But a line nonetheless. Second, decisions I make in my office don't affect my emotional health. You're

85

already exhausted, and now bruised and bloody with it.'

'I'm handling it. If I can't handle any case I catch, I've got no business on the job.'

He just looked at her. 'You wouldn't say that about anyone in your bullpen.'

'My bullpen,' she tossed back, firing up again. 'I'm the boss. I'm in charge, and that makes it different. You know that. You know it.'

'And I know this. Every day you strap that on.' He gestured to her weapon harness. 'And you walk out the door. I know what you risk, every day, and I accept it, support it, respect it, even admire it. I know what I risk, every day, because you're my goddamn world, but I stand with you. And you know that. But I question something I can see hurts you, and I have no right? I'm to back off, have no voice, no say, no opinion? Well, bugger that. I'm your husband, not your pet.'

Stunned, she took a step toward him. 'I never —'

And he stepped back, very deliberately. 'You've about a half hour before the Miras get here.'

He walked away from her, left her frustrated, furious, and flummoxed. Okay, so he was a lot more pissed than she'd realized, but that? That, she thought, was bullshit.

'Pet, my ass.' Turning to the cat, she threw up her arms. 'What the fuck is that?'

Galahad, apparently opting to stay neutral, stretched out and closed his eyes.

'He questioned my judgment. That's just what he did, so he can bugger it right back.'

She stalked into the bathroom for a shower, caught sight of herself again. Damn it, she did have a black

86

eye coming on.

She stripped, then slapped one of the cold packs on her eye before stepping into the shower and ordering jets on full.

6

She did what she could toward making herself presentable, even digging into her rarely used makeup to cover the worst of the bruising.

Probably, she admitted, not the best idea to go full-contact sparring before a dinner meeting.

But meeting was the key word, she reminded herself.

She dragged on jeans. Since Roarke wore them, they ranked appropriate. And since she had some bruising on the ribs, she used a thin cold pack on them, then chose a loose shirt.

No time for a few passes with a healing wand. Besides, Roarke usually did that for her. Not this time, she thought as she started downstairs. The best they'd manage tonight was — what would he call it? A veneer of civility.

That sounded just like him.

She stepped out onto the patio.

A table set for four with dishes of summer blue held a squat, clear pitcher full of yellow flowers. Napkins with yellow and blue stripes poofed out of pale yellow water glasses. Wineglasses had blue stems, and tea candles snuggled in clear holders.

More flowers spilled and speared from pots arranged on one side of the patio.

A portable bar and Roarke's big-ass shiny grill stood on the other side. Between them, a small table held a variety of fancy canapés.

It all looked cheerful and festive — exactly the opposite of her current mood.

Roarke poured something frothy and slushy with crushed ice from a pitcher into a birdbath glass.

'Try this.'

She decided she'd welcome anything containing alcohol. One sip gave her tart, cold, and was more than welcome.

'It's good. It looks nice out here.'

'We should think about having a cookout for friends before we go on vacation.'

Veneer of civility, she thought. He was a master, but she could coat it on, too.

'Okay.'

'Summerset's seen to the rest of the meal. We have it in the cold or warm compartments of the grill, so we've only to set it all out once we're ready for the meal.'

Though the droid hadn't delivered any gut punches, her stomach felt knotted up and far from interested in food. But she said, civilly, 'Sure.'

'You might want to come up with more than one-word answers or statements when the Miras get here.'

She gave him cool look for cool look. 'I will. See? There's two words already.'

She decided it proved lucky for both of them when Summerset brought the Miras out.

To show her mettle, Eve stepped up first. 'Thanks for coming on such short notice.'

'More than happy to. Everything's so pretty!' Mira, pretty herself in a breezy summer dress blooming with little purple flowers, gave Eve a quick hug before turning to Roarke.

'Nothing like a cookout on a summer night.'

Dennis Mira wore khakis and a green shirt Eve thought his wife had picked for him, as it matched his wonderful eyes.

His gentle kiss under her aching eye told her the makeup deal hadn't really worked. His follow-up hug wasn't quick, and Eve had to stop herself before she burrowed into the comfort of it.

He smelled like orange slices.

'Right this minute I'm envying you all this space. Your gardens!' Mira took the glass from Roarke. 'We'd never have the talent or time to maintain it, but I can stand here, admire, and envy. Well, this is delicious,' she added after a sip from her birdbath.

Dennis smiled his dreamy, distracted smile as he accepted his own, but kept an arm around Eve just another moment.

Her stress level plummeted; her stomach unknotted.

The veneer wasn't as hard to maintain as she'd feared, over frothy drinks on a warm summer evening. She got through what she understood as required small talk.

Flowers, summer plans, Mavis's new house project.

If she thought about the board and book she'd yet to set up in her home office, she did her best to lock it down.

Then with the grill smoking, and Roarke and Dennis hovering over the steaks, Mira opened the door.

'I've read the files. I'm sorry we didn't have the time or opportunity to consult today. Or I would be if I wasn't getting a steak dinner out of it.'

'That was mostly on me anyway.'

'No word yet, I assume, on the second missing girl?'

90

'Nothing. We've got the alert out, and we're plastering up her photo.'

'You're afraid they caught her — or worse.'

She couldn't discount it, but . . . 'If it was worse, if they killed her, we'd have found the body. No reason to hide it, or try to, since they left one out in the open.'

'I agree. If she managed to get away, it's more likely she'd go home than to the police. And it's very unlikely she'd go home.'

'Some of the blood was hers,' Eve began, then saw Roarke transferring steaks to a platter.

She did her duty, pulled platters and bowls from the compartments. Grilled vegetables, roasted potatoes, slices of tomato and mozzarella, crusty little rolls.

'Everything looks amazing.' Mira lifted her glass of the red wine Roarke poured. 'Compliments to the chef.'

'You did the vegetables on the grill?' Dennis asked.

'Those compliments go to Summerset. But I may give that a try next time. We're going to put together a party, a cookout, hopefully before we leave for Europe.'

'It's all in the marinade,' Dennis told him.

'Is it now?'

'It's key.' He sampled some of the grilled zucchini Eve hoped to avoid. 'Summerset knows the key.'

More small talk, Eve thought, resigned, and focused on her steak.

'Do you eat out here often in the good weather?' Mira wondered.

'My office, usually.'

'Working dinners.' Mira reached over to pat Dennis's hand. 'We often do the same. If not my work, Dennis's, or both.'

91

'We live the lives we live.' Dennis just smiled at her.

'We do and, so, I agree with your conclusions, Eve, that the second girl — Dorian Gregg — did not kill Mina Cabot. Morris's report, the forensics all lead to those conclusions. Although the evidence isn't conclusive, and we may find Dorian was and is a willing participant, my profile of her says differently.'

'Why? Here's where I get hung up on that,' Eve continued before Mira answered. 'Even though I lean, and lean hard, away from her willing participation. She came from a crappy apartment in a crappy building in a crappy neighborhood. She has a history of petty theft. Her mother was abusive, and Jesus, her caseworker ranks even worse for me.'

'Yes, and we'll discuss that and her.'

'So they snatched her, yeah, off the streets most likely. But once she's in it? French manicures, pretty underwear, good food — and I bet decent living conditions. All she has to do is go along, pay for it by doing some porn — if we're right on that. Pose for some pictures, maybe end up in some fancy house somewhere.'

Eve shrugged a shoulder. 'She's a kid, what does she know about it? It might look and feel pretty damn good after what she got away from.'

'She had no choice with her mother — and the caseworker failed her, the system gave her no choice. Why would she accept, even with the questionable advantages, having no choice again?'

Mira paused. 'And I believe she knows all too much about it, more than a child that age should in a perfect world. More, I'd imagine, than Mina did when she was taken.'

'It had to be a lot riskier to abduct someone like

Mina than Dorian. And that tells me they're not the first, the only.'

'I agree. It all strikes as very organized and sophisticated. The outlay to keep young girls — to feed them, and well, to house them in a way to prevent discovery or escape, the clothing, all the rest. It would be considerable.'

'So the profits have to make it worth the outlay. The porn trade, you can make some serious money — but not enough for this. It has to be trafficking.'

'I agree again. If you consider these girls a product for profit?' Mira shifted to Roarke. 'As a businessman, you'd have to invest — time, effort, money — into creating that product.'

'Of course. You'd also create a budget for that investment based on profit projections, otherwise your outlay may — likely will — eat into those profits, even erase them.'

'What if you have a lot of the same product — kind of product?' Eve wondered. 'Like a vehicle. A car. You can have different paint jobs, accessories, and all that. They're all basically the same — built the same, but you can customize them, right? Same basic budget, but you factor in the cost — and profit — on the fancier add-ons. Right?'

Studying her, Roarke sat back with his wine. 'You're meaning a sort of assembly-line operation. A car — a girl. Same basic make. Young, female, human. But your victim was white, the second girl mixed race. Choices for the . . . consumer.'

'I'm thinking maybe it doesn't cost twice as much to feed and clothe and house two girls instead of one. Or ten times as much for ten. You've already got the housing, so that doesn't change. Food spreads out. I guess clothes multiply per cost per kid, but —'

'Not necessarily,' Dennis put in. 'We sponsor some sports teams, right, Charlie? Grandchildren,' he added with that sweet smile. 'If you order two dozen jerseys, they cost less per item than if you order one, or six, for instance.'

'A quart of paint costs more per volume than a gallon,' Roarke said.

'More product, more profit?'

'In theory. But these are children, not cars or widgets.'

'I'm aware,' Eve responded in the same flat tone. 'I'm trying to get a handle on a possible business plan.'

'And the human element must be factored in,' Roarke countered. 'They're abducted, so not willing participants. They may not eat what they're told when they're told.'

'Take food away for a day or two and most children will eat what you provide.'

Roarke nodded at Mira. 'True enough,' he said, as he'd known hunger as a child.

'With the victim,' Mira continued, 'they had months to control her, to indoctrinate her. Evidence indicates she was killed during an attempted escape, so indoctrination failed. But as there were no indications of restraints or physical punishments, I conclude she was controlled — or careful enough to allow her captors to believe her controlled.'

She held up a hand as Roarke poured more wine into her glass. 'Just half, thanks. Now, as to the second girl. Dorian. She may have betrayed Mina, helped stop the escape.'

'Narc on another kid,' Eve added, as she'd thought of it. 'Get a reward.'

94

'Yes. However, Dorian's personal experience leads toward a distrust of authority, and one very unlikely to report on another child. My opinion is they worked together. While Dorian may have enjoyed the attention, the food, the nicer materials, and so on, freedom is a driving force with her personality. Distrust of authority, and freedom.'

'No freedom when authority's in control.'

'Not in her experience. I believe she was certainly cagey enough to fully understand her fate if she remained held.'

'She'd be sold,' Eve concluded.

'With no choice in the matter. No ability to refuse the whims and wishes of whoever bought her. And that brings me to the blood, hers on Mina's clothing. She may have been hurt during the escape, but —'

'Mina wasn't wearing those pants when she got out.'

'Exactly.' Mira nodded at Eve. 'Tending these — in their view — products would also require medical attention. Tests to be certain of the girls' health, regular tox screenings, I'd think.'

'Blood tests.'

'Most certainly, which would make it a simple matter to plant the blood.'

'After they transferred the body from the kill zone to where she'd be easily found. The kid got away,' Eve murmured. 'She got out. Why else try to set her up for the murder? Wouldn't it diminish her worth as a product to have the cops ID her, search for her? It damages her. I should've thought of that. You can't sell a damaged product for full price. She got out, and that makes her the perfect fall guy.'

Eve closed her eyes a moment. 'She doesn't trust

cops, why would she? They'd know that. They might even have a shrink on tap — bet they do. She's not coming to us. We're as much the enemy as the people who grabbed her up. She'd already been tossed in juvie once, why risk it again?'

She looked at Mira. 'Freedom's the driver, I get that. She'll find a hole and hide, or she'll run. Anything else is a cage, one kind or another.'

'You understand these girls in a way few can, not just from training or a natural insight, but from your own experiences. That makes you uniquely qualified for this case. And makes it very, very difficult for you. Both of you,' Mira qualified. 'You can see and feel through them. You may struggle to maintain your objectivity as well as your emotional balance.'

'I have to see and feel through the victim to do my job. It's how I do my job. Through the killer, too. This isn't any different.'

If she heard the defensive tone in Eve's voice — and of course she did — Mira let it pass.

'Your empathy is as key to your process as your instincts and training. But this is different, and it's deeper. I hope you'll come to me if you feel the need.'

'I'm fine. I'm good. I can handle it.'

'You don't have a choice.'

She'd closed her hand around her water glass before Dennis spoke. Now simply sat very still.

'They don't give a choice. They speak to you, these girls. They all speak to you, every victim you stand over and for. But you hear these girls in your head, your heart. How could you ignore them, pretend not to hear?'

Her chest went tight, and she breathed out. 'I can't.'

'You wouldn't be who you are if you could, or did.

96

It costs you, of course it does, but turning away would cost so much more.'

He poured more wine into her glass, then a tiny bit more into his own. 'Charlotte and I often talk through our day and our worries. Sometimes we have to do that hypothetically, but we have our codes. Don't we, Charlie?'

'Yes.' She closed a hand over his. 'We do.'

'I can't count the number of times over the years I've worried about her. What she does, what she sees. It often hurts her, what she does, what she sees. And so I hurt. You understand.'

'I do, yes,' Roarke said.

'We don't have a choice, either, do we? We fell in love with strong, courageous women, women dedicated to facing down the monsters in the world, whatever the cost.

'We tell our children monsters aren't real. But they are. You'll find this girl, I'm sure of that. And you'll find the monsters. Roarke and Charlie will help you. You have to let them.'

'Sometimes it's easier to close off help than to open up to it.'

Now he smiled, and his eyes danced. 'I could tell you stories.'

Mira laughed, leaned over to kiss his cheek. 'Don't.'

They had strawberry shortcake with fresh whipped cream and coffee, then at Mira's request took a walk around the gardens.

Roarke guided them through the grove of fruit trees to the pond.

'Now I have serious envy.' Mira sighed. 'What a beautiful spot.'

'I could dream away a day right there on that bench.'

97

'You're welcome to,' Roarke told Dennis. 'Any time at all.'

Following the path lights, they walked back to the house. At the door, Mira kissed Roarke's cheek. 'Thank you for a wonderful dinner.' Then Eve's. 'I'll write up the conclusions and profiles.'

'I appreciate it.'

When Dennis hugged her, she spoke quietly in his ear. 'Thanks for what you said before.'

He simply drew back, pressed a light kiss to the bruising under her eye. 'Next time, duck.'

'Got it.'

When Roarke closed the door, Eve stood where she was a moment. 'It was a good idea to have them over like this. Thanks for taking care of it.'

'It was nothing. No trouble at all.'

'I still have to . . . I haven't set up my board, started my book here.'

'Then we'd best go up. I can set up your board if you like while you do the rest. You can adjust it as needed,' he added when she didn't respond.

'That'd be great.'

When she stepped into the office, she glanced toward the sleep chair, but Galahad wasn't sprawled over it.

'He's likely with Summerset, as we deserted him for the evening.'

'Right. I have to generate the photos and data for the board.'

'I can do it on the auxiliary.'

Of course he could, she thought, and went to her command center, opened operations. And programmed a pot of coffee.

For a time they worked in silence. Such silence, she

thought, and keenly missed the cat's presence.

Roarke broke it as he arranged her board. 'This Pru Truman, the Child Services caseworker. We didn't get around to her at dinner.'

'Peabody's report — copied to her supervisor — is there, too. Who also got a call from me. Stupid, careless, lazy bitch.'

The outrage ripped back, tearing her out of her chair to pace.

'It's all the kid's fault, as she sees it. So much the kid's fault she doesn't do a goddamn thing when the neighbors tell her the mother smacks the kid around. Or check the mother's bullshit about home-schooling. Or do the least amount of work and demand to see and speak to the kid directly. Which she couldn't have done because the kid took off last summer. And the pathetic excuse for a mother's been collecting her professional parent stipend all along.'

'Where is she now, the mother?'

'Well, she didn't make bail so she's in a cage in Freehold, New Jersey, and facing fraud charges. Had illegals in the apartment — and the caseworker fuck never screened for them.'

'And where is she now, this caseworker fuck?'

'I can tell you where she won't be tomorrow. She won't be sitting at her desk collecting a paycheck for doing fuck-all. She ought to be in the cell next to the mother. I get the don't-tell-me-how-to-do-my-job, and the watch-your-language, and the you-don't-understand bullshit from her.'

Roarke just stood and watched her pace. 'And she walked away on her own power? I suppose the sparring droid made a reasonable substitute.'

'Almost. I don't know where to start with Dorian.

99

We don't know if she came to New York on her own, got grabbed up here last week, last month. If she got snatched a block from that crap apartment the night she took off. Anytime, anywhere between. Because nobody gave enough of a damn to look for her.'

Eve's breath shuddered out. 'Nobody cared.'

'Now someone does. You'll find her.'

'She could be dead.'

'You don't think so.' He crossed to her now, laid his hands on her shoulders. 'Trust your instincts. I do.'

'It hurts.'

'I know.' He drew her in, held her close as she wrapped her arms tight around him. 'I know. Just as I know Dennis was right.'

'Don't say you're sorry.'

His lips curved against her hair. 'That wasn't top of my head.'

She sighed, then rested her head on his shoulder. 'Can we both be right?'

'I think we are, this time in any case. Both right, both wrong. That makes it a wash, doesn't it?'

'It hurts you, too. I can't even wish it didn't or it would mean you didn't love me the way you do. And then I feel stupid and selfish, and —'

He cut her off, kissed her, soft and slow. 'I didn't fall in love with a stupid, selfish woman. It's insulting to imply otherwise. Shutting me out would be stupid and selfish, but you're not going to do that.'

'I'm not, even though it'll be hard on you.' She stepped back but took his hands. 'You didn't like it when I talked about these girls as products. Like cars.'

'I didn't, no, even understanding you looked at them through the eyes of the monsters. That's a good word for them.'

100

'It's the business — the profit angle. It doesn't feel personal, like someone taking girls for personal reasons, personal perversions, right? Mina was still a virgin. Sure there are other things somebody could do, but no signs of physical abuse, restraints, drugs in her system. And they kept her polished up.'

'Polished up?'

'Manicure, pedicure, skin care, the expensive silk underwear, good nutrition. Harvo said her shirt was tailored to fit — and no label. I mean never a label, okay? What does that say? The shirt.'

'That it was made for her, and they have a source.'

'Right, and that costs, doesn't it? It's not — what do you call it?'

'Prêt-à-porter. Ready-to-wear,' he elaborated. 'Off-the-rack.'

'Yeah, that. Why do that, go to that expense? Nothing elaborate, either, just a white, short-sleeved shirt. But what if it's something like Mr. Mira said — you order a dozen, it's less per? They had Mina for months, potentially had Dorian for months. If there are more? Plain, well-made white shirts.'

'Like a uniform.'

'Like a uniform. You go into the military, what do they do? Put you in uniform. You're not an individual, you dress alike. School uniforms, team uniforms, cop uniforms. It's part of the training, right? It's part of being trained to eat when you're told, sleep when you're told, follow orders.

'She had good muscle tone,' Eve continued, pacing again. 'She got exercise. Yeah, maybe she did that on her own to keep in shape, stay strong, but if you're grooming a girl for sale, you don't want pudge, right? You want in shape. She used some product in her hair, too. They had to buy it for her, or provide it.'

She turned back to Roarke. 'When you go to market a product or sell it, you want it to shine, right?'

'You do, of course.'

'Do you know anything about this kind of business?'

'I've stayed well away from anything of the sort, always.'

'I know that, but you might know somebody who knows somebody who knows somebody.'

'I can promise you, if I'd heard a whisper of such a thing, I'd have told you. But . . .' He walked over, poured himself coffee. 'We have the shelter, the school. I can also promise anyone who works there would do the same, and report it to me if not to you straight off. But I'll ask.'

'I don't think this is a new operation. Whether it's a couple girls at a time, or a lot of them, it's not a damn start-up. Mira said sophisticated, and that feels right. The kid might've gotten out because she was damn smart, or because they got a little careless.'

'Why not both?'

'Yeah, why not? When you've run a business smooth for a while, you might get a little careless. Then you get somebody pretty damn smart who figures out how to take advantage of that. She got out.'

Eve went back to the coffee herself, and with it turned to study Mina's ID shot. 'She got outside, in the rain. The shirt's trashed, but the pants. Probably cost a bundle, and maybe you're frugal there. More likely you put her own back on her so it looks more like she's been on the street. She's way too clean for that, way too clean and polished up, but you do what you can.'

She walked to the board, tapped one of the crime-scene stills. 'Take her shoes. Take everything, but you put her own necklace back on her. Break the chain like somebody tried to grab it, then just had to run. Use some of Dorian's blood. It's not a bad setup.'

'They'd have moved the body well away from wherever she escaped, wherever she died.'

'Yeah, a good distance. The murder weapon's real wood — Peabody said maybe an old stud somebody ripped out. You wouldn't find that on the ground in the park.'

Now she slid her hands into her pockets, rocked back and forth on her heels. 'High-end suburb of Philadelphia, and the wrong side of Freehold, New Jersey. Maybe Dorian headed toward Philadelphia, got grabbed there. But why would she?'

'No connections for her there?'

'No connections anywhere. She got busted a couple times for theft. If you were a kid running off from a lousy situation and liked to steal, why not head to New York? It's closer, full of tourists, plenty of places for a street kid to hide out.'

She started wandering again. 'Easier to snatch a street kid, less risk, and less likely anybody's looking too hard for her anyway. Maybe she got snatched in New Jersey, maybe she did head to Philly. Or maybe she made it to New York.'

She turned back to Roarke. 'For me, that makes it only one out of three the same person grabbed both of them.'

'Scouts.'

She pointed at him. 'Exactly. Assembly line, you said before. You have to keep the products rolling on that line. I've got nothing on another kid — male or female, wide age range — missing from Devon, Pennsylvania.'

103

Following her logic, he went back to studying the board.

'You wouldn't want to dip in that pool too often. It's far too small.'

'And you know why you dip in that pool in the first place? Street kids aren't generally all that healthy, they may have addictions by the time you get to them. They're unlikely to be virgins. You want prime product, you have to hunt for them where they're more plentiful.'

After dragging her hands through her hair, Eve blew out a breath. 'I have a detective who deals with this sort of thing. McNab knows her. I'm going to pull her in for a consult tomorrow.'

She looked back at him. 'How would you put together a business plan for all this?'

'Well, Christ Jesus.' He dropped into the chair at her auxiliary station. 'All right then. You'd need a location, a place to keep the girls. Even if you started small, one, maybe two, you'd need a secure place.'

'It's not going to be a house, not a private residence. Mina wasn't kept in a basement like Mary Kate Covino was. She was too healthy, too clean. No restraints. You're keeping them for months. Privacy and security, absolutely.'

'A retrofitted warehouse, perhaps, or if you've the wherewithal, an apartment building or the like.'

'All those windows in an apartment or office building.' It just didn't gel for her. 'It's hard to keep all those windows secure.'

'True enough, but with that wherewithal, it could be done. You'd need a way to prepare food, and I'd want that on-site, so some staff — not only to prepare food, but to shop for what's needed to prepare it. So kitchen facilities and staff. A way to find, take, transport the girls. Guards, of course, once you've done that. You talked of grooming, so you need those products and someone to apply them, or teach the girls how to do so. You'd want some medical staff.'

'Medical staff. Right. You'd have to check them out. Keep them healthy.'

'Someone to clean,' Roarke added. 'You'd certainly need at least one disciplinarian.'

'Because no way a kid's going to do everything you say right off.'

'Someone in charge of acquiring or manufacturing clothing, laundering,' Roarke continued, building the business in his mind. 'And marketing. Photographs and vids, certainly to attract potential clients, so a professional there would be best if you want to showcase your product well. An IT man or team to set up and maintain the online areas. Office workers — you need records, after all. Banking — you need a way to invest your profits and enjoy them. It's a considerable outlay, Eve, even for two or three girls at a time.'

'It's going to be more. Say eight to ten. You make some bucks off the porn, but the major profit's in sales. Sell one girl for five, six million, what do you do?'

'Put the bulk of it back into the business. You have salaries to pay. Mortgage or rent, food, and so on.'

'Keep one girl for six months, it costs — just say — half a million. Keep eight, it doesn't cost eight times that. Like the car, right?'

He could follow her line of thought easily, as it simply made good business sense.

'Some of the expenses and outlay remain steady. The mortgage or rent wouldn't change. If you're heating or cooling the building, that wouldn't change appreciably.'

'So, sell a couple of girls every few months — bumping that some with the porn — you're going to see an annual profit. Millions in profit if you do it right.'

'You're talking about a network, highly organized, with potentially dozens of people involved in the day-to-day.'

'Yeah, and maybe it's a lot smaller than that. But you'd still need the elements you said. You'd need all that. French manicures, grilled fish and brown rice with veg. Her dinner,' she explained. 'She stuck her fingers down her throat to boot some of it up.'

'Is that how she got out?'

'I'm betting it is. Who's going to think some girl puking up her dinner's going to run? Smart. Maybe she and Dorian pulled that together. I'll find out when I find her.'

'Which you won't tonight. I think you should call it. You're tired and you're hurting. Physically,' he continued. 'Not just the eye, the jaw, but you've started favoring your side. I expect your ribs took a pounding.'

'I've got an ice pack on them. Well, it's not cold anymore, but I put one on it.' She lifted her shoulders. 'I needed to feel it.'

'I know. And in your place, I'd have needed the same. I'm not sure what that says about either of us. But you could use a round with the healing wand.'

'Yeah, well, I'm definitely feeling it. I was a little pissed you didn't offer when I came up from the gym so I could tell you to bite me.'

'I was much too pissed myself to give you the satisfaction.'

He held out his hand; she put hers in it.

106

7

In the bedroom Eve stripped off her shirt while Roarke got a wand. Sprawled on the bed like a chunky gray ribbon, Galahad opened his eyes, gave her a long and clearly disapproving look as she peeled off the gel pack.

'That droid had a sneaky left,' Eve insisted.

Annoyed, she reactivated the pack, then pressed it to her jaw as Roarke came back in. He gave her ribs a long and clearly disapproving look before he shook his head.

'And was it worth it then?'

'Not really. I didn't get enough out, I guess. I thought programming the female would make it more like I was pounding Truman, but that bitch is built. The droid, not Truman.'

She let out a hiss as he passed the wand over her ribs.

'Truman wouldn't have landed any.'

He said, 'Mmm-hmm.'

'She's a bag of bones. The droid's solid muscle, an easy buck and a half. With a sneaky left.'

'You dropped your guard.'

'I did . . .' Damn it. 'Maybe. How do you know?'

'Even if I hadn't watched for a moment or two, I can see the results, can't I?'

'In some circles, that's considered spying.'

'As you like,' he said easily. 'After I saw it land this one?' He tapped a finger lightly on the cold pack on her jaw. 'I took a shower and changed for dinner.'

She couldn't bitch about that — she sort of wanted to, but she couldn't find a logical way to bitch about that.

'The comp said I won on points. And it was actually minor to moderate repairs.'

'Well, sit down now, and we'll finish your minor to moderate repairs.'

When she sat on the side of the bed, Galahad rolled over, squiggled forward, and nudged his head under her hand.

'I should've held off, just let Mr. Mira level me off.'

As he passed the wand over her jaw, Roarke's eyes met hers. 'He has a way.'

'I don't know how he just gets to the core of it, right off. And he said what I didn't know how to explain, really. I don't have a choice, Roarke.'

'I know it. I know it as I know you. I wonder how it is it twists me up so much more seeing you tired and hurting inside than it does seeing these bruises. Then again, these bruises heal quick enough.'

He switched from her jaw to her eye. 'We're never going to be all the way done with all the before. It made us who we are, after all.'

'I guess. Mira said . . . She said I understood someone like Dorian because, basically, I've been there. That distrust of authority? I know where it comes from.'

'And still, you chose authority. You chose the police not just as a vocation but a kind of home, and I, for a very long time, chose the opposite of that.'

'We both needed to be in charge, to take the power back. I'd be more than halfway into a burnout if I hadn't found you. You'd probably have stolen all the art and jewelry in the galaxy if you hadn't found me.'

'Ah, but that was meant, wasn't it now?'

She smiled, and with the cat now stretched over both their laps, touched Roarke's cheek. 'Irish woo-woo.'

'Pure fact, and one that speaks to me. What does she say to you, this young girl? Can you tell me?'

Closing her eyes, Eve stroked the cat.

'When I stood over her today with Morris . . . She looked so perfect, so young and perfect except for . . . I could hear her think: What would I have done, who would I have been, if they hadn't taken me? How would I have coped with what they did, if I'd gotten away? I know it's me thinking it, but —'

'Is it?'

She let it go because the wand felt soothing now instead of achy. 'They damaged her where it didn't show, where you can't see. But she had a foundation, she had a family, and she'd have gotten through it. Maybe not over it because you don't. We know that. But through it. They stole that from her.'

'And the other, the one you need to find?'

'Her foundation's cracked and rocky. I looked at — into — her mother today, and I saw Stella. Parts of her. I'm not going to beat myself up for that.'

'Nor should you. There's a type, isn't there? Stella, Meg Roarke, this woman. A mold that makes them vile and vicious.'

'Truman fits it — mostly. She's not going to smack a kid around physically, like I damn well know Jewell Gregg did with Dorian more than the neighbors ever saw. She's the type that punches the heart, the self-worth, the trust until it's all broken and bleeding.'

It made her sick inside, the thought of it, the memories of it.

109

'It's worse. She's not required or expected to love them, right? But she has a duty, and she uses that, twists that to batter where it doesn't show.'

'You'll see she's fired.'

'Absolute priority. But it's not enough. She's already damaged Dorian Gregg, and God knows how many others.'

Fury simmered inside her again.

'I recognized her, too, damn right I did. I had a couple like that. Like a wrong cop, they fuck it up for all the ones who do the job.'

He rose, walked to open the panel that held the bedroom AutoChef. Eve checked her ribs — definitely better. Her jaw — absolutely less swollen.

'I'm making time to dig into it, see if I can hang her up on anything illegal. She's going to lose her job — Gregg defrauding the PPO, and Truman not verifying? Yeah, she's gone, but unless she took a kickback, not a crime on her part. Even if I find something, it's probably a slap on the wrist. Not enough.'

Roarke came back with two glasses filled with a peach-colored liquid.

'Is this a soother? I don't need a soother.'

'We're splitting one. It's a new flavor. It should taste a bit like a Bellini.'

She knew he'd found a way to get around her with the whole splitting thing, so she took a sip. 'I haven't had that many Bellinis.'

'We'll have to remedy that.'

'Anyway, it's okay.'

'Not bad at all,' he agreed. 'Civil suit.'

'What?'

'When you find Dorian, she can file a civil suit against Truman. CPS will get dragged in, but they should have done a better job overseeing this woman, shouldn't they? And a good lawyer's bound to find a few more children — perhaps adults by now — who have similar stories. Class action suit.'

The idea added a zing to the soother. 'Sue her lazy, fucked-up ass.'

'I'll wager a court would levy more than a slap on the wrist. Unlikely she has the funds to pay off a judgment, but it would make her life hell for quite some time. Then, you have a good friend who excels at exposés.'

'Nadine.' As she rolled it around, that simmering fury turned to satisfaction. 'She'd lap this right up. Why didn't I think of that?'

'Because you have to focus on finding her, and on finding who abducted her and Mina, who killed Mina, and if there are others being held. This is extraneous.'

'Also brilliant. It's handy having a business genius around.'

'Absolutely true. Finish that up now. We'll do another round with the wand in the morning after you've had some sleep.'

He shifted the cat, then got up, set the wand aside.

Eve considered as he took off his shirt. 'I think since you did the wand thing, the soother thing, you should finish me off.'

He angled a look at her as he took off his shoes. 'Emotionally, physically, or sexually?'

She wound a finger in the air. 'All of that.'

'Feeling better, are you now?'

'Nothing hurts.'

'I'd like to keep it that way.'

'If you don't think you have the finesse . . .' She lifted her shoulders.

111

'Aren't you the clever one?'

He unhooked his belt, then gestured for her to stand as he took off his jeans. He stepped forward to unbutton hers, added another gesture for her to lift her arms.

She wore a simple white sports bra, wiser, he thought than her usual support tank that would have put pressure on the ribs. Eyes on hers, he peeled it up and off, slowly, before cupping her breasts, sliding his thumbs over them.

She wrapped her arms around his neck, met his mouth with hers. He tempered the heat she put into the kiss, kept it soft, gentle, deep. When his hands glided down her — butterfly wings — her arms tugged to take them both to the bed. But he held her in place so they stood, body to body, as he nudged her jeans over her hips.

His mouth moved from hers to brush lightly, lightly over her jaw, then to her throat where her pulse beat. She ran her hands over his shoulders, then they locked there when he skimmed his lips over her breast. A feather of a touch that tripped her heartbeat while her hands skimmed through his hair to press him closer. Closer until he took more, until he felt her heart sprint under his lips.

When once again she would have pulled him down to the bed, he turned her until her back pressed against the bedpost. Then his hands, his lips traveled down so he treated himself to the taste of her skin. He could never get enough.

The length of that narrow torso, the hard body under soft flesh, and the quiver he could bring inside that tough, disciplined body all enchanted, aroused, overwhelmed him.

She felt those clever fingers ride her jeans down her legs, then slide back up her thighs until her legs went weak and wobbly.

He could make her float, make her want to float, weightless and weak and willing.

Then she was bared to him as his mouth found her, as his tongue slipped over, around, into her.

'Okay. Okay. God!' She had to wrap an arm behind her, around the post to stay upright. 'Wait until —'

But he didn't wait, so the orgasm spread like a fever, so it rocked through her, left her gasping. Helpless, desperate, thrilled, she moved against him and took more.

'Again.' He nipped at her inner thigh, then soothed that tiny, glorious pain with his tongue. He'd take all she had, then find more. When she came again, quaking with it, crying out from it, he slid slowly up her body and set off a storm in her with his fingers.

'Take me now,' he said as he slipped, slowly, slowly, into all that heat. 'As I take you. Where we stand. Together.'

She saw his eyes, only his eyes, that wild, wonderful blue. And she knew love so keen she wondered it didn't slice through them both.

Perhaps it did.

So she wrapped around him, her body pulsing like a heart, and took him as he took her.

Eyes open and locked.

When he dropped his forehead to hers, when he found the ability to draw breath back into his body again, he gathered her up. Her body felt so lax, he wondered she didn't just pour like rainwater through his hands before he got them both in bed.

There he drew her against him, stroked her back.

113

'Enough finesse for you?'

'Any more, I'd be in a coma.'

He felt the cat leap back onto the bed, take his place. All's well then, he thought, as she fell asleep in his arms.

★ ★ ★

The dream didn't surprise her. She'd expected it. But even in the dream she willed herself to handle it, not to let it weaken her.

Maybe she hadn't expected to find herself in that room in Dallas with the red light blinking, the air so goddamn cold. But it didn't hold the terror for her it once had. She wasn't a child now, and Richard Troy was dead.

She'd killed him, after all.

She stood there, in the room of so many nightmares, dressed in black, her weapon in place, and waited for Mina Cabot to speak.

Mina stood in her school uniform, her hair bright and shiny and smooth, her eyes bold and alive.

'You think you understand me? You came from this. I didn't. I had family who loved me. You didn't. I had friends and a nice room of my own. You didn't have anything. What do you know about me?'

'I know they took all of that from you. I know what that's like.'

'You didn't have anything to take.'

'Tell me something I don't know. Something I don't know I know.'

'They wouldn't have taken you and dolled you all up. You weren't pretty.'

Eve glanced over as Mina pointed, saw the pale,

114

skinny child she'd been. The dirty hair, the hopeless eyes.

'Guess not.'

'He'd've sold you on the cheap. All broken and used up.'

'He's the one who broke me and used me up. They didn't break you, did they? Not until the end.'

'I had brains, and something to get back to. You didn't save me.'

It hurt, even in the dream, it hurt. 'You've got me there.'

'She's not going to save me, either.' Dorian stood beside Mina now, her hair groomed into perfect curls. She wore the same school uniform.

That was wrong, Eve thought. She hadn't gone to private school.

'She doesn't even know if I'm dead or alive. What does she care?'

'I'm here because I care.'

'Bullshit!' Rage, Eve recognized it as it slapped out at her. 'You're here because they pay you. Like they paid the cops to drag me back to that shithole so my mother could collect her stipend.'

'I put your mother in jail.'

'A lot of good that does me now. You can just fuck off. I can take care of myself.'

Were teenage girls really that bitchy? Eve wondered. Or did she just see them that way?

'You want to be pissed at me? Fine, but I'm what you've got. You think I don't understand you? She does. And she's me.'

She looked at the child she'd been, cradling her broken arm while blood dripped from her hands.

'It's going to get better,' Eve told her. 'You'll be okay.'

'Bullshit!' Dorian shrieked it this time. 'You're lying to her. How's it better to get tossed to strangers who don't give a shit? If they'd known what she did, they'd have tossed her in a hole. Killer! Killer! Killer! At least I never killed anybody. I didn't do that!'

Mina stood, the blood turning her shirt red around the spear through her chest.

'This really sucks, and you didn't stop it. You didn't stop any of it. So . . .'

'Just fuck off,' the girls said together.

She woke with sunlight trickling into the bedroom and a fully dressed Roarke sitting behind her.

'There now, just a dream.'

'I know, I know. I'm okay. Damn it.' She sat up, laid her head on his shoulder when he put his arms around her. 'It wasn't that bad. Well, bad, but not . . . I don't know.'

She eased back, pressed a hand to her head.

'Headache. Not a question, I can see it.'

'It'll be all right.'

He rose, went to the AC for coffee. And bringing it to her, took out a blocker. 'Take it, or no coffee.'

'That's just mean.' She took it, and the coffee.

'You got a full night's sleep before it hit you,' he commented, and had her checking the time.

'Shit! I've got to get moving.'

He simply put a hand on her shoulder to hold her in place. 'You'll take a moment to tell me about it.'

'I need to wake up, grab a shower. I'll tell you.'

'All right then, with breakfast.'

'Can it be waffles?'

He pressed curved lips to her forehead. 'It can. Get your shower.'

Not as bad as he'd feared, he thought when he

walked to the AutoChef to program breakfast. He'd checked on her during his early-morning conference calls, and she'd slept peacefully.

So it had hit sometime after he'd left his office and come back to the bedroom to find her muttering in her sleep, and the cat butting his head against her shoulder.

But not that bad. She hadn't been shaking, and the request for waffles meant she didn't feel ill.

He dealt with breakfast, and telling himself — perhaps with partial honesty — he'd save her time, laid a work outfit on the bed for her.

When she came out wearing a short, cream-colored robe, he sat with the cat curled in his lap while the morning stock data scrolled on the wall screen.

'This thing's silk, right?'

'It is, yes.'

'Is it sexy?'

He gave her a studied look and sipped his coffee. 'What's in it is.'

'Come on. Is it like fuckwear?'

With a laugh, he sat back. 'A loaded question if I ever heard one, but we'll treat it seriously. In my view it's subtly sexy.'

'Kind of classy, right?'

'As I see it, yes. It suits you.'

'Nobody's going to accuse me of being classy.'

'You're in a class by yourself.'

After a quick snort, she grabbed her PPC. 'Look at this underwear.'

'What a fascinating start to the day.' He took the PPC, nodded at the image. 'Yes, I remember this from your board.'

And if he hadn't, he thought, the bloodstains on

the bra would serve as a clue.

'Set that aside a minute. Is it fuckwear?'

'Ah, Christ.'

'I know, I know, but put that aside. Just judge the pieces on their own right now.'

'All right then. They're provocative, certainly, and designed to enhance the body. Given the color, the touches of lace, I'd say subtle again, and yes, classy, even romantic. On an adult woman.'

She punched his shoulder. 'Yes. On a kid, not subtle or classy because just wrong. But they still have that . . . Mavis would say vibe. I get that vibe. Or it hit me when I put on this robe. It's not bang me against the bedpost.'

'Did that.'

'That wasn't banging,' she corrected, taking the PPC back. 'And maybe I'm putting too much into a couple scraps of silk, but I think they wanted more from her than banging. Banging's easy. You don't have to spend a couple grand on underwear for that. And this had to be like daily wear, right? Like you buy me stuff like this — and some of it's straight fuckwear. I'm not stupid. But for work? I'm not going to wear anything like this on the job.'

Thinking, thinking, she set the PPC down again. 'Anyway, I'm going to get dressed before waffles.'

Roarke pointed toward the bed. She looked at the clothes laid out, then looked back at him.

'Seriously?'

'A time-saving offer only.'

'Accepted,' she decided, and took his coffee, finished it off. 'I've got too much jumbling through my brain to think about clothes anyway.'

'Let me see the ribs first.' When she rolled her eyes

and opened the robe, he set Galahad aside and rose to give them another pass with the wand.

'Bruising's nearly faded off.'

'They feel okay. Not bullshit,' she said quickly. 'If somebody punches me in the ribs, I'm going to feel it, but otherwise they're okay.'

'Don't drop your guard. Swelling's down,' he added as he passed the wand over her jaw. 'Your eye's bloomed a bit more, but it's not swollen. I'd tell you to give the eye another pass this afternoon, but you won't.'

'I will if I remember.'

He kissed it lightly. Just, she thought, as Dennis Mira had.

'You'll do.'

He went back to sit as she wiggled into the simple cotton briefs he'd set out.

'See,' she said as she pulled on the support tank. 'You know.'

He'd gone for brown trousers. Not Feeney's shit brown, but something that edged toward copper. And the shirt — nearly the same cream color as the robe — had needle-thin stripes of the copper and some navy. Navy, she assumed, because of the navy jacket. She strapped on her weapon, added the belt — also navy, with a copper buckle — the navy boots with thick copper soles, then the jacket that hit at her waist.

'This jacket has the magic lining, like the coat.'

'It's a prototype,' he told her, removing the domes on the breakfast plates. 'Removable, so transferable. Something we're working on.'

'Huh. It's really light.'

'In testing and simulations it blocks a full stun, a

119

blade, and, should it come up against someone who's managed to get hands on a gun, a bullet. Of course, I'd prefer you not put any of that to the test, but in case.'

He poured her coffee. 'Now, tell me about the dream.'

'Right. Mostly annoying,' she began as she drowned the waffles in syrup. 'It was in Dallas, in the room in Dallas.'

'Ah, Eve.'

'No, it doesn't hit me like it used to. They're dead, they're dead and gone. I'm not saying it was sex on a tropical beach, but I handled it. First it was just the victim, just Mina.'

She told him as she ate, occasionally stabbing a fat berry between bites of syrup-soaked waffle.

'They were pretty damn bitchy,' she added, waving a piece of bacon that had Galahad's nose twitching as he started casually toward the table.

And stopped dead at Roarke's warning look.

'I know it's me bitching at me, really. My subconscious and all that. Or how I figure thirteen-year-old girls would bitch. I mean, what do I know? The only thing I remember about being thirteen was it meant five more years until I could get out.'

She crunched into the bacon. 'But I figure my brain worked out some truths. Mina had something to get back to. And if Dorian felt — feels — anything like I did, getting out's enough.'

'You put them both in school uniforms.'

'Yeah, because I think that's probably how it works. You've got a couple of girls or a handful, they're all the same. Products. The underwear though, that's different. Major expense. Investment,' she said again. 'It's

120

like the robe. It feels good against the skin. You feel a certain way when you have it on. I put on my underwear for work, I feel a certain way. Put on the fancy stuff for under the fancy stuff, that feels a certain way. Maybe you don't really think about it, but you feel it.'

'The uniform strips the individuality. Under it, the silk, the sexy accustoms you to that feel, that mood?'

'There you go. A kind of mind game. Some want someone they have to force, even hurt. That kind of power and dominance. But you can get an LC to role-play.'

'Not the same,' Roarke commented. 'You don't own an LC.'

'Okay, true enough. But why pay big bucks — and it has to be big bucks — to rape and brutalize when you can grab up a street kid for nothing? If you want a sex slave, a product, wouldn't you pay more for one that does what you want, how you want it?'

'You think this is some kind of training. Target attractive young girls, lock them away from the familiar, indoctrinate them. The uniforms, the food, the hair and skin products.'

'Punishments, too. The carrot's no good without the stick. Think of the military again, the old 'drop and give me twenty.' They have to break you down to build you up in their image, for their needs.

'A girl like Mina, who looks like Mina, who sells as a virgin, but one with sexual knowledge, one who's gotten used to being photographed in the sexwear, or naked, or in sexual situations. You program a sex droid to be and do what you want, right? This could be like that, but with human girls.'

With a shrug, she polished off the waffles. 'Or I could be way off base. But . . . Coincidence is bullshit, and it's not bullshit that Mina Cabot and Dorian Gregg, same age, no prior connection, were both abducted, most probably from different areas, and both ended up in New York.'

She pushed up and began to load her pockets for the day.

'I'm pulling Willowby in, the SVU detective McNab knows. She may have some insight. I've gotta go.'

Roarke shot the cat another warning look before he rose, rounded the table. And laid his hands on Eve's shoulders. 'Take care of my cop.'

'I've got a magic shield.'

'I haven't come up with one for that face of yours yet.' So he kissed it. 'Wand that eye.'

'I will.' If she remembered, she thought, and left him.

In the car, she contacted Detective Willowby, asked for a meet, then drove through the gates.

122

8

While Eve battled traffic, Dorian stirred out of a fitful, feverish sleep. She'd managed to pry a thin board off a broken window and crawl through into what looked like an abandoned storefront.

Nothing in it but dirt, spiders — probably rats — but she'd needed to lie down, just try to sleep. Even with the pills and ice packs she'd stolen, everything hurt.

And under the hurt, fear bubbled. She didn't know of what, or who, but she'd crawled through that window, cutting her hand on some of the broken glass, because everything in her had said: Hide.

She'd curled on the floor, shivering and sweating herself in and out of sleep for the day. Once, during the endless, miserable night that followed, she'd started to crawl out, to steal some food, but she'd just given up until she'd slept again.

Now she saw sunlight eking through the cracks of the board she'd tried to put back in place. Another day, she realized, and every instinct told her she needed to get up, to move, to find food and a better place to hide.

But everything hurt.

'Wondered if you'd wake up.'

The voice had her jolting, so her head seemed to balloon, then pop.

'Take it easy, squeezy.'

Since it was a kid who crab-walked over to her, the

123

worst of the fear ebbed.

He had big brown eyes, an unruly thatch of purple-streaked brown hair, and a round, pink scar in the middle of his left cheek.

She thought he was younger than she was, though her blurry brain couldn't pinpoint her own age.

She tried to tell him to go away, but her voice just croaked.

'You look sick. Beat up some, too. Hungry?' He held out a piece of untoasted bagel with a hand not altogether clean. 'I ate the rest.'

She took it, gnawed on it.

'I call myself Mouser, 'cause I'm fast and sneaky.'

When she just stared at him, he shrugged. 'I guess you can come with me if you want, 'cause you don't look so good. We've got a place, lots better'n this. And cops might check in here like I did, 'cause you left blood on the window.'

'Where?' she managed.

'Not that far. Cops after you?'

'Don't know.'

'Come on with me if you want. We can fix you up. Got beds and all, and food, too.'

'No shelter.'

He snorted, swiped the back of his hand under his nose. 'Not like you mean. We look out for each other. Rule is — 'cause we got some — see a kid needs help, you help if you can. So you can come with me if you want.'

''Kay.' The cough hurt when it racked her. 'Leg hurts.'

'Don't look broken or nothing. Anything,' he said with an eye roll, as if some internal teacher corrected him. 'You can lean on me. I'm stronger than I look.'

He had to help her get to her feet, and twice, she had to just sit back down because her head swam.

When she did, he sat and waited.

But when she stood, she found she could put more weight on her bad leg than she'd feared.

Not a lot, but enough to limp, and to lean against Mouser.

They got out the way they'd come in, but Mouser laid rags over the window to protect their hands.

They came out in an alley.

'What you do, see, is you just walk along like you're going somewhere, got some business, check? Nobody pays attention much around here.'

The sunlight hurt her eyes, made them water, but she tried to look like she had some business as they came out of the alley onto the street.

'Got a name? You can make one up.'

'My head feels wrong. Everything's all messed up, and I can't remember stuff.'

'Like your *name*? No shit? That's kind of frosty.'

'Doesn't feel frosty.'

'You know two plus two?'

She sent him a look well-known to teenage girls. 'Like four? My head's messed up, not stupid.'

He just grinned at her. 'You sound like a frog.'

'Throat's sore. Where are we?'

'Down to the downtown.'

'Downtown where?'

'Jeez peas. New York.'

'New York,' she whispered. 'I was in New York. I think. I think. It hurts to think.'

'So stop.' Then he sighed, dug into a pocket of his dingy baggies, and pulled out a mini tube of Coke.

'You can have it. I just snatched it and the bagel.'

125

She chugged some down, coughed violently, chugged again.

'You're all sweaty. Maybe from being sick or whatever, 'cause it's not so hot yet. Down this way.'

He led her down another alley, then pulled up a break in a security fence. Her leg hurt more now, but he kept going until he stopped in a skinny, scabby-looking lot and dragged up a metal cover.

'Now we go down.'

'Down there?'

Heat washed over her, and cold swept after it.

'Tunnels.'

'Best way to get there. They don't use 'em anymore 'cause they changed the grid or the something, and don't need this one.'

'Tunnels,' she repeated.

'They ain't — aren't scary. It's like a secret, okay? You can't tell. Hurry up.'

Her mind turned off. She saw walking, walking. Running, walking. Had to hurry, had to get out.

Away.

Everything echoed, outside her head, inside.

She stumbled.

'We're almost there. Swear to God. Come on, get up.'

'Can't.' Curling into a ball on the rough concrete, she let the tears come.

He tried patting her head, patting her back, but the tears didn't stop.

'I'll be right back, okay? Here, here, you take the light. I know the way.'

Then she was alone. She'd sleep, she told herself. And if she didn't wake up, okay. She was so tired, so sick, so scared. She didn't need to wake up again.

She thought she heard footsteps coming fast.

They'd found her, she thought as she drifted away. She'd known they would. But they couldn't hurt her now because she was going to sleep. Forever.

She didn't feel the hand cool on her face, hear the voice speak.

'Poor thing, she's burning up.'

'Leg's hurt. She could hardly walk on it.'

'Mmm. Well, we'll see what we can do.'

Arms lifted her. Somewhere inside she flailed out. But she only moaned and muttered.

'All right now. We've got you, and no one's going to hurt you.'

⋆ ⋆ ⋆

Because she beat her way through traffic in good time, Eve went straight to her office to write out her thoughts and theories. A kind of boot camp, she considered, for sex slaves. Training facilities.

She pushed up, got coffee. She knew something — something from the dream. Something connected to it.

'Not pretty enough.'

Squeezing her eyes tight, she willed memory back.

Troy, Richard Troy. Did he say that? Something about her not being pretty enough, never going to be pretty enough to bring the big bucks?

Rent instead? Rent her out, use her up, sell her off?

'Am I making that up? Just projecting?'

She walked to her window, stared out, stared down.

'Needed seasoning. Goddamn it, I'm not pulling that out of the air. You need some seasoning, little girl. I can *hear* him say that.'

127

Because it made her sick, she pressed her forehead to the glass. She needed to stay steady. If something pushed through, she'd still stay steady.

But if *not pretty enough* meant something — something relevant to the investigation — she'd need to dig down for it.

She turned at the tap.

Detective Willowby stood in the doorway, her knuckles still resting on the jamb.

'Lieutenant, Detective Willowby. I'm a little early. I only live a few blocks away, and thought I'd come right in.'

'No problem. Coffee?'

'Yeah, sure. A little milk, one sugar. Do you mind?'

Eve nodded when Willowby gestured to the board.

While the detective studied it, Eve programmed the coffee.

She didn't look like her name, Eve thought.

On the short side with a compact, athletic body, Willowby hooked her thumbs in the front pockets of black, straight-legged pants. With them, she wore red high-tops, a white T-shirt — with confetti-framed sunshades hooked in the neck — and a red bomber-style jacket.

She sported a colorful braided cloth bracelet on her right hand, and a tattoo — a crescent moon and three stars — on the back of her left. Her hair, a razor-sharp short bob, read ink black except for the crown and thick fringe dyed dark blue.

The quick research Eve had done said Willowby's paternal side had come to the U.S. from England a couple hundred years before. Her maternal side had its roots in Iran, and she favored that with golden brown skin, amber eyes, sharp features.

'Thanks,' she said when Eve offered the coffee. 'I read up on the case when McNab gave me the nudge. I want to say good job getting Jewell Gregg charged. If we find Dorian, she'll have a chance now. Second.'

She paused, sipped coffee. Her eyes, heavily and beautifully lined and lashed, popped. 'Okay, wait.' She sipped again. 'You're married, right?'

'Yeah.'

'If you weren't, for this coffee, I'd get down on one knee right now. So, second, I want to offer my personal as well as professional kudos for kicking that useless Truman in the crotch.'

'You know her?'

'No, or I'd have given the crotch kick a solid try. But like I said, I read up. People like her screw up the system, screw up all the ones who work their asses off, and most important, screw up the kids. Dorian Gregg didn't have much of a chance as things were. We find her, she does.'

'No sightings yet,' Eve said. 'Not here, not back in Freehold.'

'She won't go back there. Nothing there for her but misery. She won't come in. She's got no reason to trust the system. You think the same, that came across in your report. But you figure she got loose.'

'Why set her up for murder if you have her?'

'A couple possibilities. You keep her as a slave or you sell her off-planet or overseas. But . . .' Willowby gestured toward Dorian's ID shot. 'You could do that without the setup. You don't need the setup. Mina's dead. Making it look like a street crime, okay, but adding Dorian's blood?'

'Vindictive,' Eve concluded. 'Add the hope that would discredit her if and when she's pulled in.'

129

'That's how I see it. They — and no way this is a single abductor, or even a partnership — they've invested in these girls. The clothes, the food, the care. The time. Months for Mina. We can't be sure how long for Dorian, but long enough for them to have formed an alliance.'

''Alliance,'' Eve repeated.

'Friendship's possible, but an alliance absolutely. I've worked with victims who've gotten out of bondage or bad homes that way. It's going to piss you off to lose that investment — times two. And it's not impossible more got out. Maybe I think you'd have gotten wind of more, but not impossible.

'Can I sit?'

'Don't sit there. Use the desk chair.'

'Okay, thanks. Siblings, for instance, may work together to get away from an abusive parent. Women or girls — because it usually is — held against their will may work together, even if it means just one getting out.'

Willowby cocked an ankle over her knee. 'We can bust up, with time, trafficking operations that ship in a half dozen at a time, say. Bring them in on boats, mostly — the occasional charter — house them in some dump. Some put them right to work, the forced sex trade. A lot of times they're promised a legit job to get them here. Modeling's a classic for a reason, then they're crammed together in a shithole, rented or sold. Drug them up, get them addicted. But that's not this.'

'No, not a shithole, no drugs, no visible signs of physical abuse.'

With her eyes on the board, Willowby bounced her cocked foot. 'Psychological abuse and torture. Lock

130

them up in a dark room for a few days, or in a room where the lights blast and never go off. Run constant propaganda on a wall screen. Shock collars, shock sticks, something that doesn't damage the product.'

She drank more coffee, savoring. 'Offset that with rewards. Toys or games for younger ones, ice cream, candy. Affection. They're going to crave it, especially the younger ones. A hug, a smile, a kiss on the head. It doesn't take long for a kid — six, seven, eight — to fall in line. It does take consistency, a secure location, vigilance. Even then, some of these kids are tough customers, and they find a way out.'

She pointed toward the board again. 'Those two? On the older edge for the kiddie porn racket, but they hit the Chicklet sweet spot.'

''Chicklet'? I've heard that term.'

'Usually ages eleven to fourteen — boy or girl — starting to develop. Attractive — on the boys side usually at least somewhat androgenous. The user or buyer or viewer, depending, isn't into the young kids, but wants that youth, the freshness. If it's a sale, they'll likely get sold again when they hit sixteen or so, unless the buyer develops an attachment. It can happen. Or finds other uses. But trade-ins are common.'

Back to the assembly line, Eve thought. 'Like a fucking car.'

'You got it. The way this reads to me? You've got a syndicate with a lot of arms. Scouts to find the kids. They may double as the pick-ups. They're going to look harmless, ordinary, may be or look pretty young. Kids trust other kids more — that helps me get their trust. I look like one of them. Alternately, they might look or pose as authority. A cop, a teacher, first responder, someone a kid's taught to respect.

'Then you've got the keepers — who take the kid in. You might have more than one location for that. You need medical people, you need people to get food or prepare it. If you take your business seriously — and this one does — you maintain records. Outlay, profit and loss, cost per product. You're probably going to want some sort of studio and the equipment to shoot vids, take photos — and somebody who knows IT well enough to get them onto the dark web without leading us right to them. Business manager,' she continued. 'You have to calculate what to charge the pervs for viewing, what to charge if you rent out the product, what to charge when it's time to sell or which ones should go up for auction.'

Willowby shrugged. 'And I'm not telling you anything much you haven't already concluded. I'm probably not adding anything much by saying if whoever took them has a solid business model, financial backing, and contacts, those two girls would go for top dollar. With those looks, that age bracket? Eight to fifteen million on the block after some smart marketing.'

'Explain the marketing.'

'Photos, anywhere from provocative to hard porn. Same with some short vids. No penetration, so if they used a male partner, everything but that. Some girl-on-girl, some solo. We've come across actual brochures listing kids. They give them names like Candy or Hank, list their data, their skill set, set a price or, if it's for auction, a minimum opening bid.'

'Can you copy those to me?'

'Sure.'

'Explain *skill set*.'

Willowby shifted, brought up her legs to sit cross-legged in the chair.

'They're going to hype, but if they want to grow the business, want return customers, not overhype. Rate them on their skill in giving or receiving oral sex, coming or bringing to orgasm, fondling, masturbation, seduction techniques. If they're dominant or submissive, or can do both, and all that. If they're not selling or renting as virgins, how they rate as full sexual partners — vaginally or anally for the girls. More than one partner, group sex, role-playing.

'Then there's Domestic Slaves, Pets, Whipping Boys, Party Favors.'

'Okay, wait.' Since she wanted it, Eve got them both more coffee. 'Domestic Slave's easy enough to figure. Round up the rest.'

'Pets, usually the younger ones, but not always. Somebody wants a kid they can dress up, play with, train, like a pet. Whipping Boys — girls there, too — for sadists. Somebody they can knock around, torment, torture. You know, had a bad day? Here's your punching bag. Party Favors tend to be somebody they can pass around to guests and friends.

'Those probably aren't going to look like our girls up there,' Willowby added. 'Unlikely to be virgins, as rape would be part of breaking their will. Regular physical punishment, too. And they sure as hell aren't going to put them in high-dollar silk underwear. Not enough return on the investment.'

'Not pretty enough,' Eve muttered and began to pace. 'That's where that came from. Okay. Not adolescent beauties who'll draw top dollar. Kids broken down enough to serve other needs.'

'Rent 'em and rape 'em, buy 'em and beat 'em. I'd really like a shot at helping you crack this one open, Lieutenant. If I could work with somebody from

133

EDD. McNab or somebody as good?'

'Work with how?'

'I've been working on prying open a door in the dark web, and I'm really close. I've got a handle, a persona, I've filtered in some data. I'm a rich bastard toying with the idea of buying a product. Just testing the waters, right? If I have some tech help on it, I really think I can break through, but I need that background solid. Any organization like this is going to do serious checking. I need to look like I've got the money to buy a prime product.'

'Have you cleared it with your LT?'

'He's waffling some, so I've been putting most of my time on it when I'm off duty. A word from you would make a difference. Especially if Captain Feeney got on board. I'm close. I know I'm close. And one more thing? They had Mina Cabot for over eight months. She was thirteen. They had to be about ready for auction. She wasn't the only one about to go on the block. They've got to have an auction coming up.'

'And if we're right, they've lost two returns on their investment.'

'They need to recoup that. Not only bring in new girls, but prep any they have for sale. And I've got some street contacts. I already put the word out on Dorian Gregg. If she's in New York, we've got a shot at finding her.'

'I'll talk to your lieutenant, and to Feeney.'

'I appreciate it. Almost as much as this coffee.' She got to her feet.

'Why SVU? Why minors particularly?'

'Me? I had a perfect childhood, good as it gets. My dad's uncle was a cop, in Queens. He had the best stories, like fairy tales to me. I wanted the Academy.

134

My parents weren't thrilled, let me tell you, but they gave me a year to get it out of my system. I didn't. Then my second week in uniform, we find this kid, seven years old, beaten half to death. His father did it before he passed out drunk. Mother was doing her second round for fraud down in Virginia where she'd taken off when the kid was about five.'

She shrugged. 'That was it for me.'

'Where's the kid now?'

'Evan? Evan Hawkins. He was lucky. He had grand-parents living upstate who wanted him, with no idea he even existed. He just graduated high school. He's going to fricking MIT. Too many aren't lucky, but now and again.'

'I'll be in touch, and so will somebody from EDD.'

'Great. I'll send you those brochures.'

When she left, Eve sat to update her notes and reach out to Willowby's lieutenant.

When she heard Peabody coming, she rose.

'Read my updates. You can use my desk. I'm expect-ing some data from Willowby. I've cleared it so she's attached to the investigation.'

'Oh. Okay. How —'

'I have to go up to EDD.'

'Did something break? How long have you been here? Shift just started.'

'I got in early. Read the notes. Do you know if McNab's clear?'

'He closed one yesterday afternoon, but —'

'Read the notes,' Eve said again. 'And yes to the damn coffee.'

She swung through the bullpen, tried to avoid eye contact with Jenkinson's tie as he stood by his desk slurping coffee.

She failed, had her retinas blasted by what might have been a depiction of the big bang.

She just kept going.

She'd known, of course, she thought as she jumped on a glide. Willowby's general information hadn't been news. But she hadn't known, not fully, the details. The terms used for the children in trafficking. The categories, she supposed.

She needed a hook, and Willowby might help her find it. She saw some openings now. Dorian Gregg could bust those openings wide, but she'd begun to see.

When she stepped into the carnival of EDD, Jenkinson's tie seemed tame, almost ordinary. Colors blasted and clashed, neon baggies, polka-dot suspenders, screaming T-shirts, and crazed airboots.

She spotted McNab standing in his cube, hips twitching, long blond tail of hair swaying as he worked on whatever he worked on.

She moved quickly into the sanity of Feeney's office.

He sat at his desk, scarred brown shoes up, baggy, crap-colored suit reassuring. As was his explosion of ginger, gray-threaded hair.

His basset hound eyes slitted in concentration as he studied his wall screen.

'Got a minute?'

'Barely got my ass in the chair, this crap coffee in my hand, and already caught one. Fricking cyber fraud, already hauled in five mil inside twelve hours, targeting centenarians. I get that old and stupid, stun me.'

'You'll get that old, but you'll never be that stupid. I need McNab, or somebody on his level you can spare.'

'I just tossed the boy one.' Frowning, Feeney

slurped coffee. 'I could have him pass it off, maybe. You need an EDD man on the dead kid?'

'It's a ring, Feeney, I know it. A trafficking ring.'

As she filled him in, he put his feet on the floor.

'You got him. I can shut down this scam in an hour — it'll pop up somewhere else, but I can shut it down. You can have me, too. Sick sons of bitches. Give me the data on the kid you think's in the wind. I can put some of my uniforms out there.'

'Thanks for that.'

'We've got some channels into porn sites, helped bust a trafficking case — adults though — a couple months ago. Bringing women — eighteen, twenty, twenty-couple — over from Eastern Europe on a cargo ship, jamming them into two or three rooms on the Lower East, then renting them out to pervs, using the better-looking ones for underground porn sites.'

'Yeah, this is like that, only bigger. More rooms, I think. Slick, sophisticated, Mira called it. I'm going to copy you on what I've got. Anything pops for you, I'm ready to hear it.'

'You got that. I'll pull Willowby up here, have her and McNab work in the lab. Let me shut this damn stupid shit down. I'd pass it on, but one of the suckers who tossed in five K is the wife's grandmother.'

'Are you kidding me?'

'You think she'd know better.' He shook his head in disgust. 'Promised Sheila I'd take care of it myself.' He grabbed one of the candied almonds from the rickety bowl — crafted by Sheila — on his desk. Popped it.

'Stun me,' he repeated. 'Put me down.'

'Solemn oath. Thanks.'

She headed out and back to Homicide.

Peabody, her eyes horrified, looked up.

'Oh, Jesus, Dallas. They're like sales kits. Like brochures. It's . . .'

'I know. Send them to your unit and get me some printouts. Send them to McNab and to Feeney. I need the desk. Come back in ten.'

'Yes, sir.'

'Take your coffee.'

Peabody just shook her head. 'I think I'll get some water right now.'

Rather than look at Willowby's data, Eve engaged her 'link.

Moments later, Nadine Furst, not exactly camera ready, Eve noted, but ready for something, came on-screen.

'Dallas. I'm in the last few hours of a thirty-six-hour moratorium on work of any kind. I'm about to have an elaborate breakfast with my moratorium companion.'

Jake Kincade, rock star and Nadine's lover, angled on-screen. 'Hey, Dallas.'

'Hey. Sorry to interrupt. Nadine, why don't you give me the contact of your top assistant or researcher and I'll give this to him or her.'

'Give what? Damn it.'

'Go, Lois,' Jake said, and kissed her cheek.

'I haven't had any media source in my life for twenty-four hours. Twenty-seven,' Nadine corrected. 'It's a record. I bet Jake I could make it thirty-six. I bet extreme sexual favors.'

'Win-win,' Jake said off-screen, and made her laugh.

'What did I miss?'

'Get to Central and I'll tell you.'

'Off record until?'

'Some of it. Some I'll want you to break, and fast.

Bring a camera.'

'On my way.'

Eve noted the skinny black straps on Nadine's shoulders and the froth of black lace visible below.

'Maybe change into something less comfortable.'

'To use your term, bite me.'

When Nadine cut her off, Eve rolled her shoulders. She decided Peabody had a point about water, rose to get some.

Then sat and read the brochures.

9

Despite the black lace, Eve knew Nadine would double-time it to Central. She did the same to the bullpen and Peabody's desk.

'Shake it off,' she ordered. 'I need you to do the coffee thing in the conference room. I hooked the same one. I want to set up the electronic board in there, so I can give Nadine some details, then shut it down for her camera.'

'Nadine?'

'I want as many hands and eyes on this as I can manage. She's coming in cold.' Eve gave Peabody a come-ahead so they could walk and talk. 'She had some bet with Jake about her taking a media blackout for thirty-six hours.'

'Nadine?' Peabody repeated, but with a laugh. 'What did she bet?'

'She almost made it, and serious sexual favors.'

'With Avenue A's front man?' Peabody executed a sexy shoulder wiggle. 'That's a no-lose situation.'

'However that goes, she can and will dig in, and maybe do a big deal about child exploitation — including by some bitch-ass rep in CPS.'

'Oooh, an in-depth story on Truman? That would be even better than a punch in the face.'

'Punching her would've been — momentarily — a lot more satisfying. A big-ass Nadine story lasts longer. Meanwhile, I'll give her a one-on-one, get Dorian's face out there. We'll set up a tip line, put some experienced drones on that.'

'She could've rabbited right out of New York.'

'Could've,' Eve agreed as she swung into the conference room. 'So I've got some uniforms hitting transpo stations, showing her photo. But where's she going to go? She's got nobody.'

'Her great-grandmother,' Peabody began.

'Dead — three years ago, traffic fatality. So, nobody.'

She switched on the board to start on the transfer of data and images. 'With Covino and the others Dawber took, they had people, they had jobs, residences. And he took them for himself, not for profit. Mina Cabot had the same, but they still managed to hold her, without a trace, for months. Dorian, and others like her? They've got nothing and nowhere.'

'Easier pickings.'

'Probably, sure. But someone like Mina represents more projected profit. That's my take, anyway, after a glance at the sales packets.'

'Do you want me to finish that?'

'No, I want you to start a search, nationwide, using Mina Cabot as a template. The age range, the good, solid family/neighborhood/schools angle. No history of running away, no trouble. And start with the seriously pretty type. Factor in missing for at least two months.'

She continued as she worked. 'Filter out any with more than a sixty percent probability they were taken by a parent, family member, or other individual, any with conclusive ransom demands at the outset.'

'Nationwide?'

'If you don't get a break in the next twenty-four, we'll take that global. But for now, I want to whittle down whatever you get to highest probability, see if

141

we can map it out, pinpoint areas, hunting grounds. When Feeney shakes free, he wants in. He can take this end over from you, but get it going.'

Peabody puffed out her cheeks, released the air. 'Do you need me in here with Nadine?'

'Did you do the coffee thing?'

'Done. And if you don't need me, I'd do better on a search of that scope at my desk. And I could tap one of the techie-type uniforms to assist.'

'Go do that. And have Nadine's camera wait in the lounge until I clear him or her in.'

When Peabody left, Eve stepped back to scan the board. A lot of data already. Hadn't done Mina Cabot any good, she thought, but they wouldn't have the data without her.

'An alliance,' she said to herself, thinking of Willowby's term. 'I can see it. Same age, good brains. Your idea, I'm betting,' she added, looking at Mina's ID shot. 'Somebody like Dorian's more used to going it on her own. You? Solid family, soccer team, friends. So you reach out to somebody you figure has some street smarts, somebody who wants out as much as you.

'And you're the distraction.'

She thought, paced, thought, paced.

'Make yourself boot up dinner. There's a mess. Do they call in a medical, take you to whatever sort of medical facility they have on-site? Have to have one on-site. It's smart, took some guts and . . . trust,' she decided. 'There had to be trust between the two of you. More than two of you?'

She rolled that around, but she just didn't see it. Bring too many in, you widen the possibility somebody breaks, says or does the wrong thing, screws it all up.

Not impossible, she thought, but unlikely.

She stepped up, looked into Dorian's angry eyes. 'Where the hell are you?'

* * *

Dorian woke in a bed, and under the hurt, under the fog, panic cut like blades. They'd found her. They'd taken her back to . . . She couldn't remember, not all the way.

But she surfaced swinging, slapping out.

'Easy now, you're safe now.'

The voice, male, older, quiet, had a steady calm. But her breath kept jumping in and out of her chest.

'You're hurt, and you've got a fever. We're going to help you.'

She saw the man, the wavy mass of brown hair, the little beard, the blue eyes, calm and quiet like the voice.

'Who are you?' Her voice sounded wrong, all croaky and hoarse.

'We're friends. Mouser found you, and helped bring you here. It's a safe place. Your ankle's not broken, but you have a very bad sprain, and your knee's banged up. You hit your head, or someone hit it. It's probably a concussion. Do you understand me?'

'I guess.'

'We have another friend, and he's a doctor. I sent for him, but if you want, we can get you to the hospital or contact someone. Your mother? Father?'

'No, no, no!'

'All right. We won't do that. Drink a little water.'

When he held a cup to her lips, she grabbed it, tried to gulp it all at once.

'Not too much too fast. You'll just sick it up. I'd like Dr. Gee to have a look at you before we give you anything more than the water. Do you want to tell me what happened to you?'

'I don't . . . it's all messed up in my head.'

He nodded as if he understood, and she saw something in his eyes she hadn't seen in many in her life. Kindness.

'That's the concussion,' he told her. 'Don't worry about all of that right now.' He set the water glass aside, then took her hand. 'Do you want to tell me your name? It doesn't have to be your real name if you're not ready.'

She had a fresh moment of panic when nothing came, then it did, at least that did. Her relief rose so fast she didn't think of making up a name.

'I'm Dorian.'

He smiled at her. 'Hello, Dorian. I'm Sebastian.'

★ ★ ★

Nadine Furst powered into the conference room in a sharp blue dress paired with a short white jacket and towering white heels. She carried a bag approximately the size of New Jersey with big blue flowers over a white field.

Her streaky blond hair fell in a new style to swing, ruler straight, at her chin. Cat-green eyes scanned the board before shifting to Eve.

'I filled myself in on the way over. Mina Cabot, age thirteen, missing from a Philly suburb since November. Her body was found yesterday morning in Battery Park, impaled. You're primary. Early reports suspect a mugging gone wrong.'

144

She scanned the board again. 'Which is bogus or you wouldn't have tagged me. Who is this?' She gestured toward Dorian. 'Who is Dorian Gregg, and why is she on your board?'

Eve walked to the AutoChef, programmed coffee for both of them. 'None of this goes on the air yet. I'm turning off the board before I give you the one-on-one.'

'I've got that part, Dallas. Give me the rest.'

'What do you know about Chicklets, youth sex trafficking, sex traffic in general, and kiddie porn?'

'For one thing, if you ever watched *Now*, you'd know we devoted an entire show to the bust a couple months ago. Importing women from overseas, locking them into the sex trade, selling them. Chicklets are generally between eleven and fourteen. Too old for the Kiddie circuit, too young for the adult. A prime spot for certain types of predators.

'Why do you think this is that?'

'Two twelve-year-old girls — twelve when Mina was taken, and when we project Dorian was — were abducted. Devon, Pennsylvania, and somewhere, we believe, between Freehold, New Jersey, and New York for Dorian.'

'Beautiful girls,' Nadine commented. 'Strikingly pretty girls. Was Mina raped?'

'No, she died a virgin. One in very good health, who'd recently used high-end hair products and was wearing a custom-tailored white shirt, her old school uniform pants, and silk underwear that retails at a couple grand.'

Nadine opened her mouth, and Eve pointed to the conference table. 'Don't ask, and I'll tell.'

She ran it through with the respect and trust that

145

had built through friendship. She ran it through, Eve realized, almost as she would for another cop.

'An organization,' Nadine commented. 'What you see as a structured and sophisticated, even practiced one. Do you think it focuses on girls in this basic age range?'

'Can't say, can't know. But it's a hard swallow for me to believe these were the only two.

'Selling in bulk, either auctions or choosing and grooming a girl for a specific client or client type. You have the setup, the structure, the staff, the facility, and some of that is steady outlay. Additional girls only cost to feed and clothe, essentially.'

Nadine sat back, held her coffee mug in both hands. 'Jesus, Dallas, if you're right, and they have scouts in other areas, it could draw girls in nationwide, even import them from overseas. Or have other locations like the one here in New York.'

'There has to be a money man. You can't start up an organization like this without serious financial backing. Money to buy the property — you're not going to rent unless you're renting from a head guy. You need money to hire, for a security system, for medical, for food and clothes.'

She'd already pushed up as she'd briefed Nadine, and now continued to pace in front of the board. 'And that money man expects to make a profit, so you've got somebody keeping an accounting.'

'And how do you hide girls — however many — without anyone noticing? How do you keep them contained without restraints or drugs?'

'They might use either or both at first. 'Want these bindings off, kid? Behave.' And still . . . my best guess is they have a solid front. Maybe run some business

146

out of part of the property, or have the look of it. Some people coming and going, so it looks like it's a business or residence. Some property that has a garage or a shipping dock or something that allows them to bring the girls in, take them out when it's time without drawing notice.'

'And you're confident this second girl, Dorian Gregg, not only didn't have a part in killing Mina Cabot but got out with her?'

'It's unlikely she'd have the strength to drive the weapon clean through the victim, and she sure as hell wouldn't have been able to move the body to the dump site alone.'

Once again, Eve studied that young, angry face. Shook her head. 'Add her blood was planted. No reason for that but to throw suspicion on her. No reason to throw suspicion on her unless she got out.'

'I'm trying to think of an argument to that, but really can't.' Nadine set the now empty mug aside. 'If you're right about the setup, you're right on the rest.'

Like Eve, Nadine studied the face on the board, the pretty girl with the angry eyes. 'You want me to get her name and face out there.'

'I want you to do that, and do whatever you can to have her name and face out in as many media markets as possible. How long she's been missing, all of her data, and as a material witness to the murder of Mina Cabot.'

'You want to implicate her?'

Eve angled her head. 'Is that what it sounds like?'

'It will to some. They wanted to throw suspicion on her, you said. Won't calling her a material witness solidify that?'

'Be nice if it works that way. And I've already gone

there,' Eve said before Nadine commented. 'They'll look for her, too. They already are. If they have any contacts in the NYPSD, the local government, the media — and they likely have some whether the some know it or not — they'll try to push to see what we have.'

'But they won't get anything unless you want them to,' Nadine concluded. 'You run a tight ship.' With a nod, Nadine looked back at Eve. 'How much of this can I air?'

Eve crossed to the AutoChef to get more coffee for herself.

'Other than the data on Gregg, I'll give you a one-on-one on Cabot, as much as I can, and that's going to include the angle that she and Gregg met up, hooked up, ran into each other on the street so we believe Gregg may have witnessed the murder, or have some salient information on it.'

'Whoever killed her will think you're hedging, but you're hedging about finding Gregg's blood, about her being your prime suspect.'

'Again, it'd be nice. Either way, we get Gregg's face out there, and that could be how we find her. I'll give you a tip line for viewers to contact. We'll get a lot of bullshit, a lot of cranks, but it only takes one genuine sighting to give us an opening.'

'You think she's still here, in New York.'

Now Eve turned to the board again. I know you, she thought as she studied Dorian. I know you.

'Where's she going to go? How's she going to get there? She's got no one, and most likely nothing but the clothes on her back. She might be hurt. She's thirteen, and if she isn't scared, she's not as smart as I think she is.'

148

'All right.' Pushing away from the table, Nadine rose. 'We'll get this started.'

'One more thing. You maybe want to take a look at Pru Truman, CPS, Freehold.'

'And why would I want to look at her?'

'Dorian's caseworker, or shitbag excuse for her caseworker. Could be a big, juicy story on neglect, abuse, and how some — even one — inside the system designed to protect can corrupt that system and lead to the exploitation of those they've sworn to protect.'

Nadine's eyebrows winged up. 'You've given this some thought.'

'Yeah, I have.'

'All right. I'll take a look.'

'Good.' Eve shut off the board. 'You can bring your camera in.'

It took longer than she'd wanted — Nadine was thorough — but if it paid off, well worth the time.

When she walked back into the bullpen, Peabody hailed her.

'I've already got nine — using your filters. I pulled in Officer Jonas, and she's running west of the Mississippi, while I'm doing east.'

'Nine — I figured more.'

'That's nine on my area, and with the filters — so far. But I wondered about the runaway filter. We would've figured Gregg for a runaway, so maybe —'

'Good thought,' Eve said before Peabody finished. 'Add them in, then we'll work through them. Some, maybe even most, probably took off on their own. But so did Gregg.'

'That puts my number up to seventeen. The other thing is the pretty level. It's, you know, in the eye of the beholder and all that.'

'Use your judgment there. We have to start some-where, Peabody. Odds are they've snatched up others who aren't as physically striking, for other levels, pur-poses. But we start with — what is it? — the high-end. When we bust this open, we bust it all.'

'I get you. Stupid for me to think: You're not pretty enough, like she didn't count. That's not it.'

'It's not. We keep the focus tight, we have a better shot. Keep at it.'

As she walked back to her office, it occurred to her she wouldn't have made her own cut. Too skinny, bony — what was the word? Gawky? She supposed it applied. Definitely not a high-end product.

Had he raped her to 'season' her or because he enjoyed it?

Probably both, she concluded. And it didn't mat-ter, she reminded herself. Unless her own experience somehow applied, somehow helped the investigation, it didn't matter.

She got more coffee, sat, and thought: Location.

But where did she start? What kind of building/facility? Not abandoned, condemned, up for sale, and not — she believed — recently acquired.

What type?

An apartment building, converted office build-ing or warehouse, factory. Something that could be tightly secured.

Apartments and office buildings had windows. Sure, you could install one-way glass, break-proof.

A big expense, she considered. Less glass in a warehouse or factory, and either of those might have — likely had — shipping docks, garage access.

She'd do a search, for what it was worth, and take

150

a hard look at anything that seemed remotely hinky. She admitted Roarke would have a better system, but she didn't want to ask him.

Stupid, she admitted. Like Peabody feeling guilty about judging girls on their looks. But she just didn't want to put him into this one. It hurt him, brought too much stress and worry with it.

So she'd get it started her way, and while she ran properties, she'd pull up Peabody's search results and start digging into missing girls.

Too many, she thought, too many lost, angry, scared young girls. She needed to find one to have a chance at helping others.

She glanced back at Dorian Gregg.

'You're the damn key, Dorian.'

★   ★   ★

She felt better. A lot better. One of the other kids, a girl named Chi-Chi (totally made up), helped her into a shower. It didn't embarrass her to get naked in front of Chi-Chi. Her months at the Academy had killed any modesty in her.

And it felt so good to get clean.

They gave her clean baggies, a T-shirt, and the doctor — if he was a doctor — used a healing wand, a cold pack, put some sort of wrap on her ankle. Whatever he did to her knee hurt like fire for a second, then eased almost all the pain.

He said she had a concussion — the worst of it — a sprained ankle, and had knocked her knee out of alignment. He'd aligned it again. She was supposed to keep the knee and the ankle elevated as much as possible, and rest.

She didn't see Sebastian for a while, but that was okay. She was tired, and since Mouser — he seemed to think since he'd found her, he was in charge — brought her a grilled cheese sandwich and ginger ale, she wasn't hungry.

Mouser chattered away while she ate, but since her head didn't hurt very much, she didn't mind. He said they got to stay there as long as they wanted. But they had rules and stuff. No fighting, no bullying, no stealing from each other.

They could steal from marks, sure, but had to be careful so they didn't get caught. No illegals, no alcohol.

What came into the family — they thought of themselves as family — belonged to the family.

Everybody took an oath to keep it all secret. Most were runaways, like her, or abandoned, like him.

Mouser's mother had left him in a flop and hadn't come back again. After three days, he ran out of food, and went out, wandered the streets.

She drifted off as Mouser told his story, and drifted into dreams.

Her mother, her mother. She could see her mother, hear the raging voice, feel the hand crack over her cheek. Even in the dream it burned like her knee had.

Like fire.

Then it wasn't her mother, but someone else. Cold, hard face, cold, hard eyes, not raging hot like her mother's. She jabbed something into her side, and the fire blazed. Bigger, bigger than the knee, than the slap, than the dozens of slaps of her life.

She cried out, but only in a piping gasp as her lungs burned, and her legs gave way.

'Spare the rod, spoil the child. We don't spare the

rod here. Follow the rules and you'll have lovely clothes and good, healthy food — even cake. Break the rules and feel the rod.'

Another jab, another blast of fire that turned her vision bright white, then dull gray.

Someone touched her. She didn't want to be touched, not that way. They probed inside her. It shocked and hurt almost like the rod, and somehow worse.

She threw out all her curses — and she knew plenty. The rod struck again. Again. Again.

She ran, ran and ran, through the dark. Through the tunnels. Someone took her hand, and she gripped it like life. Running, climbing, falling, everything so mixed up and horrible. Pain and fear, pouring rain.

She saw a face, pale against dripping red hair.

'Don't go! Don't go!'

But the hand pulled away; the face faded.

She woke crying and calling. Someone held her, and she shoved and pushed. But the hands didn't slap or probe. They stroked gently down her back, over her hair. And the voice spoke as gently as the hands.

'Hush now. You're safe. You're all right. It's just a bad dream.'

'Is she okay, Sebastian? Is she? Is she going to be okay?'

'She'll be fine, Mouser. You go get her some water. She had a bad dream.'

'I used to have them.'

'I know. But you're okay, aren't you?'

'Bet your butt! I'll be right back.'

'Try to relax now,' Sebastian told Dorian. 'Do you want me to let go?'

'I — no.' Nobody held her or stroked her hair. It

felt strange, made her a little ashamed that she liked it, and made the awful less.

'Do you want to tell me about the dream?'

'I don't know. It's all mixed up. Everything's all messed up, all mixed up. And my head feels too big or something.'

'It's no bigger than it should be, but you knocked it hard. Is there pain?'

'Not really, not like before. I'm so tired.'

She rested her cheek on his chest, heard his heart beating. And her eyes filled and spilled because — in that moment — she felt safe.

'And no wonder, so you rest as long as you need. And here, quick as a mouse, is our Mouser with some water. Sip a little.'

When she did, she looked up at the man who brushed tears from her cheek. She should've felt shame that she'd shed them in front of him, but she felt relief.

He looked smart, she thought, looked like somebody who knew lots of stuff. But why was somebody smart living with a bunch of kids? Why was he giving her a place to stay when he didn't even know her?

'The wheels are turning,' he said, and tapped a finger on the side of her head. 'You can't know the answer to a question if you don't ask it.'

'I wondered . . . Why are you helping me?'

'Why wouldn't I?'

'Mostly people don't help.'

He smiled, but she thought his eyes looked sad. 'Only the wrong people don't help. You've met too many wrong people, I think.'

'We help each other.'

Now, when he smiled at Mouser, his eyes smiled,

154

too. 'Absolutely. Go on now — you're a good boy. I need to talk to Dorian for a minute, then she can rest.'

'I can stand guard in case she has another bad dream.'

'A good boy and a good friend. It's all right. Go out, get some sunshine. It's a bright summer day.'

'I'll be back later.'

Sebastian waited until Mouser shut the door. 'It might help if you'd tell me about the dream, even if it's all mixed up. Or if you've remembered anything else and want to tell me.'

'What is this place?'

'It's home for now. A building I came by. A small apartment building once, and now home.'

'Are you rich?'

'Not the way you mean, but we've got enough. And there's more to be had when needed.'

'I ran away, I remember that. My mother hits me all the time, and gets high and brings men in. I ran away from that, and I'm not going back. If you try to make me, I'll just run again.'

'I don't believe in making people do things. I especially don't believe in making children stay with people who hurt them just because they share blood.'

'I'm not a child. I'm thirteen.'

'From my advanced age, that makes you a child. Did you run away to New York or live here already?'

'I came here, but it gets mixed up. I remember some now, but it's all blurry and jumbled up.'

'Why don't you tell me what you remember, and we'll see where that takes us?'

When she did, he listened. When she spoke of the prod, or the probing, he took her hand, held it.

She cried again. She couldn't help it.

'I can't remember more. I don't think I made her up, the girl with red hair. I think — I think she's my friend. But if she's my friend, why can't I remember her name, or how come we were running together?'

'Sometimes the mind protects us from what we're not ready to remember.'

'But I want to!'

'And you will. You're so much better already than you were just hours ago. A little patience, Dorian.'

'I don't like patience.'

Now he laughed, and she liked the sound of it.

'I can't think who does, and still we need it. Why don't you rest awhile?'

'I — can I get up? I don't want to stay in bed. Can I get up and see more of where we are?'

'If you promise to tell me if you get dizzy or feel sick, or if you have pain.'

'I can promise. I don't lie after I promise, so I don't promise if I think I'll need to lie.'

'That's a very clever philosophy. I follow a similar one myself. Well then, let me give you a tour. We can start here. This is your room as long as you need it.'

It wasn't very big, but she'd never had big. It was clean, and had a window where the sun shined in. It had a bed and a dresser with three drawers and walls painted a bright, bold blue.

'I like the color. It's pretty.'

'The last girl who stayed here painted the walls her favorite color.'

'What happened to her?'

'She moved on. She liked to cook, and got a job in a restaurant kitchen, and a little place of her own. It's how it should work, the moving on when the time comes. Until it does, this is your room.'

156

'Do I have to pay for it?'

'You do, by following the code, helping to keep it clean, sharing what you have or acquire with everyone.'

She got up slowly, then stood in her borrowed pajamas — sweats shorts and a T-shirt. 'I don't feel dizzy. I promise.'

'An excellent start. Let's continue our tour.'

★ ★ ★

While Dorian got her tour, Eve walked into the bullpen.

'Listen up! I need volunteers to take shifts manning a tip line.'

She ignored the collective groan because she — sincerely — sympathized. 'We're looking for information on this girl. Peabody, put Dorian Gregg's ID shot on the main screen.

'Dorian Gregg, age thirteen — you can read her data. A runaway and likely abductee. We believe she was held in the same child trafficking facility as Mina Cabot. Cabot, also thirteen, was found early yesterday morning, impaled.'

She briefed them quickly.

'Officer Carmichael, if you'll select four uniforms to assist on the tip line. Detectives, you can rotate, two hours on unless you're running hot.

'We need to find this girl before whoever killed Mina Cabot finds her. Any tip that doesn't include her being carried off by alien overlords gets a follow-through. Even the alien overlords get documented. The media's about to cut loose on this, so we'll get the leading wave of calls in the next twenty-four.

'Any problems, I'm in my office till end of shift, and working this at home when I get there.'

Because, Eve thought as she went back to continue her searches, if they didn't find her in the next twenty-four, odds were she went rabbit, or got herself caged like one.

10

In her office, Eve pored over search results.

She knew the expression was 'finding a needle in a haystack,' but that was bogus. Who the hell would put a needle in a haystack? Plus, she wasn't entirely sure what a haystack was, exactly.

Still, she accepted trying to find probable, even possible buildings that fit her requirements in the whole of New York equaled the damn needle.

On the other hand, if somebody was stupid enough to toss a needle into a stack of hay, the needle was in the stack of hay. So she adjusted some factors of the search, started another run.

While that worked, she shifted to Peabody's progress, and McNab's, and Feeney's.

Too many girls, she thought. Too many names and faces. But she believed she had a better shot at finding a pattern.

She separated the potentials into two categories. What she thought of as the Mina type — solid family, good neighborhood, no history of trouble. Then the Dorian type — basically the opposite. She added a third category for a mix. The girl from a good home who fell into trouble anyway. The girl with a crappy homelife who kept her head down.

She divided those into subcategories: rural, urban, suburban.

With that, she began the arduous task of picking through the case files, looking for similarities.

And found some.

She looked at her board, considered the size of her office. She thought about the conference room, then grabbed what she needed before walking out to the bullpen.

'I'm pushing an angle,' she told Peabody. 'I already see four girls snatched on the way home after a post-school deal. Sports practice, a play rehearsal, a tutoring thing — all regular schedule stuff.'

'That's a good angle.'

'Maybe. I'm going to take it home, work from there. You can do the same.'

'I think I'll kick it up to the EDD lab with McNab. Primo equipment there. You know, I kind of thought this was a needle in the haystack, but once you get into it, you can see, with some — like the after-school stuff — a kind of pattern.'

'Right. Why is there a needle in a haystack?'

'I don't know. Someone dropped it?'

'Seems dumbass to look for it. I mean, a diamond in a haystack, okay, but who can't get another needle? Anyway, send me whatever needles you find.'

She let it roll around in her head on the way down to the garage. First you have to spot the kid, so — most likely — scouts troll schools. Once you spot the kid, you just spend some time stalking — not even that if an opportunity jumps in your lap.

Snatch the kid, transport the kid, collect your fee. Had to be a sizable fee, Eve thought as she got into her car. Kidnapping a minor would get you a very long stretch.

The scouts had to blend into their hunting ground, she concluded as she swung out of the garage and into snarled traffic.

160

Good clothes, decent haircut in an upscale area. Or a uniform — delivery person for instance. Repair guy. Cop.

She put more weight on cop. Wouldn't a kid tend to go with a cop — and not tend to go with some random stranger?

An authority figure anyway.

Or.

She let it roll around a little more as she dealt with the stop-and-go. Why not use another kid — or someone younger? Not so threatening, as Willowby suggested.

She played around with the idea. A teenager, or someone who looked like one. Nonthreatening.

Hadn't she recently used Jamie Lingstrom — college boy — in a ruse to get a murderer to open the door?

So maybe at least some of the scouts were young — or some worked in pairs.

The runaways or troubled kids made easier targets. You spotted them on the street and grabbed them up. Maybe offer them some Zoner, or a place to flop, whatever. They might possess more canniness than the Mina type, but they wouldn't stand a chance against an experienced abductor.

Transportation. Had to have it.

A closed van, a fake (or not) cop car. A vehicle trunk if you could work fast enough.

She had dozens of angles, questions, possible answers circling in her head as she battled her way uptown.

On impulse, she detoured, and after a hunt for parking, doubled it on Forty-Ninth off Fifth.

She hiked her way to a stall selling I HEART NY caps

161

and T-shirts and other tourist paraphernalia.

The kid had had one of those growth spurts, she realized as she watched Tiko make a sale. The young entrepreneur still had a baby face, but he now wore his hair in short dreads and sported a pair of the wrap-around shades on sale in his stall.

He shot Eve a grin when he spotted her.

'You need these.' He plucked up a pair of the shades — mirrored lenses and black frames.

'I've got shades.'

'Why'n you wearing them?'

She'd probably lost them again. No, left them in her desk.

No, in the car.

Shit, who knew?

'I want to show you a couple pictures.'

His grin faded. 'You got trouble.'

'Someone does. I'm going to show you, then I'm going to send copies to your 'link so you can show them around.'

'Hold it. Buy three,' he told a potential customer, 'you get the third half price. Shorthanded today,' he said to Eve. 'Girl who helps me went and sassed her mama, and she got herself house arrested.'

He made the sale, turned back to Eve.

Then studied the photo of Mina Cabot.

'That's the girl got dead. Saw about it on-screen. It's sad.'

'Did you ever see her before that? Before on-screen?'

'Uh-uh. Hard to miss that hair, check it? And the looks with it.'

'Right. How about this one?' Eve swiped to the photo of Dorian Gregg.

Tiko frowned, turned his head side to side. 'I

remember her.'

Eve felt a lurch in her gut. 'Don't tell me what I want to hear because I want to hear it.'

'Why'd I lie to you? You're the good cops. I took my granny to see your vid, about the clones? Frosted supreme. I remember her, but it's back during holiday sale time. Maybe December, maybe November — but late in that, 'cause I had turkey stuff on clearance.'

'Turkey stuff. So after Thanksgiving.'

'For sure after.'

He held up a finger, walked over to a couple fiddling with the shirts and caps, made his pitch.

Damn good pitch, Eve decided, as he sold and bagged three shirts, two caps, some sort of purse thing, and sunshades.

'For sure after,' he said again when he stepped back over to Eve. 'And not here. I got a second stall downtown. I expanded.' The grin popped back. 'I got five em-ploy-ees.'

Two stalls, five employees, Eve thought, and he was younger than the child in the morgue.

'Do you have any trouble, anyone trying to hassle or hustle you?'

He married a snort with a shrug. 'Maybe they try, but I handle that. Plus, I made friends with the beat cops, even the droids. I just show them the card you give me, say Dallas is a friend of mine. They look out for me and my staff.'

She decided the kid would likely give Roarke a run at owning half of New York one of these days.

'Okay. Tell me how you remember the girl from months ago.'

'She is fine,' he said simply. 'Gotta look twice at that kind of fine. And she's staking out the stall. I

163

got scarves and hats — good quality, good prices — gloves and bags. I know a street thief when I see one, check it?'

'Yeah, I check it.'

'So, even if she's fine, I give her a look that lets her know I know, and she better not try lifting from me. And I think might be she's cold, so I tell her if she's got five, I've got a few scarves under my table got some flaws, and she can take one for five. I think she's pissed I made her so easy, but she dug up the five, and took a scarf — an orange-and-black one.'

'Jesus, you remember all that? You're absolutely sure?'

'Hundred percent. Hold it.'

He dealt with a trio of customers already loaded with shopping bags.

'After Thanksgiving,' Eve said the moment he freed up again. 'But before Christmas.'

'Had to be. Scarf she took was like Halloween and Thanksgiving stock, and already on discount, so I could break even selling it to her so low. I had the Santa stuff, and snowflakes, and the good-quality gift scarves and hats and all.'

'Did you see her again, after that?'

'Once, not long after — few days maybe. She had on the scarf and was stalking some tourists. I didn't say anything to the beat cops.' He shrugged. 'I figure she's just trying to get through, right? That's different than the bad guys.'

'All right. I'm going to send the pictures to your 'link, and I need the exact location of your downtown stall.'

'She get dead, too?'

'No.'

'She do something you gotta arrest her for?'

'No.'

'In trouble then?'

'Yes, she's in trouble. I want to find her, get her out of trouble.'

'Anybody can, it's gonna be you. But you need these shades. They're badass. I'll give you a cop discount.'

She bought the shades, got the stall location, transferred the photos to his 'link.

'Thanks for the help.'

He just pointed at the shades she'd slipped on. 'Badass.'

'Check it.'

On the way back to her car, she ordered up some uniforms to canvass a four-block radius around the downtown stall location. If Tiko had spotted Dorian twice, someone else must have seen her.

The orange-and-black scarf wouldn't hurt pinning a sighting.

Tiko added weight to what she already firmly believed. Dorian had been abducted from New York. And now, the most logical conclusion targeted that abduction after Thanksgiving and before Christmas.

Wouldn't she have roamed the same area? And if so, Tiko — sharp eyes, quick brain — would've seen her again.

Either way, she thought, and launched the battle with traffic again, Mina's abduction came first, and by at least a few weeks.

She contacted Peabody to relay the information.

'Tiko? Jeez! That's a serious break. I never thought of him as a possible source.'

'I nearly didn't. We might get lucky, hit more sightings, pinpoint the abduction time and location. At least get closer.'

'And if she got away, maybe she'd go back to the familiar, to that area. Maybe she had a hole downtown, and near enough to Tiko's stall for him to spot her twice.'

'We'll see what the uniforms dig up.'

'We're going to stick in the lab awhile, then take a break and go by the house. We'll run some auto-searches from home after.'

'Just keep it coming. I'm nearly home. I'll pick it up from there. If anything pops from the uniforms, we'll follow up in the morning. I'll let you know.'

Eve clicked off. It felt like movement, she thought. Maybe a direction.

And when the gates opened for her, she thought of Roarke.

How much did she include him in this one? She had Feeney and EDD all over it, but . . . He had his own way, and that way proved invaluable time after time.

What felt like movement meant she couldn't afford to push aside anything or anyone who could inch the movement forward.

She studied the house, the elegance, the fantasy of it against the summer-blue sky. Almost always, just the wonder of it lowered her stress level.

This evening, it lifted it.

Stupid, she admitted. Roarke would deal just as she would. As they would.

But with this, she didn't bring only death into their house, but the misery of the past with it.

It weighed on her as she went in.

But instead of Summerset and the cat looming in the foyer, she saw Roarke with Galahad.

166

'It's a visual illusion. Like a holo.' She peered down at the cat as he jogged to her. 'Maybe you're not you, either.'

'Summerset's having an early dinner with Ivanna before a night at the theater.' Now he walked over, kissed her.

'Even an illusion or holo tech couldn't make Summerset do that, like that. I guess you're you.'

'On the other hand, look at you, Lieutenant, in those shades.'

'Badass, right? That was the sales pitch.'

'Definitely.'

Studying her face, he skimmed a finger down the dent in her chin. 'Let's have a glass of wine on the patio. You can tell me what's brewing in here.' He tapped a finger to her temple. 'Then we'll go up and deal with it.'

'I didn't want to bring it home to you.'

'Bring yourself home to me, and anything that comes with you is fine.'

More her problem, she thought, so much more hers than his. So she leaned into him, held on to him. 'Let's just do this for a minute first.'

'Are you hurting?' he murmured.

'I'm not. I promise, I'm not. It's in there, I know it, but I have a grip on it. It's different now that I know I can get a grip on it. I'm okay if you are.'

'And I am.'

'Then I'd like to sit outside for a bit. I think, maybe, we caught a break. I don't know if it'll open it up, but I think it's a break. And,' she continued as they began to walk to the back, 'I could use your help. I wasn't going to ask — didn't want to — because I didn't want to bring it home.'

'Does it make it easier if I tell you it helps me when you ask?'

'I guess it does.'

She waited until he'd selected a bottle of wine, opened it.

And when they sat together amid the tumbling flowers, she took her first sip of something white and bright.

'I'll start with the break. I went by Tiko's Midtown stall.'

Roarke sat back, stretched out his legs. 'Tiko. Well now, of course — and explains the sunshades. The boy has the eyes, the ears, the instincts. Did you know he has a second stall downtown?'

'I do now. How do you know?'

'I happened to go by one day a few weeks ago. I told him, when he's ready for a shop, I'd find him a space and back him on it. Did he see either of the girls?'

'Dorian Gregg.'

She told him, all of it, winding back to Nadine, the ongoing work in EDD, the frustrating and unproductive search on properties.

'You've too many variables on buildings, it seems to me.'

'You think?' She blew out a breath, tipped her head back to the sky. 'Got nowhere, really. I changed some of those factors, running it again. I'm inclined to think downtown. Not too close to the dump site, but not too far, either. It had to be a rush job, right? 'Oops, dead kid. How can we get rid of her, and use her?' But.'

'But she may have escaped from a location farther away. They may have transported her a longer distance in hopes of doing more to cover tracks. Add,' Roarke

168

continued as she scowled and drank wine, 'without a solid idea of how many girls might be held, you can't judge the size of the building. Two girls, three or four, you'd need one thing. A dozen or more, surely you'd need another.'

'Yeah, yeah.'

'However, your call on windows, for instance? The lack of them, or minimal number, seems logical. One-way glass as an alternative, shatterproof. The shipping dock or something of the kind seems logical as well.'

'I go back to that lunatic Dawber, and the three women he held. We knew, all the arrows pointed to a private residence, single occupancy, probably with a basement, and in a fairly narrow target area. And that wasn't a snap to run searches on. This? I'm punching at shadows and know it.'

'I could punch at some for you if you like.'

'I didn't want to bring it home to you,' she repeated. 'Are you hurting?'

'I'm not. I'm worried for you, and you shouldn't expect otherwise. You've barely come off another case involving abduction and brutality that brought back hard memories. And this, on top of that, involves children.

'But we'll get through it. And you'll find who's hurt these girls. I have every faith there. In a bit of a while, we'll have a break, a nice long one in Greece and in Ireland. We'll get through it.'

Greece and Ireland seemed, at that moment, like some floating fantasy.

'I feel we've got some movement with Tiko spotting her. A time frame, a location where she was almost certainly snatched. We know she was taken from here, from New York. For Mina, blocks from home in the

169

Philadelphia 'burbs. And if we can solidify any of the other missings into a pattern, we have something to build on.'

'And now you have Dorian's face out there through Nadine.'

'Unless she lucks into someone with a vehicle who'll drive her out, she's unlikely to get out of New York without being spotted. We've covered all the transpo stations. I've got them monitoring for her at the bridges and tunnels. She can get out if she's determined, but I don't know where she'd want to go or why.'

'Away from her captors.'

'Yeah, there's that. But where?'

Desperation, Eve thought, could send you rushing into the dark. No plan, no destination, just away.

'She had a window to get out before we ID'd her. If she jumped through it, she's in the wind. But she's barely thirteen. I'm thinking her first instinct would be to hide. Tiko made her as a street thief,' Eve added. 'And yeah, he's got the eye for that. Wouldn't she need a little time to get enough funds to buy a bus or train ticket? Unless she managed to steal some money before they got out, she'd have nothing.'

'Why not be optimistic at this point, assume she's still in New York?'

'Optimism likes to kick you in the ass, and panic could've shot her straight out of New York into any-where else. But we find her, we find them. Otherwise, we punch at shadows until we hit something solid.'

'Why don't we go up and get started on that?' He rose, held out a hand to her.

'You know what?' She took his hand, pushed up. 'I've got these badass shades. If optimism tries to kick this badass, I'm kicking back.'

'I'm not at all sure how that works, but we'll go with it. Why don't you send me your property search results,' he said as they went back inside. 'I'll take a look, see how I might refine them.'

'Yeah, good luck with that.'

'She said, optimistically.'

She gave him an elbow jab as he called for one of the elevators she'd forgotten they had.

'I'll get something started while you do your updates. We'll have some dinner while all that brews.'

'I need to look over what EDD's come up with. I need that pattern. And I want to check in with Willowby if she hasn't sent me anything.'

'We'll start and see where it takes us.'

When they stepped into her office, he walked over, opened her terrace doors while she went to her command center. Galahad, sprawled over her sleep chair, yawned.

'Do you want the search results in your office or here?' she asked Roarke.

'My office for now. You take the room. Let's try for an hour.'

She sat, sent Roarke the whole damn mess, then remembered to take off the sunshades. Before she started her updates, she pounced on a report from Harvo.

And optimism kicked her in the ass.

No exact matches on the underwear from any outlet. Similar designs with the same or similar materials? What Harvo rightfully called a 'slew.'

She'd keep working it, but opined the products had been designed, manufactured, and sold off-book.

'Yeah, so dead end there, or close to it.'

Hoping for better, she read a quick report from Willowby.

The detective monitored some chatter about upcoming sales, auctions, import, exports. The fact children were nothing more than products to move on the market sat hard in her gut.

And carrying that, she did the initial updates, board and book, before bringing up Peabody's data.

She added more names and faces and files to her categories.

'Computer, run probability on category one. Highest to lowest with current data, subject abducted by same party or parties as Mina Cabot and Dorian Gregg.'

Current data is insufficient for top-level accuracy . . .

'Run it anyway.'

Acknowledged. Working . . .

While it worked, she programmed more coffee, put her boots up, and with her eyes and mind on the board, let the whole thing circle.

Slick, sophisticated, structured organization. Considering the quality of Mina's clothing, well-funded and/or profitable. Multiple employees — had to have multiple employees, had to have a secure property for housing. Almost certainly had to have some sort of studio to generate photos, vids. Had to generate healthy food, the grooming crap. Medicals on board? Highly probable.

Guards — matrons? She thought of her years in

172

state schools. Matrons — they didn't call them guards, but hell, same deal. But female for the females. They sure as hell didn't want some perv (though they came in female varieties, too) screwing around with the students.

Or vice versa, she remembered.

Female guards, she decided. Couldn't have the staff devaluing the product.

Who paid them? Who headed the whole thing up? An individual, a syndicate, a partnership?

Probability complete . . .

'Results on-screen,' Eve ordered. 'Well, son of a bitch.'

She dropped her feet, leaned forward. In the first category run, the Mina category, she had three who hit over ninety percent.

'Computer, run second category.'

Acknowledged. Warning: data insufficient for top-level accuracy. Working . . .

Eve pulled out the three case files, then held up a hand when Roarke came back in.

'Wait, okay. I might have something. Nydia Lu, age twelve, West Bloomfield, New Jersey. Missing since September 2060. Left school — private — after orchestra practice. Plays the violin. Walked a block with a couple friends, peeled off to walk the next three blocks home. Never made it. No ransom demand, no trace.

'What do you see?'

'A striking young girl. Mixed race, gorgeous, happy

173

eyes, a shy smile.'

Eve ordered a printout. 'Put her up on the board, will you?'

She brought up the next.

'Aster McMillian, age thirteen, Potomac, Maryland. Missing since February. Play practice, vanished on the four-block walk from school. Private — exclusive, too, this one looks like. Wealthy family, one older sib, one younger. No ransom demand, no trace. You'd say striking again?'

'I would, yes. Blond hair, blue eyes, bright, confident smile.'

'Got one more who hit over ninety probability. Insufficient data, my ass. Liberty Stone, age eleven — twelve now — Pike Creek, Delaware. Missing since October 2060. Choir practice — school choir. Private. Two fricking blocks from there to her house. Solid family — one sib. No ransom, no trace.'

'Another young beauty,' Roarke said. 'Golden brown skin, green eyes, hint of dimples. If these girls were taken by the same people, that's up to five.'

'It's going to be more. These are just the over ninety in the Mina category. I've got it running the Dorian type. Then I did a mix on a third. Plus, the insufficient data crap. It's factoring locations, distances. When we open that up?'

She pushed away from the command center, began to pace.

'Coincidence equals bollocks. These three popped because this is the goddamn pattern. For this type. Jesus, we could have a dozen, more, just from the northeast and mid-Atlantic. Toss in Pennsylvania, and what would it be . . . Ohio? Maybe they have more than one location — West Coast, Midwest, South,

174

Southwest. Or they bring them all here to New York.'

'A port city,' Roarke pointed out. 'If I set up a business to smuggle out any sort of illegal product, I'd want port cities. Busy ones,' he added. 'Major ones with a variety of transportation hubs.'

She looked back at him. 'You did have a smuggling business.'

'We could call it that,' he said easily. 'More, I'd say, interests, but it comes to the same for logistics.'

He glanced over as her comp signaled. And Eve pounced.

'It only gives me one over ninety here, Lottie Crug, age twelve, from the Heights. Got a juvie sheet. Truancy, shoplifting, chronic runaway. Comp's basically matching her up with Dorian. But she fits. Missing since April, suspected runaway. She's got the looks.'

'She does. You have six in the eighty-percent range.'

'Yeah, I see. I'm going to add the two that hit between eighty-five and ninety. One from Queens, one from Baltimore. Baltimore — foster kid. Queens, abusive father's how it reads. Mother filed restraining order, blah blah.

'They slide right in from where I'm standing. It's a goddamn pattern, Roarke. It's a fucking system.'

'I agree. Run your third. I'll see to dinner. You'll eat,' he said before she could object. 'Think it through, talk it out. And we'll talk about how my own search is going.'

'If you've got —'

'If I had something definitive, I wouldn't be programming dinner.' He kissed her forehead. 'Run the third.'

11

She thought it through, and when the next results came in, printed out more young faces. She had ten now, ten she considered mid to high probability, from Boston to Baltimore.

'I'm going to set up another — start with Mina's category, but take out the physical appearance factor. Follow me here, objectively, okay?'

'All right.'

'Richard Troy intended to sell me off, but not like Mina, for instance. I didn't have the looks. Don't,' she said quickly. 'You see me the way you see me. But reality is, I sure as hell didn't have the looks. I was bony, scrawny, awkward. They're called Slaves or Pets, depending.'

'I'm aware,' he said flatly.

'I'd have fit one of those. You don't need to invest so much, so you can sell for a lot less, but it's steady profit if you're just snatching them. And I need to start working on younger. Say, eight to eleven, all categories. If we're going in the right direction, an operation like this would probably diversify. Say some of the potentials for major sales just don't pan out, you sell them as a Slave or Pet or whatever the assholes call them.'

She could see, actually see, him work to set his personal feelings aside. Sometime, she thought, some way, she'd show him what that — just that — meant to her.

176

'All right, well then, a good foundational business plan might have what you'd call their private label — very high-end — and work down to the more accessible. You might say store brand.'

'That's what I'm saying.' He just said it better. 'So I want to work on that, going with the basic pattern.'

'I can help with that.' He walked to her when she didn't respond. 'Now you don't.' Taking her hand, he pulled her to her feet. 'We get through this together, remember? And I'm better at this sort of thing than you.'

'Faster doesn't always mean better.' But she shrugged as he led her to the table. 'Maybe better and faster. I'm thinking maybe Peabody and McNab — or Feeney — can do runs like this, but other regions. If they find a similar pattern, if — I know it's if — but if it's the same organization, do they transport them here, or have those other locations? Other port cities, other transportation hubs? Or are they sticking to this region?

'The more data,' she continued as Roarke removed the domes from the plates, 'the better.'

On the plate she saw a colorful pasta salad — some of the color came from vegetables, but she'd handle them. In addition, he'd come up with some sort of fish (she thought) that looked a little burned.

'AC going wonky?'

'It's blackened swordfish. You should like the heat.'

'Maybe. Who decided to eat some fish with a sword? You have to wonder if the first guy who caught one thought: Holy shit, this damn fish has a sword.'

'En garde,' he said, and made her laugh before she sampled it.

'Okay, I can see why he decided it was worth it.'

Before he could do it for her, as he invariably did, she broke one of the rolls in half, offered it.

'Thanks. I've done some categories of my own. Small office buildings, keeping it to twelve floors and under. Warehouses, converted or others. Factories — same there. Businesses attached to same that may serve as a front.'

He stabbed some pasta. 'From there, we'll look at ownership. Assuming this is a major, sophisticated operation, I lean toward ownership of the property. Renting or leasing leaves too many problems. The owner might opt to sell it out from under you, or send in agents for evaluation, inspections.'

She hadn't thought of evals and all that, so nodded. 'Okay, that makes sense. Owning a building like that in the city takes deep pockets.'

'Those or good financing. Once I see ownership, I can potentially eliminate.'

'How?'

'Well, I can certainly eliminate any I own. I hope you'd agree.'

'I can go with that.'

'I can also eliminate, or at least downgrade, any owned by people or groups I know well enough to know. Trust me on this,' he said when she frowned. 'And there may be some that send up a flag for me. Because I know them to be on what you'd call the shady side of things. Others I may not know at all — I don't know everyone, after all — and those I could look into more deeply.'

'It won't be quick.'

'It won't, no. As you've already learned from your own look, there are potentially hundreds of properties that might fit, and more yet that might fit after

178

another round. If it's attached to a business, a front, that front might run on perfectly legal means. It's what I'd do in any case.'

Since he'd put it in front of her, she picked up her wine.

'You'd run a business out of the front. Sell something, or make something, run a small factory, whatever. Keep those books, pay those taxes, keep it clean. Behind it, you run the real business.'

'Exactly so. Smuggle the girls in, warehouse them, so to speak, and when you deem them ready for the market, sell and transport them out again. You'd need vehicles. Potentially boats or shuttles.'

'Long haul trucks hauling human cargo.'

'Possibly. Risky — road accidents, traffic stops. But possibly. Private air shuttles, if you have the funding, would be smarter and safer. And faster.'

'The victim's shirt — good fabric, tailored to her size. The fancy silk underwear. No labels, and Harvo reports no match on any legit outlet with the same design, same materials. They have to have a tailor on board. Maybe the front's something like that. Fabric and clothing?'

'I can look for that.' He considered. 'It's an angle. Front with something you already use or need, and make a legitimate business out of it to cover the rest.'

'Okay, yeah. What else do they use or need? Photography and vids. You've got to market the product. Maybe that, or selling equipment for it. Transportation. A fleet of trucks or vans, a delivery service, moving company. You have to deliver the product once sold, so invest in transpo — the vehicles, ships, shuttles — and do regular business to cover. Food or medical supplies. But those don't fit as well,' she decided. 'Perishable and trickier to license and run. Regular inspections required.'

'Agreed there. The business, if it exists, may be something completely unrelated. But, again, if I ran the operation, I'd prefer the double-dip and lower overhead.'

'If you factor that in, it narrows the field. Still a big-ass field, but we have to start somewhere.'

'Then I'll do just that and get started. You've got the dishes.'

'Yeah, I got them.'

* * *

While Eve dealt with the dishes and thought through her next steps, Auntie rang the bell at the entrance of her partner's stately Georgian mansion on Long Island.

She'd enjoyed the drive — he'd sent a limo, as always. She wore a formal gown, as he'd expect, and knew she looked her very best in the formfitting bold red and metallic silver. She wore diamonds, cold and white. This chapter of her career had proved profitable. Her hair, meticulously colored and styled in the Academy's salon, swept back from her pampered face.

The techs on staff routinely eradicated any lines, smoothed the surface of that face, added fillers. While she'd never have the dewy freshness of nineteen, when she'd launched her career as an escort, her beauty remained, polished and perfect to her mind, at a ripe sixty-four.

The woman who opened the door wore a black skin suit, one that plunged deep between her breasts. The glittery choker at her throat ensured — with an electric jolt — that she didn't step outside the house.

She wouldn't, of course. Auntie had trained her personally five years before, and knew Raven — so named for her thick fall of black hair — devoted herself to her master.

'Good evening, Auntie.' The full lips coated with slick red dye curved in greeting. 'You look stunning.'

'Thank you.'

Auntie glided into the soaring entrance hall with its desert-sand marble floors, its lavish gold-and-crystal chandeliers, its bold slashes of art.

The lush roses, white and pure, on the central table perfumed the air.

'Master will join you shortly. May I escort you to the parlor?'

'Of course.'

The parlor, lavish as the rest, held a white grand piano, a marble fireplace, divans, settees, oversize chairs, all in patterns of white on white. White roses flowed from vases; ornately framed mirrors of all shapes and sizes reflected the cold splendor of the room.

'Champagne, Auntie?'

'Please.' So saying, Auntie arranged herself on a divan and watched her former trainee lift the bottle from its bed of ice in gleaming silver, pour it into a flute.

Perfectly done, she thought, and congratulated herself.

'Is there anything else I can do to make you more comfortable while you wait?'

'No.' She flicked a hand. 'You can go.'

'Enjoy your evening.'

She intended to. Her partner invariably served the

finest wines and food perfectly prepared. Their long association benefitted them both.

Some bumps, of course, along the way. Including now the despicable, ungrateful girls. But a successful business accepted certain losses as part of doing that business. A certain percentage of trainees failed, and that was the reality of it.

She and her partner would discuss it all over dinner.

He'd been a client once, she mused. Long ago, and long ago he'd seen her potential. He'd financed her when she'd launched her own escort service.

A hugely successful one, one that had catered to the wealthy, the exclusive, the famous and infamous. That partnership had done exceedingly well.

Then the government legalized the sex trade — and regulated it. Those regulations, inspections, screenings, taxes cut deep into the profits.

Licensed companions, she thought, disgusted, as if you could license sex and passions and desires. But they had, so no more party packs of drugs to keep an escort fresh — and no more taking the cost — plus service charge — out of the fee. If a client got a little too rough, put some marks or dings on the rental, the girl filed a complaint — and her company had to pay the medical.

Oh, and the medical, she thought. Those steep monthly payments to ensure her stable passed all those annoying screenings.

Now and then, of course — rarely, but now and then — a client might do more than mark or ding. But that added on a hefty disposal fee.

No more of that, and no more standard confidentiality fees added on to the client's bill.

182

Worse, many she'd brought in, groomed, trained, decided they no longer needed a madam, and struck out on their own.

Ah well, she thought as she sipped more champagne. When things change, the wise adjust. And innovate.

She heard him coming, angled toward the door, and smiled.

He wore black tie so well, she thought, and always had. Though he'd let his hair go white — and it suited him — it remained thick around a face that had weathered nearly seventy years very well.

It remained angular and sharp with hooded eyes of deep, dark brown. Though he stopped a few inches short of six feet, he had the presence of a tall man.

Perhaps it came from being born into wealth, then inheriting it all before he turned twenty-five.

Jonah K. Devereaux possessed a sharp and canny mind for business, and, she thought, whatever else he wished.

In their long association, she'd seen him burn through lovers — one literally, as he'd ordered the cottage in Switzerland where she'd fled to torched. With her inside.

Auntie admired his decisive ruthlessness, because it melded so well with her own.

Once, she'd bedded him — and others for his viewing pleasure — had jetted and sailed with him. While they remained genuinely fond of each other, their sexual relationship had ended some two decades before.

She knew she'd simply aged out of desirability for him in that regard, and cast no blame.

'Iris, my flower. How lovely you are.'

She rose so they kissed cheeks.

'How was Majorca?' she asked him.

'Warm. I wish you could have joined me, even for a few days.'

'As do I, but it's all so busy right now.'

'What would I do without you handling all that busy? Let me get you more champagne.'

He topped off her glass, poured his own before lifting it.

'To friendship, and profit. Why don't we sit, get this discussion out of the way so we can talk of more pleasant things over dinner.'

'Jonah.' She sighed as she sat. 'I can't tell you how angry and disappointed I am. I knew 238 posed some challenges, and I *know* I was well on the way to overcoming them.'

'You have a sense for these things.'

'I already had two buyers in mind for her. Ones who enjoy a bit of feisty, a touch of sass. We'd already started the marketing plan for her. But 232? The lying bitch.'

Closing her eyes a moment, Auntie held up a hand. 'You know I try not to take it personally when one of them doesn't meet expectations. But honestly, I feel duped. It doesn't go down well.'

'It's a rare occurrence.'

'Clearly they plotted together. I blame 238 entirely there. She had a slyness in her, and I admit I admired it to a point.'

'They have her name, her face. The media as well as the authorities.'

'Yes, I know. We should consider that an advantage. I have hunters out, naturally. I expect she'll run, far and fast, another advantage. With her history, she'd never go to the police, and if they manage to find her,

her history and her blood on that wretched 232 go against her.'

'Is there any way she could lead them to the Academy?'

'I don't see how. She was unconscious and contained when brought in, as is SOP. They fled through the tunnels, a considerable distance. We believe we know where they came out, and in a rainstorm — another advantage. Clearly, she'd already run, leaving 232 to fend for herself.'

Auntie drank again. 'Just another street rat, one who killed a foolish runaway for her shoes. Even if they suspect abduction on 232's part, there's no trace to us, and the results are the same.'

'It's a concern.'

'Yes, but one we'll manage. If the police find her — and I very much doubt it — the network will hear, and we'll deal with her. With no family behind her, she'll be forgotten quickly. This is a bump in the road, darling Jonah. We've had them before.'

'Haven't we though?' He laughed, then leaned over to kiss her cheek. 'Adds the spice, doesn't it? Smooth gets boring after a while, and I do enjoy the spice. And the hall matron? The medical?'

'Both terminated. I won't tolerate that sort of incompetence on staff.'

'I told you investing in the crematorium would pay for itself, and more.'

'You did. I should always leave the investment decisions in your hands. I have a candidate for the medical position. We're screening and vetting her now.'

'And I leave the staffing decisions to you. Which reminds me, I'm ready to trade in Athena. No fault of hers, really, but she's becoming a bit of a bore. It's time for a change there.'

'Of course. I'll need to check the records, but she's . . . about twenty-five, twenty-six now?'

He didn't have a taste for the Kiddies or Chicklets, she thought as she tried to form a mental picture of his current sex slave.

'You'd know better than I.'

'I'll take a look at her before I leave, get an estimate of value in a trade. Tell me what you're looking for as a replacement.'

'Oh, perhaps something a bit more interesting. Something with some of that spice.'

'I'll check the market. With the auction coming up, we can work a deal, especially since you prefer the experienced, slightly older type.'

'Send me one to try out.' He patted her hand. 'Let's go into dinner. I'm famished.'

★ ★ ★

Eve added more girls to the pattern. When she hit twenty, she started a second board and transferred all of them there.

She shifted regions and began again.

She was about to get up, just walk off the sitting, when her 'link signaled.

Willowby.

'Dallas. What have you got?'

'I've been cruising the dregs. EDD deepened my cover, so I moved up a few slots. I'm getting some chatter about an auction, a major one, multiple sellers. And a couple of them did some previews, like advanced marketing.'

'Do you have faces?'

186

'A few. Like I said, a preview. I've got two — so far — in our age group. One Chicklet, and one Ripe. Ripe's like fifteen to twenty, maybe twenty-two, depending. One Full Flower — those usually go up to maybe thirty, usually for trades or a tagalong. Ripe and Full Flower go as Breeders, depending.'

Jesus, Eve thought, but only nodded. 'Let's see the ones from our age range. Let's start there. I've got twenty-odd potentials. Maybe we'll get a match.'

'Sending now. Can you send me yours? I can look out for them as the marketing gears up.'

'Yeah.'

When they exchanged data, Eve studied the photos on her screen.

'The second girl — the blonde,' Eve said. 'They changed her hair — cut it, dyed it. But I've got her. Jaci — J-a-c-i — Collinsworth, age twelve, Detroit, missing since April. The first one hasn't popped for me yet, but I'll run her through.'

'Got it, I'll pull her file and dig in.'

'When's the auction?'

'We've got three days. If I can work it, I'll get some shipping, transfer, and/or delivery locations. Problem there is, a winning bidder gets a special code sent to their comp to access that data. We can spread it out, bid on some, but we're never going to get them all that way. Most of these buyers are going to be plenty rich and plenty savvy, so they'll get around Compu-Guard like it was nothing. It ain't that much anyway.

'We can bust some of the dumbasses, but what we're after? They're not going to sell to the dumbasses.'

'Let me think about that.' Eve glanced toward Roarke's office, then glanced at the time. 'Pretty late, Willowby.'

'Is it? I guess. Or it's considered late if I had anything resembling a social life. Which, at the moment, I
don't. More, I want to get these fuckers, Lieutenant.'

'We're going to. Lots of little cracks now, and little
cracks make big breaks. Keep in touch.'

'Count on it.'

Eve sat, studying Jaci's photo.

'Did those bastards bring you in from Detroit, or
did you get scooped up by some other asshole? Cut
your hair, made you a blonde, painted you up so they
can sell you to the highest bidder.

'We'll fucking see about that.'

'Eve.'

'Jesus! Make some noise!'

He'd come up behind her, and now laid his hands
on her shoulders, rubbed at the knots.

'All of those?' He nodded at the new board.

'Yeah, going with the pattern. The one on-screen?
Willowby got wind of an upcoming auction, and she's
one of the previews. I had her, so we matched her.'

He kept rubbing, felt her give a bit under his hands.
'I have roughly eighty properties that hit the highest probability. Another twenty or so that skim just
under.'

'Still a lot, but more workable. Send them to me,
okay?'

'I will. One hour more. It's near to midnight now.'

'Willowby said three days. We find Gregg, pinpoint
the location, bust down this auction, or Christ knows
how many get sold. This kid, this one who played soft-
ball and the piano, sure as hell will be.'

'An hour more,' he repeated, 'and you'll push
through it tomorrow.'

She swiveled toward him. 'They send the buyer a

code. You have to buy to get it, and it gives you the pickup or delivery info. She said for ones like this one? You're going to be rich and tech savvy — or have the tech savvy at your disposal to get through Compu-Guard.'

He sat on her counter. 'You're thinking of using the unregistered, and fine enough, but you could hardly buy them all.'

'One, just one, if it comes to that. We get a code, we track it back to the source. Put the auction site out of business, get their data.'

'Track the girls, the sellers, other buyers. Possibly,' he said. 'The site won't have a location, not a physical one you'll track. It'll be mobile for the very reasons you've outlined.'

'EDD set Willowby up as a potential buyer. They can do a couple more, you do a couple.' She shut her eyes. 'And an operation like the one I'm after is going to be really careful about new buyers. We'd need a lot more than three days to set up solid bona fides. Shit.'

'Your brain's tired. We'll think about it more when it's not, see if we can work something. I'll talk to Feeney, bat it around a bit. It may be we can work it another way.'

'What other way?'

'We'll work on it.'

'Is your brain tired?'

'Tired enough.'

'Can I see your results? Just run them through with me, and we'll call it.'

'There's a deal.' He reached around her, keyed something. 'On-screen,' he ordered. 'All right then. The first, a pre-Urban factory in the Garment District.'

They went through them all, and though they ran over the hour, he thought she'd sleep easier for it.

* * *

Sebastian didn't. He sat in what he thought of as the family room — a jumble of furniture in a space that had once served as a lobby.

He'd seen the media reports with Dorian's face flashing over the screen. The fact Eve Dallas, a murder cop, looked for her, termed her a material witness in the violent death of another child, worried him.

He'd promised Dorian she could stay, and he intended to keep his word to her. He doubted many others had kept theirs to her in her short life. But with Dallas on the hunt, that promise carried considerable weight.

More, if she hunted Dorian, others — much less concerned with law and order — might hunt as well. And that put them all at risk.

Even as he considered options, alternatives, precautions, she wandered out.

He set the book he hadn't been able to focus on aside. 'Can't sleep?'

'I had these dreams. I can't even remember, they were all mixed up. Maybe I could sit out here for a while.'

'All right. It's what I do sometimes when I can't sleep. Like tonight.'

She took a couch covered with wild orange flowers someone had set on the curb.

Tall for her age, he thought, and very, very lean. Even with her sleepy eyes and disordered hair, she made a picture.

'You like to read books?'

'I do,' he told her. 'Do you?'

'We got to read them on a tablet in school. But I never brought mine home.'

'Why not?'

She yawned hugely. 'She'd've sold it, probably. I don't want to ever go back there. I don't know what happened to my backpack. I had it when I left.'

Memories eking back, he thought. Piece by piece.

'When you left home?'

'Uh-huh. I had my stuff in it, and some money. Enough for the bus. I had to get farther than I had before, so I took the bus. I told a lady I was going to visit my grandma. I don't really have one, but I can lie good when I have to.'

'Where did you go?'

'I . . . went to Staten Island first. I needed to get more money, and I found a basement to stay in awhile. A guy chased me out, but I still had my backpack. I had it when I got to New York. I like it here. Except . . .'

'Except what?'

'I don't know . . . They lock the doors. I don't like when they lock the doors. I don't want to think about it.'

Because she'd curled into a ball, Sebastian didn't press. He'd have to, he knew, but not tonight.

'Why don't I read to you? I can start the book from the beginning.'

'What's it about?'

He smiled. 'Let's find out.'

12

Eve woke before dawn. She saw Roarke working on his tablet in the dim light he'd ordered in the sitting area. She felt the cat stir, uncurl himself from her lower back.

Her guards, she thought, and couldn't decide if that annoyed or reassured.

Roarke glanced over when she sat up.

'You could take another hour.'

'No.' She shook her head. 'I'm good.'

He set the tablet aside, rose to go over and sit on the side of the bed. 'You had a restless night, and not much of that.'

'Sorry.'

Now he shook his head, took her hand.

'Dreams,' she admitted. 'Irritating mostly, and faded now. Except the last one. I was a kid with a bunch of other kids, all of us chained on some sort of platform or stage. And you know how they have that guy, the one who talks real fast and calls out bids?'

'An auctioneer?'

'Yeah, that guy. The dream decided he'd be Richard Troy, and there are all these people sitting there — a lot of them I've put away, others all blurred. And they're bidding on us, and he says he'll start the bidding on me at a dollar because I'm not worth much. Got a lot of laughs out of that.'

When he pressed his lips to her forehead, she squeezed his hand.

192

'No, there's the thing. After that, I was me. Now, not a kid. And I broke the chains. I broke them, and I woke up.'

He kissed her again. 'As you did. As you would.'

'Damn right. So you don't have to sit in the dark in your zillion-dollar suit keeping watch when you should be in your office buying Australia.'

'I don't believe it's for sale, and this suit only cost a quarter of a zillion.'

He rose to get them both coffee.

'I can get a jump on the day,' she continued. 'And you can get back to yours. It didn't really cost a quarter of a zillion, did it?'

He smiled, brought her coffee. 'One day I'll have to calculate your exact equation for a zillion.'

'As long as it's enough to keep me in coffee, we're good. I'm going to get a shower. No laying out my clothes. I've got it.'

She rolled out of bed. 'Go take a meeting or whatever.'

'I'll do that. We'll have some breakfast in about thirty.'

When she went into the bathroom to shower, Roarke stroked the cat. 'She's steadied right up, so you're off duty. Have another catnap.'

As Roarke left, Galahad stretched out and did just that.

She took a long, hot shower with jets on full to pummel some of the restless night away. She had those cracks, she reminded herself, and needed to be sharp to widen them into breaks.

The biggest break would be finding Dorian Gregg, but it wasn't the only one she could work.

She had other names and faces now, and they gave

her other trails to follow. She had locations to probe. Too many, sure, and the one she needed might not be among them. Yet.

But she had cracks.

The upcoming auction.

'Break the fucking chains, every one,' she muttered as she stepped out of the shower and into the drying tube.

Another robe waited for her, this one the color of the peaches ripening in the orchard.

Who the hell had an orchard in New York City? Roarke did.

The cat slept on when she came out, and apparently Roarke had taken that meeting, or decided to buy Australia after all.

For a moment she debated. Grab clothes and get dressed before he got back or program breakfast, because maybe pancakes?

Clothes first, she decided, and maybe she'd still beat him to the AutoChef.

In her closet she blew out a breath. There were times, like right now, the magnitude of choices made her head spin.

She started to grab black pants, then calculated.

He'd expect that.

She shifted to gray, which was almost as easy as black, eliminated a white shirt — also too expected — then got lost in the hues and colors and tones.

Blue worked, she decided. Nothing wrong with blue. A blue T-shirt, gray jacket — and hanging in plain sight, the magic lining. Gray boots. And anticipating him thinking she'd gone too heavy on the gray, grabbed a blue belt.

Christ, exhausting.

And time-consuming, she realized when she came out and found him at the bedroom AC. With Galahad busy inhaling his own breakfast.

The odds of pancakes plummeted.

'I was going to get that.'

'Done now.' He carried the domed plates to the table in the sitting area.

She set the jacket aside, then sat, poured more coffee from the pot he'd already put on the table.

When he removed the domes, she saw she'd been right about the pancakes. But the omelet, the bacon and berries and croissants didn't leave room to bitch.

Naturally the omelet had spinach in it, but also plenty of cheese to offset it.

'I thought about working here for an hour or so, but I'm going straight in. I'd beat the worst of the traffic, and it'll be quiet there, for a while anyway.'

'All right. Would you like to hear my take on the auction, the unregistered?'

'Yeah, I would.'

'I can come in later today, help EDD set up three fake accounts with all the background data necessary. You already have Willowby on one, so three is all, I think, we'd risk. And those we'll spread out, geographically.'

'Okay. That'll get us in, but bidding —'

'Each will have somewhere between, say, twelve million to fifty million. The lower numbers will appear to have other accounts, if anyone digs that deep. I would. This account would appear to be set up, offshore, for precisely this purpose.'

'Okay, I follow that. But you can't toss that much money into an op.'

'I could, and would if necessary, but it isn't. I said

'appear.' Just as we'll make it appear, whenever we win a bid, the money — I assume it would be a down payment, the rest on delivery — has been transferred.'

'But it won't be?'

'There won't be any funds to transfer, but the amount will appear in the seller's — or their agent's — account. We'd likely have about twelve hours to identify the sellers, their locations.'

'How do you do all this?'

He ate some bacon. 'Trade secret.'

'No, seriously.'

'I am serious, Lieutenant. I haven't had to run this one for a very long time, but, well, riding a bike.'

'You're going to ride a bike?'

He turned, grabbed her face with both hands, and kissed her. 'I simply adore you. 'Like riding a bike,' they say, when you haven't done something in a while, as you don't forget how to ride a bike.'

'You could forget how to ride a bike. People forget all kinds of stuff.'

'Be assured, I haven't forgotten how to run this con. And the tech's improved considerably since last I did, so it'll only be easier — as long as the NYPSD doesn't arrest me for it.'

'You're covered there. Twelve hours, from the transfer to the cutoff?'

'It may be longer, but I wouldn't want to risk it. Meanwhile, we could work on hacking the other bidders' accounts. It's unlikely, you have to understand, we'll get all.'

'We get the sellers, they'll have records. Twelve hours, who knows how many girls sold and shipped out? I'm going to have to call in the feds. Teasdale's good, she's solid. I want to wait another day —

196

thirty-six hours max. I'll clear that with Whitney. I want to see how much of this we can put in place, what progress we make on the other angles, but I need to pull in the feds within the next thirty-six.'

She rose to put on her weapon harness. 'We narrow potential locations, even by twenty percent, that's major progress. We track back the abductees I've matched, maybe we find some crack, some little mistake.'

She swung on the jacket, began to load her pockets. 'If we find Dorian Gregg, it blows wide open. If we don't by end of today, I've got to figure she's way into the wind, or they found her first.'

She turned back, looked at him.

'I'm going to say I was wrong.'

'It can happen. About what?'

'About pushing you back, or trying to push you out of this one. I worried about you worrying, and I didn't want you hovering over me.'

He gave her a long, deceptively neutral look. ''Hovering,' is it now?'

'That's how I justified trying to block you out, and I'm saying I was wrong. I'm steady, and I need you to believe that.'

'I do.'

'Part of the reason I'm steady is because of you. And when we find some of these girls — I know we won't save them all, but every one we do? You're part of the reason, too. We break the chains, you're part of that.'

'I need to be. For you, for myself, for them. I need it.'

'I know that, too. If any of these cracks widen or break, I'll let you know. If we find these bastards, and you want in on the bust, if I have time to notify you, you're in.'

'Yes.' He rose, went to her. 'I would.' He brushed his mouth to hers. 'Take care of my cop.'

She wound her arms around him, held for just a moment. Then stepped back, put on the badass shades she hadn't managed to lose already.

'Take care of the guy in the quarter-zillion-dollar suit. He looks damn good in it.'

She beat the worst of the traffic, and the morning cacophony of ad blimps. She cruised a three-block area around Tiko's downtown location, circled the blocks, did it again.

She didn't expect Dorian Gregg to jump out and wave, but she took the shot.

Even if she came back to her old territory, Eve thought as she continued the drive to Central, no reason for her to be up and out so early. Far too early for tourists, so the sidewalks opened for the dog walkers, the domestics heading to work, the street joggers, the street-level LCs finally calling it a night.

If she remained in New York, and Eve held on to that as highest probability, she had a hole, cobbled enough together for a flop, or had a contact they hadn't unearthed as yet.

But Eve banked on her having the smarts to know whoever snatched and held her hunted her. And still, and still, she was barely thirteen. Scared, probably traumatized, possibly injured.

Crawl into a hole, she thought, pull it closed, and stay put.

Come out when the sidewalks teemed with people, she decided as she drove into Central's garage. Snag a wallet, a bag, get enough money to buy some food, and crawl right back into the hole.

Nowhere else to go, no one to go to.

She rode the elevator all the way up, with very little traffic there as well.

Her lucky day.

Then she walked into Homicide, and Jenkinson's tie assaulted her senses.

'What the hell are you doing here? And what the hell is that on your tie?'

'They're dragonflies.'

'From what galaxy?'

'Unknown. We caught one. Zero-four-freaking-hundred. People ought to have the courtesy to kill each other at reasonable hours. We already bagged him — asshole. Knifes a guy right outside a sex club, both of them sky-high. He runs off, but we're on scene when the fucker comes back, bloody shirt, pinwheel eyes, because he figured he could get back in to finish jerking off.'

'Sometimes they make it too easy.'

'Not at four-freaking-hundred. Reineke's escorting his sorry ass down to Booking — probably catching a quick nap in the crib now. I just wrote it up.'

'Well, good work. You can catch a nap of your own.'

'Actually . . . You got a minute?'

'I've got one.'

'Maybe back in your office.'

She gave him the come-ahead and started back. 'Are you angling for coffee?'

'Well, boss, if you're offering. Frosty shades you got there.'

'As long as that tie's in my office, I'm keeping them on.' She programmed the coffee. 'Have you had enough time to think about it?'

'Yeah. I thought about it, talked it over with the family. Thought some more. I appreciate you putting me up for the promotion, and if I can keep doing what I do, just add more damn paperwork, I'd like to take a run at it.'

'Good. It's the right call, Jenkinson.'

'Feels right, once I thought it through. I told Reineke. You gotta tell your partner, but if we could keep it with the three of us? If I tank it, I'd as soon avoid the ribbing or sympathy.'

'We can keep it between us, but you won't tank it. Just brush up on some of the bullshit.'

'There's always plenty to go around. Anyway, thanks.'

And with that item off the list, Eve checked on the status of the search for Dorian Gregg.

Plenty of tags on the tip line, with none of them panning out. But, she noted, a couple of shopkeepers in the area of Tiko's downtown stall recognized her from around holiday time.

Nothing recent, and nothing after Christmas, she concluded after wading through all of the reports.

She shifted to Peabody and EDD's search.

More names, more young faces. The efficient team not only grouped them in the categories she'd laid out, but geographically, added timelines.

Though it crowded her office, she started another board, and added the faces that hit the ninety-percent probability. Now she had twenty-three spread across an area under an hour's shuttle flight from New York. Sixty-two outside that margin.

But the pattern, she thought. When you laid it all out, put it all together, the pattern came through.

Did they select and abduct nationwide? she wondered. Transport all to New York — or have other locations for holding the girls?

Did they specialize in this age group? Just Chicklets, no Kiddies, Ripes, and so on?

'I wouldn't bet on that,' she muttered. 'No, I wouldn't bet on that. When you've got this slick a system, you don't narrow it so close.'

She went back to her computer, ordered the search, same markers but changed the age range to six to ten years, limited it, for now, to New York, New Jersey — and, thinking of Mina, Pennsylvania.

While it ran, she shifted to the long, complicated list Roarke had generated.

With a city map on-screen, she began to place each property. With that done, she started runs on owners, and members of boards or groups that owned the properties.

Something else to bring EDD in on, she thought, as working solo, it would take her days to thoroughly investigate all of them.

Since she'd come in early for a reason, she got more coffee and stuck with it.

She heard Peabody's pink boot clump just as her missing child search results came up.

'Jenkinson said you'd been here about an hour already.'

'I thought he was going to catch some sleep in the crib.'

'He caught a catnap at his desk.' She glanced over at the second board. 'You've got them all up.'

'We're going to need a third board. Goddamn it.' She had to push up. She gestured to the computer and paced to her window.

'We didn't get —' Peabody broke off, then slowly sat in Eve's desk chair. 'These are younger kids.

Younger girls. You've got eleven of them. Eleven in the last year.'

'Eleven that fit the pattern, in this geographic area.'

'Dallas, how could they hold that many girls? Eleven in this age group, the ones on the board in the younger group.'

'They likely have older teenagers. We'll cross off adults, even young adults for now. But we're going to run fourteen through sixteen. There's going to be a mistake in there, goddamn it, some mistake in all of these abductions. Someone else who got out besides the two we know. Another body somewhere we haven't tied in.'

'I'll run the next group. I'll do it.'

Eve said nothing, just nodded.

'Do you want EDD to spread out over these age groups, too?'

'Yeah.' Eve went to the AC, programmed coffee for her partner. 'Let's get that done, then I need them to assist in refining the properties Roarke's earmarked.'

She took a moment, studying those pretty young faces.

'If this is the pattern, and it damn well is — a pattern, a system, a fucking business model — they need room, a lot of room to securely hold, what, maybe forty or fifty, and could be more, at any one time.

'Figure it, Peabody. You auction two or three times a year, maybe. Hell, maybe you have monthly sales like at the Sky Mall, you're pulling in hundreds of millions. Two or three locations nationwide? You got yourself a billion-dollar enterprise. If it costs you, I don't know, ten million or twenty million — hell, double that — in outlay, you're fucking rolling in it.'

She got more coffee for herself. 'You have the front

or fronts to wash the profits when you need to. But you've got direct payments, and they're going to be in places that don't regulate. You infuse the business, sure. Need the food, the clothes, the payroll, and all that, but you've got the fronts.'

'And if you factor what Willowby said — the ones they call Pets or Slaves or Domestics? You'd have more.'

'We've got less than three days now before at least some of these girls get sold off. I'm damned if we'll let that happen.'

'I'll get started on the next age group, and I can let EDD know about the assist.'

'I'll take care of that. I have to send Feeney the file anyway.' Eve rubbed at her eyes. 'Hold on a minute. Roarke's working on an idea to infiltrate the auction. It's setting up fake accounts and backgrounds, and maybe hacking into the accounts of buyers we might identify to get locations.'

'How many warrants are we going to need for all that?'

'I'm leaving that to Feeney. It's an e-geek area. But we need to put everything we have together, cohesively, convincingly. We're going to have to bring in the feds at some point soon. And we'll need to give Feeney all the weight we can for authorization to run this e-op.'

She turned back to the board. 'If we find Dorian Gregg, we can bust this organization, put a big hurt there. But even if that happens, I want to go through with the rest. This may be a big one, but it's not the only.'

'Damn right. All the motherfuckers need to pay.'

Amused, heartened, Eve looked back at Peabody.

'Listen to the mouth on the Free-Ager.'

'I'm a cop, and a goddamn girl.' Peabody hissed out a breath. 'Hell, there's going to be boys, too. Maybe not the assholes we're focused on, but there's sure a hell of a market with these perverts for little boys.'

'And when we bust through this, we're giving a hell of a lot of data to the feds to bust through that.'

'Okay. I'll get on it.' She rose. 'If it's going to take another board, at least, you're going to run out of room in here.'

'Yeah, I'm holding the conference room. It annoys the hell out of me. I like my space. But we'll need one for full briefings, and when we pull in the feds. I'm going to request a meet with Whitney to discuss that part, and bring him fully up to date.'

'Maybe ask him to come down here. Set up the room, powerful visuals, right? If you need help with it —'

'I've got it, and that's a smart thought. The visuals speak louder than a verbal report. Let's get to it.'

'I'll get your coffee set up in the room.'

'Another smart thought. You're on a roll.'

And so was she, Eve thought as she went about the — for her — laborious task of transferring new data from her machine to the conference room, ordering printouts.

She took backups, just in case, and headed down to set it up.

Once she had, she contacted Whitney's office, requested he meet with her, then did the same with Mira's office. More backup, she thought.

And because she was there, she sat down with the conference room comp to continue her research and runs on the potential target properties and owners.

She had about thirty minutes in it when Mira came in on heels made up of lots of crisscrossing blue straps. Summer-sky blue, Eve noted, like her trim, knee-skimming suit.

'Thanks for making time,' Eve began, and Mira waved that off.

'I wanted to catch up, and I see even with your writtens I have considerable catching up to do. Good God, Eve, so many? It's stunning, even knowing how many children are taken, it's stunning to see them grouped together.'

'And they do, group together. I'm as sure of that as I can be. It's not just gut, it's pattern, and type, and system.'

'I don't disagree. While that coffee smells tempting, I think I'll stick with tea.' Before Eve could rise to get it, Mira waved her off again. 'You said the commander would be briefed as well, so wait for him, do it all at once. You're working, and I don't want to interrupt.'

'It's possible locations. A lot of possibles, even though Roarke culled them down more than I could.' She gestured to the screen. 'I've got them marked on the map. I'm digging into who owns them. The site could be rented, but if it is, it's going to be part of the business plan. Whoever owns the building has to be part of it. It's too risky otherwise.'

'Because?' Mira asked as she programmed her tea.

'The owner or owners may decide to sell. They may send him agents or reps to inspect the property, make sure it's in good repair, or appraisers if they're considering selling.'

'Yes, I see. And with the sort of enterprise you're outlining here, purchasing the building is a business investment, with much higher security.'

'And if you own, you can outfit as you need. Rooms, facilities, that security.'

Even as Eve spoke, Whitney came in. She got to her feet.

'Sir, I appreciate you coming down.'

He wore a dark gray suit over broad shoulders that carried the weight of his command. The silver in his close-cropped black hair added a kind of dignity to his wide face. He said nothing for a moment as he stood and studied the boards.

'So many,' he said at length.

'I believe more, Commander, but these are highest probability generated by Peabody and myself, and Feeney's team in EDD. All fit the pattern, including three types of victims within the age range eleven to thirteen. I've begun, and Peabody is continuing, to factor in others between the ages of six and ten.'

'Geographically,' she began, but he held up a hand.

'Let me get some coffee, and first tell me where we are on the second girl you believe escaped.'

'Sir, the canvass in the area of the witness's stall turned up two shopkeepers who ID'd Dorian Gregg, from sightings last December. Both were sure of the ID, and reasonably sure of the time frame. December, prior to Christmas. We've yet to find anyone who's seen her since then. We're still canvassing.'

'And the LEOs in Freehold?'

'Are on watch for her. But she won't go back there.'

He got his coffee. 'Dr. Mira?'

'I agree with the lieutenant on that. She has nothing there. She may have found a way out of New York between the time she escaped and we identified her and put out the alert to transportation stations, but

206

that would be awfully quick work even for a bright young girl.'

'If Mina had a plan,' Eve added, 'it would have been to get to the police and/or contact her parents. Dorian Gregg wouldn't do either. Possibly, last resort, but she has no reason to trust either her mother or the authorities.'

'You're putting a lot of weight into the stand she got away because of the planted blood.'

'Yes, sir. If they recaptured her, she remained a valuable product, but on the loose, she's a liability. Smarter to discredit and implicate the liability, especially one with a history of trouble and some violent behavior while you continue to hunt for her. Find her, sell her off cheap, or eliminate her.'

Eve paused.

'Which they might have done,' she said. 'She's smart, and she's been on the streets before, but these people are organized and experienced, and very well funded. They had several hours' head start on us in the hunt.'

'And knowing all that, you want to continue to deploy the manpower to canvass.'

'Yes, sir.'

He nodded. 'I agree. I read her file, and your report. She's had a raw, rough life. You should know Truman's been terminated from her position at CPS.'

Now he sat. 'Geographically?'

'Geographically,' Eve repeated, and brought him fully up to date.

He stopped her several times, questioned, consulting Mira for opinions. And when Eve finished, sat back with a second cup of coffee.

'Authorizing and running this e-op would be easier

with the FBI already on board.'

'Possibly, Commander, but we've got the best on it, and we have movement. I'd like the next thirty-six hours to refine it. I would also request we go through Agent Teasdale. She's not only proved capable, but she knows the team we'd have working that area. It's not for credit for the bust, sir.'

'I know that very well. Why another thirty-six?'

'For the chance to find Dorian Gregg, that's primary. An opportunity to find her, to gain her trust before the bureaucracy crowds in. We may get more cooperation from her if we offer her a choice.'

'A choice of what?'

'The foster system, or a place in An Didean.'

As Whitney's eyebrows lifted, Mira smiled.

'Very good,' Mira murmured. 'Very good. First, a choice gives her some personal power, and second — you don't believe for a minute she'll go for the system. The school offers some freedom, some boundaries, of course, but a way out of the cycle she's been trapped in.'

'The feds may not have that choice to give, or may not want to offer it. I think I could convince Teasdale on it, but she wouldn't have the full authority, as I see it, to give that the green.'

'So you'd preempt them, make a deal with her, which we can use to block — or attempt to block — other avenues. You have to find her first.'

'Yes, sir, and if we don't in the next thirty-six, the odds are we won't, at least not before this auction. But there are a lot of lives at stake. If we find her, any information she has leads us to this organization, the location of many of the faces on these boards. We shut it down without alerting any other locations, any

208

other sellers, buyers. And we follow through with the e-op, with the feds, to break the backs.

'Mina Cabot remains central. I want the person who ended her life. If I can get the person who abducted her, the people who held her, the ones funding it and profiting from it, that's gravy. But it's fine with me if the feds take them down. I'm still looking for a child killer, and I'm hoping we find Dorian Gregg alive, and she points the finger.'

'All right. We'll see where you are in twenty-four. If your progress justifies it, you'll get the thirty-six, and I'll authorize the op. I need to be kept tightly in the loop on that.'

'You will be, sir, and thank you.'

He rose. 'Find the girl, Dallas.' He looked back at the board. 'Let's find all the girls.'

13

Dorian woke in bed with sunlight streaming through the privacy-shielded window. It took her a moment to orient herself, then she realized she must have fallen asleep on the couch downstairs with Sebastian reading. And he must have carried her up to bed.

The idea felt odd and oddly . . . nice.

Why couldn't someone like him have been her father? Did she even have a father? It didn't feel like it, or how come she ended up hurt and hiding?

Why couldn't someone like Sebastian have taken her away from all the crap and into the nice?

Because things didn't work that way, she decided. Maybe she didn't remember lots of stuff, but she remembered that. Never had, never would work like that.

Not for somebody like her.

Still, she lay there a few minutes fantasizing about it. She couldn't remember if she'd ever lain around in bed before on a sunny morning.

Get your lazy ass up!

She heard the voice clearly inside her head. A woman's voice, harsh and raspy. Mother? Yeah, yeah, mother, because the face started to come clear, too.

She didn't want to hear it, see it, so she just blocked it out.

Because she could stay here now, Sebastian said so, and nobody seemed to care if she remained in bed awhile in the morning. He could be — sort of — her

210

father, couldn't he? As long as she stayed.

So she lay there for a bit and took inventory. Her head didn't hurt or feel wrong anymore. Her ankle felt sore, but not as bad. Same with her knee.

Maybe they felt a little twingy when she got up, but she could walk okay. Nobody had said she couldn't take a shower, and she wanted one. She had the little bag — toothbrush and stuff — Mouser had brought her, so she went to the bathroom she shared with Chi-Chi and some other kids.

It felt so good to wash, to put on clean clothes, even if the pants were a little too big and a little too short.

Hungry, she started downstairs. She could hear people talking, hear at least somebody playing a game. She thought she'd get something to eat and see what chores she had to do.

She'd be happy to do them — if she did her chores, didn't bitch and whine, she could stay. Stay with Sebastian and Mouser, and all the other kids. She'd always have somebody to talk to, to hang out with.

Then, when she did whatever Sebastian said, maybe Mouser or Chi-Chi or somebody wanted to go out for a while. She wanted to see the city.

She had little flashes of it — icy cold, lots of lights and people — and wanted to see if she made them up or remembered something.

Maybe she didn't want to remember the woman with the angry voice, or why she'd had to hide in the dark, but this was different.

She liked having her name — Dorian — and she liked being here. She felt sure she liked being in New York even though that was blurry and cold.

She saw Sebastian in the family room, just like the night before, but today he talked to one of the kids — a

211

girl, maybe a little younger than she was — while he scooted three little red bowls around a table.

'Keep your eye on the shiny silver ball, Bets, while we go round and round. Find the ball, win five dollars.'

Then he stopped. 'Where's the ball?'

She tapped, decisively, on the middle bowl. But when he lifted it, no ball.

'But I know it was there. I watched really close.'

'Hand's quicker than the eye.' And he held out a hand with the silver ball in the palm.

'But I saw you put it under the bowl.'

'You thought you saw because I told you to see it.' Idly, he shifted the bowls around the table. 'You have to be very quick and smooth in the old shell game.' He smiled at her. 'Oops, where's the ball?'

'In your other hand.'

He held both out, empty, then lifted the left bowl to reveal it.

'But — how did you do it? Can you teach me?'

'I am.' He spotted Dorian. 'Practice awhile. You have the hands for it.'

He rose. 'Good morning. I bet you're hungry.'

'I could really eat.'

'Let's see about that.'

They had a communal kitchen with a big table, and a bigger table in the room right next to it. She knew the rules already. Everybody took care of their own dishes. If you ate the last of something, you had to tell the one in charge that week. It rotated.

'I'll take care of your breakfast this morning.'

Like a dad, she thought, and yearned. 'You don't have to.'

'You get one more day's grace,' he told her. 'How

about an egg pocket, and it looks like someone for-aged in the great city woods and found some berries.'

'That's chill. Is Mouser around? I thought maybe we could go out today. I feel a lot better.'

'That's good.' As he programmed what looked like an ancient AutoChef, he glanced around. 'Give us the kitchen for now, Howl.'

When Howl, a gangly sixteen with a mop of hair falling over his eyes, shrugged and slumped off, Dorian said, 'I don't mind if he's here while I eat.'

'I'd like to have the time and space to talk to you for now.'

At the table, she gripped her hands together in her lap. 'Did I do something wrong? I'm sorry! Don't make me go. I can —'

'Dorian, you did nothing wrong, and no one will make you go anywhere.' He set the egg pocket in front of her, and the berries, then something pretending to be orange juice.

'You said you trusted me.' He programmed coffee for himself, or what came as close to coffee as they could manage.

'I do. I really do.'

'Eat some of that now. Did you sleep better the rest of the night?'

'I didn't dream at all after. I want to do chores, like you said.'

'We'll get to all that. Doc said your ankle would be sore.'

'A little, but it's not bad. I wrapped it again like he said after I took a shower, and I can walk on it without it hurting.'

'Young bones.' He smiled at her. 'No headaches, dizziness?'

She began to relax and eat as she decided he just wanted to check on how she felt.

'Uh-uh. I want to go out and walk around, see if I remember anything, you know?'

Watching her, he sipped some coffee. 'You haven't remembered anything more?'

'Not exactly.'

He nodded, then took a 'link out of his pocket. 'I want you to look at something. Someone. And tell me — you'll be honest because we trust each other — if you remember her.'

'Okay, but I don't think I really know anybody except you guys.'

Her first thought when she looked at the screen was she liked the girl's hair, all bright and red. And then . . .

Her heart began to bang, and her skin went ice-cold. For a minute — it seemed like forever — she couldn't breathe, only gasp for air that wouldn't come.

It all fell onto her, a collapsed building hurtling down with bricks and steel and jagged glass rushing to bury her. From a distance, she heard a voice, but just kept shaking her head.

'No, no, no, no.'

'Dorian, you're safe. Dorian, no one's going to hurt you. Look at me now, just look at me.' Sebastian had a grip on her arms, kept talking as he leveled down to draw her wide, shocked eyes to his.

The panic attack ripped, turning her face sickly gray, racking her with shudders.

'You need to breathe in, breathe out.'

'Can't.'

'Yes, you can. Look at me, look right at me and breathe, nice and slow. There you go now, that's the

214

way. In and out. You're safe. I'm right here with you.' He flicked a warning glance at one of the kids who started to wander in — and sent her scuttling away again.

'Good girl. You're all right. Everything's going to be all right.'

He watched the first tear slide down her cheek and considered it an improvement over the wild-eyed shock.

'I'm going to get you some water. I'm just going right there and getting you some water.'

'I remember. I remember.'

'Yes, I can see that. Just sit, sit and breathe.'

As he got the water, he cursed himself. Had he gone too fast? Should he have given her more time? And what in God's name would he do if this child was somehow responsible or complicit in the death of another child?

He brought her the water, sat, looked at her face. And simply couldn't believe it. Yes, even children were capable of killing, he certainly knew that to be tragically true.

But not this one. Not this one with the desperate eyes shedding mournful tears.

'Can you tell me what you remember?'

'Mina.' Her hand shook as she lifted the glass, so she gripped it with both. 'Mina. I forgot.'

'What happened to Mina?'

'She got away. Did she get away? She ran, she ran so they wouldn't find me. In the rain. I fell, I fell, I hurt my leg, my ankle. I fell, I fell, and she ran so they'd run after her. We got out, we got out, but they were coming, and I fell. Did she get away?' She put the glass down with a rattle, grabbed his arm. 'Is she here? Is Mina here, like me?'

'No, she's not here. You and Mina got out? Of what? Of where?'

'Of the Academy.' Tears flooded now, and she laid her head on the table, racked by them. 'Oh God, oh God, I remember.'

She told him pieces and in fits and starts. He clamped down on his outrage, knowing if he let it come, he'd only frighten her.

Finally, she knuckled at her swollen eyes, and those eyes pleaded with him. 'Can you find her? Can you help me find her? She's going to call her parents. She said they'd come.'

He stroked her hair. 'You need to be strong. It's so much to ask after all you've been through. But you've already shown you're strong. I'm so sorry, Dorian. Mina didn't get away.'

'They caught her? No, no, we got out, and if they took her back . . .' Her face went blank, and those pleading eyes blank.

His felt his heart break as he watched something inside her die.

'She's dead, isn't she? They killed her. Those fuck-ing bastards killed her. She ran so they didn't catch me, and they killed her. I couldn't run, and now she's dead.'

'I'm sorry, more than I can say. None of this is your fault.'

'I fell and couldn't run.' Life came back to her face, but it was hard, and it was bitter. 'She helped me, and nobody ever did. Now she's dead.'

'She was brave and thought of you. You have to honor her, and the first way is to put the blame where it belongs. On the people who hurt her, and you, and

216

all the others.'

'I want to kill them.'

'I find it hard to blame you for it. Do you trust me?'

'Will you help me kill them?'

Looking into those young, bitter eyes, he sat back. 'I can't do that. As much as I understand, I can't take a life, even a vile one. I have others here who trust me, who need this safe place because they've been hurt or betrayed or abandoned. But I have another way, another way you can honor Mina, and make them pay for what they've done, what they're doing.'

'Pay how?'

'By losing everything but their lives. And that's a deeper punishment. Losing everything and having to live with the nothing. You can help take it from them, take their freedom like they took yours.'

He took her hand again, leaned toward her. 'I know someone who can help do that.'

'You.'

'In my way, but someone else.' He tried a little smile. 'Do you know who Mavis Freestone is?'

'Yeah, who doesn't? She's pretty mag, I guess. I couldn't listen to music at home, but I stole some buds so she wouldn't hear, and I listened to her sometimes.'

'She's a friend of mine.'

Some of the young girl eked back. 'Step out. She's like a total celeb, and way rich and all of it.'

'She wasn't always. Once she was like you, like the family here. A girl who needed a safe place.'

'Serious? No bull? She stayed here?'

'Not in this place. I didn't have it then, but in another.'

'But she's . . . somebody.'

'So are we all.'

'Even if, how's she going to help make them all pay? She's a singer.'

'She has a friend, a very good friend, who's police.'

Dorian snatched her hand away. 'Cops. Fuck that, fuck them. They'll ship me back to Freehell, or toss me in juvie again, and I'm not ever —'

'Hear me out. We listen to each other here, Dorian, so listen to me now. I'm going to promise you not to do anything, talk to anyone unless you agree. That's first. I promise you.'

'I'm not going to agree, so forget it. I'll leave first and take my chances.'

'They're looking for you, Dorian, these evil people, and the police.'

'Because of Mina? They don't think I —'

'I said you're safe here. And if you choose, I'll get you money and find a way to get you out of New York. But if you choose that, they will never pay, and never stop. Never pay for Mina, never stop hurting all the other girls.'

He put a hand on her cheek, gently, and felt relief when she didn't jerk away.

'It's too much, too terribly much to put on your shoulders, but that's the reality of it. Before you choose, I'm asking you to hear me out.'

'I'm not going to the cops.' She folded her arms. 'But whatever.'

'I'm going to tell you how I met this cop. Lieutenant Eve Dallas. And why her friend and mine, Mavis, brought us together. There were girls,' he began, 'like you and Mina, years ago. Someone hurt them, killed them, and hid their bodies behind a wall. One day, not very many months ago, a man broke down that wall because he wanted to build something new, something good, and those young girls, what remained of them, were found.'

★ ★ ★

At Central, Eve paced the conference room.

She'd put most of the morning into looking for ways to cut down the number of properties on Roarke's list. The problem remained he'd done too damn good a job doing that already.

It left her with far too many that could fit what she envisioned. And worse, her vision might be off.

Frustrated, she'd switched to potential victims, and began scouring files looking for that one tiny, overlooked mistake.

Now she paced. She'd find the mistake, she'd damn well find it. She'd only been through six files so far. The fact that she hadn't found it there didn't mean she wouldn't find it in any of the others.

She'd rather be out on the street, doing something that felt like action, like progress. But the simple fact remained on this one, the action and progress lived in files.

More coffee, she decided. She just needed more coffee.

She heard Peabody coming seconds before she caught the scent. She turned to see her partner carrying in two plates.

'You got pizza?'

'One pepperoni, one veggie — the veggie's my excuse to have pizza. Out of your office AC. And the only reason I got out of the bullpen alive with it is everybody knows what we're working on.'

She set them on the conference table. 'We gotta eat, Dallas. Roarke told EDD he'd be in soon, and he'd push you to eat anyway. Probably not pizza.'

Peabody had a point. And a check of the time told her morning had somehow become two in the afternoon.

Peabody pulled a tube of Pepsi out of one pocket, one of Diet out of the other.

'Time's slipping away.' Frustrated, Eve cracked the tube and drank. 'One way or the other, I've got to call the feds in tomorrow. Hell, maybe that's best. Either I'm not seeing something, or it's just not there.'

'We've hit a little wall. We'll push over it.'

Thinking of that, Eve mentally shifted back to locations. 'I'm going to have Uniform Carmichael put together a team. They can start paying the properties a visit. Just need a bullshit excuse. Community outreach should work. Just get in and sniff around. Going in knowing the possibility it's a front, you might just smell something off.'

'Couldn't hurt.'

Peabody sat, took a slice.

Giving up, Eve did the same.

'I'm wondering if some of the abductions come from scouts that root in a certain area. Service people, repair people, delivery people. Fucking cops — and I hate that one, but we have to let it in. People get used to seeing them, don't look twice.'

'Plumbers,' Peabody speculated, 'IT people, handymen who cover an area, or even if they don't, people don't usually look twice at a work truck or van driving through the neighborhood.'

The pizza hit the empty places in exactly the right way.

'Maybe you live in a neighborhood and take a kid from it,' Eve considered. 'Get the kid, drive off, travel to a pickup location, or all the way to the target area.'

'The business there would have to be a front, too,' Peabody pointed out, 'or most likely, for that to work.'

'Yeah, but if it's connected with the front here, say the outlet where they make the underwear, the uniforms. It feels smart, and this is a smart operation. You wouldn't pick up a kid every day, or even every week. You go about your business, pick the kid, and have all the time you need to watch until you hit at the right time. Street kids — the Dorian type — that's a different system.'

Pizza, Eve thought as she ate, answered almost all needs.

'Let's try this. Plumbers, like you said — so we look for a big operation here with our probabilities. Plumbing supplies, commercial plumbing operation. Same with IT. General repairs, I'm not sure what you attach that to, but we'll find it. The sewing, tailoring operation. Delivery services — plenty of big operations for that. Utility shit. You know, solar installation and repair. It's an angle.'

'I'll tell McNab to plug it in, too. The more, the better. I've got more kids, Dallas. I started on open cases where the girl didn't hit that physical beauty level. I found seventeen more, so far, from six to sixteen, that fit the abduction pattern. I'm going to put them in the categories — ages, good neighborhoods, runaways — but I needed the break.'

'Seventeen. I'm going to get Carmichael started, and hell, maybe I'll tug on Teasdale today. We've got the cracks, but we're not widening them.'

She took a second slice. 'We should've had a solid

sighting of Dorian Gregg by now if she stayed in the city, if she went back to her former territory. She's either gone, they grabbed her back, or she's dead somewhere.'

'Gone's most likely,' Peabody commented. 'She had a window before we ID'd her blood. She climbed out and booked. We could get lucky, and she'll get picked up somewhere.'

'No relying on luck there.'

She thought of herself at eight, and how terrified she'd have been if she'd ended up with federal agents surrounding her. But it was coming down to the wire on no choice there.

She pulled out her communicator, contacted Officer Carmichael, gave him the assignment, sent him the necessary data.

That, at least, felt like action, however weak.

She looked over as Willowby came in.

'Hey, thought I'd bop down from EDD and fill you in.'

She'd dressed for EDD, Eve thought, in a rainbow shirt and neon-green bibbed baggies. And bopped over on pink low-top air kicks.

'That pizza is not Vending crap.'

Eve waved a hand at it. 'Go ahead.'

'Either one,' Peabody told her. 'Or both.'

'Veggie pizza's the only way veggies go down easy. I'll take a slice of both.' She sat on the table, laid one slice over the other, and bit in. 'So, your man's up there now,' she told Eve. 'Sizzle.' She gave a little shiver. 'If you don't mind me saying.'

'You already did.'

'I got a weakness for the sizzle, and the smarts. I don't care what chromosomes somebody's got, I just

222

go for sizzle or smarts. Somebody's got both? I'm a goner. He sure has both. Anyway.'

She paused to take another bite.

'He's working with the e-geeks on this op, and I'm going to say, it could work. It'll take some doing, and some damn good cover. It's pretty late in the game for this auction, but you do get some buyers who don't move in until late in the game.'

She looked at the board, at the faces as she ate. 'If we do it right, pull it off, it could work for some of them.'

'Did you get any sleep, Willowby?'

'Zonked a few z's. Pizza's better than the z's. We're down to two days and change. I'll sleep after.' Then she gestured to the board. 'Some of the girls you've got up there are starting to pop up in more previews. If it goes the way I think, full sales kits go online by this time tomorrow. You've added some of the Kiddies.'

'Yeah, they fit the abduction pattern.'

'Fuckers. I want to take them down as much as you. The thing is, however slick, however major this organization is, there are others. The op up in EDD? Maybe, just maybe, we take down a few more.'

'How many you figure?' Eve asked her.

'On this scale?' Willowby shook her head. 'Not many, but you'll have smaller organizations, maybe holding three or four to put up for an auction like this. A few more that specialize, and likely import rather than snatch. The Brutes — just my term for it — the ones who use and abuse, then sell off — more of those, but they'd need good financing to participate in this level of auction. The entry fee's half a mil, and that's just to get in to sell. Then twenty percent of the sale price goes to the auction.'

'Seems like busting that wide would be a good move.'

'Doesn't it just? Maybe this'll give us a shot at it. It'd be a hell of a thing, wouldn't it, if these two kids blow it all down.'

'No trace of her yet? Dorian Gregg?'

'No. We're hitting on the kooks and the overeagers, but nothing that's panned out. I'm calling in the feds, tomorrow latest.'

'Shit, figured that was coming.' She ate more pizza. 'I hate to see them horn in on what we're starting up in EDD. We're going to do it clean,' she added. 'No way we're going to let any of these bastards slide out on technicalities. But feds can be harsh on a little wiggle.'

'I can't hold it off longer than that. Right now, I'm not sure I should.'

'I hear you. Whatever it takes. I'm going back to the circus. Thanks for the pizza. Most mag-o.'

As she pushed off the table, Trueheart, the earnest, tapped on the doorjamb.

'Sorry, Lieutenant.'

Even as he spoke, Willowby turned back to Eve, widened her eyes, tapped her hand on her heart.

'Detective?'

'Mavis is here. I didn't want to send her back without getting your go.'

'She got the kid with her?'

'No, sir.'

'You can send her back.'

'He's so cute!' Willowby said when he went out again. 'Got the cute sizzles. Got brains?'

'He's a solid cop, a good detective. Tamp it down

224

some, Willowby.'

'Just saying. Not married or anything, is he?'

'He's not,' Peabody filled in when Eve just closed her eyes. 'But he's just off a relationship. She took a job in East Washington. He's really sweet.'

'I like sweet, especially with cute sizzles. I'm in a serious dry spell, you know? Maybe after we bust these bastards, I can — Holy shit!'

Mavis stepped in on purple sneaks, pink skin pants, and a purple shirt that clung to her little baby bump and sported a pink arrow pointing to it that read: guess who?

Her hair was a curling mass of both colors.

She would, Eve thought, have fit in very well in EDD.

Willowby actually squealed. 'Mavis Freestone. Holy shit. I'm a mega fan.'

Mavis put on the high beams, but Eve knew her.

Something's up, she thought. Something's off.

'Thanks! Great to meet you.'

'Willowby. Zela Willowby. I hit your concert on Fire Island. Man, it was beyond. And the vid you just released, backed by Avenue A, dueting with Jake Kincade? Frosted supreme.'

'I'm babbling. Sorry.'

'Hear me complaining? Juices me to hear somebody likes my music.'

'Love it. This is a moment for me. Anyway, gotta go before I drool or something. Jesus,' she said as she headed out. 'Two sizzles and a Freestone. What a day.'

'Okay.' Mavis let out a breath, and the high beams dimmed. 'Can I shut this door?'

'Yeah. Is Bella okay, Leonardo?'

'Yeah, yeah, all totally.'

'Then come sit down and tell me what the fuck. I can see it all over you.'

'I'm going to.'

'Want some tea or something?' Peabody asked her.

'No, I'm good. All good.' She crossed over but stood looking at the board. 'So many,' she said quietly. She pressed a hand protectively over the child inside her, then sat. 'I need you to hear me all the way out, and not get pissed.'

'Why would I get pissed?'

'I just need you to listen all the way. You're looking for one of those girls, especially. Dorian Gregg.'

'That's right. What do you know?'

'If you listen all the way, and don't get pissed, I can get her to come to the house, where you can talk to her.'

Eve struggled not to lurch up and shout. 'You know where she is?'

'No, but I can do what I said if you listen, don't get pissed.'

'I need to know where she is, Mavis.'

The hand rubbing circles over the baby bump went into high speed. 'You're already pissed. I know what all this means to you, and you know what it all means to me. I know you want to know where she is to keep her safe, and to find a way to help all those girls.'

Her voice broke as she looked at the board again.

'Please, let me help that happen. I had to give my word to get this far. Solemn promise mode — most solemn. I'm going to have to ask you and Peabody to give yours to get more. But I can help, if you hear me all the way.'

'I'm listening.'

'Sebastian tagged me. She's with him.'

226

14

She wanted to explode, to spew hot, molten, electric fury, so did the opposite. She went ice-cold.

'Where is she? Where's he keeping her?'

'I don't know. Dallas —'

'Don't fuck with me, Mavis, not on this. Where's his hole?'

'I don't know! Even if I did, I couldn't tell you because I had to promise. But I don't know. It's been a bazillion years since I ran with Sebastian and his kids, Jesus, since before I met you. You know that.'

'He's holding a material witness to a murder, and the key to a hell of a lot more. What does he want for her?'

Mavis's eyes went hard, went hot. Her voice matched it.

'It's not like that. I knew I'd piss you off. I didn't figure you'd piss me off, pulling out the hard-ass goddamn cop.'

'I am a hard-ass goddamn cop. A hard-ass goddamn murder cop with a thirteen-year-old girl in the morgue.'

'Okay.' Peabody held up both hands. 'Why don't we —'

Both Eve and Mavis rounded on her with looks that burned to the bone.

Peabody lowered her hands. 'Nothing,' she muttered. 'Nothing at all.'

'You need to shut up for two damn minutes and

227

fucking listen,' Mavis snapped. 'He didn't tell me much because he wants her to tell you, get it? He didn't want it all filtered out through me. So I know one of his kids found her, and she was hurt. The kid brought her in.'

'Hurt how?'

'I don't know, okay?' Mavis snapped it back again. 'I don't. He saw the media reports, and he's been working on convincing her to talk to you.'

'So he tags you up, puts you in the middle of it.'

'Yeah, he tagged me up because he figured I'd have a better shot at getting you to agree to her conditions than he would going direct. Tell me he's wrong.'

'Conditions, my ass.'

'You're really being an asshole, so Number Two and I are going to take a walk around the room and simmer it. Peabody, could I get some water?'

'Sure.' And reading the room, Peabody left it rather than using the AC.

'He didn't tell me a lot,' Mavis continued as she walked. 'But I saw the reports, too. And he told me enough for me to figure out it's more than that poor dead girl and this scared-out-of-her-shit one. It's all these. We know what it's like.'

She turned back, eyes still hot, but brimming now. 'I don't know exactly what this is, but I can buy a fricking clue, and we know what it's like, you and me. So you're really pissed off, and I'm really pissed off. And all I can think is what if somebody took Bella, took her and hurt her, and —'

'Don't. Don't do that.' Struggling to find her calm again, Eve pressed her fingers to her eyes. 'He had no business bringing you into it, because you know what it's like, and because you'd go there.'

'You don't get pissed for me.' Mavis jabbed a finger toward Eve. 'I can do that all by and for myself. And if you stop being pissed for a minute, you know why he came to me.

'You don't have to like him. You don't have to like or get what he does. But I know without him at that point in my life, I could've been on that board. He was what I needed when I needed it. Right now he's what this girl needs.'

'What she needs is medical assistance and police protection. And those girls on the board, what they need is for her to tell me every goddamn thing she knows.'

'Great, mag, awesomelutely.' Mavis sat again, one hand running light circles over her belly. She glanced over as Peabody came back. 'Thanks. So here it is.'

She took the moment to crack the tube, sip some water.

'She's agreed — and I get the impression he had to tap dance, do backflips, and juggle at the same time — to talk to you, at a neutral location. Which is the house, our house.'

'Mavis —'

'Please.' Reaching out, Mavis took and gripped Eve's hand. 'She won't come into Central. Jesus, neither would I back in my time. But she'll meet you, talk to you at my place if you make some promises. Sebastian knows — and he's convinced her — you won't lie to me. And I won't lie to them.'

'What promises?'

'You don't arrest her. Dallas, she didn't kill that other girl.'

'I know that. Peabody?'

'Whoever did,' Peabody began, 'tried to throw it on

Dorian. We know that. She's a witness, not a suspect.'

'You have to promise not to arrest her,' Mavis repeated. 'Or send her back to her mother, or yank her into the system, a foster home, a safe house. She feels safe right now.'

'You want me to promise to let a key witness go off to an unknown location with a guy who runs a gang of kids who grift and steal?'

'It's not a gang, really. It's more a kind of family. But wait. Sebastian thinks, once she's talked to you, we'll be able to convince her to go to an official safe house until you find who murdered Dorian's friend. Especially if you let one of the kids, the kid who found her, go with her.'

'Dallas?' Peabody, very carefully, dipped a toe in again. 'First priority is to find her, talk to her, get everything she knows. We can work out the rest. EDD's still working on the op in the meantime.'

'You can't charge or arrest Sebastian, either,' Mavis said quickly. 'She trusts him, Dallas, and if you go after him for this, she's not going to trust you.'

'You know if I agree to this, I'd have to go around command for it. More, they'll know where you live, or will live.'

'I know what you think of him, but I know what I know. Sebastian would never do anything to hurt me or mine. And guess what? That includes your stubborn ass.

'We've both been hurt and alone. How scared were we?'

This time Eve pushed up to pace. Maybe, okay maybe, what ran through her was primarily anger, and a knee-jerk distrust of the man Mavis put her faith in. Beyond that, it blurred so many lines, left too many gaps.

And yet. Those faces on the board. All those faces. And the young girl in a drawer in the morgue.

'How do you know Dorian and Mina Cabot were friends?'

'He told me they made a pact, and they ran together, but got separated. That's all he said about it because he wants her to tell you.'

It fit, she admitted, with her own deductions.

'If we agree to this, he gets one shot. If she balks, if she lies, deal's off.'

'That's fair.'

'When?'

'We can set it up as soon as I tell him you gave me your word. I gotta say something else.'

'Sure, hell, why not?'

'I know what you think of him, and I get it. But he was upset, really shaken. I can figure what this is, at least some of it. And I can tell you he wants whoever's doing this as much as you do. If this didn't work, he was going to talk her into making a recording for you, laying it all out. But he wants her to talk to you direct, you know? For her to see you, for you to see her. But either way, he wants to get you what you need to catch these bastards. Enough, he's putting himself on the block for it.'

'I don't like you in the middle.'

Smiling now, Mavis rose, walked over, wrapped around Eve. 'How about I tell you if I help you help this girl, all these girls, I'll feel solid on it. Could've been me, could've been you. Let me help fix it.'

'Tag him back.'

'You have to say it.'

'Christ. Fine. You've got my word.'

'Peabody?'

'You've got mine.'

'Okay. Most of the crews on the house will knock off soon, so I'm going back, and getting the nanny to come in, take Bellamina to the park. I don't want her around this.'

'What nanny?'

'We hired August — you can run him if it makes you feel better, but Peabody already did.'

'August Fuller,' Peabody said. 'Age fifty-eight, Special Forces, retired. Divorced, one offspring, male, age twenty-six, captain, army intelligence, who is currently dating Mavis's head of security's daughter. They're clean.'

'And this guy wants to be a nanny?'

'He said it was time for some light and bright in his life, and he missed too much of his son's growing up time. It's just on-call mostly for now. But he's more than a sitter, so nanny.'

'Okay, make the contacts.'

'You won't be sorry. I've got a good feeling about it. Give me a few.'

When she walked out to make the contacts, Eve headed straight for coffee. 'I can't say I've got a good feeling about it.'

'I think I'm somewhere between the two of you. But like you always say, every detail matters. She's going to give us a lot of details.'

'Maybe.'

She gulped down coffee as Roarke came in.

'Did you get it set up?'

'For the most part, yes, and Feeney's filling in the gaps. I thought I'd leave it to them for now and see what I could do about the location search.' He glanced

232

back. 'I saw Mavis in what seemed a very intense 'link conversation.'

'Yeah, there's that happening.' And Eve considered. He'd met Sebastian, and he sure as hell knew every angle of every con. Maybe she didn't really suspect one here, but . . .

'We may not need the location search. We've got a line on Dorian Gregg.'

'Well now, that's excellent news, and yet you don't look pleased about it.'

'I don't like the catches and contingencies. Sebastian — Mavis's Sebastian — found her. Or she found him. Unclear at the moment.'

'Ah.'

'Yeah, ah. I think maybe you should come along for this. You've got a rhythm with him I don't. It could be we have to convince him Dorian needs a safe house to get her to go in one.'

'How long has she been with him?'

'Unclear. Damn it. He didn't tell Mavis enough to give me a jump, and claims he wants the story to come straight from the kid.'

'That would make good sense, actually.'

'Yeah, but —' She broke off as Mavis came back. 'Roarke's going with us on this.'

'Sure, but he has to promise.'

'Fuck it all, Mavis, he can't arrest anybody. He's not a cop.'

'And thank the gods for it' was Roarke's fervent opinion.

Mavis laid one hand on her belly, the other on her hip. 'He has to promise anyway.'

Eve pressed her fingers to her eyes, breathed in what she could of calm. 'Fine. Roarke give Mavis your word you'll stick to the deal I made.'

'I'm to give my word on a deal without knowing what I'm giving my word on?'

'I'll fill you in,' Eve snapped. 'Just give it.'

Ignoring Eve, he turned to Mavis. 'Do you need this?'

'Yeah, sorry, but yeah.'

'Then you have it. I'll adhere to what the lieutenant's agreed to.'

'Mag. Whew. We need about an hour. I really want Bella away from the house, plus the crew'll be gone. Better that way. I'll go on back now, and you can come in like an hour.'

'Peabody, go with Mavis.'

'You don't trust me!'

'I trust you. I just don't know enough about all the rest to feel good about you heading back alone. That's all. Peabody's with you.'

'Okay, iced. They're into the master baths, Peabody.' Mavis pointed at Peabody, at herself, then shot two thumbs up.

'Oh boy, oh boy!' Peabody scrambled up. 'Can't wait.'

'Well, cha,' Mavis said. 'See you soon.' She glanced at the faces on the board one last time. 'You're doing the right thing.'

As she walked out with Mavis, Peabody glanced back at Eve and mouthed, *I've got her.*

After they'd gone, Roarke turned to Eve. 'All right then, what did I just give my word on?'

Eve scrubbed her hands over her face. 'I hope to all those gods you called on it's the right thing.'

And told him.

He listened, waited, watched her pace it off.

234

'I understand completely why you distrust the man, and feel you're being pressured — with Mavis as the vise — to agree to something that doesn't feel quite right to you.'

'You're going to say 'but,' and I'm going to want to punch you for saying 'but.''

'But,' he said, nonetheless, 'you know she's alive. You know she wasn't found by the people who abducted her, held her, who killed Mina Cabot. However you feel about Sebastian, she has been and is safe.'

'And we've devoted how many men, how many hours into finding her while he's had her hidden away? It's very likely she started running with his gang when she got into New York last year. Then she goes poof, but he doesn't report it. Those kids come and go — how many come to hard ends?'

'That's one way to look at it. Another is, at least for a time, they have somewhere to go where they're not beaten, raped, or otherwise abused. You have your stand on it,' he continued, 'and it's natural for you. Mine's a bit more flexible. Regardless, Eve, you'll soon know what she knows.'

'That's the only thing keeping me from kicking him in the balls.'

'Let me give you something to lighten the mood you're completely entitled to.'

She shot him a simmering look. 'You're pandering.'

'Well, I am, but it seems fair enough. On the other hand, in addition to the profile Willowby — who's a sharp one — already established, we have three more. And, not to bang my own drum too loudly, they'll stand. Each has a nice deep financial pool to dip into — varying amounts, of course,' he continued, as he got coffee for himself.

Fizzies equaled the drink of choice in the EDD lab, and he'd had enough fake sugar for the next six months.

'Varying backgrounds as well, and some with a whiff of trouble with law enforcement. Some with a history, minutely created, of pedophilia and/or purchasing from other outlets.'

'That's quick work.'

'Time was a factor, after all. And now the team in EDD is working with some hack we devised. More work there, but we've enough time, I think, to complete it. And if so, we'll be able to hack into other buyers' accounts, pull out the information you'll need to break this all down.'

'Or the feds will.'

'I'm sorry?'

'Hey, me, too. But tomorrow, I call them in. I'm going to push hard for a joint op with the NYPSD in the lead. I can make a case for that, especially if we're able to hand over data that turns into arrests — by those feds — outside of New York. And more, that leads to finding and rescuing victims — these and, with more luck, at least some who came before.'

She drank coffee, paced. 'Dorian changes some of it, maybe. She gives us the New York location, we put together an op to take them down — without alerting the auction, the other buyers. We can work on that. We can make that happen. We put EDD on it, inside the location, keep up the appearances of the sales. We could hand the data to the feds for an assist there if we need it. We locate the auction site, the people involved there.'

'Thinking ahead.'

'Yeah, I'm thinking ahead. It's like that thing with

the things.' She held up her hand, made a space in the air with her thumb and forefinger.

Roarke decided he knew her mind as well as he knew his own when he understood. 'Dominoes.'

'Yeah, yeah, those things. Line them up right, knock one down, and they all fall. We just have to line it up right, knock down the right one.'

In under two days, she thought. But no pressure.

'Then let's consider finding Dorian this way a stroke of luck.' When she snarled, he smiled. 'You worried for her. You dreamed of her and worried. She's alive and safe. You'll help keep her that way. Meanwhile.'

He glanced at the time.

'I'll let Feeney know I'm on a related project with you.'

'You can't tell him about Dorian. I'm not bringing more people into the gray area mess of this.'

'And I won't. I can work with them remotely, come back in, or set up the team in the home lab. Whatever seems best. We'll know more, won't we, after we talk to the young witness?'

'Let's walk over there. It'll help clear my head. We should probably have a vehicle, but I need to walk.'

'We'll walk, then walk back for it. I'll just sign off with Feeney.'

'Do that. I need to swing through the bullpen.'

When they started out, using the glides, as she needed physical room as well as head space, she considered how to handle a teenage witness, a likely traumatized one.

'If I push her too hard, she'll pull back. If I don't push her enough, she'll leave things out we need. I'm going by her history with cops and authority,' Eve added.

'You'll find the way, and there's Peabody to soften it up if need be.'

'Kids are tough. Especially . . . I should bring Mira in.'

'And I agree, but take this round first. The girl's already outnumbered, isn't she?'

'Plus, I'd have to ask Mira to take this goddamn oath. It just puts her in a squeeze. Mavis is getting the kid out — Bella — and that's the right call. She's got some guy cruising toward sixty, used to be Special Forces, doing the nanny thing.'

'August.'

As they walked outside, Eve stared at him. 'You know about that?'

'I met him, briefly, a few days ago when I went by the house to check on things. Bella's very happy with him.'

'Peabody ran him.'

'Of course.'

'You did, too.'

'Of course. I'd have mentioned it, but it slipped my mind, and we've been busy the last couple of days.'

'You should be at your fancy office in Midtown.'

He took her hand before she could avoid it. 'I've been there. All's well. And I admit the challenge of this particular op has been very satisfying. I detest the reason it's needed, but the work itself? Fascinating.'

'How many laws have you broken?'

'Not a one — after I took the template of it all in to Feeney. I may have bent a few to get there.'

'I'm bending a few right now,' she muttered.

'Not laws,' he corrected. 'Regulations. They may come to the same to you, but you'll soon bend them right back again.'

238

'If she refuses to go into a safe house . . . Not an option,' Eve decided. 'We have to convince her. I've got a thought on that, now that I'm thinking.'

'I'll pray to those gods that thought isn't bringing her home with us.'

'Jesus, no. No way in hell. She's a victim, sure, and a wit, but she's also a troublemaking hard case. I've got an idea what might work. Maybe.'

She glanced toward the playground as they reached it. Bella, in her pink-and-blue shorts, her sunny curls flying, squealed as a man pushed her on a swing.

He looked fit, Eve observed, with his sturdy boxer's build and carved biceps flexing. He wore jeans and a T-shirt, and his hair close to the skull. Like his body, his face was carved, sharp angles with deep brown skin tight over them.

Sunshades hid his eyes, but his lips curved in an easy smile as he pushed, with apparently inexhaustible patience, the little girl on the swing.

'He looks military,' Eve observed. 'And like if anybody tried to mess with Bella, he'd chew them up, then spit out their gnawed bones.'

'Mavis took the body found here to heart. He's as much bodyguard for Bella as nanny. More, I'd say.'

'Good then. That's good.'

As she spoke, Bella spotted them.

'Das! Ork! Das! Ork!'

She tried to scramble out of the safety seat, then lifted her arms to August as she babbled with glee.

He hefted her, then with a nod to them, set her down so she could run.

When she reached them, Bella wrapped around Eve's legs, then tried climbing up them.

'Okay. Okay.' Eve hauled her up, received wet,

239

enthusiastic kisses in return.

'Wing! Wing with Aug.'

'Yeah, I got that.'

'Lieutenant, I'm August Fuller. Roarke, good to see you again.'

'Aug,' Bella said, beaming. 'Wing Das, Aug. Wing Das!'

'Yeah, well, thanks, but we've got to work.'

'Aw!' She gave Roarke a side-eye with a flirtatious smile. 'Wing, Ork.' Then patted his cheek.

'You're hard to resist, darling, but I have to go with Dallas.'

'Aw.'

'Why don't you show them how you can slide?'

'Whee!' She scrambled down. 'See, see, see!' And ran to the little slide.

Eve thought of the dream she'd had where the child she'd been discovered the thrill of a slide.

Bella wouldn't dream such dreams, she thought. Because she lived them.

She watched Bella climb the steps to the smallest slide, settle her butt, lift her hands high, and squeal all the way down. Laughing her crazy laugh, she raced around to do it all again.

'She's a pistol, that girl. I won't let anything happen to her, believe me. The kid stole my heart inside five minutes.'

'Are you from New York, Mr. Fuller?'

'Me, no. I'm from nowhere, really. But my son lives here, and I'm trying to make up for some lost time. You can't get it back, but you can try to make up for it. Landed a bonus with Bella. She sure brings the sun to a cloudy day.

'Come say goodbye, Bella. Dallas and Roarke have

240

to go to work. Good luck,' he added. 'I don't know what's going on, but I know it's something. So good luck.'

When they finally got away, Eve nodded. 'He's solid. Good choice. I figured if they ever went for somebody to help out there, it'd be some fresh-faced girl the kid would run all over and back again.'

'If they'd gone with fresh-faced, I believe she'd have had martial arts training and a security background.'

'You're right. They're careful. Now they'll have two cops living on premises, a security system you designed, and this August guy in addition to the security team when Mavis has a gig.'

'Still you worry a bit.'

'Only because she does shit like she's doing now.'

When they approached the gates, she paused, looked through them. 'They've got actual grass now, and some of those flowery things Peabody's been dying to put in. A couple trees.'

'Considerable work done on the backyard as well, and the interior. Still a work in progress, but progress is moving right along. Even a bit ahead of schedule, though that may change.'

He pressed the intercom, entered a code. 'We're at the gate. We walked.'

'Two seconds!' Mavis's voice came through clear.

The gates opened, and once again taking Eve's hand, Roarke walked through.

'They'll want you to see some of that progress, before or after. Pressed for time, I know, but take a moment or two. Their hearts are in this place, and it shows already.'

'I don't know how this is going to go, so I can't promise. But I can say it all looks great, amazing,

241

mag, whatever.'

'There's a start.'

Mavis came out, stood on the porch as they walked up the drive. 'You're a little early, but they're on their way. I promise. You can take a look around some, right? The kitchens are basically done. They're both abso-mag.'

'Relax,' Eve ordered. 'I gave my word.'

'I know, I know. I still got jitteries.'

She pulled Eve inside. 'Looking good, right?'

Eve saw mostly empty space, a lot of tarps, tools neatly organized, workbenches, some strips of paint on a wall.

And light, a lot of light.

'This part's not much different from when you saw it last, but come back. Okay, they've gutted the powder room, and started — what's it — stripping down and repairing the molding and stuff in I think it'll be like a music room maybe. Or a sitting-type room or reading-type room. I keep changing my mind.

'But back here! Ta-de-da-de-dah!'

Color. It saturated. The light poured through the glass wall in the rear and saturated the saturation.

The counters, enough acreage of them to feed a battalion of starving soldiers, softened the bold — a little — in a creamy, lightly blue-grained white. The tiles behind them formed a crazed but visually stunning patchwork of colors. Eve couldn't think of any left out, with the reds, blues, greens, yellows. Orange and pink and everything else.

The cabinets above them picked up the theme, with some glass fronted to break it up.

It should've been too much, Eve thought, and yet it was just right. It was Mavis.

242

The walls picked up the faint blue graining in the counters, and woodwork gleamed, rich and natural. Light fixtures dripped with teardrops in all the colors.

They'd gone down to the original wood on the floors, and it worked.

Somehow it all worked.

Add the eating space to one side, the lounging space on the other, where sofas and chairs already lived, and it was somehow perfect.

'Okay, wow.'

Mavis bounced on her toes. 'Do you mean it, or is that covering 'Holy shit, what's she done?''

'No, I mean it. It's completely you. It's stupid happy.'

'I am stupid happy.' Sobbing with it, she threw her arms around Eve. 'With hormones! I love it so much. We can't stay here yet. Too much for Bella to get into, and too much left to be done. But when we get the screen installed in the lounge, we're having a vid night and snuggling on the couch. Oh, my studio. You should —'

She broke off when the gate signaled.

'Okay, okay, that's going to be Sebastian. Let me open the gates.'

'I'll do it,' Roarke told her.

'Thanks. I'll tell Leonardo — he's upstairs doing some organizing in his design center — which is total. And Peabody. She just went next door to bask a little.'

'Get Leonardo,' Eve said. 'I'll text Peabody.'

'Okay.' But she gripped Eve's hand again. 'It could've been you or me, remember.'

'I've got it.'

15

She didn't have to like it, Eve thought as she signaled Peabody. She just had to get the details, the location, all the information she could out of the kid. Then secure the kid safely.

And they outnumbered her, Roarke had that right, Eve thought. So she scoped out the area, considered the best way to conduct the interview. Whatever she thought of Sebastian, Eve admitted — and she didn't think much — he'd brought Dorian in, or this version of in.

If, as seemed apparent, he had Dorian's trust, Eve determined to use him in any way possible.

'I can hear the wheels turning in there.' Roarke tapped the side of Eve's head. 'I don't suppose it would do any good to suggest you handle this a bit organically?'

'Organically, my ass. I'm already over a line here. I can justify it, but I've crossed it. The kid sits in that chair, I take that one, facing her. Peabody in the third. You and the rest on that big-ass couch.'

'You don't want her leaning too heavily on Sebastian.'

'No, I don't.' She turned as the glass doors opened and Peabody hustled in. 'You there, kid there,' Eve said. 'When we need the soft touch, come into it.'

She heard the murmur of voices, turned again. Waited.

Leonardo, tall as a tree in his long red shirt, towered

over the rest. His hair, a gleaming copper, tumbled down, and eyes nearly the same color were dark with concern.

Eve hoped the look she sent him — *we've got this* — settled his nerves.

She flicked a glance at Sebastian, saw worry on his aesthetic face, and his hand loosely curled around the girl's arm.

She favored her left leg a bit, Eve noted, but otherwise looked fit, even strong. Longer hair than in her ID shot, and carrying some expertly done highlights, deep gold against the raven black.

Resentment and defiance simply radiated from her. No less than expected.

'Dorian,' Sebastian began, 'this is Lieutenant Dallas.'

'Yeah, I know. If you try to send me back —'

'Dorian.' Sebastian spoke again, gently.

She only shrugged.

'Let's get you a drink.' Leonardo, obviously struggling to play host, gave her a wide smile. 'Do you like fizzies?'

'I like them okay. Cherry mostly.'

'All right. Sebastian?'

'Just water, thank you.' He aimed a look at Dorian.

She did a half eye roll. 'Yeah, thanks.'

'Take a seat.' Eve gestured Dorian to the chair. 'Sebastian.' And to the next. Though it grated, she nodded to him. 'I appreciate you bringing Dorian here to talk to us.'

'She's been through an ordeal.'

'I'm aware. We've been looking for her for a couple days because we're aware.'

He simply held up his hands, let them fall, then

took his seat.

'You can just blow off giving him grief about it,' Dorian snapped. 'I'm only here because he talked me into it. And he said you swore you wouldn't send me back to Freehold. I'm not living in that rathole with my mother anymore. If you try —'

'Your mother's not living in that rathole anymore because I arrested her, and she's currently living in a jail cell. Take a seat.'

Dorian's eyes narrowed. 'What do you mean you arrested her?'

'I mean I put her in cuffs, charged her with multiple offenses, and handed her over to the Freehold PD. Now sit down.'

'What offenses?' But she sat, and so did Eve.

'Child abuse and neglect, and since she continued to collect the professional parent stipend after you took off, failed to report you missing, fraud. You should know your neighbors stood up for you.'

'Tiffy, sure, but —'

'All of them. They'd also reported the abuse and neglect to CPS through Truman.' At Dorian's snort, Eve nodded. 'And now Truman's been fired. It'll be up to the PA, following an internal investigation at CPS, if she's also charged and arrested.'

Dorian took the fizzy from Leonardo, muttered a thanks, but kept narrowed, suspicious eyes on Eve.

'It's easy to say all that shit. Cops lie all the time.'

'Believe it or don't. You left home sometime in August. We're unsure of the exact date.'

'I don't know. Who remembers? I'd had enough of getting knocked around, and getting the eye from the guys she dated. I can take care of myself.'

'If that were true, you wouldn't have been grabbed

off the streets. When and how did that happen?'

'It wasn't my fault a couple assholes jumped me.'

'When and how?'

'How the hell do I know? I was just walking.'

'Night or day?'

'Night. I was just looking at the Christmas lights and all, minding my own. Somebody jabbed me with something from behind, and . . . I don't remember, okay? I think I tried to run, but my legs wouldn't work, and I passed out. In a van or truck. I don't know. Nobody gave a shit anyway. Nobody until . . .'

'Mina?'

'You don't get to talk about her.' Rage reared up, burning at the tears. 'You don't know anything about it. You don't know what it's like and don't give a flying fuck. She's dead. And you're just another asshole cop who thinks she's some big deal and can do whatever the hell she wants. I got beat most days all my life, then I got out, and I could do what I wanted. Then I got smacked and shocked and had stuff stuck up inside me, and you don't know. You don't care. You're just one more bitch trying to push me around because you can.'

'Where did they take you?'

'Just fuck you.'

'That's it.' Mavis, leading with her baby belly, surged off the sofa and rounded on Dorian. 'You don't get to speak to her that way, not in my home.'

'I don't want to be in your damn home.'

'Well, you are, and you'll show some goddamn respect.'

'Mavis,' Eve began, but Mavis snapped back at her.

'You be quiet.' And to Dorian she continued. 'She puts her life on the line every single day. She works

247

herself into the ground to help someone like you because she does know. You think you've had it rough, well, join the crowd. I asked her to give her word, and she did. If she wasn't who she was, Sebastian would be in lockup right now, and you'd be in a box at Cop Central.'

'Okay.' Eve started to rise. 'Let's just —'

'I'm not finished! Sebastian asked me to go to Dallas, so I did, and when I did, she and Peabody had dozens of faces, young girls like you, on their board. Girls they're trying to find, to help, because nobody in this nasty damn world cares more. Consider yourself lucky she's the one who stood over your friend, who's working to find out who hurt her and killed her, because she won't stop until she does.'

She took a long breath. 'This is my home. And you won't sit here and speak to my friend that way. Apologize.'

Eve started to speak again, got a laser flash out of Mavis's eyes, and kept silent.

'Jesus, lady.'

'I said apologize.'

'Fine, sure. Sorry. Jesus.'

Now Eve got to her feet. 'Here's an idea. How about the rest of you get some air, and give Dorian and me the room for a few minutes?'

'Sebastian said he'd stay with me.'

'And I'll be right outside. I think some air is just the thing. You've vented your spleen, Dorian, now be the smart girl I know you are, and listen.'

'Peabody, you, too. A few minutes,' Eve added. As she waited for the room to clear, she sat again.

Let the silence hang.

Dorian broke first.

'Man, she's like totally whacked. I thought —'

'Say another thing about Mavis Freestone,' Eve invited. 'Go ahead.'

Dorian shrugged, looked away.

'I've got a feeling,' Eve said, 'just a feeling right now because I don't have any firm data, that Mina would've stood up for you that way. I've been friends with Mavis a long time. Busted her the first time I met her.'

That got a glimmer of interest. 'No shit?'

'She was grifting back then. Older than you, but she'd have recognized your mother. So would I. Anyway, we've been friends a long time. You and Mina didn't have that chance. They tried to frame you for her murder.'

'What?'

'They tried to make it look like you killed her. Planted some of your blood on her body. That's how we ID'd you.'

Dorian bared her teeth. 'You think I killed Mina.'

'Is that what I said? I said they tried to make it look that way. I'm good at my job, and so's my partner. No, I don't think you killed Mina. I know you didn't. If she meant a damn to you, help me find the ones who did so I can stop them from hurting all the others.'

'I don't know!' The tears rolled now. 'I can't remember mostly, and I don't know anyway.'

'Tell me what you do know, what you do remember.'

'I got away from her, and I got to New York. I liked it. I can take care of myself, I can. I was. I found places to sleep.'

'You hooked up with Sebastian?'

'Not then, no, no. That was after. I was just walking, and they got me, and the next thing I knew . . . Can he come back? Can Sebastian come back? Please. I already told him when I remembered. When he showed me Mina's picture and I remembered. He can help me.'

'All right, but no more bullshit, Dorian.'

Eve went to the open doors, signaled. 'We're all good here.' She waited, then put her arms around Mavis. 'Appreciate it,' she murmured. 'But you were pretty scary.'

'She better straighten up or I got more.'

'I've got it. Keep calm for Number Two.'

Eve went back, sat again. 'Tell me.'

'I felt sick and dizzy, and I was in this room. Like a hospital room or something. And — God — Sebastian. Can you, please?'

'She told me when she came to, she was naked, strapped down, and there was a man — he was the doctor they used — examining her. Verifying virginity, taking blood.'

'I fought, and I screamed, but they gave me something else and I passed out again. Then I was in another room, and I had on some kind of nightgown, but I was strapped down again, and she was there.'

'Who?'

'Auntie. That's what we had to call her. She was in charge of the Academy.'

'The Academy.'

'They kept us there. You couldn't see outside, you couldn't go outside. You got locked in at night. She said I belonged to the Academy now, and if I was good, if I obeyed the rules and improved myself — shit like that? — I'd be treated really well. I'd have good food, good clothes, I'd learn manners, learn to be well-groomed. I'd eventually get my own pretty room, my own private bathroom. I'd be educated.

'I told her to fuck off and let me go. She jabbed me with a shock stick. I yelled at her, and she shocked me again, and again, until I stopped. It hurts so bad.'

'I know.'

'She didn't let me out for — I don't know how long. They had needles in me — for nutrition, she said. When I learned to behave, I'd get real food. So I said I would be, I pretended, and I got a uniform. You had to wear it during the day unless you were in the studio or had the sex classes.'

She knuckled her eyes. 'They made you take off your clothes, or wear underwear and stuff so they could take pictures and vids. I tried to get away, but you couldn't, and you'd get the stick, or they'd put you back in a room, the Meditation Box, in the dark, alone, locked in until whenever. They made you get into bed with another girl and sometimes a man and do things. I didn't want to.'

'How many girls, Dorian? Can you tell me?'

'I don't know, but a lot. They'd bring in new ones, and younger ones. Just little kids, and they were so scared. Or they walked around like droids, you know? We had to learn how to take care of our bodies, our hair, our skin — their way. If we screwed up, the stick. Even if you didn't, sometimes one of them jabbed you anyway. They liked to.'

'How many of them?'

'I don't know. We were on the Pretty Ones floor, and there were day matrons and night matrons. Usually one at night. And instructors. And the doctor, and some men — like guards. You had classrooms, I guess, and some of the girls from other floors got brought in for some of it, but they didn't sleep on our level.'

She hitched in a breath, let it shudder out. 'Can I have another fizzy? It makes my throat burn to talk about it. I'm sorry about before. I'm sorry.'

'Sure.' Mavis rose. 'I've got it, honey bear,' she told Leonardo, then crouched down in front of Dorian. 'I'm so sorry about what happened to you. They're evil. They're not even people, they're just made of evil. You leave it to Dallas and Peabody. They'll make them pay for all of it.'

'Do you need a minute?' Eve asked Dorian.

'No. I want to get it out. I want it over. I couldn't get away. There wasn't any way to get out, and I just mostly stopped fighting. They told us how we'd get rich masters and live in beautiful places. How lucky we were.'

She hitched in breaths as Mavis brought her another fizzy. Drank deep, breathed out.

'I'm not stupid, I knew what all that meant. I thought maybe when it happened, I'd kill myself if I couldn't get away. Then Mina . . . I — I never had a friend like her before, not like Mina. She helped me, she talked to me, and it all felt better. She said we'd find a way out, and how her parents would help me. She has a little brother, and a family, and . . .'

She gripped the fizzy in both hands and rocked.

'Do you want me to finish it for you?' Sebastian asked her.

'No, no, I'm going to say it. Honor her, like you told me to.' Dorian swiped at her cheeks, drank again. 'She figured out a plan. It was scary, but she figured it out. I had to steal the elevator pass from the night matron — that was my part, because I'm good at that.

And she faked being sick so they'd take her down to the infirmary. I had to sneak out, go down in the elevator. If they caught us . . . But it was a good plan. She puked on the night nurse and put gum on the lock of the sickroom. And we met up at the elevators and went all the way down to the tunnels.'

'Tunnels?' Eve repeated.

'They brought girls in that way, and took out — Some of the girls died. Killed themselves, or they hurt them too much, and they took them out that way. We didn't know where to go in them. We didn't even know where we were, okay? We didn't know we were in New York or, you know, freaking Alaska.

'We got down there and walked and walked, then we heard them coming, and we ran. There was a ladder on the wall, and we started up. But I fell. I fell and ruined everything.'

The words tumbled out now as she rocked and rocked.

'Mina got me out, and we hid, and it was raining so hard, but they were coming. I couldn't run, so she did. She said she'd run and lead them away, and she'd get her parents to come and come back for me. She ran so they wouldn't find me, and I heard her scream, but when I tried to get up and run to help, my leg . . . I fell and I hit my head.

'When I woke up, I didn't know what happened. I didn't remember any of it. I just hurt so much, and I didn't know where I was. I walked and walked, and I stole some ice packs and meds and hid. I was so cold, so hot, so sick. And Mouser found me, and took me to Sebastian. He helped me. It's not his fault, because I didn't remember Mina or Auntie or anything. He helped me and nobody but Mina ever had before.'

253

'I saw the news reports.' Sebastian looked at Eve. 'And put some of it together. I know my word is difficult for you to take, but you have my word Dorian didn't remember until I showed her Mina's picture.'

'I have no reason to doubt that.' Not when she'd lived it. 'It's hard, Dorian. I'm going to need to get as many details as you can remember about where they held you. Any names — other girls, the people who work there. I need the exact location where Mouser found you, so we can try retracing your steps. We're going to stop them, we're going to help all the others. You're going to make sure that happens. You and Mina are why we're going to be able to stop them.'

'Auntie has a partner.' Dorian sniffled, wiped at tears. 'Mina heard her talking to him. Mina was good at pretending, and Auntie liked her. She was like a favorite.'

'Do you know the partner's name?'

'No. Nobody used names. I was Trainee 238. I was a number.'

'They only tried to make you believe that.' Roarke spoke for the first time. 'You've never been a number. You're an incredibly brave young woman, and you bested them.'

'They killed Mina.'

'We'll make them very sorry for it.'

'Tell me about the tunnels.'

Dorian looked back at Eve. 'They were big, I guess, and dark, like a yellowy light. We just guessed which way to go, because we didn't know. I don't remember. I just don't. And they were coming, we could hear them coming, so we ran and tried to be quiet. And there was the ladder, but it was old and slippery, and I fell.'

'What was it like when you came up?'

'It was raining really hard, and we couldn't see, and we were scared. There were buildings, but we didn't know where we were, okay? There was all this old wood and stuff.'

'Wood?'

'Like broken boards or whatever, I don't know. We tried to hide, but we could hear them, and they were looking for us. And Mina told me to stay down, stay quiet, and she'd run. She picked up one of the boards, a pointy one. I said no, but she said she'd run fast and get her parents, but . . .'

'Like a construction site?' Eve prompted. 'Like a place where they pull old stuff out of old buildings and pile it up?'

'I guess maybe. I don't know!'

'Okay, okay. You fell down again,' Eve reminded her. 'And hit your head. When you woke up, what did you do?'

'It's all fuzzed up. I hurt so bad, everywhere, and I didn't know what happened, or where I was. I felt really sick, and I . . . I used one of the boards, I think, like a crutch so I could walk, and I walked. I don't know where. I kept walking, and I stole the meds, and I kept walking because I wanted to hide. I just knew I had to hide.'

'All right. Okay, let's go back some. Tell me more about this Auntie.'

'She's mean and horrible and everybody's scared of her. She pretends to be nice, if you do everything she wants, but she's not.'

'Can you describe her? How old, Black, white, Asian, mixed, anything. How tall, anything.'

Dorian sat back and sucked on the fizzy. 'I guess.

I can see her in my head. I'm always going to see her in my head. She's taller than me. Taller than the night matron bitch.'

Eve got to her feet. 'Taller than me?'

Dorian angled her head to the side. 'Maybe about the same, but bigger. I mean, you're kind of skinny. She isn't. Big boobs and all. White, I think. Maybe a little mixed, but mostly white, with really blond hair she always wore kind of pulled back.'

'What color are her eyes?'

'They're blue, but not like his.' She looked at Roarke. 'They're dark and mean.'

'Good. Here's what I need. I have somebody who can draw her if you describe her.'

'I don't know how —'

'He does. It's what he does. He's not mean. And if he can draw her picture, we'll get her name. We'll find her.'

'Just from that?'

'It'll go a long way. And if you can describe anyone else, but we're going to start with her. She's in charge.'

'Totally. She has an office, and she wears fancy suits, and everybody does what she says.'

'Okay. Here's what else. I have some pictures, and I need you to look at them. If you recognize anybody, if any of them were or are at this Academy, you can tell us.'

'What's going to happen?'

'We're going to do our jobs, and you're going to help. And you?' Eve shifted to Sebastian. 'I need the location where this other kid found her. Exact location, exact — or as close as you can get — time.'

'A building on Watts off Hudson — condemned. I'll get you the precise location. Mouser brought

256

Dorian in yesterday, about eleven in the morning. She was feverish, dehydrated. She had a concussion, a severely sprained ankle, and a dislocated knee. We got her medical attention. Yes,' he said before Eve could speak, 'you would say we should have taken her to a hospital or health center, but she was terrified, and said no. My sense was she hadn't had a choice before, and I gave her one.

'She remembered nothing at first,' he added. 'Then remembered her name. Her first name. She came to you of her own volition when she remembered the rest.'

'No, I didn't. Not really,' Dorian said. 'I didn't want to, but Sebastian said I had to honor my friend. Honor Mina, and help the others. If you're mean to him, I won't talk to the artist person. I just won't.'

'You will,' Sebastian corrected, 'because you're not going to let all the other girls go through what you and Mina did. So you will. Don't disappoint me, Dorian.'

'We're going to start with this. Peabody, contact Yancy, see when he can work with Dorian. Contact Feeney, have him factor in what we've got. Piles of old wood, possible construction site or derelict buildings, tunnels.'

'I'm on it.' Peabody rose. 'Dorian, what Roarke said — about being brave. It's true. You're doing the hard here.'

When Peabody left, Eve pulled out her PPC. 'I want to show you some pictures.'

'Why don't I set up the screen,' Roarke began, 'so she can see them that way? It'll be clearer than your portable.'

'Great, do that.'

Dorian sent Roarke a look as he walked over to the

257

wall screen. 'He can do that? He's wearing a suit and stuff.'

'He can do that. He's wearing a suit because he can do that and a lot more. Let's take a walk.'

'I'm not leaving Sebastian.'

'Just outside. He has my word, and so do you.'

'Her word's as good as they come,' Sebastian assured Dorian. 'Remember the girls behind the wall. Go with the lieutenant, and listen.'

He got an eye roll, but Dorian walked out with Eve.

'I'm going to show you those photos. But until we get to that, do that listening thing.'

Eve looked out at the gardens already just beginning, at the play area just cleared, at the tumble of rocks and lines of pipes that would be, she knew, Peabody's water feature.

Home was where you made it.

'You can't go back with Sebastian.'

'I can do what I want.'

'No, you really can't, but — Shut the hell up and listen. But I can give you some damn good choices. First, I'm going to make sure you never have to go back to your mother. I can find a way around you going into foster if you're against it. I said shut up,' she repeated when Dorian started to interrupt. 'I was in the system once — it can work, but it depends on who's in charge. Now I am the system, so I'm going to make it work for you.'

'Why?'

'Because it's my job. And because I've been where you are.'

'How?'

'Not your business, so that's all you get.'

Eve turned, stared into the young defiance.

258

'They're after you, know that, fear that, and believe me. If they find you, they'll do one of two things. Kill you outright, or sell you. Either way, you're done. That's not going to happen.'

'There're more of them than you.'

'You think it's just me? I'm in charge, and there's not a cop under me who wouldn't put his life on the line for you. And one of your choices is a safe house — a place to stay where they can't find you, with cops I pick to watch out for you. That's one choice. I got another, and if you're smart, you'll grab it.'

'What?'

'There's a school.'

'Like they won't find me in a school. Jesus.'

'They won't in this one. The guy in the suit? He started it, and what he doesn't know about security doesn't exist. It's a damn good place, and the woman in charge? She's the opposite of Auntie. You have to have a cop go in with you, and you're going to give your word — you break it, I bust Sebastian — you won't leave the building until I take down these fuckers.'

'Like prison.'

'If prison's having your own room, an education, good food, nobody walking around ready to jab you with a shock stick and strip you down for porn before they sell you off to some perv, yeah. If it's being able to play music, paint, hang out, learn, be treated like a human being and not a number, yeah, just like prison.

'I was in a state school a lot of years,' Eve added. 'It was decent enough. Compared, this is goddamn paradise.'

'Why were you in a state school?'

'Not your business,' Eve repeated. 'There's a roof-top garden, there's counseling if you want it, you don't have to wear a uniform or sexed-up underwear or wonder when somebody's going to ship you off to some pervert. And when this is done, if you don't want to stay, we'll figure out what. Sebastian's not an option. It's a line I can't cross. Take your choice.'

'If I said the school, can Mouser come with me?'

A crack in the wall, Eve noted, but shot Dorian a suspicious look for form. 'Who the hell is this Mouser?'

'He found me, when I was sick and hurt, and he could've left me, but he didn't. He helped me. I don't care what you think about Sebastian, he helped me. They all did. If Mouser wants, can he go?'

'I'll see what I can do. Take the school, then listen to me. When this is done, you're going to sue the living shit out of Truman.'

Dorian poked at some sort of plant. 'As if. Like I'll call my lawyer, right?'

'That's right, the lawyer the guy in the suit's going to get for you. The lawyer who's going to sue her ass off. She probably doesn't have money, or much, but it's not about the money. It's about making her pay. She was responsible. If she'd done what she promised to do, you'd never have ended up where you did. She pays.'

'Why would the guy with the voice and the suit get me a lawyer?'

'For the same reason he started the school. Because you matter. Take the school, start there. If Sebastian's not a complete asshole, he'll say the same.'

'He's not an asshole! Maybe, I guess, maybe, if he thinks so, I can try the school. With Mouser if he wants. If I don't like it, I don't have to stay.'

'We'll start there. Now let's look at some pictures. You're going to help me save some lives and bust these bastards.'

16

Dorian identified three almost immediately, two from what she said they called the Pretty Ones, and another from the Slave/Pet area.

In the middle of another group, she burst into sobs. 'She's dead, she's dead. I didn't know her name, but they said she hung herself, with her sheets. And Auntie was really mad, and somebody said the floor matron on her level got beat up bad. It's how Mina heard about the tunnels, I think. It's hard to remember, but I think, because Mina heard they took her body out that way to where they burn it up.'

'This is so hard, and you're doing so much.' Peabody's voice soothed like a cooling balm. 'Can you remember when this happened? How long ago?'

'I don't think I'd been there very long. I mean not like right away, but I think it was when some of the matrons and guards bitched about how cold it was, for this time of year or something.'

'Okay, that's good. That really helps.'

'She's dead. Mina's dead, and that other girl's dead, too. How does it help?'

'It helps all the others,' Peabody told her. 'Everything you can tell us helps all the others. But if you want to stop, we can stop and come back to it.'

'I want to forget it happened. I was happy when I forgot.'

'But it did happen,' Eve reminded her. 'So let's pay them back. But we can give it a rest. You've given us plenty to start with. We can do more tomorrow.'

Eyes still flooded, Dorian turned to Sebastian. 'She said I can't go back with you.'

'She's right.'

'It's not fair.'

'It doesn't feel fair, I know. Too much isn't fair. But we all need to do what's best for you.'

'She said there's this school, but —'

Holding up a hand to stop Dorian, Sebastian turned to Eve. 'Do you mean An Didean?'

'That's the idea,' Eve confirmed, and Sebastian sent her a look of profound gratitude.

'Dorian, this is a gift, an opportunity I hope you'll be smart enough to embrace. I've been to this school.' He flicked a glance at Eve. 'I was curious. It's not just safe, and that's incredibly important right now. It's everything you could ask for. A superior education, and you'll be taught by people who care. Practical education as well, the arts, everything. Nothing, I think, can truly make up for everything that's happened to you, but this is your crossroads. Do you understand? It's your chance to try a new, exciting path. I believe, absolutely, you'd be very happy there.'

'I'd rather be with you.'

'Mavis, I think you might have said the same at one time. But —'

'But.' Mavis nodded. 'Sebastian gave me something I'd never had before. Somewhere no one wanted to hurt me. He gave me fun, and a freedom I needed so much. But it's only a kind of springboard. I never had the chance to choose something like this. I might've been too scared to take it. I hope you're tougher than I was.'

'She said maybe Mouser could go with me, but

only maybe.'

'You would take him?' Sebastian said quietly. 'Knowing nothing of him?'

'I said I'd see what I could do,' Eve began.

'Consider it done,' Roarke said. 'But there are rules, and you'd both have to obey them. What you're doing here is for all of them.' Roarke gestured to the screen. 'What you do at An Didean is for all who go there. You and your friend have to agree to that.'

'We'll need to put a couple cops in there,' Eve added. 'For protection.'

'I'll contact Rochelle. We'll work it out.'

'Can you come see me?' Dorian asked Sebastian. 'She says I can't leave until they get Auntie and all of them. It could be forever.'

'I'll check in on you, but it won't be forever. You're helping make sure of that. I'm very proud of you. I'm going to go talk to Mouser now. If he agrees, and I think he will, I can bring him to the school. Is that acceptable?'

'I need a name — a legit name,' Eve insisted. 'If he has family —'

'I believe he does, but not the sort you, being who you are, would subject him to. He's only eleven, and though he's pushed his way through most of the emotional scars, he still has physical ones. I expect that's something you'll want to deal with at some point.'

'At some point,' Eve agreed. If the kid made the difference for Dorian right now, she'd take the kid. 'If he was abused or endangered, we'll deal with whoever's responsible. I need his legal name to do that. Tell him no bullshit.'

'So I will.' Sebastian rose, held out a hand to Eve. 'I know our methods are dramatically different, but we

264

have considerable common ground on the ultimate goal. Thank you for your . . . creativity and flexibility in this.'

'It only goes so far.' But she took his hand.

'Understood. Mavis can contact me when you're ready for Mouser. Thank you all.' He opened his arms for Dorian. 'You're strong and brave, and you have such a bright future ahead of you. I'll see you soon.'

She clung to him another moment, and whispered in his ear, 'I'll never tell them where you are.'

'I know. Strong, brave, and true.'

He left quickly. Dorian shoved tears away with the heels of her hands as she looked at Roarke. 'She says you can get me a lawyer to sue the shit out of Ms. Truman. Can you really?'

Roarke lifted his eyebrows. 'First, she has a name, and it's polite to use it. Second, I can arrange for that, yes. We'll get you settled in the school first.'

'I guess you've got lots of money.'

'It happens I do. It also happens I spent the first years of my life very much like you. On the streets, and getting the boot or fist at home. I decided I wanted a different kind of life, so I made one. You have a chance to do the same.'

He rose. 'I'll contact Rochelle and she'll take care of what needs doing.'

When he walked outside, Dorian turned to Eve. 'I can do more, I guess.'

'Peabody, arrange for a detail at the school. We'll take one more group,' she told Dorian. 'And that's enough for tonight. Detective Yancy — that's the police artist — will come to you tomorrow. One more group, then Roarke and I will take you to the school.'

'If Mouser doesn't come —'

'One thing at a time, kid. Let's do the next group, then call it for now.'

Eve ignored the headache while Dorian identified two more.

'Okay, that's it for now. We're going to walk back to Central, get my ride.'

'I had it brought down,' Roarke told her. 'It seemed easier.'

'Yeah, great, fine. Thanks for all this,' she said to Mavis and Leonardo. 'I'll be in touch.'

'If anyone can help those children, it's you.' Leonardo enfolded her before Eve could evade. As he embraced her, Mavis pinned Dorian with a look.

'Somebody just handed you a mega op. Don't blow it. I'm saying that as somebody who might've been whacked enough to blow it in the back time.'

'You weren't that whacked,' Eve said simply. 'Let's go.'

When they stepped outside, Dorian took one look at Eve's DLE. 'Man-o, that's one totally out car. Doesn't look like it'd drive over five.'

'In the back, strap in.'

After the required eye roll, Dorian settled in. 'Hey, you got an AC back here. That's prime. I can get another fizzy.'

'No.' Eve shot through the gates and prayed to any deity who'd listen to help her carve her way through traffic and get this done.

Roarke shifted. 'There'll be a meal for you and your friend at the school.'

She sneered at that. 'Like veggie hash or soy surprise.'

'The surprise there is that anyone would eat either of those if they had a choice.' As that got a grin, Roarke

266

did what he could to engage Dorian in conversation while Eve pushed through traffic.

Eve figured she owed him all kinds of monkey sex.

Still, when they pulled up in front of the quietly dignified building that housed An Didean, Dorian's shoulders hunched.

'Give it a day,' Roarke suggested. 'If you're unhappy, we'll try something else.'

Not wanting to risk the chance of having to chase the reluctant kid down the street, Eve hit vertical, shot over several vehicles, and dropped into a loading zone.

'Frost-tee!'

'A lesson in judging by appearances,' Roarke said as Eve flipped on her On Duty light.

'Don't make me chase you,' Eve warned, and got out on the sidewalk. To make sure, she took a good grip on Dorian's arm with Roarke flanking the other side as they walked to the front doors.

Roarke buzzed in, and Rochelle waited in the entrance hall, with Crack beside her.

As far as imposing went, they hit top level.

He owned and ran a downtown sex club, but obviously hadn't dressed for work. Worn jeans and a black tee showed off an ultra-fit body. His shaved skull gleamed in the lights.

'Hey, skinny white girl.'

'Hey back, buff Black man.'

Before Eve could say more, he grinned at Dorian. 'And hey, cutie.'

Rather than speak, Dorian edged a little closer to Roarke.

'Welcome, Dorian. I'm Rochelle Pickering, and this is my friend Wilson. Why don't I show you around? The day students are gone until morning. We have summer classes and activities,' she explained. 'The live-in students have finished dinner and have free time.'

'They said Mouser would come.'

'Yes, your friend Tom. He's on his way. I thought you'd want to wait and have dinner together when he gets here.'

'He's really coming?'

'Yes, he is. It'll be good for both of you to have a friend as you start a new school, but I think you'll make more friends here. Why don't we go up, take a look at your room? I can show you some of the classrooms and other areas on the way.'

Eve decided, with considerable relief, to let Rochelle handle things as Dorian stepped toward her.

Rochelle, in a quiet blue suit, her hair wild dark curls, took Dorian's hand. And continued to talk, in a voice as quiet as the suit, as she led the girl away.

'She's got it,' Crack said. 'My Ro knows what to do.'

'I need the kid secure. I've got two officers coming in to make sure of it.'

'Yeah, we got that, too. I'm staying until they get here. No one's getting through me to hurt that child.'

And that, Eve could trust and believe.

Still she stayed, walked through areas, noted kids gathered here and there in the common areas, others jamming in the music room. A lot of space to secure, she thought, but then Roarke had secured it.

She could trust and believe that, too.

She sized up the two officers in plain clothes when they arrived, and decided Peabody had chosen well. Though Peabody had briefed them, Eve briefed them again.

Then got her first look at Mouser.

Sebastian led him in. A scrawny, sharp-eyed kid a full head shorter than Dorian. Obviously hastily cleaned up and carrying a small duffel.

'I need to look in there.'

Mouser stared holes in her. 'Got a warrant?'

Sebastian merely tapped his shoulder.

'Cops,' the boy muttered, but opened the duffel.

She found some rough clothes, a tablet with a cracked screen, a tattered graphic novel, a magnifying glass, a toothbrush, a little tin box holding some shiny rocks, a half-empty bag of gummy candy, and a hidden pocket with thirty-two dollars in cash along with an obviously homemade beggar's license.

She pulled out the license, said, 'Really?' and pocketed it before she handed him back the duffel.

'Bogus' was his opinion.

'Name's Crack.' Crack shot out a hand, took the boy's, shook it. 'I'm going to show you around. Dorian's up checking out her room.'

The kid drew himself up to his full height, poked out his chest. 'Anybody messes with her messes with me.'

'Get in line,' Crack advised. 'I've got him,' he told Eve.

'Don't disappoint me.' Sebastian laid a hand on Mouser's head. 'And, more important, don't disappoint yourself.'

Sebastian watched them walk off, then took a disc out of his pocket. 'His legal name is Thomas Grantly. You'll certainly run his file, but this has most of it. He survived and escaped a nightmare. I'm trusting you not to send him back to one.'

'I'll make the determination when I read his background, but until we shut down this Academy, he's

269

here. If Dorian takes off, manages to get out and find her way back to you, I'll find her, and you and I will be on opposite sides of this.'

'And rightfully so. You can't save them all, and neither can I, but we each try in our own way.'

He handed Eve a small bag. 'This is what she was wearing when Mouser found her. We didn't wash any of it as I normally would have because it all seemed off. And the shirt and pants were torn in any case.

'I'll leave it at that, and leave those children in good hands.'

Eve watched him go. 'How many street thieves, B and E men, grifters, and frauds has he trained over the years?'

'How many lost children has he saved from abuse and misery?'

'That's not his job.'

'Perhaps not, but it's certainly his vocation. And he's given two into your care because he knows he isn't enough to keep them safe. Let that part go for now, Eve. You've enough to deal with.'

'You're right.' She opened the bag Sebastian had given her. 'Uniform — with the sex gear under it. It's all already been handled, damn it, but Harvo might find something. I need to take these to the lab, call her back in, and . . .'

She paused as she riffled through. 'Something stuck in the pants pocket.'

Using the fabric, she pushed it out. 'Jesus, it's a swipe. A broken swipe. Just a piece of one. Broke when she fell, maybe in the tunnels, maybe outside. And we've got a piece of it.'

'Let's have a look.'

'Don't touch it!'

'I know the ropes, Lieutenant. It might be enough to give us some data.'

She zipped it all back up when she heard footsteps and voices.

Like a little damn parade, she thought. Rochelle, Crack, the two kids, the two cops, all chatting away.

'We're heading to the kitchen for some dinner,' Rochelle began. 'Can you join us?'

'No, but thanks. I need to get back to it.' Eve looked at Dorian. 'Detective Yancy will be here in the morning. If you remember or think of anything more in the meantime, either of these officers can contact me.'

'I like my room.'

'Yay.'

'It doesn't lock from the outside.'

She felt that, deep in her guts, but spoke casually.

'It's a school, not a prison. Tell me about the swipe card in your pocket.'

'The swipe?' The puzzled frown went to wide-eyed shock. 'Matron's card! I forgot! I — I was going to drop it on the ground, like maybe she just dropped it, but then I thought we might need it again, so I kept it. Maybe if I'd dropped it, they wouldn't have known we got out. Maybe if —'

'Ifs mean dick, but here's another. If you don't think they had cams and alarms in the tunnel, you're not as smart as you look.'

Mouser put an arm around Dorian. 'Cops blow wide.'

'Oh, golly, the sting!' Ignoring him, Eve met Dorian's eyes again. 'There's no ifs on anything you did with what happened to Mina. It's all on them. Whatever you forget, don't forget that. Go eat.'

271

'Crack says they've got cow burgers. We've never had one.'

'Go have a cow burger. Any questions, problems, you know how to reach me,' she told Rochelle. 'Thanks for making room.'

'We always do.'

Eve stepped outside, pulled out her com. 'I'm going to bag the clothes, have a pair of officers take it to the lab. Contact Harvo on it. I'll bag the broken card, take it home. Contact Feeney.'

'Make the contacts. I'll play Peabody and bag your evidence.'

It took time before the black-and-white pulled up for the pass off, but Eve thought she'd bought a little of that time.

She had the kid secured, and a fresh flood of information, fresh evidence in the clothes and the broken card. And if anyone could finesse a description out of a wit that led to an ID, it was Yancy.

When Roarke got behind the wheel, she settled into the passenger's seat.

'Maybe I should push for Yancy to start with her tonight.'

'No. Give her the time there. A good meal, her friend, time to feel safe and get a decent night's sleep. She'll be clearer on it tomorrow.'

'Maybe, maybe. I need to tie this up tight so the feds can't unravel it. Putting her in there rather than a safe house or in the system, they're going to make some noise.'

'You'll make the case it's safe and secure, and your victim, your witness, will be more cooperative. And emotionally steadier — Mira would back you there.'

'Good thought. I'll talk to her.'

Roarke stilled her hand before she could pull out her 'link. 'Take a blocker for the headache.' He flipped open a little case. 'And close your eyes for five damn minutes.'

Rather than argue, she took the blocker, but then shook her head. 'I can't stop. I need to get things nailed down.'

She contacted Mira.

'I'm sorry to interrupt your evening, but I need to bring you up to date. I'll write it up as soon as possible, but I've taken some . . . liberties.'

She ran it through, start to finish, answering when Mira questioned, holding nothing back. She felt it pushing, pushing, pushing, the desperate need to break. Just break.

Couldn't. Just couldn't.

'The child is safe, secured, guarded?'

'Yes.'

'Moreover, the child feels safe, and is with trained professionals after a horrific and traumatizing experience. By securing her in this environment, you've gained her trust, and her cooperation. I'd strongly recommend she continue to stay in that environment and work with the very skilled counselors, instructors, and therapists provided to students. I would like to speak with her personally tomorrow, and will make the time to do so.'

'Thanks.'

'You did what was right for her, this minor child, in these circumstances.'

'The other kid —'

'Is helping your victim and key witness feel safe,' Mira finished. 'And has no bearing on the investigation otherwise. I would like a copy of his file, but see no reason to include him in any report to the FBI as applies to this specific investigation.'

'I have to leave that up to the commander.' Another hole in the gut, Eve thought. 'I'll be bringing him up to date shortly.'

'Of course. Suggestion?'

'Sure.'

'Request a holo-briefing. It's closer to in person. And take some time to clear your head.'

'All right. I'll get you the written as soon as I can.'

'Take your time with that. I have enough from the oral to back you on this, and I will. Take some time.'

Haven't got it, Eve thought, but said, 'Thanks. I'll be in touch.'

She saw, with twinges of both exhaustion and relief, the gates to home open.

'How much of her advice will you take?'

'The holo-briefing's a solid idea. And she's right about the other kid. Right now, he's none of the feds' business. I gotta read his file, make sure I'm not getting smoke blown up my ass.'

He stopped the car, shifted to her. 'You're going to take a breath, and you're going to have a meal.'

'I'll eat something after I brief Whitney. I can't, okay, I can't. Nothing would stay down until I know how he reacts, what he orders.'

She'd gotten paler and paler on the drive, and not just from fatigue, he knew. From the stress of blurring her rules and regs. From the sickness he imagined lived inside her from hearing Dorian's story.

So he nodded.

'Then we'll set up the holo first.'

'You can start on the swipe? See if you can dig anything out of it.'

'I will. But I can't be expected to do my best work if I'm worried about you.'

'That's a cheap way to get me to eat.'

'Not when it's true.'

They walked inside together to the looming Summerset and the cat. Whatever Summerset started to say, he swallowed it back after one glance at Eve's face.

'Welcome home. The pasta and meatballs is particularly good tonight.'

'Just the thing,' Roarke said as he steered Eve toward the stairs. 'Thank you.'

Summerset looked down at the cat. 'I expect the lieutenant could use your company. She will push herself beyond reason,' he added as the cat streaked toward the stairs.

'Let's just get this done.' Get it over, Eve thought. 'I'll make the request, and hope he's available.'

'He'll make himself available when you tell him you've secured Dorian Gregg.'

'Yeah, I'll lead with that.'

She used her comm, on text mode.

Commander, Dorian Gregg has been located and is now secured. I have conducted a lengthy interview, and will write up same. I would prefer to give you an oral briefing as soon as possible by holo, as I made several concessions and agreements in order to secure Gregg and obtain her full cooperation. Dallas, Lt. Eve.

Roarke handed her a glass. 'Water — just water. Coffee later.'

'Fine.' She gulped it down while she studied the

board and waited. 'A lot of updating to do here.' Because she wanted more information, she plugged the disc on Thomas Grantly into her comp.

'The kid's from Buffalo, for God's sake. He —'

She broke off, read. Then sighed it out as Roarke set up for the briefing.

'Father liked to beat the crap out of the kid, and the mother. Mother liked to self-medicate. Looks like she tried to clean up a couple times, and they put the kid back with her. A lot of medical on both of them. Broken bones, concussions, then he took to burning the son. Getting back with the mother, then going on his rage-fest. Jesus, we got photos of the burns. Favored the torso, the belly. Finally got busted, he's still in. It's looking like the mother went back on the juice, took off. OD'd in some flophouse. When they found her — dead a couple days — ID'd her, went to look for the kid, he was gone.'

She broke off again when her comm signaled.

'Whitney says five minutes.' She took a long, slow breath. 'All right, I've got it from here. You should hit the lab.'

'He may have some questions for me regarding the school and its security.'

'Right.'

'Stand with the board behind you, Eve.'

'What?'

'Stand with the board behind you, the young girls behind you. Stand there as you stand for them.'

17

Rather than one of his dignified suits and conservative ties, Whitney entered the holo wearing khakis and a navy golf shirt. It threw Eve off for half a beat before he spoke.

'Lieutenant, you bring welcome news.'

'Sir. Dorian Gregg, through an intermediary, sought the protection of the NYPSD, and has provided us with a great deal of vital information. She's currently in a secured location and under the watch of two handpicked officers. Detective Yancy will meet with her at oh-nine-hundred to begin the process of identifying the female we believe is in charge of the child trafficking operation.'

Eve remained standing as Whitney took a seat.

'We installed Dorian Gregg at An Didean.'

Whitney's eyebrows winged high. 'The school? And why would you choose a civilian location, one with other minors and considerable civilian staff in residence?'

'To secure her cooperation first and foremost, Commander. Secondarily to give her both a physical and emotional break from the trauma endured over the past several months. I take full responsibility for this decision, and for giving my word, as a representative of the NYPSD, on several points. It was my call.'

'And you didn't find it necessary to contact and receive authorization of this call from command?'

'I felt, and continue to feel strongly, that I had to

make this deal with Dorian or lose her. Her cooperation, finding a way to gain at least some trust from her was and is key to identifying and locating those responsible for Mina Cabot's murder, for the abductions, forced imprisonment, and sale of dozens of minors.

'Sir, if I could detail the events that led to where we are now.'

'I think you'd better.'

She watched his eyes narrow as she relayed the contact through Mavis, the connection to Sebastian, the unorthodox meeting.

It didn't do the knots in her stomach any good. She expected the battery of questions, point by point, and he had them and more.

'You believe these initial memory gaps?'

'I do, yes, sir.'

Wandering the streets of Dallas, broken and bloody, mind a blank. Yes, she believed.

'And I believe she came forward, reluctantly, because she remembered Mina. Her attachment and trust in Sebastian came quickly because he helped her, and no one else had. Not the police, not the social workers, not any authority who had the responsibility to do so. If he hadn't persuaded her to talk to me, we wouldn't have the information she provided.'

'Which doesn't include the location of this Academy.'

'No, sir, but it gives us a great deal to work with, details we wouldn't have otherwise. It's verified the status of several of the victims on this board. Ones she saw there, and one she states self-terminated. We have knowledge that the woman known as Auntie has a partner, or a financial backer, perhaps a superior.

278

We know the building where the abductees are held consists of at least seven floors. We have a portion of the swipe card she used to access the elevator to the tunnels. The existence of the tunnels narrows our search for the location. The clothes she was wearing when she escaped are now at the lab and may offer more evidence.'

'The end may — may — justify some of your means, Lieutenant. However, by circumventing the chain of command, placing a minor victim and key witness in an unauthorized and civilian location, you've left a lot of cleanup.'

'Yes, sir. It's my responsibility. I made the decisions based on the circumstances of the moment and the emotional state of the minor. She's also mine, sir. She came to me.'

'And you answer to the department,' he reminded her. 'While you've given your word to this girl and her — we'll stick with intermediary for now — I haven't given mine. We have a network of safe houses, we have trained child protection professionals.'

'Like Truman.' Eve used all her will to push back emotion, to keep it out of her tone. 'I'm fully aware Truman doesn't represent the majority of CPS professionals, Commander, but Dorian Gregg has only that individual in her experience. If I'd called in CPS, we'd have lost her. Rochelle Pickering is also a trained professional, and Dr. Mira has requested at least a session with the minor child.

'I could have given her no choice, pulled her in, installed her in an authorized location with CPS and a few cops. Maybe we'd have gotten this information from her, in time. I wasn't willing to do more damage to her to get it.

'She's spent her life being beaten, abused, neglected, and the last several months being forced to submit to physical exams, punished with shock sticks, being forced to perform sexual acts with other girls trapped as she was. She made a friend in Mina Cabot, and now blames herself for her friend's death. She fell, she couldn't run, and her friend ran to protect her and died.'

Everything inside her wanted to shake, to break, but she wouldn't allow it. She'd done the right thing, as a cop, as a human being, and she'd stand by it.

'No, sir, I wasn't willing to pile onto that, so I used my best judgment, and gave her a choice. If I don't protect and serve Dorian Gregg and every girl on this board behind me, I don't deserve the badge. I stand by my actions, Commander, and again, take full responsibility for them.'

'I wonder if she knows the advocate she has in you.'

'It doesn't matter. Protecting her, finding Mina Cabot's killer, and busting the organization that exploits and torments, that sells girls like her into slavery is all that matters.'

'When we're done here, I'll have a discussion with Dr. Mira. Meanwhile, I'll need chapter and fucking verse on the security and setup at the location you chose. The chain of command, Lieutenant, doesn't stop with me.'

'I'd be better suited to address that area.' Roarke stepped into the holo. 'I can answer any questions you have, and I'll send you the schematics and blueprints.'

Eve stayed where she was, just stepped back in her head and let the technical talk roll over her. If Whitney pulled Dorian out of An Didean, it would leave a scar. On the kid and, Eve admitted, on herself.

Because she knew what it was to be shuffled around, all in the name of the best welfare of the child. And, she could admit as well, she'd made some of the decisions she'd made because she knew.

Too close, too deep, no question. Now all she could do was wait, accept the command, the consequences, and see it through.

If Whitney pulled her off the case, and he had every right to do so, she'd turn over every scrap of data she had to whoever took her place, to the feds.

They'd bust it down, she believed that absolutely. But Dorian Gregg would never trust a cop again. She wouldn't believe she mattered. And the first chance she got, she'd run again.

Living on the streets and, one day, invariably, she'd sell the body the bastards had abused, pampered, and trained.

And, Eve thought, she'd be responsible for that. She'd crossed the lines.

'That's a great deal of high-end security for a school,' Whitney commented.

'The students, their parents or guardians, the staff, guest instructors all deserve a safe place. You may also wish to speak with Rochelle, as she can provide you with the day-to-day precautions and protocols, and the schedule she's planned for Dorian.'

'And when we close this case?'

'Dorian will remain a student at An Didean as long as she wishes. Rochelle will begin the process of speaking with her contacts at CPS, arrange for a caseworker, and the necessary guardianship. This is part of the services offered.'

Whitney said nothing for a moment. 'I'll contact Dr. Mira. Meanwhile, Lieutenant, you have a matter

281

of hours before you'll call in the feds. I suggest you put this report together carefully, and push — push hard — on nailing down the location of this hellhole, get data off that broken swipe. Get a damn name. One name that can break down the door to the rest.'

'Yes, sir. Commander, I apologize for —'

'Save it,' he snapped, and faded off.

'Ouch,' she murmured.

'You handled that very well,' Roarke began.

'Did I? Did I handle any of it well?'

Letting go, she sat on the floor in front of the board, pulled her knees up, pressed her face to them, and rocked.

'Eve.' Roarke lowered down beside her, put his arms around her. 'It's all right now. I don't think he disagreed with anything you did, he's just a bit annoyed at being out of the loop.'

'It's not that, it's not that. It's not even that he didn't pull me off the investigation. It's all of it, just all of it. Locked doors, locked in the dark, beatings, rapes. Trapped.'

He stroked her back, her hair as Galahad ran over to rub against her.

'She's safe now, as you are, as all of them will be when we're done.'

'You were probably right, back at the start. I should've passed this on.'

'I wasn't right. Not wrong, either, as it was worry for you, for this exact thing. You working yourself so thin, feeling too much, and hurting. But, my darling Eve, I never worried you wouldn't find your way to push through it and stop this evil.'

He lifted her face, kissed it as she curled an arm around the cat.

'You did what was right for a murdered child, for a desperate and frightened one, and for all the others. You put them first, and as I know the commander, he knows that.'

He brushed tears away. 'That's who you are. That's who I love.'

'I look at her, I listen to her, and my insides shake. I need the mad, I need the furious, but I can't get through the shakes.'

'When you need to, you will. No one does the pissed-off cop half so well.'

With a watery laugh, she cuddled the cat and leaned into Roarke. 'I need to think straight. I know I need to think straight, do the job. I have to think straight and write up this report.'

'So you will. They can't break you. You won't let them. Neither will I.' He kissed her again. 'Or him, come to that.' And gave Galahad one long stroke.

He wanted, deeply, to bundle her up, pour a soother into her, and put her to bed. But he knew what she needed.

'You do that now, Lieutenant.' Again, his lips brushed hers. 'I'll get a start in the lab with this swipe. An hour will do it, then you'll eat. That's non-negotiable.'

'I have to find the building.'

'And we'll focus on that after a meal. I'm in this, too. The boy? Mouser? Looking at him was like looking at pieces of myself in the past.'

'Fake beggar's license.'

'Well now, even at that age, I'd've done a better job there, but . . . I was about to say he'd learn.'

She laughed again and held him close.

'Instead we'll aim him in another direction. Oh,

and I'm to get a lawyer for Dorian so she can —
I quote — sue the shit out of Truman. I'm pleased
you ran with that idea.'

'It was a good one. It's not the money.'

'She'll see the system can work, and those who
abuse authority can be punished. Now.' He got to his
feet, pulled Eve to hers. 'Let's get to it, as I've a yen
for that spaghetti and meatballs.'

'Thanks.' Still holding the cat, she leaned in one
last time. 'Thanks for not coddling me.'

'I know my cop.'

When he left, she stood another moment, nuzzling
the cat. Steadier, she decided, she felt a lot steadier.
'Thanks.' She pressed a kiss to the cat's head as she
carried him to her sleep chair. 'I'm okay, and I've got
work.'

And no, they wouldn't break her, she thought as
she walked to her command center. She'd damn well
break them.

✶ ✶ ✶

While Eve wrote her report, Jonah K. Devereaux
examined his newest possession.

The female he'd decided to call Luna had beautiful, perfect skin the color of midnight and eyes of
almost feral green. She stood straight, naked but for
her collar as he studied her. He approved the slash-
ing, razor-sharp cheekbones, the full lips dyed a bold
and blooming red. Her hair tumbled to her shoulders,
all glossy black curls touched with that same bold red.

They'd augmented her breasts, but subtly. He didn't
care for overstatements. Long legs, good muscle tone
throughout, slim, but not thin.

'Teeth,' he said, and she opened those full lips so he could check them.

White and perfect.

He circled her, found no flaws, and decided Iris had done it again. The woman was a treasure, no question.

Luna — yes, he enjoyed the name — had come from Tunisia, taken at the age of fourteen and shipped, along with others on that acquisition trip, to New York for her training. Iris's meticulous accounting listed precisely what financial outlay had gone into her — the dental work, the breast work, and so on, and what the investment had earned through photographs, vids, rentals.

All of that had proved lucrative enough to keep her rather than sell. Now at twenty, he considered her prime for his purposes. He preferred the experienced slave, and one he'd have to discipline only rarely.

'You're Luna. Who am I?'

'You are my master.'

He smiled, pleased with the musical touch of accent on her precise English.

'Why are you here?'

'To serve at your pleasure in all things.'

'And if you serve me well, I'll treat you well. I have no desire to mar your beauty. This is my room. You only enter it when I bid it. You'll wear what I give you to wear, eat what I give you to eat. I may, on occasion, share you with others.'

He turned to circle her again, and didn't see the momentary despair in her eyes.

'If you displease me, I'll hurt you. If you anger me, I may kill you. You are mine to do with as I wish. When I have no desire for you, you'll remain in your suite of rooms. You are not to leave them until I deem you've earned that privilege.

'Do you understand?'

'I understand, Master. I am your property, and grateful to serve you.'

'Good. Get on the bed. I'm going to fuck you now. I like enthusiasm.'

He used her, then took a pill to revive himself so he could use her again. He liked the feel of her, the sound of her moans and gasps.

Pleased, he ordered her on her knees to test her oral skills, and as she served him — and very well — he decided to send Iris flowers, with something shiny tucked into them.

'You'll do, Luna, for now.' He gave her breast what he considered an affectionate squeeze. He went to his intercom and signaled one of his domestics.

The blonde in a red skin suit and collar answered promptly. 'You're to show Luna to her quarters. She may have a meal. A salad, some grilled halibut, brown rice, and asparagus.'

'I'll see to it right away, Master.'

'Shower thoroughly,' he ordered Luna. 'Use the lotions I've provided you. When I call you back, answer promptly.'

'Of course, and thank you.'

He waved them out, and didn't see the tear spill down his newest possession's cheek as she kept her head down.

Well satisfied, he took a shower himself. He groomed, pampering his skin, studying his face and body in the wall of mirrors.

He found no flaws.

He dressed in lounge pants and a loose silk shirt, then left his bedroom suite to go to his private office.

There he opened a vault and studied other possessions.

Cash, of course. He could never get enough of it. And those shiny things he loved to own and — when the occasional called for it — give out like party favors.

He selected a bracelet, fiery rubies meshed with icy diamonds. He'd order roses — red and white — and tuck the bracelet in with them.

He closed the vault, poured himself what he considered a well-deserved brandy, then sat at his massive desk. 'Contact Iris, personal 'link.'

He started to frown when the 'link signaled a third time.

Then her face came on-screen. 'Jonah, how lovely to hear from you.'

'I was about to cut the call.'

'Oh, I'm so sorry. I needed to move to a quiet spot. I'd just taken a scouting report.'

'And?'

'There's no sign of that ungrateful girl. Infuriating when I think of the potential there, the waste of our time and efforts. But I'm determined it's for the best. An obvious troublemaker. Simply a defective product.'

She sent him an easy smile. 'I hope you haven't found the selection I made for you defective or unsatisfactory.'

'On the contrary, I called to congratulate you on your invariably exquisite taste. She's very much what I had in mind, and performed very well. I've named her Luna.'

'What a beautiful name. How kind of you.'

'I'm going to send you a little thank-you gift.'

'Oh now, that's not necessary.' And she laughed.

'But I'll take it! While I've got you, I'll tell you the preliminary marketing and plans for the auction are going exceptionally well. I expect us to see a major profit with this event. Enough we may want to discuss, more seriously, opening an academy in England.'

'Great minds. I've been toying with a manor house in the Lake District. It would need some work, of course, a considerable investment, but if you don't grow, you stand still.'

'I couldn't agree more.'

'We'll take a closer look after the auction. Let's be sure to replenish our supplies.'

'Not to worry. We acquired a new trainee tonight — or will have acquired when she arrives. A Pretty One. Supply and demand, Jonah, we meet both.'

'It's a fine life we have, isn't it, Iris?'

'Couldn't be better. Enjoy your evening, and Luna.'

'Believe me, I will. Good night.'

He sat back with his brandy, gently swirling while he reflected on just how perfect his world was.

His parents, of course, would have been appalled. But then their world, their vision, had been so narrow, so staid. They'd never known the thrill of taking whatever you wanted, doing whatever you wanted, indulging every whim.

Then they'd died. He shook his head, sipped brandy.

They'd died never having stepped out of that narrow world, and left him — their only child — all the money, the properties, the business, the power.

He'd done as he'd wanted with it all, and now look at him. He had so much more.

In his world, his wide-open world, he was a god.

He lifted the snifter in a toast to self. In his world, he ruled, and no one could stop him.

★ ★ ★

Eve continued updating her board when Roarke walked back in.

'Anything?' she asked him.

'We'll talk about it over dinner.' He moved straight through to the kitchen.

Sneaky way to get her to eat, she thought. Still, they'd had a kind of deal, so she stepped away from the board when he came back carrying two domed plates with a basket of bread balanced on top of one.

'I considered various ways to persuade you to take a soother.' He set the plates down at the table by the open balcony windows before backtracking to the wine rack behind a panel. 'So let's skip all the debate and arguing and compromise on half a glass of wine.'

'I'm okay.'

'Good.' He chose a bottle. 'Let's keep it that way. Food, a little wine.' After opening the wine, he brought it and two glasses to the table.

She'd sat on the damn floor and cried, Eve reminded herself. If she couldn't admit to having a bad moment, she'd just end up having another.

So she walked to the table, took a seat, then looked down at the plate he uncovered. 'Pretty clever to pick one of my weaknesses.' She picked up a fork, then it hit her. 'Summerset did that. Jesus, how bad did I look?'

'If you can't drop the stoic cop face inside your own home, then where?'

'That bad.' Accepting it — what choice did she have? — she wound the first bite of pasta around the fork. 'I'm over it — enough,' she qualified, and ate. 'So tell me what you got.'

289

'Not much to work with. It's a high-security-level swipe, something you might use in a prison or highly sensitive facility. Not a standard level as you'd have in, say, a hotel, a residence, or an office building.'

'It is a prison,' Eve said, and stabbed a fat meatball.

'Agreed. We have approximately twenty percent of the swipe, the lower right corner. The data's secured under several layers and encoded.'

'You can't get anything off what we've got?'

He gave her a gimlet eye as he wound pasta. 'I can tell you, first, a swipe like this would be programmed and developed in a handful of places — if we stick to the U.S. Since most of those would be government contractors, those are most likely low probability.'

'Not out of the question,' Eve considered, 'but lower than a private contractor.'

'One of those private contractors would be Roarke Industries, so I've started a search there on clients.'

'What kind of clients?'

'Asks the cop.' Roarke broke a hunk of bread in two, handed her half. 'Financial institutions, private labs, high-end resorts, security-minded individuals and businesses with deep pockets. And no, we wouldn't vet a client for this. Why would we? But I'll be doing that now, and it'll take a bit of time.'

'Okay. That's all you got off the piece of swipe?'

He gave her that gimlet eye again. 'I've got partial codes, which I'm now running on auto through a series of decoding programs. Once I see how far down those can take it, I'll dig down on that.'

'Wouldn't you be able to tell if it's one of yours?'

He picked up his wine, took a long, slow sip. 'Eve, we make millions of swipes at this level, design, encode, personalize, after which, any client may add their own layer of programming, and then layer on the data for the individual who'd hold the swipe.

'Smaller companies may ask us to do that final step, with photo ID included. However, consider turnover. Someone resigns, is fired, or simply damages or loses the swipe. So most that want this level have the ability — as, say, a hotel on the lower levels has with room swipes — to erase the previous data and reprogram.'

'So that's a no.'

'If I had the top portion of the swipe, I'd find our signature coded in. But I don't have that, and have to work with what I do have.'

'I'm not giving you grief. I just don't get this stuff.'

'Your master, for instance. If it was stolen, lost, damaged, what's the procedure?'

'I report same, asap. Ah, they disable it, administer a new one after a big fat headache of paperwork.'

'Precisely. At the level we're dealing with, the swipe would be automatically disabled when dam-aged. No doubt, when they discovered it had been stolen, they'd have disabled it, but breaking it? They obviously didn't have the time or foresight to wipe it — which is a much simpler process when the swipe is in hand — before that level of damage. Now they can't.'

'They can't wipe the data?'

'I'm going to say the girl took a hard fall, as the swipes aren't fragile, and when it snapped, it's done, you see. It can't be used, and the data on it simply carries the name of the holder and their clearance level, the company or individual who owns or runs the building where it's used, the programmer, the manufacturer.'

'Couldn't somebody access the data — like we're

counting on you to do — then forge a swipe, access those areas?'

He smiled, sipped more wine. 'There was once an exquisite Van Gogh. But . . . we don't need to go into all the details. I'll say I had weeks for the planning, the setup, and so on, and a necessarily quick execution. Years ago, darling Eve. But we — and surely most others — build in fail-safes for such mischief now.'

'But you could get around that.'

He went back to his pasta. 'Given time, and a less strict wife. But circling back, we have what we have, and we'll do what we can do.'

'What you've done so far confirms things we either knew or believed. The Academy has deep pockets, is run like a prison, likely has various levels of security. Sophisticated — Mira called that from the start. Dorian lifted the swipe from a floor matron, according to her statement. Someone like that had access to the elevators — or at least the one on that floor — and that security clearance ran all the way down to the tunnels.'

'And it's unlikely all would. Food providers, for instance, general cleaning or clerical, that sort of thing. The matron's just another term for security in this case.'

'Agreed. They use a crematorium. Use the tunnels to get the body or bodies out, transport to a crematorium. Whoever runs that is part of this, or someone there is part of it, taking a fee or more. It gives us another angle.'

'And likely hundreds of mortuary businesses to run,' Roarke added. 'What would you look for?'

'First, for a mortuary in New York that provides this dead service owned or run by or that employs

292

someone with a criminal history. Leaning into crimes against minor females, but not exclusively that.'

'Why not exclusively?'

'Blackmail and/or payoffs work. Somebody wants to hide the fact he's gotten busted, maybe done time. Then you look for those somebodies who might have more money than they should, or the business itself is more flush than it ought to be.

'I can't take time to dig into all that, so I'll pass it on.'

'I could have the time.'

'If you have any, I'd rather you use it to get everything off that swipe that's getable, and help me narrow down locations for the Academy. And I seriously regret they co-opted the name of a place that helped make me a cop.'

She was back, he thought. She was definitely back. 'That's the thing, Lieutenant. Through all of this, I'd wager they have no idea how many areas of your wrath they've lit.'

'It can't be about wrath.' She wound more pasta around a bite of meatball. 'Maybe a little,' she conceded. 'Under the rest. A little more than a little, but under the active, ongoing, official investigation.'

She ate, wound more. 'I can hope, with that little more than a little personal wrath, I get to punch this Auntie and her partner in the throat. I'm okay with hoping for that — but only after we bust their asses, build the case that gives the PA enough to lock them up for the rest of their miserable lives.'

She shrugged, ate. 'It'd be a nice bonus.'

She was, yes, all the way back, he thought, and grinned at her.

18

Eve dealt with the dishes while Roarke went back to his IT lab. She considered the fact his far-reaching company might have manufactured the swipe that got Dorian and Mina out of the Academy.

Coincidences bugged the crap out of her, but after some thought, she decided this didn't qualify. Roarke Industries manufactured so much damn stuff, it would be more of a coincidence if they weren't one of the possibles here.

Satisfied with that, she went back to her command center, programmed coffee.

So many tunnels in the city, she thought. In use, abandoned, rife with squatters and sidewalk sleepers. Add the underground and its dens of inequity. Sex shops, sex clubs — the sort you didn't find on the streets, but under them. The junkies, the thieves, rapists, and those who felt wandering among them equaled adventure and excitement.

Tying in with all of that? Could be handy, lucrative, another sort of training ground.

But . . . that lacked the element of sophistication, and added an element of risk — security-wise, anonymity-wise. Maybe you had scouts troll through, looking for minor girls who wanted a taste of that adventure, or a street kid who thought she could find some work.

She wouldn't dismiss that connection, but she wouldn't put it at the top of her list. She could dismiss subway tunnels or tunnels known to house big pockets of junkies, homeless, the lost and abandoned.

Utility tunnels worked. Shut down the access to the Academy, even conceal it, and make use of them when empty. Easy enough to know. She had to believe they had the tunnels monitored. Too huge a security breach otherwise.

She'd look there, but would start with abandoned or out of use.

After a long, frustrating hour, she pushed up, poured more coffee, paced around the room.

'Give me something,' she said when Roarke came back. 'Because I've got too damn much of everything.'

'I can give you a partial name. Partial last name, and some data that might help fill in.'

He went to her unit, hit some keys so data flowed onto the wall screen.

'Iamson,' Eve read, 'vel 5, and we've got what . . . 4th, ment 206. Okay, that's going to be level five — her clearance. An address. Could be Fourth Street, Fourteenth, Twenty-fourth, and so on. Iamson — that could be a last name.'

'From the angle of the break, it's partial, then end of the surname.'

'Yeah, I see that. And is that a date? It could be a date, zero-five-seven. A year? 2057. Not date of birth. Date of employment?'

'As good a conclusion as any,' Roarke said, because as he saw it there were many. 'It could be her serial number, a number assigned to her. Or part of a longer code. I wish I could give you more, but that's all there is.'

'It's more than we had. We've also got the location

where Dorian hid after she escaped. She states she walked a long time, but odds are it just felt like it. She's hurt, in pain, dazed, in shock.'

Eve ordered the map on-screen. 'For now, I'm going to concentrate on below Houston, east and west. Let's say you've worked for this organization for the last four years, you've got at least a mid-level clearance, you're willingly working for people making money abducting, abusing, and selling children. You're responsible for locking them in at night. I'm betting you make enough to afford a decent apartment, and one reasonably close to work.'

'You're going with fourteenth.'

'Starting there,' Eve agreed. 'It still gives us a hell of a lot of possible residences, but it's an apartment, most likely a second-floor deal given the 206. We know she's female, so —'

'Run a search for a female in that number apartment on Fourteenth Street whose last names ends in iamson.'

'Maybe we get lucky, maybe we don't, but —'

'Let me have this.' Brushing her aside, he took the chair and the controls.

She could do it, she thought, but had to admit he'd do it faster. And they'd go north from there — and south into Brooklyn. Maybe matron bitch liked a little distance between home and work.

Maybe zero-five-seven wasn't a date, but part of her ID code, or 'link code, or —

'Marlene Williamson.'

'You're fucking kidding me. That fast?'

'Age forty-three, single, no offspring, no marriages on record, no cohab on record. Address 526 West Fourteenth Street, apartment 206. Employed at Red

Swan Productions as night security since April 2057.'

'Red Swan, get me the data.'

'Coming on-screen.'

'Mobile videography, what the hell?'

'No location, no fixed address. Clever. I can dig in.'

'Yeah, yeah, we'll do that, but we both know it's a front, it's bogus. Maybe they file enough, put enough data in to pass, but it's bullshit. Let's go. You drive.'

'If we're heading to Williamson's apartment, she'd be at work, wouldn't she?'

'Yeah, so I'm tagging Reo on the way for a search warrant, and an arrest warrant so we bag her when she comes home. You drive, and I'll set the rest up. I'll put McNab and Peabody on the listed employer,' she said as she strode toward the door. She glanced at him as she pulled out her 'link. 'Swans aren't red, right?'

'Not on this planet.'

'Bogus,' she muttered, then pulled out her 'link and contacted the officer guarding Dorian.

'I need to talk to the kid.' She shot a finger at Roarke before he could object.

'She's in her room, sir. Should I wake her?'

'Yeah, now.'

'Just one minute, Lieutenant.'

'She IDs Williamson,' Eve said to Roarke, 'I won't have to tap-dance with Reo to get the warrants, and she won't have to do the same with a judge.'

She slid into the car Roarke remoted out of the garage as Dorian came on-screen. 'What's the what, man?'

'I'm sending an image through. Tell me if you recognize this individual, and if so, how and when.'

As Roarke drove toward the gates, Eve sent the ID shot.

297

'Oh, wow! Jeez! That's Matron. That's the floor matron bitch whose swipe I swiped.'

'Are you positive?'

'Holy crap, yeah. Like I wouldn't recognize the bitch from hell who smacked me around and jabbed me with the shocker? I didn't do the artist stuff yet. How did you get her picture?'

'By doing my job. Detective Yancy's still scheduled for the morning. Be ready for that unless I say otherwise. Go back to bed.'

'But how —'

'You want the bitch from hell to pay?'

'Fucking A!'

'Then go back to bed and let me make that happen. Put the officer back on. Now.'

'Sir?'

'Close eye, Officer. If there's another movement tonight, I'll loop you in.'

'Standing ready, Lieutenant.'

'Well, someone won't sleep much tonight. And,' Roarke said as Eve snarled, 'you were absolutely right. The eyewitness statement will grease the wheels for the warrant.'

'She might have something in that apartment that leads to the location of the Academy. If not, I'll have cops sitting on the place until she gets home. Then I'll put her in the box, break her down.'

'I've no doubt of it.'

She tagged Reo as Roarke surged downtown.

The APA came on-screen with her frothy blond hair bundled up. She wore what Eve assumed was a robe — tropical birds winging over a hot-red background.

'You know,' Reo began, 'I was having my first full

298

evening at home — a nice quiet me time. Bubble bath with wine and candles, a home facial, just snuggled myself in with a chirpy rom-com vid to top it off. You're not going to add to that lovely pattern, are you?'

'I need warrants.'

'See my shock and amazement. On the Cabot/Gregg case, the child trafficking?'

'Marlene Williamson. Gregg has identified her as the night floor matron where she was held, one who physically assaulted and abused her. Gregg stole Williamson's security swipe — it's how she and Cabot got out. We retrieved a broken piece of it from the pocket of the clothing Gregg wore when she escaped, and retrieved enough data to confirm it's Williamson's.'

'And you have Dorian Gregg's positive identification?'

'Affirmative. I showed her Williamson's photo, asked if she recognized this individual, and Gregg nailed her as the matron, no hesitation. I need search and seizure for her residence, and an arrest warrant.'

'You've got her data, send it to me. I'll get you what you need. Bag her sick ass, Dallas. Let's bag all of them.'

'That's the plan. Push it.' She clicked off, tagged Peabody, and filled her in.

'We're on our way. I can help with the search, McNab can help Roarke with the e's. This is the break we needed, Dallas.'

'Yeah, it is. Later.' Eve clicked off. 'We're going to need a place to park and wait until the warrants come through.'

'I believe there's underground parking.'

'You believe that because?'

'Unless I'm mistaken, it's one of mine.'

'Shocked and amazed.' But possibly convenient, Eve admitted.

'I can hardly keep all the addresses in my head, but I'm reasonably sure of this, as we recently completed an upgrade on the tenant fitness center.'

'An upscale building, like I figured.'

'Judge for yourself.' He lifted his chin toward the midsize tower of steel and glass before turning into a parking garage. A light blinked, then flashed on the gate before it opened.

'How does it know you're authorized?'

'There's a sensor on all our vehicles that takes care of that.' He pulled into a slot. 'We can go straight up to her floor, or to the lobby. You'll probably want to speak to night security.'

'Yeah, I do.'

'And you'll want a field kit.'

'You got that, too.'

He took one out of the trunk, then set the locks on the car.

They crossed the echoing garage to a bank of elevators.

'Does it ever get old?' she wondered. 'You know: "Hey, that's my place"?'

'Absolutely not.' He nudged her inside the car.

Eve scanned the levels as he called for the lobby. Three parking levels, the fitness and — jeez — indoor pool level, lobby, retail level, then the floors, one through twelve, topped by a rooftop level.

'How many tenants?'

'I couldn't say right off, but if you need that information, I can get it.'

300

'No, just curious.'

She stepped out in the lobby.

Quiet, she noted, the air cool and subtly fragrant. Glossy black flooring with little gold flecks added an edge that, she supposed, suited the ultramodern art — all slashes and swirls of color — the twisty black-and-gold metal lighting hugging the ceiling, and the weird-ass flowers poking out of glass tubes.

The night man pushed off his stool behind a sleek U-shaped counter and quickly came around it. He wore a black suit with a gold tie and wore his ink black hair in a modified fade.

'Sir, ah, Lieutenant. I'm Rohan, the night manager. How can I assist you?'

'Marlene Williamson.'

'I believe she would be at work. She works nights, so I rarely see her. Our hours are similar.'

'Do you know when she left tonight, and when she usually comes back?'

'She hasn't come through the lobby since I came on. At nine. But as I said, I rarely see her. I do believe she comes in most mornings at around five-thirty or six. I generally leave between five and five-thirty myself, but have occasionally crossed paths in the morning.'

Yeah, convenient, Eve admitted, and began to itch for the warrants. 'How about this morning?'

'No, I'm sure I haven't seen Ms. Williamson in the last several days, but that's not unusual.'

'Maybe you could check the lobby feed,' Eve began, then her PPC signaled. 'Never mind that for now. I have a warrant authorizing me to enter Williamson's residence.'

'I see. If there's some difficulty, or if I can be of any assistance in this matter, I'm at your service.'

301

'Great. Two officers will be coming in shortly. Send them up. If Williamson happens to come in while we're up there, do and say nothing, just give us a heads-up.'

Eve started to dig for a card, but Roarke pulled out one of his own.

'Of course. Please let me know if there's any other way I can assist you.'

With Roarke, Eve walked to the elevators — gold with black flecks. 'Where'd you find him?'

'I can't be sure, but I will find out. He never flicked an eyelash. I admire that.'

'If she's on schedule, we have several hours before she heads back.' Eve rocked, heel to toe, toe to heel. 'Plenty of time to go through her place. We find anything, we put an op together to take down the Academy, get those kids out, and I have some cops sit on her place in case she gets clear.'

'Wouldn't that be nice and tidy and in a bow?'

'Yeah. How come things hardly work that way?'

She stepped out on two. Pale gray carpet on the floors, more bold art on silvery walls. Good lighting, she noted, solid security on every black apartment door.

She paused in front of 206.

'Record on. Dallas, Lieutenant Eve, and civilian consultant — and owner of this property — Roarke. We have a warrant to enter this apartment, to search same and seize any evidence pertaining to the investigation of the abduction and murder of minor female Mina Cabot, the abduction of minor female Dorian Gregg, and the suspicion of child trafficking by Marlene Williamson, the resident, and others.'

'Very formal,' Roarke murmured.

302

'Cross every t on this.' She pressed the buzzer, waited. 'Occupant does not respond, and is believed to be on duty at the as yet unknown location where the minor females are held. Mastering in.'

Roarke laid a hand on hers. 'Before you do that, why don't I disengage any and all alarms? It's possible the occupant has an alarm tied to her 'link.'

'Okay, do that.'

While he worked, she scanned the hall. Quiet as a church, she thought. Whatever that meant. But if anybody watched screen, engaged in noisy sex, or beat the crap out of anyone behind those black doors, the soundproofing proved exceptional.

'There you have it,' Roarke told her. 'Alarms and locks disengaged.'

'Great.' She gave the door a good pounding with her fist first.

'Marlene Williamson, this is the police. We are authorized to enter.'

She drew her weapon, went in low.

She caught the scent first. Death, but not human, not animal.

'Lights on,' she ordered, and swept the spacious living area with her weapon.

Clean lined furnishings in soft colors, and nothing out of place. A dining area with a glossy white table and chairs. The death was there in a vase of flowers drooping from a clear vase that showed a stingy level of cloudy water. Withered petals scattered over the table.

'We clear it, but she's not here. She hasn't been here in the last couple days at least. Seal up, then take the kitchen, see when she last used the AC.'

Weapon in hand, she headed down a hallway, a room

converted to a home office, a small bath attached. The master, bigger, splashier — with more dead flowers on a dresser that showed a thin layer of dust.

The bed might've been made with military precision, but it had a lot of frills and fuss. In the master bath a single bud of some sort stood withered in a slim vase.

'No way,' she muttered. 'No way all those flowers died today. An organized soul,' she said when Roarke joined her. 'On the outside — the living area — conservative, even simple. Indulgent here in her personal space, fluffy pillows, frilly curtains.' She opened the closet.

'Same here. Straight lines, black or gray on one side — work clothes. And some cut-loose stuff on the other side.'

'She last used the AC on the evening those girls got out,' Roarke told her. 'At seven o'clock — almost on the dot — dinner of beef tenderloin — real beef,' he added, 'new roasted potatoes, and roasted eggplant. Iced tea.'

'That explains the dead flowers and the dust.'

'I did a quick search,' he continued as she took the can of Seal-It from the kit, used it. 'Every morning prior to that last meal? An omelet or a soft-boiled egg, with fruit and whole wheat toast. Seven a.m., again almost precisely. At, again, precisely two in the afternoon, a salad. She used the dishwasher at seven-thirty-eight on that same evening. Besides the dishes you'd expect from the breakfast and so on, a wineglass. There's a nice bottle of pinot grigio — open — in the wine fridge, and a very good selection of wine on a rack.'

'Tormenting kids pays well,' Eve concluded. 'They either relocated her after the escape, or killed her. I'm betting on number two. They not only got past her, but her swipe card got them out. Grounds for termination.'

'With prejudice,' Roarke finished.

'She still could have things to tell us. We'll start in the office.'

Since she planned to leave the electronics to him, and McNab when the detective joined in, she walked to the closet.

'Locked. I like it's locked.' She rolled her shoulders. 'Somebody's got secrets.'

'Would you like me to open the lock?'

'I've got it.' She pressed a hand to her recorder. 'Gimme your picks.'

'How do you know I have picks on me?'

'Because you always do. Gimme.'

He took out a small case, passed it to her.

Reengaging the record, she got to work on the lock. Sure, it would take her longer, but she wanted to practice anyway.

'Passcoded and fail-safed,' Roarke told her as he worked on the desk unit. 'Yes, I'll agree, someone has secrets.'

'And whoever relocated her or killed her didn't think of that. Yet, anyway. Got this big auction coming up, got cleanup to do on the escape, got hunters out for Dorian. Busy, busy. Williamson, just a cog in the wheel.'

'It hasn't been long.' Roarke sat, began to work on bypassing the security on the desk unit. 'I'd say they're not particularly worried about anyone noticing she hasn't been home. Not worried about the police identifying her, particularly if they found the rest of the broken swipe.'

'Follows.' The thin bead of sweat running down her spine as she worked annoyed the crap out of her. But she kept at it.

'She lives alone, works nights. We'll check to see if she had any daytime or day off visitors. Talk to neighbors, but— Got it!'

'Congratulations.'

'Bite me, slick.' She opened the closet. 'Standard-type office supplies, and ooh, a safe — we'll get to that. And a couple file boxes of discs.' She pulled them out, set them on the work counter, pawed through.

'Jesus, Roarke, they're labeled. Trainees — by numbers. Going from . . . sixty-five to two-fifty-three. She kept records on the girls, her own records on them.'

She paused at the buzzer. 'I've got that, keep at it.'

She hustled to the door, and snapped orders. 'McNab, check the security, see if anyone's entered the premises since the night of the escape. Peabody, start knocking on doors on this level, determine when anyone last saw Williamson. She hasn't been here since the night of.'

'On that.'

'McNab, when you're done here, assist Roarke. Peabody, contact Rohan at the desk. I want the security feeds and visitor's logs. I want to know if anyone came to visit Williamson in — let's start with the last three weeks. I want the feeds from the lobby, this hallway, the elevators, and the garage for the last five days.'

'Is she in the wind or dead?' Peabody wondered.

'I'm thinking dead, but maybe she went rabbit. She's got a safe in her home office. We'll see what's in it, if anything. Go.'

She hurried back to Roarke. 'Status?'

'Getting there. She either had the skills or hired

someone with considerable. It's a very fine job. Couple minutes more.'

While she waited, Eve selected a disc, used her own PPC. 'I'm guessing she had the skills. The discs are encrypted. We'll get through that, but it'll take more time. I'm bringing Feeney in.'

Roarke looked up. 'Eve, it's near to midnight.'

'He's a cop.' Pulling out her 'link, she walked to the master to search while she made the tag.

She found an old 'link, obviously kept as an emergency spare, a tablet, a roll of cash — two grand — in the underwear drawer.

'Like thieves never look there.'

Sexy underwear, but the only sex-type toys she found indicated solo rides. No regular bed partner, she concluded.

Soft, silky fabrics in the undergarments and night wear, some simple, serviceable jewelry, practical shoes on the business side, sex-me-up type on the party side.

'But you didn't party much, did you, Marlene? All this tells me it was more a wide and twisted fantasy life. Maybe you got decent vacation benefits. That might be party time. Cut it loose somewhere not here.

'What've you got?' she asked Peabody without turning around.

'Nobody really knew her, not on this floor anyway. I've got a little from the woman across the hall. She knew Williamson worked nights mostly because she'd see Williamson come in some mornings when she headed out to the gym. Wit works remote at home three days a week, so she'd occasionally pass her in the afternoon — going to the market, that sort of thing. Mostly just nodded to each other.'

Peabody glanced at her notes. 'She doesn't remember seeing anybody visit, but since she felt Williamson didn't want any friendly neighbor vibe, she didn't make a point of chatting.

'Down the hall guy said he rode in the elevator with her sometimes when he headed out to meet friends and she was going to work. He asked, and she said she worked nights, then sort of froze him out — according to him.'

'Okay, let's get that feed. I'm going to check on the e-team. Feeney's on his way in.'

She went back to the office, saw McNab at the desk unit and Roarke crouched in the closet, with the safe door open.

'We're in,' McNab told her. 'I'm starting on files. She's one paranoid mother, Dallas. Encrypted up the butt.'

'Feeney's coming.'

'Couldn't hurt, but we're in here, and Roarke melted through the safe in like five seconds.'

Eve crouched beside Roarke as he drew out jewelry cases. 'Those are going to be real.'

'I'd say so. Simple and elegant, good settings, good stones.' He opened cases, revealing necklaces, bracelets, earrings, rings. 'It's a lovely little collection.'

'How much you figure?'

'At a glance? Maybe a couple hundred thousand. We'll find they're insured and pin that down. And look here.' He pulled out another box, opened it. 'Nice and green.'

'She had a couple thousand in her panty drawer, this is more.'

'About . . . half a million. Smart, I suppose, not to bank it all. It's likely she's paid more than she should be, and rather than send up any flags, they do some, at least, in cash. Easier to wash that way, on all sides.'

'No way she's in the wind. You don't rabbit and leave all this behind. You want the cash — and there's a passport here, and an unused 'link. Insurance. Gotta run, grab the sparkles, the cash, the passport, the fresh 'link. She didn't get to run.'

She sat back on her heels. 'Nothing in here, nothing I found in her bedroom that touches on the Academy. We need to get into those discs, and her personal files.'

'I'm getting there,' McNab told her.

She pushed to her feet. 'Let's take it all into Central. You'll have more tools there, and it'll be quicker. Tag Feeney, tell him to go there, not here. I'll get a detail to sit on the place in case I'm wrong and she just found a hole to hide in for a few days.'

She looked around. 'Take it in. Peabody and I will do another solid sweep through, check the security feeds, then meet you. You don't —'

Roarke cut her off. 'Don't say it.'

She shrugged. 'Knee-jerk. I'll see you there.'

Eve walked away to order the detail.

But, she thought, she wasn't wrong. Marlene Williamson had certainly taken a last trip through the tunnels and was never coming back.

19

With Peabody, Eve went through every drawer, closet, cabinet, and cubbyhole in the Williamson apartment. And found nothing that pointed the way to the Academy or those who ran it.

In the security hub, they scanned feeds and confirmed Williamson's departure at twenty hundred hours on the night of Mina Cabot's murder.

No return at any time, on any feed.

The thirty-day visitor's log showed no one signing in for Williamson.

Dead end, Eve concluded. In every way.

'Coffee,' she said the minute they got in the car.

'Oh yes, please.' With a heartfelt sigh, Peabody programmed it. 'The probability she's alive and hiding is subzero. But literally terminating her for having her swipe stolen's seriously harsh.'

'So's stealing kids and selling them to pervs.'

'Yeah, it is.' Peabody gulped coffee, yawned, gulped more. 'But that's — for them — business.'

'So was this. Fire or discipline an employee, said employee could get pissy, and being pissy might try to cut a deal with the cops. Why risk it?'

''Dead men tell no tales,'' Peabody quoted.

'Sure they do, and dead or alive, Williamson's telling us plenty. She'll be telling us more when the e-nerds break her codes. That was a saying, right?'

'Yeah, it's —'

'Sayings like that are another reason people do the

stupid. 'Okay, dead now, so that's that.' And it's not. Nobody knows it's not better than a murder cop. Add to it, you know why these assholes didn't think to wipe her apartment? She was nothing to them. Just another number. Night Matron Williamson, employee number whatever. Disposable. She cost them millions, and profit's the bottom line here.'

She pulled into the garage at Central.

'She worked there a solid number of years,' Peabody added. 'I bet she kept her head down, did the job, didn't make waves. Who'd think she'd keep files on her — charges, I guess.'

'Prisoners,' Eve corrected as they crossed to the elevator. 'According to her data, she was a prison guard, Attica, for ten years before she got into this.'

They stepped into the car, and Eve called for EDD level. 'I'm betting they recruit,' she continued. 'Prison, juvie facilities. Vet them, do deep background, a psych eval, because you need the type who'd be just fine with all this. You're going to pay them a hell of a lot more, add some juicy benefits — and give them the chance to jab kids with shock sticks.'

'Psych eval. You're right because they have to know they're hiring sadists and sociopaths.'

'Maybe — probably — monitor them for the first few months, more likely a year. Spot check after that. You'd need to be careful to avoid addicts, people with spouses or close family ties. Someone like Williamson? No close relationships, organized, routine-bound, punctual, just greedy enough? I'm betting she was a model employee until she screwed up.'

'I could start a search for people with that employment background who transferred to Red Swan.'

'Do that,' Eve said as they stepped off the elevator.

'A five-year spread. We only need one, goddamn it. One live one.'

She headed straight to the lab, and through the glass walls saw the e-team at work. Feeney in his industrial beige shirtsleeves, dung-colored tie loose and crooked. McNab, bony hips twitching in red baggies paired with a T-shirt swirled with atomic colors. And Roarke, pale gray dress shirt somehow still crisp, with the sleeves rolled to the elbow, and his hair tied back.

They'd added Callendar, she noted, who completed the lineup with blue-and-green-striped baggies, a sunshine-yellow tank, with the new feature of hair ink black at the crown falling into a short, multicolored rainbow of tufts and spikes.

Eve pushed in; the noise level rose from library quiet to a night at the club.

Music didn't blast, but it sure as hell pumped. Snatches of conversation — that might as well have been Ferengi — cut through it as the e-team communicated.

Machines beeped, buzzed, clacked.

And the air smelled ripe with coffee and sugar from mugs and fizzies and a not-quite-depleted box of doughnuts.

'Jesus, how can anybody think?' Eve demanded.

Callendar glanced over her shoulder. 'Uh-oh, Mom's home. Kill music. It can actually help you think,' she claimed when it dropped away. 'Like the sugar rush.'

'Pulled her in,' Feeney said as he worked. 'Lotta data to crack, and we want it fast.'

'I'm for that. What have you got?'

'Layered it good and proper, she did.' Roarke spoke, and as it often did when he dived deep in the work,

312

his accent clicked up a few degrees. 'And bloody buggering hell, there's another. I've got it. Are you seeing this, Ian? She's sandwiched a cross jab with a roll-down and two-step.'

'Overkill, total. Need assist?'

'No, I have it. Ah, the roll-down's counterfeit, cozied with a triple slash and inverted ampersand. It's clever enough, but easily . . . And there. I've got it.'

'Got what?' Eve demanded as her brain just swirled like McNab's shirt. 'What in holy hell have you got?'

'I took the files on the girls — or two and a half years of them, going back from the now. She changed the code, so Callendar's on the next two. Feeney and McNab are dealing with her personal files.'

'Show me, show me one of them.'

He brought the first on-screen.

'I know that face. She's on the board. Show — no, send all you've got to the conference room.'

'Which room?'

'We're in one. Peabody.'

'I'm with you.'

'I need an address,' Eve snapped as she headed out. 'I need a location. Run that search,' she told Peabody. 'Get that started. We only need fucking one.'

'I can use McNab's unit up here. They're a lot juicier than what we have in Homicide. And I can have the results sent down to the conference room.'

'Do that.'

She went down alone, jogging down the glides. She swiped into the conference room, eyes on the board as she detoured to the AutoChef. The scent of her own coffee relieved her as she located the girl.

'Jaci Collinsworth, age twelve, Detroit.' She ordered the data Roarke transferred on-screen, saw the same face, the same data. Then more.

Williamson kept records on when the girl had been 'admitted,' wrote up a sketchy report on physical condition, and what she called repairs. Dental work, skin and hair regimen, exercise and nutrition.

She deemed Jaci spoiled, difficult, defiant, with poor language skills that relied on swearing. Physically aggressive and requiring discipline and chemical modifications.

Also noted were the times and dates of the discipline, the method, the times and dates and doses of the drugs.

Improvement in attitude and behavior noted at seven weeks.

She'd noted down skill levels — her scale, Eve assumed — as training continued. The trainee required small, daily doses of a personalized chemical cocktail to reach her potential. She got an eight out of ten.

Williamson estimated her value at auction at six million, with a bonus for herself as matron/disciplinarian of six hundred. Her notes indicated this as a disappointment.

She read on, girl by girl, including three she added to the board.

And Mina Cabot.

'You learned fast, didn't you?' Eve mumbled as she read Williamson's data. 'Play along and look for a way out. You went from spoiled and willful, according to this bitch, to cooperative, compliant, and eager to learn. Got a ten out of ten, and an estimated value between twelve and fifteen million. So up to fifteen hundred for your night guard, who rates you as a success.'

314

She read, paced, read, paced.

The child Dorian stated had killed herself, confirmed by Williamson's notes, cost the matron a thousand dollars. Deducted from her pay. Failure.

'She rated them,' Eve began without turning around when she heard Peabody come in. 'Scale of one to ten. She really didn't like Dorian, and I've got over twenty incidents where she used a shock stick on her. She considered the discipline did its job, and rated her a nine out of ten, potential value at twelve million, as some buyers liked the sass.

'Sass,' Eve repeated. 'She'd have netted twelve hundred dollars at that rate, as a bonus. They also deduct a thousand for any girl who dies. Smart business. Make it work, you get a piece of the action. Fail, it comes out of your pocket.'

'Are you okay?'

'Five by fucking five. I've only gotten through six months, and already added three we didn't have. Younger ones. Six to ten.'

'I think I've got two.'

'Two what?' Distracted, Eve turned, then cleared her head. 'From the search?'

'Yeah, I've got it running on auto now because I wanted to get this to you fast. Can I put them up?'

'Yeah, Jesus.'

'Okay, first one? Maxine Pryor, former army, less-than-honorable discharge, sixteen years back. She worked as a guard for Metro State, Atlanta, from 2056 to 2058. Some slaps in her file there. She took a job as a security guard at Red Swan. It says Atlanta, but the address — her residence — is bogus there, so I dug deeper and found one that matches in Chelsea. It's under L. M. Pryor, and she changed hair color, had a little work done, but it all fits. One marriage, divorced fifteen years. No offspring.'

'That's good. Give me the next.'

'Cecil B. Doggett. He was a cop in Baltimore City, terminated after twelve years on the job for excessive force, extortion, and ultimately striking a superior officer. Picked up work as a prison guard at a minimum-security prison in rural Maryland, and for the last five years has been employed by Red Swan as a recruitment officer.'

'Is that what they call the scouts in polite company? Address?'

'In Maryland, outside Baltimore. He has a black van registered in his name, no spouse, no kids. I dug down more, and he's got a damn nice house, a boat, and a Panther ZX convertible roadster. He's living pretty large on what he reports as his annual earnings.'

'Wonder what kickback the scouts get from sales? This is good, Peabody. Let's go wake up Maxine Pryor.'

'Do we want a warrant?'

'The first tag she'll make is to her superiors and their lawyers. We need to convince her not to do that. We use Marlene Williamson. You're a liability, you're dead. Then —'

She broke off as she heard McNab coming with a double-time prance.

'Got through.' His face, a little pink from the run, beamed success. 'Jesus, the layers, and obsessed much, a million separate files.'

'Location, McNab.'

As he reeled off an address, Eve ordered the map on-screen. 'I had that one. What the hell is it?'

Before she could call that up, he told her. 'It's a delivery hub and warehouse for Reliable Delivery Services. It's been around for like ever. Maybe close to ninety, a hundred years, global, but they have their headquarters in New York, always have.'

'Who owns the building?'

'Same guy who owns the business — lock and stock,' McNab told her. 'Roarke knows him, some. They're coming, but the cap told me to fly, so I did.'

He paused, let out several huffing breaths.

'Jonah K. Devereaux, inherited the whole deal from his parents when their private shuttle went down in the Sea of Japan when he was like twenty-something. He got it all.'

'Already a multi-billion-dollar industry,' Roarke added as he walked in. 'Under his eye, it's continued to run smoothly enough, though he hasn't implemented any expansions in the last decade or so. He has the family home on Long Island as his New York residence, and I believe villas in the south of France, another in the Caymans. I haven't checked as yet, but he may have more.'

'You know this guy?'

'Very slightly. The foundation his parents started when he was still a boy donates generously to some organizations I also support. I brushed up against him a few times at charity events but not, that I recall, in the past few years. The word is, such as it is, that he prefers spending his time on one of his estates. He's never married, but has been known to enjoy the company of women, usually professional women, and younger. Not children,' he said quickly. 'I've never heard a whisper of that, or I'd have passed it on to you already.'

317

'What's younger?'

'Twenties, thirties. He's in his sixties, maybe early seventies, and that wouldn't be unusual.'

'I need more on him, on the business, on Red Swan.'

'We're here to get it,' Feeney told her. 'Callendar's upstairs pushing on Red Swan. We don't need the fancy to look at Devereaux or RDS. Figured to use your bullpen.'

'Have at it. I need everything you can get me on this building. Every square foot of it you can get.'

'You'll have it. Give us another hour.' Feeney rubbed his eyes. 'And a hell of a lot of coffee.'

Eve checked the time. Somehow it had gotten to be past four in the morning.

'You're sure about the hour?'

'An hour,' Feeney confirmed. 'Maybe less.'

'Use what you need, take what you need. Peabody, keep at it. Let's see how many people you can connect to Red Swan, and add in the delivery service to the search. He'd need some there, too, even if he's running the front as legit.'

Alone in the room, she looked back at the board. She'd get back to those faces. More, she'd get them out, all she could.

To do it, she needed more than data. She needed cops.

Taking out her 'link, she started calling them in.

She tagged her bullpen, including Uniform Carmichael; she tagged Reo, Willowby, and added Lowenbaum from SWAT. She, with reluctance, woke up her commander, and considering the proximity of the building to the river, requested both air and water support.

Then she sat, used the conference room comp

318

to do some digging herself on Devereaux. EDD would get her what she needed, but she thought of wealthy — seriously wealthy — men, and how often they ended up on the society pages with some snazzy woman — or man — on their arm.

She started back, scanning for photos, names of women he escorted. He had a partner, a female partner, not a twenty- or thirty-year-old, according to Dorian. But older.

Maybe he mixed business with pleasure, or had at one time. He had to meet her somewhere, build a relationship, cement trust.

Her eyes burned, begged to shut down for just a few minutes. The back of her neck felt like wires hummed and twisted under the skin.

She'd need a booster before much longer, she admitted, and she hated them.

She scanned through photos and quick write-ups — Devereaux in tuxes, beautiful women in glamorous gowns. Slick suits, sleek cocktail dresses.

Blondes, brunettes, redheads, curvy or stick thin, but with common denominators: young and stunning.

But nothing and no one clicked, not with the socialites, the heiresses, the celebrities and high-dollar models.

When her eyes blurred, she rubbed them clear. Thought about more coffee.

Wasting time, she decided, and with her focus fading, nearly missed it.

The photo was more than twenty-five years old, a glossy report from the Met Gala. Devereaux, his hair lush and gold, had his arm around the waist of a statuesque woman in a figure-hugging red gown cut low to showcase impressive breasts and an equally impressive waterfall of diamonds and rubies. Her pale, almost silvery blond fall of hair rained down to her shoulders, and a sparkling pin swept it up behind one ear.

A ruby pin in the shape of a swan.

"Iris Beaty," Eve read, "flaunts her past as the notorious madam of Red Swan with a diamond and ruby hair clip. Will she rub elbows with clients enjoying the rarified air of the Met Gala? Discreet as ever, Ms. Beaty won't name names even now that sex workers are licensed and legal.'

'Iris Beaty,' Eve ordered. 'Official ID and data on-screen.'

As she studied the older, still beautiful face, the ice-cold eyes, Eve saw predator. She pushed up, dragged her hand through her hair, pacing now as she read the background.

'Holy shit. I've got you.' Ignoring the running footsteps, she continued to read.

'Red Swan,' Callendar said triumphantly.

'Iris Beaty.'

'Well, hell.' Blowing out a breath, Callendar looked at the image on-screen. 'We've way underestimated your e-skills.'

'Cop skills, no real e about it. I found a photo of her with Devereaux, and she had a damn red swan pin in her hair.'

'Ballsy.'

'How did you find her?'

'She wrote a damn book, can you check that? *Flight of the Red Swan*. It popped in one of my runs. High-class escort service back in the twenties. She had a good long run finding dates at a few thousand a bang for people who could afford it. According to the

320

summary I read, the book's full of juice, but she's all coy about saying who bought who and like that. She wrote it after sex work was legalized, regulated.

'And I connected her to Devereaux — old friends, right, maybe more. And he helped finance her legal LC business.'

'Is that still running?'

'No. She sold out and retired.'

'I'll buy sold out. Legal, regulated, monitored, the paperwork, the license fees, taxes? Cuts into the profit. And I'm betting some of those earlier clients paid steep to keep her — what did you call it — coy. But she didn't retire. Just changed direction.'

'I hear that. The address on her official data? Some farm she supposedly retired to in France? Bogus. And her financial data, what I skimmed, looks hinky to me.'

'Hinky how?'

'Seems like she'd have more. Plus, no credit transactions, zippo. All cash. And what goes out, comes in. Almost to the dollar — or euro. Whatever.'

'Another front. We can dig into that. She's in New York, and going to have that more. Lots of more. We'll dig, and we'll find it. But first, we find her.'

She checked the time again, and found the hour up.

'Set up facial ID, will you? Maybe we pop out another ID. Wait,' she said even as Callendar moved to the comp. 'Try Swan — it has meaning for her. Start with Iris Swan, and look in France, too.'

As Callendar got started, Eve turned to the door and Peabody.

'The others are wrapping up,' Peabody said. 'I've got five more, Dallas, over ninety percent probability.'

'On the board.'

'Ex-cops, ex-military — at least these five.' Peabody

began to put them up. 'I'm seeing they recruit the ex-cops as scouts, the military as guards and security. So far, anyway. Two female and one male as guards, I think, one female and one male scout.'

Peabody glanced back. 'What digging I did into Red Swan, I get a mobile consulting firm, pretty small change. A couple more surfaced. A dance company in Wisconsin, and looks legit. A company called Cygne Rouge in Provence — France.'

'France,' Eve repeated.

'Yeah, it's — ah — videography.'

'It's going to connect.'

Peabody paused. 'It is?'

'Any more?'

'A defunct escort service, way back. Out of business for close to a decade.'

'Depends on your definition. She ran it,' Eve said, and ordered Iris Beaty's ID back on-screen.

'Is that —'

'I'm betting that's Auntie. Iris Beaty.'

'Aka Iris Swan,' Callendar announced. 'French ID.'

'And check her data,' Eve noted. 'Same address as the videography front.'

'Are we going to France?'

Ignoring Peabody, Eve studied the side by sides Callendar put on-screen. 'Changed her hair for Swan — deeper, longer, but not much else. Vain — she likes her face. And she's not in France. She's here in New York.'

I know you now, Eve thought.

'We'll add informing the authorities over there,' she added. 'They'll want to hit that location. You want to funnel girls in Europe, it's handy to have a location in Europe. And she'd spot-check on that. Zip on over, make sure it's all running smooth. But she lives in New York. This location is the main hub.

'I need the data on the damn building. Peabody, get me whatever they've got. We've got a full briefing in ninety minutes.'

'Who are we briefing?'

'Every-damn-body. Go.'

Eve swung back to the board. 'Yeah, I think she hit with these. Callendar, let's start financial runs. Maxine Pryor first. Look for the shady, a secondary account, any —'

She broke off as she heard people coming. 'Hold that for now.' She started to complain when they came in, but she caught the gleam in Feeney's eyes.

'Me first,' she said, since Beaty was already on-screen. 'Iris Beaty, former sex worker, former owner and proprietor of Red Swan, a defunct escort service, and companion to Jonah Devereaux. You can call her Auntie.'

'Good work, Callendar.'

She lifted her shoulders at Feeney. 'Looks like Dallas and I hit with her at the same time. Different angles, same target.'

'She also has ID, French ID, under the name Iris Swan, and an address under each name in France, one bogus, the other claiming to be a videography business.'

'Another front.' Feeney hit the AC for coffee.

'Most likely, and most likely either another training location or a holding station for shipping the girls. Meanwhile Peabody's ID'd seven employees of the Red Swan in New York — which claims to be a mobile consulting firm. No physical address.'

'Handy.'

'Your turn.'

'Devereaux's got a legit shitpile of money, holdings, investments,' Feeney began. 'RDS is a private company, he's the sole owner, and he rakes it in. Doesn't seem like he'd need the two shadow accounts we dug up. Had to dig deep,' Feeney added. 'Guy's no dumbass there, so it took a while. And . . .Your find.' He pointed at Roarke.

He'd changed somewhere along the line, Eve noted. Rather than his dress shirt and suit pants, he wore a black tee and jeans.

'He's a signatory on what appears to be a business account, in Switzerland — he went classic there — for Cygne Rouge, LLC.'

'French for Red Swan.'

'Exactly. He has a second on Nevis under RS Productions, LLC. Both currently hold over two hundred million, and Iris Swan is also a signatory on both.'

'You had her, too,' Eve observed.

'Three times a charm. As money flows in and out,' Roarke continued, 'these are clearly accounts set up to cover the expenses of running their business, and for channeling a portion of profits.'

'And it hooks them together on all this, nice and tight. The building. I need the building.'

'Copied to this unit.' Roarke stepped over, reached around Callendar, and brought a set of blueprints on-screen. 'These are the official ones. As you see, there's the lobby area on the main floor where customers would bring packages in for shipping. Offices for clerical work and so on. Storage area for packaging, boxes, crates. An underground garage for trucks, vans, other vehicles. The shipping area, the shipping

324

dock. Offices on the upper floors, more storage, a conference room, employee locker room, employee break room.'

'That's not right.' Eve just shook her head. 'It's too much room for offices, and it's sure as hell not set up for holding abductees.'

'I agree. Far too much wasted space, termed here as future builds and projects. Considering the purpose we all believe the structure's used for, and the deep pockets of that purpose, it occurred to me the work needed to utilize those upper floors, all really but the front — in both senses — could be done unofficially, without permits.'

'That won't help me plan an op.'

'No, but this should.'

He brought another set of blueprints on-screen. The detailing, the use of space gave her a quick flash of her time in state schools.

'How'd you get this? I can't — we can't use data you got by hacking Devereaux's files. Nothing we do from it will stick.'

'Do I look like this is my first day on the job?' Feeney pointed at his own face. 'Remember who trained you, kid. We figured what we figured, and Roarke figured there had to be prints somewhere. Even off-the-grid, you gotta have a plan. Roarke does a little digging — not over any line — and pulls out the architect Devereaux likes to use.'

He held up a finger before Eve could speak. 'I tagged up the PA — went to the top — called in a favor. We go back some. It took some doing — another reason we ran over some — but we got a warrant to cyber-search the files, and there it is. Clean. A defense attorney might squawk, but it's clean.'

'Okay. Okay. The plans are ten years old. They've been at this awhile.'

'The building was originally a warehouse with offices on the lower levels,' Roarke told her. 'I have those blueprints, but suffice it to say they used the basic footprint, reconfigured to their needs. You have the rooms where they'd hold the girls, four floors of those small rooms and baths with a break area on each, presumably for staff. These larger areas could be training areas, classrooms. You have a single elevator on each floor. No windows. Stairs with reinforced doors and alarms.'

'Main level,' Eve picked it up. 'The delivery front lobby, its storage and work areas, access to the shipping dock and garage. A security hub. One floor up, studios, shower area, kitchen area, another security hub, classrooms. Big office at the end there, with a bathroom and an elevator — that's going to be Beaty's office. Lower floor, that's the infirmary, sickrooms, cleaning supplies, employee locker rooms.'

'Top floor,' she continued. 'You've got windows there. They'll be privacy screened, but windows. Big space. Living and dining areas, powder room, big kitchen, big bedroom and bath, home office, home gym, entertainment room. She lives there. Auntie's got herself a nice penthouse apartment.'

She slipped her hands in her pockets. Whatever fatigue she'd felt had snapped away.

'The tunnels. Both sets of plans had tunnels running under, old ones, to be filled in, according to the official ones. But they didn't do that. Where do they lead?'

'We have that, and can show you, but . . . McNab.' Roarke turned to him. 'Your find.'

326

'You have to figure if they take bodies out that way, they'd want to get close to where they dispose of them.' He reached out, finger-touched with Peabody. 'Makes you sick when you think they're doing that to kids. You take the tunnel east from the elevator, then the south fork. It's going to come out under Quiet Rest. Funeral home and crematorium.'

'Good work. Damn good all around.' Eve shoved her hair back again. 'I need everything on the funeral home.'

'I got it,' McNab told her.

'We pile that in.'

Studying the screen, she paced back and forth. And she could see how it could be done. Not fast, not easy, but she could see it.

'Okay, I've called in my detectives, Willowby, some uniforms, Lowenbaum from SWAT, the commander, Reo. I'll pull Mira in. I see how it can work, so let's talk it through, work out any kinks before they all get here.'

20

There were kinks. A building of that size, tunnels beneath, the security, unknown number of adversaries inside. More, the unknown number of minor civilians.

Then there was timing, coordinating with the authorities in France, Devereaux on Long Island, the whereabouts of scouts.

As they worked it, the fatigue crept back.

'Anyone in this room who wants in on the op takes a departmentally approved booster. Including me. Most of us have been up and at this for twenty-four or better.'

'Hate that shit,' Feeney muttered.

'Get in line. I'd say everybody take an hour down, but we don't have it, so the boost. Take ten if you want it. Take a walk, get some air, whatever works. Peabody, sign out six boosters, log everyone's name.'

As she spoke, Willowby came in.

'You're early.'

'So I get the worm. I got more on the auction, wanted to pass it on in person since you called me in anyway.'

'Did you get any sleep?'

'Caught a couple hours. Things are moving.'

'Seven boosters, Peabody. We'll brief in about ten, you can address new data then.'

Willowby scanned the screen, the board. 'Looks like you've got plenty of new.'

'We have the location. We're hitting it this morning.'

'No shit?' Slapping her hands together, Willowby focused on the screen. 'That's the where? Is that the . . . that's the RDS drop-off I use. Fuck me, I've been in that place dozens of times. Now I'm pissed. Can I get in on this?'

'It's why you're here.'

'Well, hot damn. I've got to kick somebody's ass now that I know I stood at that damn counter and there were girls . . . Son of a bitch.'

'We'll get them out. Give me ten, Willowby.'

'Yeah, sure. I gotta walk off the mad.'

When Willowby left and they were alone, Eve turned to Roarke.

'You can't worry about me. I'm talking about my mental and emotional state. I'm handling it, and I'm going to keep handling it.'

'Until?'

'Until it's done. I'm going to say, here, to you, that even though I know it shouldn't, my mental and emotional state need to get this done. And I'm going to say we wouldn't be here, where I know we can get it done, without you. I couldn't have gotten here without you. I don't only mean the e-work. I mean knowing you'd be there if I got shaky. So I'm telling you I won't get shaky. We, every one of us, have to be on top of this, every step of it, every contingency, every unknown — and there are too many of them. We have to, or it won't get done.'

He took his hands out of his pockets, where his fingers had toyed with her old gray button, and put them on her shoulders.

'You're steady as they come. If I had worries about that, you put them to rest an hour ago. Still, you're so bloody tired.'

'Hence the booster. What the hell kind of word is *hence*?'

He just gathered her in, rested his cheek on top of her head. 'Promise me something. If, after it's done, you need to feel shaky, you'll let yourself.'

'After it's done. And you're good with your parts in this?'

'I am. I'm with you, Lieutenant, before, during, and after.'

'I'm going to say I love you, then we need to break this up.'

'I'm going to say I love you.' He tipped her face up to his, kissed her. 'And now we can break this up. Temporarily.'

'Let's plan — when it's done — on getting a bunch of sleep, then having a bunch of wine, then having a bunch of sex.'

'Sex, sleep, wine, more sex.'

'I can agree to that. Break,' she said, and stepped back, stared at the screen. 'It's going to work.'

'I believe that. I had a change of clothes brought in for you. They're in your locker. You'll feel better if you take ten minutes for yourself.'

'Probably would. Shower, change, boost. Okay, thanks. Looks like you grabbed the first two of those already.'

'I did, so I can attest you'll feel better for doing the same.'

'I'll be back in ten.'

She made a beeline for the locker room, and decided if the stingy piss-trickle of almost hot water in the shower felt like luxury, she'd needed it.

And the fact that Roarke had provided, in his

330

Roarke way, a black shirt and trousers, fresh boots, a thin black jacket with magic lining told her he understood she wanted the take-no-bullshit state of mind.

In under ten she headed back to the conference room.

She caught the scent from ten feet away.

Bacon, coffee, sugar.

And from the sound of voices, cops who'd beat her back had dived right in.

Once again the Roarke way, she thought when she stepped in. Thermal dishes and platters huddled on the conference table. One look at the mountain of fluffy scrambled eggs told her he hadn't ordered the fake stuff from Central's Eatery.

Bacon, sausage, bagels, and damn it, she recognized the sticky buns from Jacko's.

She watched the e-team along with Peabody, Willowby, Baxter, and Trueheart piling plates with all of it. Before she could speak, Jenkinson and Reineke barreled in behind her.

'Now *this* is what I call a briefing!' So saying, Jenkinson zeroed in on the sticky buns.

It was hard to blame him.

With a smile, Roarke brought her one of her own.

'I'm going to have a rescue/takedown team loaded with food.'

'Fueled,' he corrected. 'Make sure you eat some eggs.'

Since it was right there, she bit into the sticky bun.

They streamed in. She gestured Lowenbaum and the two cops with him to the table. Found that nicety unnecessary with Santiago, Carmichael, and the uniforms.

Then Mira came in with Jamie Lingstrom —

Feeney's godson, summer intern, college kid. Eve just pointed at him.

'Cap asked me to come in and run the screen for the briefing,' he began.

'And I added to that.' Mira gave Jamie's arm a pat. 'He's closer in age to the victims you'll get out, and may be able to help reassure and keep them calm.'

'You can work in here, in the van, and with Dr. Mira. You're not on the takedown. Not this time,' she said when he started to object. 'But you'll free up McNab, and that's going to help. Take it.'

'Yes, sir.'

'Eat. I'm waiting for the commander, then we roll.'

It's not a damn party, she thought as Jamie spotted the sticky buns and let out a '*Woo!*'

'These girls will feel disoriented, afraid, displaced.' Now Mira laid a hand on Eve's arm. 'We can't know how deep the indoctrination goes for some of them, how deep the trauma. Having Jamie, and Willowby for that matter, as she looks younger than she is, may help. It doesn't end at getting them out.'

'I know it.'

'You do. All of you have done good work here, and when you finish that work, mine really begins. I've called in two other therapists, ones I trust, to help with that.'

'Okay. That's your end. You should get something to eat before the scavengers lick the plates.'

'So should you.'

But as Eve waited by the door, itching to start, Peabody brought her a plate with a scoop of eggs, a couple slices of bacon. And the booster.

'It's not really good to take one on an empty stomach.'

332

'Right.' She didn't think she needed one, not when she felt revved again. But she'd given the order to include herself.

She funneled in a couple bites of eggs — definitely not from the Eatery — then popped the booster with the coffee Peabody handed her.

'They're already getting the gist,' Peabody told her. 'Feeney's giving Jamie the basics so he can handle the screen. And Willowby made Trueheart blush. Twice.'

'Christ.'

'No, I think it's a good thing. She's going to be part of the op — an important part. It's good to make connections. We hauled in more chairs. Not sure if it's enough.'

'It's fine. Not everybody's going to want to sit.'

And finally she saw Whitney striding toward the conference room. With long, lean, lanky Chief Tibble beside him.

Training put her at attention.

'Chief. Commander.'

'Lieutenant.' Tibble scanned the room. 'A breakfast buffet. Excellent idea,' he added as Eve braced to take the heat. 'I've spent the last two hours in holo-briefings with the French, and the commander's done the same on the domestic front regarding the scouting suspects. I could go for one of the cinnamon rolls and some coffee. What about you, Jack?'

'As long as my wife never hears about it. We'll take a seat, Lieutenant. You can begin when you're ready.'

She was beyond ready, but gave it another two minutes, waiting until the brass took seats before she walked to the center of the room.

'Stuff it in, stand or sit. Jamie, on-screen.'

Feet moved; chairs scraped.

Roarke stood in the back, as she'd figured he would. Lowenbaum stood beside him. A scatter of others did the same, coffee mugs in hand.

'I'm not going to spend a lot of time on background. Some of you have been in on this investigation since the beginning. The rest of you are cops, and if you don't know how to keep your ears and eyes open, you shouldn't be.

'We'll start with Mina Cabot. Jamie, let's go.'

She ran through the basics, and had to admit, with next to no prep, Jamie kept up with her.

She answered questions when they came, added details when warranted, and built the framework, as she saw it, of the child trafficking organization.

'We've identified minor females abducted from New York, New Jersey, Pennsylvania, Michigan, Maryland, Virginia.' As she reeled them off, Jamie put their photos on-screen.

'Our investigation indicates they're chosen and abducted by scouts paid through the Red Swan front. Detective Peabody has compiled a priority list of suspects. Detective.'

'Cecil Doggett,' Peabody said as she got to her feet. 'That fucking guy.'

Eve zeroed in on Officer Carmichael. In all the years she'd known him, she'd never seen hot rage in his eyes, or heard him speak in that tone.

'Sir,' he said immediately, 'apologies.'

'You know that fucking guy?' Eve countered.

'I — we — had an incident once.'

'Elaborate.'

'Sir. He was a cop, in Baltimore.'

'Correct.'

'It was a long time ago. I was twelve. My parents

took me and my little sister, my baby brother into Baltimore to visit my grandma. My mother's mother. My mother, her mother, and my mother's sister went out shopping, and to a baby shower for a friend. So my dad took us — the kids — out for ice cream that night, and on the way back, we get pulled over.'

'Traffic stop?'

'No, sir, though that man there used that as an excuse. He came up to my dad's window, put his gun in his face, ordered him out of the car. My sister's screaming, the baby's crying, and I watched him drag my father out of the car, slam him against the hood so hard it busted his lip, had his nose bleeding.'

'Did Doggett have a partner or trainee with him?'

'No, sir. He said how the car was stolen. My dad's telling us to stay still, stay in the car, he's saying it's his car, and he has the registration in the car, got his driver's license in his wallet. He's begging the cop not to hurt his kids. Doggett there, he leaned down low, and I don't know what he said to my dad, but I saw the fear in Dad's eyes. Fear for us.'

The room had gone so quiet, Eve could hear Carmichael breathing.

'People started gathering, calling out, recording it. He cuffed Dad, put him facedown on the ground, and leaned in the car. I thought he was going to shoot me, but he just stared while he got the registration out where Dad told him it was. Took his time with it, checked it against the driver's license.'

Officer Carmichael cleared his throat. 'I believe, always have, if people hadn't been watching, recording, he'd have done a lot worse, but he took the cuffs off. He told my father how he got lucky, this time. Then he walked back to his car and drove off. My father's

335

face was bleeding where he got slammed against the hood. His hands shook. Some of those people came up, asked if he was okay, could they help. But he said he just needed to get his babies home. I know that face on-screen, and I know that name. I've never forgotten it.'

'Did your father report the incident?'

'I don't know if he would have, but someone who recorded it posted it all online, and the next day cops came to my grandmother's, talked to him, to me, too, and my sister. The baby was too young for that. I found out later, because I checked, he got suspended for it, and it wasn't the first time he'd done something like that. So I know that face.'

'He should've been fired and brought up on charges. It's a mark on every cop that he wasn't, right then and there. Justice can move way too slow, and sometimes the system that drives it breaks down. Not this time, Officer. This time, we're going to put Doggett exactly where he belongs.'

'Yes, sir. I trust we will.'

'Peabody, pick it up.'

'Angela Delinski.'

From the scouts, she moved to the suspected guards. Eve took over with Iris Beaty/Swan, then Jonah Devereaux.

'Those are the known suspects and their place on this wheel. We have several locations, and all will be covered, either by the NYPSD or the proper authorities. Our main target is the building where the abductees are held. Secondary are the residences of suspects in New York, the funeral home, and Devereaux's Long Island estate. Main target's blueprints, Jamie.'

336

'The building has seven floors, including the base-ment area, and has access to tunnels. Lieutenant Lowenbaum, I leave it to you where to best position your men, but I need all exits covered, including exterior tunnel exits.'

'We'll work that out,' he assured her.

'The e-team will give us the eyes and ears we need, cut communications, shut down the elevators, including the private one to the top floor and Beaty's residence. We'll have both air and water support.'

'I'm gonna cut in for a minute.' Feeney pushed to his feet. 'We worked out a little something that'll do better than the blueprints. Just a portable deal, but . . .'

He took out a remote, aimed it at the center of the room. A holo, a three-sixty of the blueprints, shimmered on. 'I can turn it. It'll be a little clunky.'

'Nice.' Eve circled it, stepped back into what would be the Hudson, nodded. 'Yeah, nice. Okay, yeah, eyes front. Here's how we take this target down, and priority is the safe recovery and rescue of all abductees.'

She went over every step, every move, adjusted when someone posited an alternative that seemed more solid. She had Feeney speak to the timing and responsibilities of the e-team. Then asked Whitney and Tibble to outline the plans for locations outside of New York.

Then she shifted to other New York locations, assigned teams.

'We'll have transportation for the abductees, and Dr. Mira will supervise that. We have a conference room where they'll wait. They must be interviewed, and Willowby and SVU will handle much of that, along with Dr. Mira and other therapists. Once

337

identified, evaluated, and interviewed, those who have families or guardians can be released into their care. The others will process through Child Services.'

She scanned the room, confident she'd chosen the best, the brightest, and the most dedicated.

'Vests, all around. Takedown teams, battering ram. Tunnel team, night-vision, masks, canisters. Rescue teams, count heads after we've got that count, and get them all out and to their transport. Questions?'

Not anymore, she thought. Each and every one knew their job.

'Gear up. Transpo on garage level one, all teams, all locations. We move out in twenty.'

She walked over to Officer Carmichael. 'After this is done, we clean it up, I'll have Doggett transferred here. But it could take some time. If you want a couple days' leave to go down to Baltimore, I'll clear it.'

'Appreciate that, Lieutenant. I don't need to see him. This is enough. Son of a bitch made me a cop.'

'No, you did. He might've turned you in that direction, because that's who you are. Somebody else, and it's hard to toss blame, might've said fuck them all. You've done credit to your uniform every day I've known you. That's you, Officer.'

'Thank you. Thank you for that.'

After Carmichael left, Lowenbaum moved to her. 'Just give me five minutes to go over our placement with you, all locations.'

She locked it in with him. Then turned to her commander and the chief. 'Are you going to observe the operation of the primary target?'

'We'll be here, coordinating the transfer of prisoners, victims,' Whitney told her. 'And coordinating with the outside locations and their operations. You

338

have the command, Lieutenant.'

'Yes, sir. Sir, Detective Yancy will be with Dorian Gregg this morning, working with her on sketches. I'd like him to bring her here when we have Beaty. I'd like her to confirm ID on her, and anyone else she recognizes.'

'Has Mira cleared this?'

'She has. She believes it will help the minor female, sir. And Reo believes it will only help nail down the legal case.'

'We'll set her up in an Observation area when it's time, with a child advocate.'

'Yes, sir.'

'Get the children out, Lieutenant,' Tibble told her. 'And let's nail the sons of bitches who profited from them to the wall.'

'That's the plan.'

She headed out, crossed paths with Peabody, who handed her a vest and her earbud. 'I'm so ready for this.'

Eve gave her a hard study as they walked to the elevators. 'How much booster did you take?'

'Just the one. It's all I needed. I want to crush them. I want them to squeal and beg for mercy when I do.'

'That's not very Free-Ager of you.'

Peabody snorted. 'I'll light some candles and meditate to rebalance later. Crush now.'

'Do you actually do that? Light candles and stuff?'

'Bet your skinny ass. Sorry!' She sent Eve a wild-eyed, appalled look. 'I'm revved up.'

'I'll let it go — this time.'

'Revved,' she repeated. 'Pissed. And cold. Ice-cold, so don't worry about me not handling it. I do light candles and stuff. It balances out everything we see and do. That and hot jungle sex with McNab keep me level.'

When Eve's eye twitched, Peabody grinned. 'I figured it was a good time to get away with that one.'

'It's never a good time. But since I need you at a hundred percent, I'll put my boot up your ass later.'

'Always something to look forward to.'

And when Eve shoved off the elevator to avoid a crush of cops, Peabody trotted after her.

On the glide, she pulled out her 'link. 'I've got to balance things,' she said, and tagged Nadine.

'Dallas,' Nadine began.

'Listen, don't talk. Here's what you can do, what you can't. I'm going to give you an address. Get there, bring a camera. No live feed. No. Live. Feed,' she repeated. 'Stay across the street. Do not cross to the location. Do not attempt to speak to anyone. Do not release the feed until I say. If you follow all those very specific instructions, I'll clear you to come into Central, do a few select interviews.'

'You found them. You're going in.'

'I've told you all I'm telling you at this time.' She paused a moment. 'You helped find a victim, and she's safe. You get this.' She read off the address.

She clicked off. And when she hit the stairs to the garage level, nodded to herself. 'Better than candles.'

'That's good, that's good and smart.'

'Feels like it. Let's be good and smart now.' She put on her vest as they crossed to the assembled team. 'Check comms,' she ordered as she fit in her earbud. 'Get it done. Take it down, bring them home.'

She climbed in the back of her assigned van, counted heads as her team followed. Peabody, Roarke, McNab, Feeney, and Jamie; Officers Shelby, Dubock, and Marshall. 'We're set. Move out.'

Detectives Carmichael and Santiago's team to the crematorium, uniform teams dispatched to suspects' residences. Jenkinson and Reineke with theirs on the tunnels.

She checked in with Whitney for status on outside locations, then with the commands on water and air support.

'Approaching our mark,' Feeney told her.

Just a normal day for most, Eve thought. Just a muggy morning in the city, traffic snarling, air blimps blasting, people on their way to work, grabbing cart coffee, tourists gawking and hitting up the early side-walk vendors for caps, T-shirts, knockoff designer bags.

Busy, noisy, impatient, and full of life.

And inside one building, one she saw on-screen now, that life filled with fear and misery, with greed and viciousness.

Time to end it.

'Numbers,' Eve said.

'Scanning now.' As he'd been briefed, Jamie started with the tunnels. 'I've got two, in a vehicle due to speed of movement and position.'

When he gave her direction and location, she relayed to the street patrol. 'Pick them up, shut down any communications, search and confiscate vehicle.'

'Basement level,' Jamie continued. 'Four, three standing, the fourth supine. Elevated. That's the infirmary. One leaving area, moving up. Elevator, bypassing main level. Five heat sources front main level, three standing, two sitting. Rear main level, we got four more.'

With the blueprints layered over the screen, Eve

341

identified the delivery front, the back offices, the shipping dock, and as Jamie scanned up, the kitchen area, the dining area for that level, what would be bedrooms, the studio.

She ran the count in her head as he worked.

'That's a hundred and seventy-two heat sources. No way to confirm how many are prisoners. Callendar, you copy?'

'Affirmative,' she said in Eve's ear.

'Take a walk.'

'Copy that.'

On the next screen, Eve watched Callendar stroll along the sidewalk with a shipping box under her arm. When she went inside the building, Eve monitored her heat source on the first screen.

Moving to the counter. Just sending off a package, one they'd scan — SOP.

Seconds later, she heard Callendar's voice — not just through her earbud, but through the monitor's audio.

'Gonna be a hot one.'

'Loud and clear,' Eve said as the clerk chatted back. 'Counter bug activated.'

'Check it,' Callendar said cheerfully as her heat source moved back to the main door. 'Cha.'

'Activate package ears.'

'Activating now. Two females at the counter, one male moving in and out the back.'

'Roarke.'

'Yes, it's coming right along here. I should have the comms down in about two minutes, the front and rear cams as well. And McNab's working on a bit of a bonus.'

'What bonus?'

'Getting a hack into their interior cam system — just the cams,' Mc.Nab told her. 'I should be able to bounce it back to us. Can't finish until the comms are shut or it's gonna show. I'm pretty damn close.'

'Can you hit simultaneous?'

'Should.'

'Feeney, if this works, I want you and Jamie to feed us as much as you can — kids priority. Numbers, locations, proximity to suspects.'

'We're on it.'

'I'm in,' Roarke told her. 'When you're ready.'

'Central Command and all teams, comms going down in five . . .' She pointed at Roarke, 'four, three, two, one.'

'Done.'

'Hack complete. Take it, Cap.'

'We're go, all teams, all locations. We're go.'

21

She jumped out the back with Peabody, McNab, and the uniforms behind her. 'Talk to me,' she demanded as they headed toward the front.

'Baxter's team moving in the rear,' Roarke told her. 'Water side of tunnels blocked. Jenkinson's team moving into tunnels. No activity in the tunnels but yours at this time.'

Jamie added, 'You've got twenty-two kids on the first level, Dallas. Two in that studio, in a bed. Three of the fuckers in there with them. The others sitting in some kind of classroom, two adults in there, two others in the hall.'

'Keep it coming. We're going in.'

Pedestrians scattered when she drew her weapon, and ignoring them, she went through the door.

'Hands up. All hands in the air. NYPSD. I'll drop you,' she warned the man who started to slide a hand in his pocket.

She heard the commotion in the back, and the pounding of cop feet as more uniforms rushed in.

'Restrain, remove, secure,' she ordered. 'Moving up,' she added, and ran for the stairs.

'Roarke's working on deactivating interior locks,' McNab called from behind her. 'It's not all one system, but —'

She took a quick look at the one on the stairway door, stepped back. 'Take it down, Officer.'

Dubock stepped up with the battering ram. It took

two solid hits, then she was through. 'Peel off,' she ordered, then stunned the suited man whirling toward her with a weapon.

Cops scattered in assigned directions. Kitchen area, classrooms, to the next level. Through the shouts, the rush of feet, the whine of discharged weapons, reports from other locations sounded in her ear.

With Shelby, she pounded her way toward the studio. Screams ripped out behind her, and she heard something big and breakable crash in the kitchen area.

Then the hard snap of shock sticks, the low hum of stunners.

She took the studio door down, standard lock, with a flying kick.

She registered the two minors in a bed, two adult males, one adult female.

'Move, I put you down. Take the girls, Shelby.'

'We're the police,' Shelby said as she moved toward the bed. 'You're okay now.'

'On your knees, now!' Eve snapped. 'Hands behind your head.'

The woman with a shock stick in hand flicked it toward Eve, then jittered and fell when the stun hit her mid-body.

The videographer swung the camera and tripod at her while the other charged. To avoid the blow, she dropped into a crouch, fired up. As the camera flew across the room, and he toppled, she pushed up to deliver a kick to the next. He went down before she gained her feet.

She glanced back at Shelby and the weapon in her hand. 'Thanks. Good reflexes. Rescue and containment, first-level studio,' she ordered. 'Two minor females, three suspects. Suspects are down. Stay with the girls, Officer, until Rescue takes them.'

'Lieutenant —'

'Don't leave them,' Eve ordered as the two girls clung to each other and wept. 'We clear this floor, then move up.'

She ran out, sweeping her weapon, separating the voices in her ear — tunnels secured, main level secured, Willowby's team in action on second level, Baxter's team responding there — from the sounds in her ear.

Girl kid screams and wailing, cop shouts.

She found Peabody with two suspects down and restrained, and Officer Marshall trying to deal with the panicked girls. She saw the look of pain on Peabody's face.

'Are you hit?'

'Shock stick — just a graze. Hurts like hell, but I'm good.'

'Listen up!' She shouted it, and most of the wailing eased off. 'We're the police, we're the good guys. You're safe now, and we're going to get you out.'

'Rescue's heading up, sir,' Marshall told her.

'Hold here until. Shelby's got two more girls in the studio, and three suspects down. Peabody, with me. We clear the floor.'

'You can't leave us! You can't leave us,' one of the girls screamed. 'I want my mom!'

'We're not leaving you,' Peabody said in her Peabody way. 'Nobody's going to hurt you anymore, and we're going to get you to your mom.'

Fuck it, Eve thought. 'Stay, stay with Marshall until Rescue gets them out.'

'Dallas.'

'Stay.'

She cleared as she went. Empty rooms, hardly more than cells, locked storage areas holding shock sticks, collars, batons, stunners.

A lot of weaponry, she thought, against a bunch of kids.

She came to another locked door — a double set. High probability, she remembered, for Auntie's office.

'Roarke, do you read?'

'I do.'

'I'm at Beaty's office door. Can you deactivate the lock? No access at this time to a ram, and it's secured like the stair doors.'

'Not anymore it's not.'

'Oh, okay then. Stand by.'

She pushed in, swept.

Efficient luxury, she decided. Fancy desk, high-end D and C, cushy furnishings, private bathroom, she recalled from the blueprints.

And with the office door shut behind her, she heard nothing from outside the room.

'EDD, give me a read on heat sources, my location.'

'Just you, LT,' Jamie told her.

'Read on top floor.'

'One.'

'There you are,' she murmured.

'Willowby, second level. We're clear. I have an injured officer, twenty-six girls, thirteen mother-fuckers. Baxter's team on assist and now moving up to the next level to assist McNab's team.'

'First floor clear and secured. Heading up. Jamie, monitor that heat source. I want to know where she moves if she moves.'

On the second floor, she found Rescue escorting girls out, weeping girls, silent ones with glazed eyes.

'Dallas.' Willowby swiped a hand over her forehead. 'Permission to bring in two more from SVU. We've got a lot of vics here.'

'Granted. The injured officer?'

'She took a baton hit to the arm. Looks broken. Medical's on the way.'

'I'm moving up.' She held up a finger as Jenkinson spoke in her ear. 'Copy that. Have medical take her, call for removal of the suspects. Infirmary level's clear,' she told Willowby. 'We got the doctor, another so-called medical, and an unconscious girl strapped to the damn table. Brought her in this morning — that vehicle driving out of the tunnels.'

'Did we get them?'

'We got them. I'm heading up,' she said again.

On the next level, she took out a fleeing woman with a bare-knuckled fist to the face. Stopped short of doing the same when she realized the one charging her was maybe twelve.

'Hey, hey.' Eve blocked the punch. 'I'm a cop. I'm here to get you out.'

'Fuck the fucking cops.'

Eve dodged the kick, pivoted, and wrapped her arms around the girl from behind.

'Stop, stop now.'

'I'll kill you!'

'Knock it off! Jesus Christ, Trueheart,' she said when he, mouth bleeding, ran her way.

'Sorry, Lieutenant. Some of the kids scattered. They're scared.'

'I get that, but — I said knock it off!' Eve snapped when the kid tried to kick Trueheart. 'We're the NYPS-fucking-D, and we're getting you the hell out of here. There are a lot of girls in here these bastards

348

snatched and hurt, and we're going to help them. If you run when I let you go, you're on your own.'

'I've been on my own my whole life.'

'Yeah, sad story.' She nearly sighed with relief when a Rescue team came through the stairwell door. 'You can go with them, help us put the fuckers who did this to you, and all the others, in cages, or you can take off and help them keep doing it.'

'Screw them, screw you, and everybody else.'

'Okay then.' Eve released her. 'Go.'

The girl rounded on Eve.

'Lottie,' Eve said. 'Lottie Crug.'

'How the hell do you know? I don't know where the hell I am, and screw you, I'm not leaving Carrie.'

'Who's Carrie?'

The girl's eyes went to molten slits. 'Trainee 282.' She snarled it. 'They took her down for vids, the fucking pervs, and —'

'Describe her.'

'She's a white girl, long blond hair, and —'

'Blue eyes, maybe a hundred pounds. Carrie Wheeler.' Another face on her board, Eve thought. 'We got her out, her and the girl they had with her. The three assholes who held them in there are currently in lockup.'

'Maybe you're lying.'

'Not everybody lies,' Trueheart said, and the girl snorted.

'What planet are you from?'

Eve watched Baxter and two officers lead a group of girls their way.

'Check with Dr. Mira,' Eve told the Rescue team. 'Have her locate Carrie, so Lottie can see for herself.'

'If you're lying, I'll find you, and I'll make you pay.'

'Well, that terrifies me. Is this level clear?' she asked Baxter.

'That's affirmative.'

'Heading up.' She released the girl. 'Don't be stupid. Baxter, Trueheart, with me.'

She started up. 'Jamie, status on top floor.'

'She's moving around, just started to. I think she was eating breakfast or something before.'

'I'm going up. Help clear the next levels,' she told Baxter. 'I'm taking the top.'

'Want backup?' Baxter asked her.

'I like my odds on the one-to-one.'

She jogged up the stairs, level by level. Fifty-eight girls secured so far, came the report in her ear. Another twelve in the process. Eighty-six suspects in custody.

'Roarke, do some magic on her door. Jamie, where is she?'

'The bathroom. I, ah, think she, you know, relieved herself. Looks like she's washing her hands.'

'Too bad. Lowers the possibility she pisses herself when I take her. I'm at the door.'

'It's got an alarm, taking it down. Hold there.'

'Come on, come on,' she whispered, bouncing on her toes.

'She's in the bedroom, Dallas,' Jamie told her.

'And the lock's down. Mind my cop.'

'You bet.'

Eve pushed in as Beaty stepped out of the bedroom doorway.

'Hi, Auntie. Hands up, turn and face the wall. Well, shit,' she said when Beaty leaped back, slammed the door. Eve heard the sharp click of the lock.

'Yeah, that'll make a difference.'

She stepped up, kicked it open, whirled away. And

wasn't a bit surprised to hear the stunner stream hit the wall behind her.

'It's a cliché, but needs to be said. The place is surrounded. You've got nowhere to go. So, you know, come out with your hands up.'

'Come and get me.'

'Dallas, Lowenbaum. We burned through the privacy screens, and have a clear shot of the subject on the top floor. Want us to take it?'

'And spoil my fun? Just hold.'

She dived, facing the opening, sweeping streams as the return fire hit over her head.

The gasp of pain brought huge satisfaction.

Beaty had dropped to her knees, her right arm shaking where the stream had grazed her. Her stunner lay on the floor.

'Go ahead, try for it. It won't be a glancing hit this time.'

'I know who you are. Bitch.'

'Yeah? I know who you are. Move another inch toward it, we'll be carting your unconscious ass out of here. You're done, get it? The girls are out, your perverted staff is in custody. Now, down on your face, hands behind your back.'

'I don't take orders. I give them!'

With that, she lunged up, charged. Eve had a split second to decide, but since she already had, it didn't take that long.

She lowered the weapon in her right hand and led with her left.

One jab in the face.

'That's for Mina Cabot.'

Beaty's head snapped back; her eyes went glassy for an instant. Then she snarled, grabbed for Eve's weapon with one hand, tried a right cross with the other. Blocking most of it — a couple of knuckles on the chin got through — Eve stomped her boot on Beaty's designer heel.

'That can be for Dorian Gregg. And this?' The uppercut had Beaty's eyes rolling back white. 'For all the others.' She stepped over to put her boot on the dropped stunner.

Breathed out, breathed clear as she studied the woman sprawled at her feet.

'Subject is down.'

Her weapon swung back up when she caught movement in the doorway. Then lowered with a shake of her head when she saw Roarke.

'Nearly took a stream, pal.'

'I trust your reflexes. I wasn't needed in the van, so I thought to see what you were up to.' He tapped his chin. 'Caught you a bit, did she?'

'Caught her more.'

'So I see. The rest of the teams are a bit busy at the moment. One of the guards got to a weapons lockup before it could be secured.' He held up a hand. 'Under control or I wouldn't have simply continued up.'

'Injuries?'

'I can't tell you, but Peabody indicated all minor on your side. Mira's already cleared about twenty of the girls, medically, so they can be taken into Central. Feeney's already having at the electronics. When do you want to leave?'

She crouched, secured Beaty's hands behind her back. 'Now's good, or as soon as I get the clear from all teams, and somebody comes up and hauls this one out of here.

'Here comes Peabody.' Eve turned to the door as

her partner, one eye swollen, rushed to the door.

'We're clear. Got the last of the girls out. Bad guys in custody, already transported, or secured and awaiting same.'

'Good. Who punched you in the eye?'

'Elbow jab. Jenkinson took a double stream to the chest. Even with the vest, it knocked him on his ass. He is pissed. But we kicked their ass a lot harder.'

'We kicked their ass. Start processing those kicked asses, and get some muscular uniforms up here to haul her out. She's no lightweight.'

'You're going? You sure you don't want me to go with?'

'Need you at Central. Long Island team,' she said into her comm. 'We're a go in . . . five,' she said when Roarke held up five fingers. Then she pointed at the stunner on the floor. 'Make sure that gets bagged and taken in, Peabody. Good work, and put an ice pack on the eye.'

'You've got a bruise on your jaw.'

'Shit.' She rubbed at it. 'Well, all in a day's.'

★   ★   ★

She hated this part, but knew the timing mattered too much to indulge herself. When she reached the roof, she took one look at the waiting jet-copter and sucked it up.

She got in, strapped in as the others — Feeney, McNab, Lowenbaum, and two of his men along with two uniforms — did the same.

Roarke took the pilot's chair while she took out her 'link and notified the Long Island PSD currently watching the estate that they were on their way.

A lot of manpower, she thought — because she wanted to think of anything but the sound of the damn flying machine roaring to life — for one rich, middle-aged pervert, but they didn't know how many they'd come up against.

The copter lifted off the roof, then shot like a bullet from a gun over the city. She sucked it up harder and turned to Feeney.

'You're sure you can do this from the air?'

'Got a few extra toys.' He flicked a glance at Roarke but didn't elaborate on those specifics. 'We get close enough, we'll jam up their alarms, their cams, their comms.'

'Somebody's going to notice that.'

'Yeah, they are, so you're going to have to move fast.'

'We can and will neutralize any targets outside,' Lowenbaum said when she shifted to him. 'It's what we do, Dallas.'

In theory, she thought, all she, the uniforms, McNab — if Feeney didn't need him — had to do was get inside, take down any guards posted in the house, get to Devereaux, and arrest his ass.

It remained a possibility, one she considered a likelihood, he had innocent civilians inside.

Maybe it was just a business to him, but wouldn't he want some of the fringe benefits?

'On approach, Feeney.'

'We're ready.'

Eve sucked up more and looked. She saw the estate — the high white walls framing it, the green lawns, the gardens where everything lined up like soldiers, the sparkling blue waters of a swimming pool, and the glass-walled house beside it.

354

She saw the greener-than-green nine-hole golf course, a small orchard, a gatehouse, another two outbuildings, the frigging jet-copter pad.

And the main house, as white as the walls that separated it from the world. Some stone terraces spread on the top three levels with wide stone steps leading up or down, all graced by lavish urns of flowers or dwarf trees.

Tall windows shined like diamonds.

'Going silent,' Roarke said, and Eve resisted the desperate need to close her eyes.

The roar snapped off — how could she know how much she'd miss it? — and though she braced for the crash, the copter glided, as Roarke had assured it could and would, over the sparkling blue water, the greener than green.

'You've got your window, Feeney.'

'And we're going through it. Jamming now. Alarms down.'

'Touchdown in ten.'

'Cams down.'

'In five.'

'Comms down. This baby is sweet!'

They didn't land on the pad like a feather, but neither did they experience the bone-jolting shock she'd expected.

Rather than bless her luck, she shoved out. 'Get the gates open for backup from the locals.'

'Smooth ride,' Lowenbaum said as he jumped out after. Then he was all business as he and his men fanned out.

Like the bone-jolt, she'd expected a flood of quick-responding opposition, but she covered the ground nearly halfway to target before she saw a single male step from an outbuilding.

He looked annoyed, then spotted her. Even as he drew his weapon, the stun struck, took him down.

'McNab, heat sources interior, how many and where?'

'Two in the kitchen area, two in the smaller dining room — one sitting — one in the entrance hall, all main level. Two on the second floor, none on the third. Cap's taking it from here, I'm moving out.'

She paused, backtracked, and with the floorplan in her head, angled toward what had to be the window of the smaller of two dining rooms.

'Son of a bitch is having breakfast. A woman with him, standing. She's wearing a collar, and not much else.'

'McNab, use the outside steps, take the second floor with the officers, secure it.' She glanced over as Roarke stepped up beside her. 'We've got the entrance and dining. Lowenbaum?'

'Only two, both in the gatehouse. Secured.'

'Take the kitchen. Nobody moves in until my go.'

'Copy that.'

'Side door down there.' She gestured. 'Can Feeney lift the locks? I want to move on him before they bust the others down.'

'Easier for me, manually.'

'Then let's do that.'

* * *

Inside, enjoying his steak and eggs and coffee, Devereaux smiled at Luna. 'You did very well last night. So well, I had the need for good, rare, red meat.'

'Thank you, Master.'

'I believe I'll find several years of enjoyment in you before I sell you off.' He ran a hand up her inner thigh. 'You put me in a celebratory mood. I'm going to host a small party tonight with a few intimate friends. I have no doubt they'll enjoy you as much as I.'

He skimmed those fingers over her center. 'Does that please you, Luna? Does it excite you?'

She stared straight ahead as he fondled her. 'What pleases you pleases me.'

'Enthusiasm,' he snapped.

She looked down at him, into his eyes. She smiled, rocked her hips.

'Better. Tonight, it's going to please me to have you laid out on this very table, a tasty entrée. It will please me to fuck you while my guests watch, then it will please me to watch while they do whatever they want to you. Use you, abuse you.'

He pinched her thigh, hard enough to mark it, then went back to his breakfast.

'Oh, not too much, just enough.

'You'll be a delicious centerpiece we can devour. One in your cunt, one in your ass, one in your mouth. I need to see your full potential while you entertain me and my guests.'

'My potential.'

'That's right. It's time I have my monthly parties again. You'll be the star.' His eyes went hard when she said nothing. 'I expect gratitude for giving you this privilege, for making you a showpiece.'

'Gratitude,' she repeated.

'Yes, gratitude, for that, and this.' He cut a small piece of steak, tossed it to the floor. 'Eat it. Get down on your hands and knees and eat it so you remember what you are. My dog.'

Her chin dropped to her chest. A dog. She'd had a dog once, and loved him so. She'd been a girl once. She'd been free once.

Her heart wept and wept.

She started to lower to her hands and knees, and he laughed.

'Good doggie.'

Then her hand was on the knife, and the knife plunged into his throat even as her collar ripped pain through her.

She screamed, against the pain, against the years of fear and humiliation. She stabbed again.

'Move in, Dallas!' Feeney shouted. 'Dining room, heat sources — one fading. Entrance subject on the run in that direction.'

'Move in!' Eve ordered, and leaped through the door when Roarke dropped the locks.

Beyond the expansive foyer with its golden sand tiles and towering ceilings a wide staircase swept. From beyond that came the screams. Eve shifted her attention right, left, up, as she rushed across the tiles into plush, empty rooms washed in sunlight.

As she did, the screams stopped. She heard a voice — female — in a tone of quiet pleading as she kept moving forward, then angled left.

And through a doorway into a dining room that smelled of coffee and blood. The man who had been Jonah Devereaux slumped in the high-backed chair, his mouth open in stunned surprise, his eyes fixed and staring as blood poured from the wounds in his throat, his chest, shoulders. A woman in a white thong and bra, a thin, transparent robe, and thick black collar stood over him.

Blood splattered her and dripped from the knife

she gripped.

She bared her teeth at Eve and raised the knife high as if to strike again.

'You need to drop the knife. We're the police.' Eve didn't shout it, but kept her eyes fixed on the woman's. 'We're here to help you.'

'Don't hurt her. Please don't hurt her.'

Eve lifted a hand toward a second woman, one in a black skin suit and collar. 'We're not here to hurt her. You need to stay back.'

'Please, you don't understand.'

'Roarke.'

'We understand very well.' Roarke moved to the second woman.

'Put the knife down,' Eve repeated, 'and step away from him.'

'I killed him.'

Had her eyes looked like that, Eve wondered, when she'd crouched over the body of Richard Troy, when she'd gripped the bloody knife she'd plunged into him again and again?

'Put the knife down,' she said yet again. 'We need to get that collar off you.' And she lowered her weapon. 'No one's going to hurt you. Back off,' she ordered as one of her uniforms moved into another doorway. 'Everyone, back off.'

'I won't go back. I won't.' Now the woman brought the knife to her own throat. 'Death is better.'

'Stop. Look at me. Give me your name. What's your name?'

'They took it when they took me.'

'Take it back. What's your name?'

'I — my name is Amara,' she said as her eyes filled. 'I am Amara Gharbi. I was. I am. I was.'

'If you use that knife on yourself, Amara, he wins. They took you from your home, from your family. Do you have family, Amara?'

'I did, in the before. But —'

'We're going to help you get back, to your home, to your family.'

'I killed him. I gave him death.'

'They stole your life,' Eve said as she cautiously moved forward. 'Let us help you take it back, Amara.'

'He said — he said he would have a party, and his guests would do what they wished to me.'

'It's an initiation.' The other woman stood shivering and weeping as Roarke deactivated her collar. 'He did the same to me when they first brought me here. I'm glad he's dead. Glad he's dead. I wish I'd had the courage.'

'It's over now. This part's over now,' Eve corrected, because it was never really over. 'You stopped him, so this part's over. Give me the knife, Amara, and let us help you get through the rest. You have to trust me. Please.'

She lifted her left hand, closed it over Amara's on the handle of the knife. She could wrench it away, use her weapon on light stun. But she wanted Amara to make the choice.

'He's finished,' Eve murmured. 'Finished hurting you and all the others. You're safe now, Amara. Let me have the knife. Let me have it so we can get you home to your family.'

When Amara let it go, Eve nodded at the uniform, held it out to him. 'Let's get that collar off you. Come over here.'

'He said — he said I was his dog. And he laughed, he laughed. I killed him. I killed him. I picked up the knife, and the pain, the pain. I didn't care.'

'I know.'

But Amara shook her head. 'No, no, no. You can't.'

As Amara wept, Eve holstered her weapon, put arms around her. 'I can,' she whispered. 'I do.'

22

She had Amara and the imprisoned domestics transported, with medical supervision, to Central. And sent the three guards Lowenbaum's team had handled back with them in another transport.

'I need to do the official on-site on the body. We're going to need the EDD team to go over the electronics, flag for transfer.'

'Place this size?' Feeney glanced around. 'We're gonna need a bigger boat.'

Due to Roarke's fondness for classic vids, she knew that one, nearly laughed. 'Yeah. First priority is any and all auction data. The more we know there, the wider the net.'

'We'll get on it. I'll pull in some of the locals to assist.'

He glanced over at Devereaux. 'I'd rather see him rotting in prison for a few decades, but I can't say justice wasn't fucking served, and on a damn platter. You want one of the locals to give you a hand with him?'

'No, I've got it. When I'm done, they can bag and tag him. Then I need to head back.'

'Another long day, but this one? It's a good one.'

She nodded and carried her field kit over to the body. For an instant, her father's face shimmered over Devereaux's.

Then it faded, and she got to work.

When she finished, made the arrangements, she

stepped out of the dining room, gave herself a minute to wander and breathe.

She supposed the estate rivaled Roarke's castle in size and scope. Apparently, Devereaux hadn't gone for antiques or what she could consider cozy spaces. Everything here was hard, bright, new.

His money — or his ancestors' money — hadn't satisfied him, she thought. It hadn't been enough for him to own a successful, respected business, to own precious things. He'd needed to own people.

Women and girls.

When Roarke found her, he cupped her face, kissed her lightly.

'I'm fine,' she told him.

'I see that. I didn't have a moment to tell you the way you handled Amara showed exactly who you are. A quick stun would've been simpler and quicker for you.'

'She'd been hurt enough.'

'She won't forget you. Now I'm more than pleased to tell you we've come across a treasure trove of data on the auction.'

'He pulled the strings there, too,' she said. 'Probably set up a different arm, shell, whatever to keep from muddying things up, but he headed that up.'

'Got it in one, didn't you?' Now Roarke angled his head. 'But I see you already suspected something of the sort.'

'Power. All of it came down to power. His. I'm curious to see if Beaty had a piece of that, too. I'm thinking no, no because it's too much power sharing, and that was his greed. But I'll find out either way.'

'With the data here? You'll have the dates of every transaction — through previous auctions and through

Red Swan. The buyers, the victims, the price paid. All of it.'

The satisfaction of that, the relief of it, had her scrubbing her face with her hands, walking around the ornate entrance hall.

'The current auction, can we still play that out? Some of the buyers could be new to this, but that doesn't mean they don't pay for attempting to buy a human being.'

'We can, of course. Feeney and McNab are already feeding data to Central.'

'Good. Good. We'll give it all to the feds. I'm going to request Teasdale use Willowby as NYPSD liaison on it. She earned it.'

'A very good call, Lieutenant. I'm not especially needed here at this point, so when you're ready, I'm with you.'

'I'm ready now.' More than ready, she admitted, to get out and away from this hard, bright house. 'And you have to change and go to work.'

'I do have to go in for a bit of time, but I don't need to change. I'm the boss, after all. But I've had a change of clothes sent in for you.'

'Why?'

'When you held Amara, his blood was still wet on her. And so on you.'

'Oh.' She glanced down, blew out a breath at the bloodstains on her shirt, her jacket. 'You know what? Let it ride. Let them see it when I have them in the box.'

She checked in with Peabody for status, then contacted Yancy to arrange for Dorian to come in to Central.

'He says she nailed Beaty,' Eve said as she strapped

in for the flight back. 'But we're going to add the flesh-and-blood ID there, and see if she, or any of them, can do the same with some of the others.'

She sat back, closed her eyes a moment. 'We may not find out who shoved that spike of wood into Mina Cabot. Not the single individual responsible for that.'

'They're all responsible, aren't they?'

'That's how I see it. That's how I expect the courts to see it. But.'

He reached over, rubbed his hand over hers. 'What that brave child began, you're finishing. There'll be payment, Eve, and with payment, justice. And with that payment and justice, some closure for her family.'

She could see them, the mother, the father, the brother, huddled together in a pool of grief.

'They'll never get over it.'

'I don't know how anyone could, but what you've done will help them get through it. And surely there's a young girl out there right now who'd be a target, tonight, tomorrow, next week. Now she'll live the rest of her life never knowing that. Never knowing she owes that life to Mina and Dorian, to you and all the rest who fought for her. It matters, I think, she'll never know.'

She looked at him, loved him. 'Maybe she'll grow up to be a total asshole.'

And he looked at her, loved her. 'Maybe she'll grow up to be a damn good cop.'

She considered. 'I guess it's all fifty-fifty.'

When they landed at Central — sweet relief — she climbed out, and he lifted off to fly to his Midtown office.

By the time she got down to Homicide through the cop buzz of a major bust, she wanted five minutes of quiet and coffee. She'd take two minutes if she could have a giant coffee.

But she ran straight into Reo.

'Good, you're back. Jenkinson and Reineke are working one in Interview A, Carmichael and Santiago have another in B, Peabody's with Willowby — who's splitting her time between dealing with the victims in conference room three and Interview. I've got —'

'Conference room — the working one.' There went two minutes in her office, Eve thought as she strode down the hall.

'I've already got one who's ready and willing to flip on the others,' Reo continued. 'Apparently, she was friendly with Marlene Williamson, and she's been ready to bolt since they terminated Williamson. She'll testify, and she's talked her ass off already.'

'What did you give her?'

'Twenty in — that's solid, no wiggle — on-planet.' Reo held up a hand. 'She's already rolled on Beaty and a host of others. Among those others are a few we don't have — but now will very shortly.'

In the conference room, Eve headed straight to the coffee.

'I've just finalized the deal,' Reo continued. 'It's a win, Dallas. You've got a lot of hard cases in this, and we're not going to get a bouquet of confessions out of them. What she's feeding us will give us a mountain for the trials.'

'I'm going to get a confession out of Iris Beaty.'

'You're going to have to go through her lawyer. Word is she's called in big guns.'

'Name.'

'Sampson Merit, great big guns with offices in East Washington, New York, and New L.A.'

366

'Did she have him on tap?'

'I'd say yes, as he's already here and consulting with her.'

'Can we freeze her finances?'

'We'd have to analyze and separate what she'd earned legally prior to the Academy, then —'

Eve waved that away, pulled out her comm. 'Callendar, whatever you're doing, stop that and do this. Sampson Merit, lawyer, New York, East Washington, New L.A. Dig in, dig deep. Find me the connection to Iris Beaty and the Academy. Get me the dirt because he's going to be dirty.'

'Got my shovel right here,' Callendar said before Eve clicked off.

'I've heard a lot of things about Merit, Dallas, but never any whiff of this sort of thing.'

Eve shook her head. 'She had him on tap, and he jumped. She's got something on him.' Eve pointed to the board. 'This is ugly stuff, and it'll get uglier in the media, and dragged out. A big deal like that doesn't need the money, doesn't need to risk his rep this way. Maybe he's just a shitbag, and he'll jump this fast at the idea of a case that's going to pay big and get him in on-screen. But it's just as likely the other way. Never caught a whiff? How much do you want to bet plenty will say the same when we start arresting the really rich assholes who buy kids online?'

'That's a fair point.'

'Catch me up, will you?'

'Doggett, the former Baltimore cop, picked up and being transferred here. Maxine Pryor, picked up and currently being grilled — she settled for a less shiny lawyer, but she's got some gloss.'

As she ran it down, Eve paced and absorbed.

367

'Let Beaty stew awhile longer. We're going to run through as many of the others as we can. I've got Dorian Gregg coming in. Plenty of the other victims can ID her, but I want to give this to Dorian first. Mira can decide if any of the others are ready to do the same.

'She's in three?'

'Last I checked. I should get back, keep it rolling. The boss and two more APAs are observing and serving.'

Eve walked down to the conference room, eased the door open. She saw about a hundred girls, some huddled together, some sitting still and quiet. And she recognized many of the faces from her board.

She signaled to Mira.

'I'm sorry to interrupt,' she began when Mira crossed to her.

'Not at all. We're making progress — getting names, evaluating, even contacting parents, guardians. The longest held we know of at this point was taken two years ago, the shortest was taken only yesterday.'

'The one we rescued from the infirmary?'

'Yes, nine years old, abducted from outside of Columbus, Ohio, walking back from her piano lesson.'

'I want to put Beaty and some of the others in lineup. I need you to decide which ones can handle that, can handle doing some IDs.'

She spotted the girl who'd fought her in the Academy sitting with her arm around a younger kid. And took a chance by crossing the room, crouching in front of her.

'Remember me, Lottie?'

'Yeah.'

'Carrie. You need anything?'

'I want to go home,' Carrie said.

'We're working on it.' She looked back at the other girl. 'Want to pay them back?'

'Fucking A.'

'Good. I'm going to send for you in a bit. You're going to take a look at some people. They won't be able to see or hear you. And if you recognize anybody, you just say so.'

'I don't leave her.'

'Okay.'

Eve started to straighten up.

'You've got blood on your shirt. Is it some of theirs?'

'Yeah, it is.'

'Good.'

Eve walked back. 'That one,' she said to Mira. 'She can handle it. The one with her, I don't know.'

'Carrie. We've notified her parents, and they're on their way.'

'You wouldn't have done that without taking a look at the parents.'

'Everything points to them being good people. They have two other children, older kids.'

'Let them know the one with her? She wouldn't leave her behind. She wouldn't leave her and fought to get to her. Let them know that if I don't get a chance to speak with them.'

'I will.'

'I'll let you know when we're ready for the lineup.'

She walked down to Observation and found her commander stepping out.

'Let's use your office,' he said, and led the way. Inside, he gestured to her AC. 'If I could.'

'Absolutely.' She programmed coffee.

369

'The operation in France rescued forty-two victims and arrested eight suspects. One officer is currently hospitalized and in serious condition. Other injuries, on all sides, are reported as minor.'

He drank coffee. 'Devereaux is dead.'

'He was dead when we got to him, yes, sir. Amara Gharbi, age twenty, was abducted from Tunisia nearly eight years ago. She was collared, Commander, as were the other victims we rescued from that location. Gharbi was in severe distress, in fear for her life when she picked up the knife from the table. She —'

'You don't need to sell me, Lieutenant.'

'We have the names of all the victims rescued from the Devereaux estate, none are minors, all state they were abducted at various ages and trained at either the Academy in New York or the facility in France before being sold and/or rented. Devereaux raped all of them upon their arrival at the estate, multiple times, and often held what he called parties where his guests could also rape and abuse them. At this point in time, all but Gharbi were designated as domestics, which their statements agree was his routine. He recently traded in another woman.'

'I see. Do we know her status or location?'

'Not yet. EDD is searching his records.'

'All right then. Some of these subjects will also face federal charges. I've spoken with Agent Teasdale. She'll consult with you when you're ready.'

'I appreciate the leeway, sir.'

'You took considerable,' he reminded her. 'And your judgment was correct.'

'Thank you, sir.' She turned at the tap on her door-jamb. 'Detective Yancy. Dorian?'

'In the bullpen, Lieutenant, with Ro and Ms. Vera,

from CPS. She did great. If I could show you?'

She gestured him in, waited while he opened his sketchbook. 'She dug on the hand sketches, so I went with that rather than comp generated.'

'That's Iris Beaty. That's damn good.'

'Did one full length.' He flipped a page, had Eve's blood pumping. She wanted Beaty in the box.

'Really damn good,' Eve murmured.

'She hits details.' Yancy pushed at his curling mop of hair. 'I've got three more suspects, and I think she could give us more, but you said it was time to bring her in.'

'We're going to line them up for her. Show me the rest. That's the night matron, the dead one. The doctor, and I don't have a name on this one yet.'

'Cyril Gum,' Whitney supplied. 'Santiago and Carmichael are interviewing him now, and he's holding his line.'

'We'll put him up for her, see how he holds it after that. Good work, Yancy. We'll get copies for the file, get the originals to the PA.

'Sir, I need to review the interviews before I bring Beaty and her lawyer up. Reo tells me we've already flipped one.'

'Let me know when you're ready, Dallas. And good work, as usual, Detective.'

'Buy me some time, Yancy, and take her through another. I want her occupied.'

'Glad to do it.'

When he left, Eve sat and began her review.

An hour into it, she paused when she heard Peabody's clump.

'Please, coffee, please.'

Eve jerked a thumb at the AutoChef.

371

'Philamenia Horowitz,' Peabody said as she got her coffee. 'Cleaning supervisor and Domestic instructor. She taught those trainees selected as Domestic Slaves. Three years in, and you know what? You know the fuck what? She has daughters of her own, teenage daughters, but she did this. Needed the job — boo-hoo — needed the money. Never hurt anyone, taught useful skills. Sniveling bitch.'

'Status?'

Peabody gulped coffee. 'Cracked her like an egg. And I got to be bad cop. Willowby looks like a kid, so I got to come in hard. She flipped on Beaty among others, tried to claim she had no idea what was really going on, and we shoveled out that bullshit. Carlyse, one of the APAs, dealt her a hard twenty. See how she likes it.'

'Where's Willowby?'

'She's checking in with Feeney, something about the auction and the change of status there. We didn't have time to talk about it. What's the change?'

'Dead Devereaux ran it. Something Beaty may or may not have been aware of.'

'So he was double-dipping.'

'That's one way to put it. He could buy, sell, trade, collect the membership fees, take the auction house percentage, and preview all the other entries. And I'm thinking an enterprising soul like him? Maybe you supplement with a little blackmail here and there.'

'So like quadruple-dipping. How about the woman who stabbed Dead Devereaux?'

'I have to check on her, but no charges. Her family in Tunisia — parents, two sibs — has been or will shortly be contacted. For now at least, we have to leave the bulk of the victims to Mira, the therapists, and SVU while we keep cracking those eggs.'

'I'm ready for that.' Seriously ready, Peabody did a quick boxer's shuffle. 'Who's up first?'

Eve checked the time and decided she couldn't wait any longer. 'I'm putting Beaty and some of the others in lineups. Check with Mira. She was going to select some of the victims she thought could handle it. I've got Dorian with Yancy.'

The battle light in Peabody's eye went soft and sober. 'You're giving them back power. The power these people took from them.'

'Positive eyewitness identification is the purpose, but that's a solid side benefit. I'll set it up, get Dorian. Meet me with the others.'

She left it to the PA to roll over defense lawyerly objections. She didn't mind the delay, as it gave her a chance to see Sampson Merit's tap dance. She started with one of the hard cases, Frank Bestor, security, an egg who'd yet to show the thinnest crack.

Dorian stood with her arms folded as behind the one-way glass men filed out. 'Number three, that one,' she said without hesitation. 'I saw him around.'

'Around where?'

'The Academy, where do you think? And some-times he'd come into the studio and watch. He'd meet with Auntie in her office, mostly during the day, but . . . Can you make him say something?'

'What do you want him to say?'

'Um. Spread out and find those bitches.'

She stepped to the intercom. 'Number three, step forward. Repeat this. Spread out and find those bitches.'

He curled his lip, but repeated the phrase.

'That's him, that's him. He was in the tunnels that

night, and outside when we were hiding. He said that before Mina ran. She ran because he said that, and I couldn't run.'

'Number three, step back. Dorian, you're going to step out with Dr. Mira.'

'Why?'

'I have others who need to look at the lineup.'

'But I said it was him. If you don't believe —'

'I absolutely believe you, but why should you have all the fun? The more of you who ID him, the more he'll pay.'

Out of six witnesses, Eve got five positive IDs. She worked her way up the chain, security, matrons, instructors, medical personnel, until she came to what she considered the grand prize.

When Beaty filed out with the next group, Dorian let out a gasp.

'Number four, four, four. Number four. That's Auntie. That's her. I swear to God that's her.'

'Okay. Take a breath. Take a few of them.'

'She has to pay.'

'She will. Look at her. She already is.'

'It's not enough.'

'It will be. You've given me everything I need to make it be enough. Now you have to leave it to me. You're going to go back to the school now, and you're going to live your life. You're going to make something of it because that makes her pay, too. Every smart thing you do, from this moment on, makes her pay.'

'How?'

'Because she wanted to take it all from you, and instead you're taking it all back. She tried to make you nothing, and you'll make yourself something.'

Tears gleamed and burned. 'Mina's still dead.'

374

'I can't change that. But everything you do now gives Mina's bravery meaning. Don't forget that. Go on out. Rochelle's waiting for you.'

Dorian took one last look at Beaty. 'Rot in hell,' she said before she walked out.

'Well done, Eve.'

Eve shook her head at Mira. 'It's not over yet.'

'No, but that young, damaged girl is already healing, and you're a part of why.'

'I didn't have half her guts at that age.'

'I completely disagree.'

Eve just took a few of those breaths herself and called in the next witness.

With Iris Beaty, she got a solid six out of six.

'We're going to wrap her up and wrap her tight,' Reo stated. 'No deals,' she added before Eve could speak. 'I'm going to love having a chair at the table at her trial, and I'd bank on us against Merit on this one, all the way.'

'I'm taking her in the box, and don't bet against me breaking her.'

'I never do.'

'I'd hoped to shake things up with the lawyer, but —' Eve broke off when Callendar ran in. 'But hell, what have you got?'

'It took a frigging backhoe, and — okay — with everybody tied up in the auction deal and the dead guy's e's, I gave Roarke a tag for a quick remote assist.'

'Results. We can talk method later.'

'Sampson Merit goes by deepdaddy online — at least as his underground handle for trolling kiddie porn sites, and for registering for the aforesaid auction. He's participated in same — using different handles — for ten years we found so far. And — got more — he has a private residence on Long Island, not far from Devereaux's, titled under another name, under a shell, under more bullshit. This is not one of the residences he shares with his wife of twenty-several years.'

'Deepdaddy?' Eve repeated.

Callendar bared her teeth. 'Yeah, and sure, ick, but he's in this. I tagged Feeney on the way down to you, and he's looking to see if Merit helped him set up the not-so-legal stuff for the Academy, the auction.'

'Enough to arrest?' Eve asked Reo.

'Let me take a look at it, huddle with the boss. Give me twenty. Maybe thirty.'

'I'm putting them in the box.' And going to consult with Teasdale, she decided. 'That'll get you twenty, maybe thirty.'

'Send me everything, Callendar,' Reo said, on the move.

'Same goes. And good work, Detective.'

'Feels good. Feels like a damn good day.'

'Let's keep that going.' Eve yanked out her comm. 'Peabody, get Beaty and her lawyer in a box, meet me in my office, and move it.'

She got Reo her twenty, worked out strategy, then stepped into the box where Beaty, not looking her best in the orange jumpsuit, sat with her distinguished attorney.

'Record on. Dallas, Lieutenant Eve, and Peabody, Detective Delia, entering Interview with Beaty, Iris, aka Swan, Iris, and her attorney of record, Merit, Sampson, on the matters of —' She blew out a breath, then read off the multiple case files.

'You've procrastinated on this matter for long enough,' Merit began. 'I've already filed motions to —'

'I don't much give a crap about your motions. Your client was arrested on-site where a hundred and thirty-six minors were held against their will, where evidence of physical, mental, and emotional abuse is mountainous, and where evidence of child trafficking, abductions, and murder are clear and present. You're well aware of all this, Counselor.'

'My client categorically rejects these accusations, and has claimed her right to remain silent.'

'Your client has been positively identified in lineup by six witnesses as the woman known as Auntie, who ran the organization responsible for these abductions, forced imprisonment, torture, sexual abuse, and trafficking.'

He smiled thinly. 'Witnesses, one presumes, who are minors, and who — by your account — have suffered emotional abuse. I doubt, very much, their coached testimony will hold up in court.'

Eve drew out a sketch. 'You know who described you for the police artist? Dorian Gregg. She just keeps besting you, Iris.'

She pulled out others, tossed them on the table. 'And all these, matrons — including the one you killed — instructors, security. Jesus Christ, I walked in — duly warranted — on a couple of prisoners, minor females, being videoed in bed. I know she's got you by the short hairs, Merit, but you know she's going down for this.'

'I have no idea what you mean.'

The brisk knock on the door made Eve smile. 'I bet that's going to explain it.' She rose, opened the door to Reo and two uniforms.

'Your warrant, Lieutenant, for the arrest of Sampson Merit on charges of child trafficking, child abuse of a sexual nature, fraud, conspiracy to commit the abduction of minors, enforced imprisonment of minors.'

He'd surged to his feet. 'What nonsense is this?'

'It's the naked truth, Deepdaddy. Officers, escort this human slimebag to Booking.'

'This is an outrage.'

'No, you are. And I bet when we find whoever you're holding for your own sick pleasures at your hideaway on Long Island, they'll agree. Get him out of my Interview room.'

When they muscled him out, Reo came in, sat.

'Reo, APA Cher, joining Interview. Well, oops, Iris, looks like you lost your lawyer. And now that we've been able to freeze at least the bulk of your accounts, good luck hiring another. You do have a right to an attorney, and we'll provide you with same if you wish. Speak now.'

'Go to hell.'

'No, thanks. I like elbow room, and you and your people are really going to crowd the place. We've got you.' Eve leaned in. 'We've got you cold. We have eyewitness identifications and accounts — and not all from minors. Several of your staff have flipped on you and others already. More will. We have your own records — meticulous ones. And your own security feed. We have your scouts, and those we haven't taken yet, we will. Oh, and we took down your branch in Provence. Last I heard, lots of people talking and rolling and doing backflips to drag you down.'

Eve let out a happy sigh. 'Now we've got your lawyer, and if he doesn't grab a deal on this, I'm a monkey's uncle. What does that mean?' she asked Peabody. 'Isn't a monkey's uncle just another monkey? Discuss later.'

378

She shrugged it off. 'You've been around the block — another stupid one — but you've been around and more than once. You know when you're cooked.'

'I'll make a deal,' Beaty said.

'Will you? We've got you, Iris. Why would we deal?'

'I'll give you who financed it all, who created it all. For immunity on all charges, I'll give you the top, and every single buyer and seller I know, and I know plenty. I could, hypothetically, start with Sampson Merit.'

'Merit's already toasted, and immunity is never going to be on the table,' Reo told her. 'Lower your expectations.'

'Why should I give you a thing then?'

'Try the prospect of doing several life sentences, without possibility of parole, in an off-planet facility.'

'Five years, on-planet.' Beaty folded her hands on the table like a woman in charge. 'You wouldn't be here if you didn't want to deal.'

'That's not a deal, it's a gift. I don't know you well enough to give you a gift. Twenty years.' Reo held up a finger before Eve could object. 'On-planet, if — and only if — your information leads to the identities, arrests, and prosecutions of those you name. That's all I've been authorized to offer you by the office of the prosecuting attorney of New York. Take it or leave it.'

'Put it in writing.'

Reo rose; Eve shoved up and followed her out.

'Um, Dallas and Reo exiting Interview. Do you want something to drink while we wait, Ms. Beaty?'

Beaty flicked a smug glance at Peabody. 'A dry martini would go down nicely. Sparkling water will suffice.'

'Interview pause as Peabody exits.'

Outside of Interview, she ditched the meek expression and did a happy dance to Vending.

When they came back, restarted the record, Beaty read the deal carefully, then signed it.

'Names,' Eve snapped. 'Work your way up to the top.'

'Wade C. Younkin, international finance, numerous residences. Alice Ann Dobbs, shipping heiress, fifth generation.'

She had a hell of a long list, and though Eve recognized some from Feeney's early report, she let Beaty state them all for the record.

When Beaty paused, Eve nudged. 'Who murdered Mina Cabot?'

'Though I hold Matron Williamson and Nurse Parks responsible for the loss of a trainee we had invested heavily in, she was killed during an altercation with Devin Kunes, night security. The girl brought about her own death, literally running into that spear of wood when Kunes got it away from her. She injured three before he did so.'

Good for you, Mina, Eve thought.

'Hit the top.'

'Jonah K. Devereaux, owner of Reliable Delivery Service. The very top. His money founded the Academy, and its smaller European counterpart. It was his concept, and a brilliant one. A training facility, self-contained — to educate, instruct, improve those selected to serve and service. He enjoys the control, of course, and the benefits of owning a few — adult, as he isn't personally into the young ones — slaves. But the revenue stream has been very rewarding.'

'From sales, rentals, the porn revenue.'

380

'Of course. A superior product will merit handsome profits. And we produced superior products.'

'You and Devereaux.'

'He had the funds, I had the experience and expertise.'

'Spell it out, Iris.'

And she did, the procedures, start to finish. Abductions, transportation, training, punishments, rewards, security. Every detail — on record.

'Devereaux, Devereaux, sounds familiar.' Eve pushed up, frowning, pacing. Then stopped. Smiled. 'Oh yeah, that's the rich, sadistic pervert I sent to the morgue this morning. He's dead.'

'Dead? That's impossible.'

'Possible. One of the women he abused decided she didn't want to be a slave anymore. She didn't want to be gangbanged at a party for a bunch of sick fucks. He got off easy. You won't.'

Her lips quivered before she firmed them. 'I don't believe you. I personally selected every domestic and consort for Jonah.'

'Seeing's believing.' Eve pulled out a crime scene photo. 'I'm full of dumbass sayings today.'

Beaty sat, several moments, staring at the bloodied corpse of her longtime partner. 'Jonah Devereaux was a visionary, and a friend.'

'One you were ready to toss over to us for a deal.'

'And a man who understood self-preservation.' She pushed the photo away with her fingertips. 'You think I can't do twenty?'

'Oh, I think you can do the twenty — though I doubt you'll ever get to it. Could be wrong,' she said as she rose and opened the door. 'Special Agent Teasdale, you're up. FBI,' Eve said to Beaty. 'Federal charges, numerous and heavy. All those abductions crossing state lines, the shipping of human minors over same, not to mention internationally.'

'We have a deal, on record, in writing.'

'And that deal holds.' Reo rose. 'For New York. Federal charges? Out of our hands.'

'Oh, one more thing before we turn this over?' Eve paused at the door. 'Your visionary friend? He ran the auction — the big one coming right up — as a side deal, charging the Academy fees, collecting them.'

'You're lying!'

'Hey, he's dead. Why would I bother? Over to you, Special Agent.'

'Thank you, Lieutenant. Always a pleasure.'

'Back at you. Dallas, Reo, and Peabody exiting Interview. Record end.'

Eve waited long enough to watch two other agents escort Beaty out while Teasdale read off charges.

'I love when a plan works.' Eve rolled her shoulders. 'And you've got to love when they just don't see it coming. Get me this fucking Kunes guy, Peabody, and let's crack him like an egg for Mina.'

'All over it!'

'That was good work, Dallas. We all did good work on this.'

'Not done yet, but yeah, all-around good work. She thought she'd skate. Do twenty, probably run some businesses from inside. They were nothing to her, Reo, those girls were nothing to her but profit margins. But she felt something for Devereaux, you could see it. She'd roll him flat to make a deal, but she felt something for him. Friendship, admiration.'

'More than she felt for the clients she gave up. Which we're going to start knocking down like

382

bowling pins. A favorite sport.'

'Bowling's your favorite sport?'

'No, knocking bad guys down like bowling pins. Tag me if you need me on Kunes. I've got to get this to the boss. Buy you a drink later?'

'Sunday afternoon, our place, barbecue.'

'Yeah? I am so there.'

'How did that come out of my mouth?' Eve asked herself. Then went to her office for a hit of coffee before she took on the murderer of Mina Cabot.

Epilogue

There were times she drove through the gates toward home that she felt euphoric. Times she felt exhausted. Tonight, she felt a tangle of both at once.

When she parked, got out of the car, she stood a moment looking at the trees, the grass, the flowers in the softening light of a summer evening. She needed this world right now, and everything waiting inside the house.

Then she walked in, saw Summerset.

Maybe not everything.

Not in the mood to swipe snipes, she thought, and headed straight for the stairs with the cat jogging behind her.

'Lieutenant.'

'Not today, Satan.'

'Lieutenant,' he said again, and annoyed, she turned.

'What?' And something on his face shook her. 'Roarke. Is Roarke all right?'

'Yes, he's upstairs. And he's fine. I saw Nadine's report.'

'Jesus.' She'd really wanted those ten years of her life he'd just scared out of her. 'Fine, good.'

'Lieutenant,' he said a third time. 'All those young girls, right here in New York. And no one knew.'

'Some knew, and the ones who did are going to do a whole hell of a lot of cage time. Listen —'

'I had a daughter.'

Her annoyance dropped. That's what she saw on

his face, she realized. A kind of grief. 'I know.'

'She was innocent, and she was loved, as those girls were.'

She started to say not all were loved, but let it go.

'They hurt her, and they raped her, and they killed her. My child. I think they wouldn't have been able to do so if there had been a cop like you, in that place and time. But there wasn't, not then, not there. For the families who have their daughters back, I'm grateful to you.'

'I didn't do it alone. It takes —'

'Leadership,' he interrupted. 'The tone is set at the top. You should get some rest.'

'Going to.' She started up, stopped. 'The one most responsible for all this, he inherited his money, and exploited it, used it to cause pain and suffering. I'm not getting into how Roarke built the foundation for his, but I know what he does with it. The shelter, the school, and all the rest he does. The tone's set from the top there, too. You gave him the chance to set it.'

She continued up, with the cat rushing ahead. She went to the bedroom first, and for the first time in what felt like days, took off her weapon.

She'd check in with Roarke, take a shower. God, a real shower. Then —

He walked in.

'I saw Nadine's very extensive report.'

'Yeah, I gave her the whole deal when Feeney said they'd cracked right through the auction data. Various LEOs and agencies are busy picking up perverts, rescuing girls and women. We won't get them all, you never get them all but . . . You know that kid who gave me such grief during the raid?'

'I do, yes.'

385

'Lottie Crug — she was on my board. She wouldn't leave Carrie until Carrie's parents got there. And they wouldn't leave Lottie. They got emergency custody, and said they're going to apply for permanent. Some people don't suck.'

'Some people don't,' he agreed, and crossed over to wrap his arms around her.

'Thanks for the assist with Callendar — and with the auction deal after. Had to cut into your time even more.'

'I have more time. And right now, all I want is time with you.'

'Handy, because I want the same with you. It started with Mina Cabot, and I ended it with her killer. Cracked like an egg. That's something that's going around today. I needed that. I know it was personal, I guess all of this was personal. But it's done.'

She held on tight to everything she needed now.

'I was going to take a shower. How about we spend some of this time in there, all naked and wet?'

'I definitely have time for that.' He lifted both of her hands, kissed them.

'Oh, just one more thing.' She kept her hands in his as she walked backward toward the bathroom. 'I sort of invited pretty much everybody to that cookout deal you talked about. On Sunday. Like this Sunday.'

He paused, angled his head. 'Did you take a blow to the head after I left Central?'

'I wondered the same, but I got caught up or something. It's a lot of people. A lot. Then I come home and end up having a conversation with Summerset. I mean, a *conversation*.'

'I need to get you naked, take a close and thorough look to make absolutely certain you're Eve Dallas and

386